Here's What Readers Are Saying about the Christy Miller series...

"I wish I could find the words to tell you what a blessing your books have been! I've learned a lot from Christy's character, and Todd makes me want to wait for a hero! ☺ Please keep writing!"

"Before I finished the first chapter of *Summer Promise* I was hooked. I had always called myself a Christian, but it wasn't until your books that I really knew what it meant to lay down my life to Jesus Christ. You would not believe what a difference God has made in my life already. Thank you!"

"If people ever tell me that being a Christian is boring, I tell them to go read your books! They helped me to start living for God and to look to my Bible for answers to everything."

"I read the Christy Miller books during a really stressful time, and they were like a calm in the storm. I have learned so much from them, too! When Doug told Christy that godliness is beautiful, it was an entirely new concept to me! I will not hesitate in saying these books changed my life."

"My best friend and I have been reading your books since we were twelve years old. We love them! They have brought us closer to the Lord, and we treasure this more than anything in the world."

"I had to read a book for school, and I chose *Summer Promise*. I never knew it would change my life. I've read the series at least six times. I now have a personal relationship with Christ. Thank you for being obedient to God."

"When I was in sixth grade, my mom gave me the first Christy Miller book. These books changed my life! Please, don't stop writing until your hand falls off!"

"I'm thirteen years old, and I love your books! All my friends are reading your books, too. We wish they were movies."

"I absolutely love your books. You are my favorite author. After I read the first one, I immediately became a Christian and turned my life over to God. I have struggled some, but your books helped me to stay on track. I thank you from the bottom of my heart for writing them."

"I wanted to thank you for all the books you have written. They have been my joy when things are hard. Every book has been amazing."

Christy Miller

COLLECTION

●●●●● VOLUME 1

SUMMER PROMISE

A WHISPER AND A WISH

YOURS FOREVER

ROBIN JONES GUNN

MULTNOMAH

THE CHRISTY MILLER COLLECTION, VOLUME 1

© 2006 by Robin's Ink, LLC
International Standard Book Number: 978-0-593-19317-4

Cover image by PixelWorks Studio, www.shootpw.com

Compilation of:
Summer Promise
© 1988, 1998 by Robin's Ink, LLC
A Whisper and a Wish
© 1989, 1998 by Robin's Ink, LLC
Yours Forever
© 1990, 1998 by Robin's Ink, LLC

Scripture quotations are from:
The Holy Bible, New International Version (NIV) © 1973, 1984 by International Bible Society, used by permission of Zondervan Publishing House

Published in the United States by Multnomah, an imprint of Random House, a division of Penguin Random House LLC.

MULTNOMAH® and its mountain colophon are registered trademarks of Penguin Random House LLC.

Printed in the United States of America

The Library of Congress has cataloged the hardcover edition as follows:
Gunn, Robin Jones, 1955-
   The Christy Miller collection.
      v. cm.
   ISBN 1-59052-584-1
   Summary: A collection of previously published books featuring Wisconsin farm girl Christy Miller as she learns about Christianity and life.
   Contents: Summer promise —A whisper and a wish—Yours forever.
   [1. Friendship—Fiction. 2. Christian life—Fiction.] I. Title.
PZ7.G972Chr 2006
   [Fic]—dc22

                                        2005025580

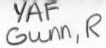

TEEN NOVELS BY ROBIN JONES GUNN

THE CHRISTY MILLER SERIES

Volume 1
Book 1: *Summer Promise*
Book 2: *A Whisper and a Wish*
Book 3: *Yours Forever*

Volume 2
Book 4: *Surprise Endings*
Book 5: *Island Dreamer*
Book 6: *A Heart Full of Hope*

Volume 3
Book 7: *True Friends*
Book 8: *Starry Night*
Book 9: *Seventeen Wishes*

Volume 4
Book 10: *A Time to Cherish*
Book 11: *Sweet Dreams*
Book 12: *A Promise Is Forever*

THE SIERRA JENSEN SERIES

Volume 1
Book 1: *Only You, Sierra*
Book 2: *In Your Dreams*
Book 3: *Don't You Wish*

Volume 2
Book 4: *Close Your Eyes*
Book 5: *Without a Doubt*
Book 6: *With This Ring*

Volume 3
Book 7: *Open Your Heart*
Book 8: *Time Will Tell*
Book 9: *Now Picture This*

Volume 4
Book 10: *Hold On Tight*
Book 11: *Closer Than Ever*
Book 12: *Take My Hand*

BOOK ONE

Summer
Promise

To all the Christys in my life.
A summer promise
can last forever—if you give your whole heart.

Off to a Bad Start

"I hate you! I hate you!" Christy Miller shouted at her reflection in the closet-door mirror. With a wild *grrrr* she wadded up her beach towel and heaved it at the mirror, watching it wobble and distort her lanky proportions.

"Christy darling?" came a shrill voice from the hallway. "Are you back from the beach so soon?"

"Yes, Aunt Marti." Christy grabbed a brush and pretended to be untangling her long, nutmeg-brown hair.

Her aunt, a slim, stylish woman in her forties, opened the guest room door and looked around. "What was all the commotion? Who were you talking to?"

"Nobody. Just myself," Christy answered calmly, trying to suppress the volcano of fiery emotions boiling within her.

"Why aren't you out on the beach, dear? It's a gorgeous day, and here you sit in your room, talking to yourself." Aunt Marti dramatically pointed her acrylic fingernail toward the door. "You should be out there enjoying yourself!"

Christy bit her quivering lip and didn't answer.

"This is California. Live a little! We didn't fly you all the way from Wisconsin so you could spend the summer hiding in your room. Get out there and make some friends."

Suddenly the internal volcano erupted with great force, spewing words with the hot tears. "I tried, all right?" Christy choked. "I tried to get in with some of the beach kids, but they're all a bunch of snobs! I can't stand them! They're rude and mean, and they laughed at me." Christy covered her face with her hands; the tears oozed through her fingers.

"I had no idea!" Her aunt switched tones and ushered Christy to the edge of the bed. "There, there. Tell me what's bothering you, dear."

It took Christy a few minutes to compose herself before she said calmly, "I don't fit in with the people here. They think I'm a nerd."

"Well, are you?" her aunt challenged.

"Am I what?"

"A nerd."

Christy didn't answer. She stared across the room at her reflection in the mirror.

"Well?" her aunt prodded.

"Look at me, Aunt Martha!" Christy jumped up from the bed and stood in front of her. "I'm as white as a frosty cone—sort of shaped like one too! If that doesn't make me a nerd in Newport Beach, I don't know what does!"

"Really, Christy. A frosty cone?"

"Well, look at me." Christy stretched out her arms to provide a full view of her 5-foot-5-inch, 110-pound frame. Her one-piece bathing suit covered her Olive Oyl torso like a bright green Ace bandage.

"Tell me I don't look like a frosty cone."

"You don't look like a frosty cone."

"You're just saying that." Christy plopped on the floor and folded her arms across her stomach.

"Oh, come now, Christy. You might be a bit of a late bloomer, but really, you're a very sweet girl, and you've got a lot of potential."

"Yeah, right. Tell that to the surfers out there. The one who said, 'Hey! It's a walking green bean.'"

Her aunt looked confused. "What's that supposed to mean?"

Christy let the tears drip and sniffed loudly. "Don't you see?"

"I see that you got upset over a little remark about a green bean. That doesn't make sense at all."

"They meant *me*, Aunt Marti! No other girl on the beach had on a bathing suit like this ugly one! *I'm* the walking green bean!"

Christy covered her face with her hands and cried until the tears ran down her arms. It was the kind of crying that comes from the pit of the stomach and brings a headache with it. The kind that makes a person snort and gasp, and no matter how idiotic you feel or how hard you try, you can't stop.

"Do calm yourself, will you, dear? It's not as bad as all that. We can certainly buy you a new bathing suit easily enough. And just think. They called you a bean, not a frosty cone. See? They're saying you're thin. That's almost a compliment."

Christy gasped in short spasms, trying to relax.

Her aunt took the opportunity to make her point.

"This is exactly the reason I told your mother I wanted you to spend the summer with us. You deserve more than your parents can give you right now, and goodness knows your mother and I didn't have much when we were growing up."

Christy wiped her nose with the back of her hand.

"Here. Use this, will you please?" Marti handed her a tissue. "As I was saying, my goal this summer is to treat you to some of the finer things in life and to teach you, Christina Juliet Miller, how to become your own person."

Christy blinked and tried to suppress a wild belch that bubbled up as a result of so much sobbing. Too late. The muffled *urp* leaked out.

"You're certainly not going to make this easy for me, are you, dear?"

"I'm sorry." Christy felt an uncontrollable urge to laugh. "Are you sure you're ready to transform a belching green bean frosty cone into 'her own person'? Could be kind of dangerous!" Christy broke into laughter.

Aunt Marti shook her head and didn't join in. "We'll start tomorrow, Christina. I'll call and make an appointment for you to have your colors done at nine, and then we'll start shopping for your new wardrobe."

Christy instantly sobered. "I didn't bring much money with me."

"Don't be silly! This is my treat. A few outfits are certainly not going to break me. And one other thing: We really should have your hair cut. Something short and stylish. My hairdresser, Maurice, does marvelous work. By the time we're done with you you'll look and feel like a new person."

She said it with such finesse, Christy almost believed her. A new wardrobe? A new hairstyle? And what did her aunt mean by "having her colors done"?

"Why don't you shower and dress, dear? Your uncle doesn't know it yet, but he's going to take you to an early dinner and a movie tonight." Aunt Marti swished out the door.

Christy approached the mirror with a new perspective. Twisting her long, nutmeg-brown hair on top of her head, she posed this way and that way, trying to imagine how she would look with short hair. She couldn't quite picture the change.

She wished Paula were there. Paula, her best friend back home, always gave her advice when it came to major decisions like this. But then, what did Paula know? She was the one who helped her pick out the dumb green bean bathing suit!

Christy scrunched up her nose and stuck her face close to the mirror, examining her skin for new blemishes. No new and ugly bumps today. But her cheeks were flushed, and her nose was bright red from crying. Even her eyes showed the effects of her crying spree; they were puffy and bloodshot.

"I have such stupid eyes," she muttered. "They're not blue, and they're not green. They're just sort of nothing—like the rest of me."

"Knock, knock," Uncle Bob called out from Christy's open door.

She immediately released her hair and turned away from the mirror, embarrassed that he had caught her in the midst of such scrutiny.

"Looks like we've got a date tonight for the movies." His merry eyes looked at her from beneath his baseball cap. He must have just come back from golfing, judging by the perspiration stains on his polo shirt. "Anything special you want to see?"

"No."

"Okay. I'll take a look in the paper to see what's playing. Your aunt's not much of a movie fan, so I hope you don't mind that it's just you and me."

"No. That's fine."

"We'll leave in about an hour, okay?"

"Okay."

"By the way," he lifted his baseball cap and wiped his forehead, "I haven't told you yet, but I'm glad you came to stay with us this summer." Then he added, "You are my favorite niece, you know."

"I also happen to be your only niece!"

"Minor detail, my child, minor detail," he quipped, politely closing the door.

With a sigh, Christy flopped onto the bed. She didn't feel like showering, and it wouldn't take her that long to change. With an hour to kill, she decided to write to Paula.

Christy liked to write—especially when she had a lot on her mind. She would get everything out on paper, and then when she reread it, it would be like looking at her own thoughts in a mirror. Usually things came out clearer on paper than when she tried to say them.

Finding the pad of stationery Paula had given her when she left Wisconsin, Christy set to work. Paula insisted that she write the first letter to her on this stationery.

Dear Paula,

Hi! How's everything back on the farm? The plane trip out

here was fun for the first hour, but then it got boring. I didn't see any movie stars at the airport, but I still have your notepad, so I can get some autographs in case I see anybody famous.

Remember when you called last Thursday and I told you I couldn't talk? It was because my parents were giving me a big lecture about my trip out here. They made me promise I wouldn't do anything this summer I would regret later. Can you believe that?

The funny part is, the only thing I regret is that I ever came here. I hate this place! There's nothing to do, and everybody is so stuck up. It's so boring. At night, all I do is sit around and watch TV.

At least one good thing is going to happen. Tomorrow my aunt is going to take me shopping, and guess what? I'm probably going to get my hair cut! Can you believe it? I'm kind of scared, but I think she's trying to give me a new image or something.

Well, I've got to go. I'll tell you how the big makeover turns out. Just think, you might not recognize me when I step off the plane next September. You'd better write to me.

Love,

Christy

2

The Makeover

Christy awoke the next morning to the steady rhythm of the ocean waves outside her window. They sounded like a giant taking deep, relaxed breaths as each wave came in and oozed back out. She drew up the window shades and watched a flock of seagulls circling the sand, scavenging breakfast. Their white bodies flashed bright and clean against the pure blue of the sky.

Opening her window to breathe in the fresh sea air, Christy found herself entranced by the ocean. Foaming waves broke on the shore, erasing the footprints of two early-morning joggers. Everything looked, smelled, and felt fresh and new.

She quickly dressed and greeted Uncle Bob in the kitchen with a cheery "Good morning!" to which he replied, "And a good morning to you, Bright Eyes! Wait till you see what I've got cooking for breakfast."

"Mmm. Smells like waffles."

"And right you are!" Uncle Bob pulled the first steaming waffle from the waffle iron. "Butter and syrup are on the table, and this one's for you. I made my own batter from scratch, and, if I must say so myself, it turned out to be a prize winner."

"I'm impressed." Christy hurried to spread on the butter so it would melt into all the little squares; then she poured the syrup slowly so each little square had just the right amount. Carefully cutting the tender waffle into bite-sized pieces, she closed her eyes and drew the first forkful to her mouth.

Suddenly Aunt Marti burst into the kitchen and shrieked, "Christy darling! What do you think you're doing?"

"Eating my breakfast."

"But, sweetheart, don't you realize how many grams of fat are in that one waffle? That certainly isn't a proper breakfast for a young lady who wants her eyes to glow, her skin to gleam, and her hair to shine!"

"I do? I mean, it isn't?" Christy looked to Uncle Bob for support as she held her first bite only inches from her mouth, the syrup dripping onto her fingers. Uncle Bob only smiled.

Bustling around the kitchen, Aunt Marti whirled something in the blender.

"Here you are, dear. This is much better for you, and it has all the vitamins and minerals you need to make the boys notice you."

She presented Christy with a glass foaming with some kind of protein breakfast drink. "Go ahead, honey. Try it!"

Christy put down her fork and picked up the glass. It looked awful. She took a small sip. It tasted awful too!

"Yuck, Aunt Marti! You expect me to drink this stuff?"

"Yes, drink it all, dear. And I've got something else for you here." She pulled from the refrigerator a sectioned grapefruit half sitting on a glass plate with a white doily underneath it.

With an air of satisfaction, Marti presented it to Christy. "There. Isn't it marvelous? The perfect breakfast. Now hurry and finish while I put on my shoes. We've only got twenty minutes before your draping appointment." Then out of the kitchen and down the hall pranced Aunt Marti.

Christy looked at her waffle and then at her grapefruit. She turned to Uncle Bob, who was suppressing a huge laugh.

"So," he teased, "vitamins and minerals, huh?"

"It's not funny!" Christy returned, trying not to laugh herself.

"I don't know. Sounds like a pretty good breakfast to me."

"Then you drink it!" She pushed the glass toward him.

"Not me. Your aunt tried to reform my diet once. Once was enough!"

Christy looked at the protein drink and then at the waffle. Quickly, she stuffed two big bites of waffle into her mouth. "You won't tell on me, will you?" she garbled.

"Your secret is safe with me." Uncle Bob winked, pulling another waffle off the iron. "She really means well, you know."

"I know," Christy said with a sigh. "Uncle Bob? Do you think I should get my hair cut?"

He joined her at the table, studying her face and hair like a photographer looking for just the right angle. "Guess

I'm not the best person to ask. I've always liked your hair the way it is. Your aunt is the one who knows all about hairstyles. Why don't you ask her?"

"That's just it. She's the one who thought I should get my hair cut today, and I'm not real sure about it."

"Well," said Uncle Bob, slicing his waffle, "the only advice I can give you is, 'To thine own self be true.'"

"To my own what?"

"'To thine own self be true.' It's a quote from Shakespeare. It means always do what you want to do, and don't try to please everybody else. Follow your own instincts. That's been my philosophy for years and probably part of the reason I did so well in real estate. I just followed my instincts, and to my own self I've always been true."

Aunt Marti entered the kitchen dressed in a classy black and white pantsuit that showed off her slim figure. Christy discreetly carried her dishes to the sink and quietly poured the protein drink down the disposal before her aunt noticed.

"I hope you also told Christy that much of your success can be attributed to that wonderful secretary you worked with in your first real estate office." She put her arms around his neck and kissed him on the cheek, leaving a smudge of fuchsia lipstick.

"You know," she went on, "that sweet young secretary you ended up marrying."

They exchanged a smile and a quick kiss.

"See what I mean, Christy?" Uncle Bob pointed out. "It always pays to follow your own inner voice."

"Well, my inner voice says we need to get going!" exclaimed Aunt Marti. She gave Christy a quick look. "Is that what you're going to wear, dear? Well, no matter. We don't have time to change. Let's get going."

Christy looked down at her long floral-print skirt and the pink tunic top that hung almost to her knees. It was one of the nicest outfits she had brought with her, and she liked it. Aunt Marti's comment made her feel so out of style. Depression surged inside her like a wave, but she didn't have time for it to overwhelm her as it had yesterday. Aunt Marti was already pulling her silver Mercedes convertible out of the garage.

"Better get going. When your aunt goes into warp drive like this, there's no stopping her."

Uncle Bob was right; with Aunt Marti steering Christy along, the day zoomed by. In the first hour and a half a striking middle-aged woman "draped" Christy with a variety of colored fabrics to determine which colors looked good with her skin tones and which didn't. She selected a group of paint chips and fabric squares and prepared them in a small packet for Christy to carry with her while shopping.

"These are your colors," the specialist told her. "Don't ever wear a color that's not in your packet."

The bright green of her bathing suit was not in the packet. The light pink of the top she had on was not in the packet. She had never realized what a fashion degenerate she was.

As Aunt Marti and Christy paraded in and out of the fancy department stores, Christy could barely keep up. When it came to shopping, Aunt Marti was in "warp drive." Nothing could slow her down, and nothing was out of her price range.

At noon they stopped for a salad at Bob Burns Restaurant, which Marti said was the only place with atmosphere in all of Fashion Island. Christy thought the place was too dark and quiet to be inviting, but she meekly followed her aunt to a booth. Dropping onto the thick cushion, Christy pushed the bags against the wall.

"I'm afraid we're making rather slow progress, dearie." Aunt Marti squeezed her lemon slice into her iced tea. "Aren't you enjoying this? You seem awfully reluctant to try on anything. Why, you haven't tried on a single bathing suit yet! What do you think the problem is, Christy?"

Christy ran her fingers through the ends of her hair and decided to be honest with her aunt. After all, Uncle Bob had told her to be true to herself.

"I just don't know if I like all the same things that you like. I mean, those two shirts and the pair of sandals we bought are pretty basic, but I don't know if I'm ready for some of those other outfits you were showing me. Plus, I don't know, I just feel weird having you pay for everything. I've never been shopping like this before."

The waitress arrived with their salads and asked Christy if she would care for fresh ground pepper on hers.

Christy stared at her blankly for a moment and then said, "No, I don't think so." She had never been asked that before.

The waitress didn't seem to notice Christy's inexperience; she was already offering to twist the large pepper mill over Aunt Marti's salad.

"Listen." Marti waved the waitress away with a swish of her hand. "I already told you: Today is my treat. Now, please don't spoil all my fun. Let's start buying things!"

Christy nodded and pushed her cherry tomato to the side of her plate. "Okay. I'll try to loosen up."

"That brings me to another subject, Christy. You must work at being more outgoing if you want to make any friends with the beach kids. Take control of your destiny, darling! Plan your goals and then go after them. Force yourself to be the one in control. Make the first move! Be aggressive! It's the only way you're going to make it."

"I don't know. That's not really me."

"Then make it you. Set your sights high and tell yourself that anything you want is yours."

Christy finished her salad and hungrily eyed the dessert tray the waitress held before them. "I'll have that chocolate thing there." She pointed to a chocolate torte. "As long as it doesn't have nuts in it."

"Christy!" exclaimed Aunt Marti.

Before Marti could scold her, Christy echoed, "You just said anything I want today is mine, and I want this piece of cake."

Aunt Marti laughed in a light, happy way that cut through her sophistication, exposing her as the simple hometown girl she once was.

"Okay, you win. Nothing for me, thanks," she told the waitress. "Enjoy your decadent fat grams in a hurry so we can go do some serious shopping."

In the dressing room of the next store, Christy had tried on a dozen bathing suits when Aunt Marti brought in one she seemed to be thrilled about.

"This is marvelous!" she gushed with renewed excitement. "It's not too skimpy like the red one, and yet it's still quite fashionable. Trust me, dear. It will look absolutely stunning on you."

The suit, a black one-piece, had thin straps that crisscrossed in the back. It was definitely not the kind of suit Christy would have chosen for herself, but she was eager to try it on and to hear Aunt Marti's reaction.

Aunt Marti had a reaction all right. "Oh, Christy! Didn't I tell you? It's perfect on you. Simply perfect! Come on, step out of that dressing room and look at yourself in this full-length mirror."

As Christy shyly emerged, Aunt Marti called over her shoulder to the dressing-room attendant, "See my niece in this bathing suit. Doesn't she look marvelous?"

How embarrassing! Christy looked in the mirror and caught the reflection of the attendant smiling and politely nodding her head.

"Should I get it?" Christy asked, staring at the $120 price tag.

"Of course!" Aunt Marti chirped. "Now let's see what else we can find. They have a superb selection here."

A half hour later, Christy watched the cashier add up her new wardrobe. Besides the suit, she had three pairs of jeans, six shirts, two dresses, a sweatshirt, a jeans skirt, and four pairs of shorts.

"The total comes to $887.58," said the cashier with a smile.

Aunt Marti whipped out a credit card and handed the cashier a pair of bright yellow earrings. "Can you add these on as well?"

"They'll go perfect with the sundress, don't you think, Christy?"

Christy was still gasping at the total of the bill. Her mother made most of her clothes, and when they did go shopping it was traumatic to spend more than forty dollars at one time. But she was with Aunt Marti now, and this was Aunt Marti's way of doing things. So she responded with, "Sure. They're great!"

Passing the cosmetic counter on the way out, Marti exclaimed, "Oh, good. I'm glad we came this way. I'm almost out of my fragrance."

She asked the clerk for the largest size of Chanel No 5 and then said, partly to the clerk and partly to Christy, "Say, I've got an idea! Let's have your makeup done while we're here."

The clerk responded graciously, and before Christy knew it she was perched on a high stool before a mirror with lights tilted toward her. The cosmetic specialist gently smoothed a cotton ball over Christy's cheeks and down her nose, explaining the proper procedure for cleansing facial pores.

This must be a dream, Christy thought as the cosmetician smoothed Autumn Haze shadow across each eyelid. A soft pencil traced the inside ridges of her lids and was gently dabbed to perfection at the outside corners. The brush across her cheeks felt like velvet, and as she pursed her lips she thought the lipstick smelled like strawberries.

"There," announced the cosmetician. "Have a look at yourself. What do you think?"

Christy opened her eyes slowly.

"Is that me?" she asked in a small voice.

It was her, but it wasn't. She looked older, more mature. And her eyes! She never noticed before, but her eyes really were kind of pretty.

"Her eyes are the perfect shape," the cosmetician said to Marti. "She can do about anything with them colorwise because they're such an unusual shade of blue-green."

"Really?" Christy looked at her eyes more closely in the mirror.

"Yes." The cosmetician tilted her chin up to look at her more closely. "I know models who would kill to have eyes like yours."

Christy couldn't believe it. Little bubbles of excitement burst inside, making her feel lovely and almost as if she had done something she shouldn't have. At home she was only allowed to wear lip gloss. But this—this was wonderful!

"You've done a marvelous job," Aunt Marti praised the cosmetician. "We'll take one of everything you used."

"Aunt Marti!" Christy gasped. "Are you sure?"

"Why yes, dear, and please don't make such a scene. We'd also like your complete line of sunscreen products."

Christy couldn't believe all this was happening to her. "Thank you!"

"You're very welcome, my dear." Aunt Marti handed her the bulging bag of cosmetics. "Now we have one more stop to make, if you're at all interested."

"What's that?" Christy asked, catching her reflection in a shiny display as they passed.

"Why, Maurice's Hair Salon, of course."

Christy flashed a smile at her cunning aunt. "I guess it's now or never!"

3

The Dream

At four-thirty they arrived home and found Uncle Bob in the den, sitting in front of his laptop with soft jazz music playing in the background.

"Ta-daaa!" Aunt Marti announced dramatically.

Bob turned around and for a moment looked shocked. Then his dry smile returned. "Well, now! I didn't realize you were bringing a movie star home for dinner. I would have worn something more presentable."

"What do you think?" Christy turned all the way around. "Do you like it? I mean, my hair? Do you like it short like this?"

It was short all right! The front layers hit just below her ears. Maurice had styled the layers around her face and cut thin, wispy bangs. At the salon, Christy had moaned that she felt like a pampered poodle, but Maurice overheard and Marti scolded her severely. He seemed offended that anyone should question one of his creations. All the stylists then came over and made gushy comments about how ravishing she looked.

Christy wasn't convinced. She wondered what Paula would think. But since Paula was several thousand miles away, Christy was anxious to hear what Uncle Bob had to say. She knew he would be honest with her.

"You sure surprised me, missy. If you didn't have on the same clothes as the girl who left here this morning, I wouldn't have known it was you. You've become quite a young lady."

Christy sighed in relief. "The guy at the salon showed me how to put this spritz stuff on my hair, and I got two bottles of it. I also got a curling iron, and he showed me how to use that, too. But that's not all I got today! Wait till you see what's in all these bags. I've never been on a shopping trip like this before."

Excitedly, she opened all the shopping bags to display her new belongings. Soon the couch was covered with clothes, shoes, accessories, and her complete makeup assortment.

"Can you believe this?" Christy asked and giggled. "I wish I could wear it all at once."

Aunt Marti looked quite pleased with herself. "This is just what she needed," she whispered to Bob. "Some new clothes and things to make her feel good about herself. I told you she would snap out of her little slump."

"You were right," Christy squealed. "These earrings go great with this outfit. I can't wait to wear it!"

"Then how about putting it on now, and I'll take my two favorite women out for a celebration dinner."

"Actually, Bob," Marti said in her take-charge tone of voice, "I've got my women's group meeting tonight, so you

and Christy go ahead. Why don't you take her to the Crab
Cooker?"

"Okay," Bob agreed. "Sounds good to me. What do you
think, Christy?"

She had already scooped up her new clothes and called
as she dashed up the stairs, "I'll be ready in five minutes."
Amazingly enough, she was.

But when she came downstairs, Uncle Bob was on the
phone. While she waited for him, Christy noticed that he
had changed into a clean shirt and combed his thick, brown
hair. A handsome man, he looked much younger than his
fifty-one years. His skin, leathered by too many afternoons
on the golf course, had settled into creases around his eyes
that deepened when he smiled. His voice, smooth and low,
contributed to his easygoing manner, which contrasted so
sharply with Aunt Marti's accelerated approach to life.

When Uncle Bob finished his phone conversation,
Christy made her entrance into the living room.

He gave a low whistle and offered his arm. "May I have
the honor of escorting you to the car, m'lady?"

Christy laughed. "Why certainly, your handsomeness."

As they walked out the door, Aunt Marti called, "Have a
marvelous time, you two!"

They arrived at the Crab Cooker to discover they had a
half-hour wait before they could be seated. Ordering
shrimp cocktails from the walk-up window, they moved
through the crowd to a long wooden bench.

"Nice breeze tonight," observed Uncle Bob.

"Smells kind of fishy," said Christy.

"That's because Newport Pier is right down that street."
He indicated the basic direction with his plastic spoon.

"That's where all the boats bring in their daily catch."

"Wow!" Christy exclaimed. "Look at that car!"

"You mean the Rolls Royce?"

"Yeah!" Then, lowering her voice, "Do you think movie stars are in it?"

"Not likely."

"I've never seen a car like that, except on TV."

Christy rose from the bench and tossed her plastic cocktail cup into the trash can. As she did, a convertible sports car roared past her into the parking lot.

"Now that's my kind of car," Bob said when she returned to the bench. "TR6, wire wheels, overdrive. I'd guess that's a '68."

"Oh," Christy responded. Now it was her turn to be unimpressed by a car. However, she considered the college-age guys who were getting out of the car worth noticing. She studied them as they walked toward the restaurant and decided they represented everything she liked about California. Tanned and wearing shorts and T-shirts with surf logos, they stood nonchalantly a few feet away, looking very cool.

For a moment Christy thought they were studying her. She must be imagining it. But then Uncle Bob confirmed her suspicions.

"Those guys are sure checking you out."

"No, they're not!" Christy nervously tucked her newly styled hair behind her ear.

"Sure they are. Must be the new outfit and hairdo. Do you want me to ask them to join us for dinner?" he teased.

Christy turned her back to the two guys, who were definitely looking in her direction. "Stop it!" she whispered. "I can't believe you said that."

"My, my. Your cheeks look awfully red for someone who wasn't even in the sun today."

Just then the hostess called out, "Bob, party of two, please."

"Guess we only got a table for two," Uncle Bob said. "Your boyfriends will have to wait till next time around."

Christy turned her head away as they walked past the guys. She watched as Uncle Bob smiled and gave them a nod.

Through clenched teeth she threatened her uncle, "I'm going to kill you."

After ordering, it took about twenty minutes for the food to arrive.

"Thank God," Bob pronounced when it did come. "I'm starving."

His comment prompted Christy to ask something that had bothered her for a while. "Do you and Aunt Marti believe in God?"

Uncle Bob paused for a moment. "I guess we feel religion is something personal. Something internal based on what you believe. It's not something you publicize."

"Do you ever go to church?"

"Sure, sometimes. But I've always felt that since God is all around and part of everything, you can worship Him wherever you are. You don't have to go to a church to do that."

For as long as she could remember, Christy had gone to church. All her family and friends back home in Wisconsin went to church. As a matter of fact, that's where she had met Paula—in the kindergarten Sunday school class—and they had been best friends ever since. She had never known anybody who said that he believed in God but didn't go to church.

"So," Uncle Bob said, taking a deep breath, "sounded like you and Martha had quite a day shopping. How do you feel about your new look?"

Skewering a plump shrimp, Christy thought for a moment. She liked feeling grown-up and stylish, and secretly she had loved the attention from the two guys out front. Feeling mysterious and attractive pulled her toward a way of life she had never experienced before but had certainly fantasized about.

"You know," she began in her most mature-sounding voice, "I really like it. It's much more the real me, don't you think?"

He smiled one of his wonderful smiles. "If you're happy, Christina Juliet Miller, that's all that matters."

That night she washed her face and obediently applied her new astringent and moisturizer before slipping into her nightshirt. The astringent had an antiseptic odor, but the moisturizer smelled like fine perfume as she smoothed it on.

"I even smell rich," she thought, crawling into the four-poster bed and pulling the white eyelet comforter up to her chin.

Uncle Bob's words from the restaurant echoed in her head as she lay in the stillness: "If you're happy, that's all that matters."

Today she had felt happy. Happy in an outside, thrilling sort of way. But the feeling of excitement brought with it a new sense of fear. She had felt this way once last summer on the way back from the Dells. Paula's older brother had let her drive his pickup. She remembered how she hadn't particularly wanted to drive the truck, but both Paula and her cousin had taken their turns, and so Christy couldn't say no when it was hers. She had only gotten up to about forty-five when the others laughed and challenged, "Go faster!" She had felt as if her stomach were wadded up into a tight ball that would bounce up into her throat at any minute. Fun? Maybe. Scary? Definitely.

She turned off the light on the oak nightstand and fell asleep, thinking of how she would try to be outgoing tomorrow on the beach—take her destiny into her own hands and all that.

At about two in the morning, Christy suddenly sat up in bed, her heart pounding and her nightshirt damp with perspiration. She quickly turned on the light and tried to slow down her frantic breathing.

"Fresh air! I need fresh air!" She couldn't jump out of bed fast enough to open the window. Inhaling the brisk salt air, her mind began to clear. The roar of the ocean soothed her with its constant curling and uncurling sounds.

"What a horrible nightmare!" She shivered in the night breeze at the memory of her eerie dream.

She had been lying on the beach, when all of a sudden a big wave came up on shore, crashed on top of her, and pulled her out to sea. She struggled and gasped for air, and when she finally thrust her nose above the waves, in every direction all she could see was water. The land had disappeared. In the distance she saw a rowboat. She tried to swim for it, but long, slimy tentacles of seaweed wrapped around her legs and tried to pull her down. Each seaweedy arm had a voice, and in garbled union they all chanted, "Now-we've-got-you, now-we've-got-you."

At last she reached the boat and frantically grasped the side, ready to pull herself in. Then for one terrifying moment she couldn't decide if she should hoist herself into the boat or give in to the seaweed's persuasive pull. She was paralyzed by indecision at the crucial moment. That's when she woke up.

"It was just a dream," she told herself. "A silly, meaningless dream."

She took another deep breath, closed the window, and anxiously paced the floor. "It was just a dream."

Then, leaving the light on, Christy dove under the covers and prayed, "Dear heavenly Father, please protect me and keep me safe. Be with my mom and dad and David. Amen."

Praying for her family reminded her of the promise she had made to her parents before she left home. So she added, "And, dear God, please help me keep my promise to my parents not to do anything I'll regret. Amen."

Within minutes Christy fell fast asleep.

4

Surf and Seaweed

Had there been a contest to see who could spend the most time in the bathroom getting ready, Christy would have won first prize the following morning. After nearly an hour and a half of preparations she opened the door to find Aunt Marti standing in the hall, ready to knock on the guest room door.

"There you are, honey. We were just wondering how you were coming along. Let's see how you look."

Hoping for some sign of approval, Christy asked, "Well? How do I look?"

"Your hair, dear...your hair looks...well, I'd say you did a very good job for your first try."

"I think I used too much spritz; my bangs all clumped together."

"Yes, maybe you should use a tad less next time. And perhaps go a bit easier on the eyeliner. But the bathing suit looks marvelous on you with your long legs, dear. You won't always have thighs like that if you take after your mother's side of the family, so watch the starches and keep those legs slim as long as you can."

"Yes, Aunt Martha." Christy's voice showed her irritation at the endless advice.

"Well, you know what they say," Marti quickly added, "nobody can ever be too rich or too thin!"

They both laughed and headed down the stairs.

"Do you have any good books I could take with me to read on the beach?" Christy asked.

"Sure, all kinds, darling. They're on the bookshelf in the den. Take your pick. Are you ready for your breakfast drink?"

Christy shuddered at the thought. "No, I'm not hungry. I'll just take something with me to drink." She pulled a paperback novel from the shelf.

Marti returned from the kitchen with two bottles of flavored mineral water and tucked them into Christy's canvas bag. "There you go. Have a wonderful time, and remember: Make an effort to be friendly so you can get to know some of the other young people on the beach."

"Yes, Aunt Martha." Christy ducked into the kitchen, where Uncle Bob was reading the paper. "Shhhh," she hissed, holding her finger to her lips. Then, opening the refrigerator, she exchanged the mineral water for two cans of Coke.

Uncle Bob winked and went back to reading his paper.

As Christy shuffled through the sand twenty minutes later, a few thin clouds sailed across the late morning sky. The "young people," as Aunt Marti called them, clustered together down by the jetty where the surfers hung out. The jetty, as Christy had learned from her uncle on her first day there, was a long, man-made peninsula of rocks that stuck out into the ocean, creating a calm harbor inlet on one side and the beach's biggest waves on the other.

Christy stopped and watched the morning waves smashing against the jetty. The northern waves first swelled some distance out; then, pressing in like a wall, they crashed straight down on the rocks with powerful force.

"Take control of your destiny!" Christy's aunt's words echoed in her head and pounded against her nerves. She lifted her head high and walked straight toward the same group that had laughed at her a few days earlier. With the new haircut and swimsuit, she hoped they would think she was a different girl.

Spreading out her towel, Christy noticed a few of the guys looking in her direction. *So far, so good!* Then, stretching out on her stomach, she began to read her paperback, playfully wiggling her toes in the sand. She didn't know what would be worse: for them to ignore her again or for someone to come over and actually talk to her.

A few minutes later she cast a shy glance toward the guys to see if she still held their attention. She didn't. They all fixed their eyes on an unbelievably gorgeous girl coming their way.

Tall and thin, clad in a bikini and sunglasses, the girl waltzed through the sand. Her blond hair fell to her waist, swishing behind her like the mane of a wild horse. She stopped a few feet away from Christy. Then, as everyone watched, the model beach beauty settled into the sand and gazed out at the ocean as if posing for a swimsuit ad.

What's she trying to prove? Christy pretended not to notice her. *Why is she sitting near me? What if the guys come over here to talk to her? What if they talk to me?*

A strong urge to run away swelled up in Christy. But she ignored the way her heart raced and fixed her eyes on her book. Her aunt's voice pounded in her head: "Take control of your destiny. Make the first move! Be aggressive!"

The sweet smell of coconut oil floating from the girl taunted Christy until she looked over and, with great effort, forced out a weak "Hi."

The girl responded eagerly. "That's a good book. Have you gotten to the part where they get stuck in the taxicab in Hong Kong?"

Christy was startled at the girl's friendliness. "No."

"Then I won't spoil it for you," the girl said with a smile. "But that part in Hong Kong is great, and it's so intriguing."

"Oh." Christy turned to study the girl more carefully. She seemed awfully nice—for a snob.

Then the girl asked, "Have you been in the water yet? Is it very cold?" Christy noticed that she had an unusual accent when she said certain words.

"No," Christy said. Then, realizing she wasn't adding much to the conversation, she stammered, "I mean, no, I haven't been in yet today, and I didn't go in yesterday, so I don't know if it was cold then, but the day before it was really nice." She hesitated and then asked, "Were you out here yesterday?"

"No. We arrived yesterday. My name is Alissa. What's yours?"

"Christy. Where are you from?"

"We've just come from Boston, where my grandmother lives, but this past year we lived in Germany."

"You're from Germany? Really?" Christy asked in

amazement. "My dad has some relatives in Germany. I always wanted to go there."

"We only lived in Germany for the past two years. Before that we lived in Argentina, and before that, Hawaii."

"Wow, that must've been something."

"It has its good points and its bad points. My dad was in the air force. What about you? Do you live here?"

"No. My aunt and uncle do, and I'm staying with them. I live in Wisconsin."

Wisconsin sounded pretty boring compared with Argentina or Hawaii. Alissa didn't scoff, though. Instead she suggested they go in the water. Christy felt the gaze of the surfers as she and Alissa started in slowly, moving out till they were up to their waists before diving under the foamy waves.

The cool water hit Christy's every pore. *There's no other feeling in the world like this!* To Alissa she said, "I love the ocean, don't you?"

"Definitely!" Alissa replied, bobbing over the top of a mild wave. "You would love the beaches in Hawaii. The water is so warm and clear. You can stay in almost all day, it seems. And the waves are perfect for bodysurfing."

"I wish I could bodysurf," Christy lamented. "I'm just too uncoordinated."

"It's all a matter of catching the wave at the right time," Alissa explained. "Like, see this one coming? If you wait too long, it will break on you and take you right to the bottom. You have to start kicking and paddling as the wave crests behind you. Then let it carry you to shore, like you're part of it."

The wave behind them rose too big for them to float

over, so they held their noses and dove down to the calmer water below. Up they came, treading water as the wave pushed its frothing curve toward the shore.

"Now that would have been a perfect wave to ride," came Alissa's evaluation as she smoothed down her soaking hair. "See, those guys over there caught it. I was told in Hawaii by some surfers that every seventh wave is the one to catch."

They floated over four smaller swells before Alissa pointed out, "See the seventh wave building out there? It should be the best one in this set to ride. You go over it, and I'll try to ride it in. Maybe you can see what I mean about starting to kick before it crests."

With a powerful swell the wave lifted Christy with the ease of a parent lifting a baby. She watched Alissa gracefully ride the wave all the way to shore. *She makes it look so easy!* Christy thought with a sigh.

The guys down the beach were equally impressed with the graceful Alissa. As she emerged from the water, four of them left their surfboards and jogged over to talk to her.

Christy watched with twinges of jealousy as Alissa, dripping wet, gathered her long hair over her shoulder and wrung the water out. *Oh, to have a body and a personality like Alissa's. She has it made in every way.* Christy both admired and disliked her at the same time.

Absorbed in watching the scene on the shore, Christy didn't notice the huge wave rising behind her. Without warning it broke, pulling her down with its crashing force. She turned a complete somersault under water and, panicking for air, gulped in a choking mouthful of saltwater. The terror of her dream the night before rushed up, causing her to fight something greater than the ocean. Mercilessly the wave dealt her a final blow, spewing her onto the shore and scraping her elbow in the coarse sand. The wave receded, leaving Christy like a beached seal only a few feet from none other than Alissa and the surfers.

"Oh, no!" she gasped as the group began to laugh. Water dripped from her nose, sand trickled from her ear, her bathing suit straps were all twisted in the back, and a long strand of seaweed had wrapped around her ankle. Worst of all, her hair stood straight up in the back, and the whole right side lay plastered across her cheek, covering her eye. She blinked, looking to the group for some support, but they all kept laughing. Alissa laughed the longest.

A tall, good-looking surfer with long, bleached blond hair stood next to Alissa. "Gnarly! That was totally thrashin'!"

Blood trickled from Christy's elbow, stinging almost as much as her hurt pride. *This is the absolute worst moment of my entire life!*

Then one of the surfers who had just ridden a wave into shore came over to Christy. He planted his orange surfboard into the wet sand and reached out to help her untangle the seaweed from her ankle. "You okay?"

"Yeah." Christy looked up into the face of the cutest guy she had ever seen. He matched exactly the description she had given to Paula months ago of "the perfect guy": sun-bleached blond hair falling across a broad forehead, a strong jaw, a straight nose, and screaming silver-blue eyes.

He took her by the elbow and helped her stand.

"I feel so stupid," she confided softly.

He stood at least five inches taller than her, making her feel small.

"Yeah, I can see how you would." It didn't sound cruel the way he said it. He seemed to understand how she felt.

The others went back to flirting with Alissa while Christy made her way through the hot sand to her towel. The cute guy tucked his orange surfboard under his arm and followed her. He just stood there while she dried herself off and tried to shake the sand from her ears.

Finally, Christy broke the silence. "Thanks for helping me."

"Sure." He carefully laid his board on Alissa's towel and sat next to it in the sand. "Will your friend mind if I borrow her towel?"

Christy glanced at her "friend," who was so involved in flirting with the surfers that she acted as if Christy didn't exist.

"I don't suppose so."

"I'm Todd." He smiled a fresh, clean smile.

"I'm Christy." She was surprised at how calm she acted around this unbelievably adorable guy. "Do you live here?"

"Yeah, during the summer—with my dad."

"Where's your mom?" Christy asked.

"Tallahassee, Florida. My parents are divorced, and my mom lives in Tallahassee. I live with her during the school year and spend the summers and some holidays with my dad."

Just then Alissa and one of the surfers sauntered over. They looked as though they were getting along very well. He had his arm around Alissa's waist, and they each held a beer bottle.

"You want some?" the guy offered Christy.

"No, that's okay," she answered, feeling caught off guard.

"Oh." He looked at Todd. "You must be one of his kind of friends."

"Well, actually, I brought some Cokes with me," she stammered, not sure what he meant by "one of Todd's friends."

"I've got two." She turned toward Todd. "Do you want one?"

"Sure."

Todd moved over next to Christy on her towel and then introduced the other surfer as Shawn. Christy introduced Alissa. Shawn moved Todd's board off the towel and sat down with Alissa beside him.

This is too wonderful to be true. She knew her aunt would be thrilled.

For the next hour they sat and talked. Alissa pretty much carried the conversation. She had lots of stories about what life was like in Germany. Christy liked her accent, which must have been a combination of all the places Alissa had lived and all the languages she had been exposed to.

"And the cars go so slow on the autobahns here," Alissa said. "But that's not the right word. What do you call them? Freeways?"

"No," said Christy.

"Yeah," said Todd at the same time.

They looked at each other.

"In California we call them freeways," Todd explained.

"In Wisconsin we call them interstates," Christy said.

"You still drive very slowly here," Alissa said. "In

Stuttgart it was nothing to drive at 120 kilometers an hour."

Todd and Alissa talked about cars, and Christy listened. She barely knew the difference between a Jag and a Jetta and was afraid she might say something foolish. Shawn seemed quiet too. He looked as though he wasn't all there, and his eyes were glazed. Whenever he did focus his gaze on Christy, she felt uncomfortable.

"Check it out," Shawn suddenly exclaimed, waving an arm toward the water. "That dude can shred!"

"What's that mean?" Christy asked Todd quietly.

"See that little kid out there on the white board? He's only about eight years old, and he's a really good surfer."

"How old are you?" Alissa asked Christy.

Thinking she was probably the youngest of the four of them, Christy started to lie. "Fifteen." But then she caught herself. "Well, actually, almost fifteen. My birthday is in a few weeks. How old are you, Alissa?"

"Seventeen."

Christy wasn't sure if she was lying or not. Alissa looked that old, but whenever she laughed she seemed like a junior higher. Plus, why would she be hanging around someone as young as Christy if she really were seventeen?

"You guys haven't said how old you are," Alissa pointed out.

"Ah, I forget," Shawn said.

"We're both sixteen," Todd said.

"Thanks a lot," Shawn said. "Now Alissa's going to leave because she doesn't go out with guys who are younger than her, do you?"

"That all depends." Alissa gave Shawn a look that embarrassed Christy.

She wasn't sure why, but she felt as though she were intruding on a private game. Shawn must have known all the rules to this game, because he leaned over and whispered something to Alissa. Christy turned to look down toward the jetty.

"Waves are picking up," Todd said. "Let's go surfing, Shawn."

Shawn stood and offered Alissa his hand, pulling her up with him. "Naw. We're taking off."

Alissa grabbed her towel and slipped her hand into Shawn's. "See you guys later," she said. "Nice meeting you both." The couple moved quickly through the sand toward the row of beach houses.

"Are they going to get some lunch or something?" Christy asked, confused by their sudden exit.

Todd looked at her strangely. He didn't answer.

Christy wasn't sure what she had missed, but she knew Todd wasn't exactly thrilled about Shawn leaving. She didn't mind. She would love to spend the rest of the day sitting here, talking to Todd, looking into his gorgeous blue eyes. She had never liked a guy as much as she liked Todd, and she only met him today! Did he like her? He seemed to, even though he hadn't tried to hold her hand or anything like Shawn had done with Alissa.

Actually, the thought terrified her. *What if Todd tries to hold my hand? What if he tries to kiss me?*

"Well, do you want to?" Todd interrupted her thoughts.

Christy's heart skipped a beat. "Want to what?" *Did he just read my thoughts?*

"Do you want to go surfing?"

"Oh!" Christy laughed. "I don't know. I'm not very coordinated in the water, as you may have noticed."

"I'll teach you."

"What I really want to learn is how to bodysurf. That's what Alissa was trying to teach me earlier."

"I'm not the best bodysurfer around, but I'll teach you what I know."

They dove into the water, and Christy was met again by that fresh exhilaration. Only this time it was magnified by the excitement of having Todd beside her. Like a pair of dolphins they faced the waves together, talking and laughing. Patiently Todd tried to teach her to bodysurf, but she couldn't get the timing right. Every wave rushed past her, taking Todd with it and leaving her behind, drenched.

After a while another surfer paddled to where they were bobbing over the wave, and Todd introduced him as Doug. He was cute, and Christy thought he was much friendlier than Shawn and the other surfers she had encountered earlier.

"Try this." Doug offered Christy his body board.

"How do you use it?" Christy asked, unsure of what to do with the soft, short, blue and white board he held out to her. It was much shorter than a surfboard and looked less threatening.

"Well...you just hop on and, ah...I don't know. You hold on and ride it to shore," Doug said.

"Here." Todd strapped the Velcro end of a leash around his wrist. "I'll show her."

As the next wave swelled behind them, Todd lay across the body board on his stomach and began kicking furiously to get ahead of the wave. Christy and Doug floated over the wave and watched Todd as the wave broke right behind him, lifting him and the body board, pushing them to shore.

"Looks fun!" Christy exclaimed. "I think I can handle this."

"Sure you can!" Doug agreed. "Use it all you want."

"Thanks!"

Todd paddled back out and handed the body board to Christy. "Here you go. Remember to kick yourself ahead of the wave and hold on once it begins to carry you."

Christy self-consciously lay on the board. Todd and Doug's instructions and demonstrations suddenly eluded her. All she could think was, *I hope my rear end isn't sticking up!*

"Okay," Todd called out, "start kicking!"

Christy kicked and kicked and didn't look behind her. Suddenly, the force of the wave caught her, starting at her feet and then lifting her, pushing her upward, forward. Before she realized what was happening, the wave had enveloped her. As she hung on to the board for dear life, she felt the force of the ocean tide rushing toward the shore. For one triumphant moment she felt as if she were flying. Then the belly of the body board slid onto the coarse sand at the shore, and immediately the wave receded.

Christy stood up, unscathed, and waved to Todd and Doug, who were waving their congratulations to her.

That was so fun! No wonder surfing is such a big deal. I can't imagine how it would feel to do that standing on a board! Just lying on the body board was enough to take my breath away.

She fought the waves, getting back out to the calm swells where Todd and Doug were treading water.

"Awesome!" Doug said when she joined them.

"Awesome?" Todd echoed. "Nobody says *awesome* anymore."

"I do!" Doug laughed. "And, Christy, that was an awesome ride! Took you all the way to shore." He had such a boyish look of joy on his tanned face that for a moment Doug reminded Christy of her little brother, David.

"Hey, what time do you think it is?" Todd asked.

Doug squinted up at the angle of the sun. "Probably close to three-thirty."

"That's my guess too. I gotta jam," Todd said. "I'm picking up Tracy from work."

Then he turned to Christy. "Will you be here tomorrow?"

Christy nodded, shivering a little from the cool water.

"Maybe you'll be ready to try surfing tomorrow," Todd said.

"Hey, this looks like a good one." Doug motioned toward the huge wave that was building behind them. "Let's all take it in."

While Christy lay on the body board, Doug and Todd held on to the sides, and they all kicked together. As soon as the wave caught up with them, the force tore the three of them apart, pushing Christy the fastest. She gave a tiny scream as the powerful surge thrust her forward, yanking the body board out from under her. She tumbled just once under the wave and came up behind it. The leash around her wrist allowed her to pull the board back. Todd and Doug, both now ahead of her, were rising out of the water at the shoreline.

Christy stretched back onto the board and let the wave behind her, a smaller and more tame one, nudge her to shore. She watched as Todd tilted his head back, shaking his sun-bleached hair so that all the salty droplets raced down his back.

"See you tomorrow," Doug called out as Todd headed up the beach toward where he left his surfboard in the sand.

"Yeah, later!" Todd called after them.

"You going back out in the water?" Doug asked Christy.

She was still watching Todd, hoping he would turn around and give one last wave meant only for her.

"No, I'm kind of cold." She unstrapped the Velcro leash around her wrist. "I think I'll lie out for a while. Thanks for letting me use your board. It was really fun!"

"Sure," Doug said, taking it from her. "Anytime."

Christy stretched out on her towel and let the sun warm her. The salt water dried in little spots on her legs, and she felt scratchy and dry and terribly thirsty. She lasted on the towel only about half an hour before deciding she couldn't stand it any longer. Doug was still out in the water, riding his body board, and Todd wouldn't be back for the rest of the day. Alissa was long gone. There was no reason to wait around, so she gathered her belongings and hurried back to the house.

This whole day has been "awesome," to use Doug's word, she thought as she picked her way over the hot sand. *My aunt is going to be so proud of me! She was right. All I needed was the right kind of bathing suit and hairstyle. I love being part of Todd's group. Todd. Oh, man, Paula is never going to believe this!*

5

The Invitation

Early the next morning, Christy marched out to the beach. Her hair washed and styled, her eye makeup in place, she anxiously looked for Todd. Except for a few surfers she didn't know, hardly anybody was on the beach. None of the group she had met the day before was there.

Slipping back into the silent house, she checked the clock: 8:27. No wonder nobody was on the beach yet. Christy dropped into a chair and snapped on the TV. A children's program was on. She sat there numbly watching the brightly colored puppets as a green one with shifty eyes tried to talk a big, fuzzy yellow bird puppet into buying a pickle and sardine ice cream cone. The bird kept saying he didn't like it.

"How do you know you don't like it unless you try it?" The green puppet pressured his friend until he finally gave in, paid his quarter, and took a lick.

"Yeech!" The bird squawked. "I tried it, and I don't like it."

"Heh, heh, heh," laughed the green fellow. "I knew you

wouldn't like it! But too bad for you because now I've got your quarter. Heh, heh, heh. You just made my day. Heh, heh, heh."

Oh, brother! Christy clicked off the TV. *To think that that's supposed to be educational for little kids! Sheesh!*

"I tried it, and I don't like it," she mimicked in her puppet voice.

"Don't like what?" Uncle Bob's voice came from the doorway.

"Oh! A pickle and sardine ice cream cone."

"Then how about a pickle and sardine and cheese omelet?"

Christy laughed at her uncle's humor. "Okay—if you skip the pickles and the sardines!"

Over breakfast Christy talked with Uncle Bob about Todd. "He is the absolute cutest guy I've ever known, and I'm pretty sure he likes me."

"Any guy would be crazy not to like you, Christy."

Uncle Bob was so easy to talk to. Christy wished it could be the same way with her own dad, but he was a serious, hardworking farmer. Conversations with him consisted of him pondering a subject for hours, and then he'd tell Christy, "This is the way it is." Not much room for free thought or discussion. He was the dad; she was the daughter. He said; she did. That was that. She liked this feeling of being able to give her opinions, to talk things through, to feel capable of making wise decisions.

Her self-confidence lifted, she headed back out to the beach around eleven o'clock, ready for anything. She was so exuberant that when she saw Todd she ran to greet him, not realizing he was talking to another girl. A very cute girl.

"Hey, Christy," Todd called out. "How's it going? This is Tracy."

"Hi," Tracy said with a quick smile. Petite with shoulder-length, light brown hair, Tracy had a heart-shaped face that gave her a sweet, innocent look.

Christy's eyes darted from Todd to Tracy, then back to Todd. Had she intruded or what?

"Do you guys mind if I put my towel down here?"

"Of course not," Tracy answered. "Todd told me that two new girls were out yesterday while I was at work. Is your friend coming?"

"I don't know. I just met her yesterday, and she took off with Shawn. I didn't see her the rest of the day."

"I saw them both this morning," Todd said in a low voice. "They'll probably be down later."

"I don't see how you can still be such tight friends with him," Tracy said to Todd.

"Shawn and I have been friends a long time."

"I know, but you guys don't have anything in common anymore."

"I can't just ignore him," Todd defended.

"Don't get mad," Tracy scolded. "I only wondered why you still do things with him, that's all."

"Where do you work?" Christy interjected, trying to clear the air. She couldn't quite tell if Todd and Tracy were talking to each other like brother and sister or like boyfriend and girlfriend.

"At Hanson's Parlor. It's an ice cream shop down by the Pavilion. Do you need a job? They're looking for someone else to work nights."

"No. But thanks anyway," Christy answered, still trying

to discern Todd and Tracy's relationship. Todd and Tracy. Their names even went together! Did he like Tracy? Christy felt jittery, wanting to know where she stood with him.

"What time do you work today?" Todd asked Tracy.

"Noon to six. Can you still give me a ride?"

"Sure. We probably should leave pretty soon. Hey, there's Shawn and Alissa."

Now Christy definitely felt like a fifth wheel. Shawn and Alissa came up with their arms around each other, clearly orbiting in their own private galaxy.

What am I doing here? Christy thought.

"Are you all coming to the party tomorrow night?" Alissa asked.

"What party?"

"Shawn's. His parents are going out of town for the weekend."

"Are you going, Tracy?" Christy asked.

"No. I'm not much of a party person. Besides, I've got to work."

"What about you, Todd?"

"I'll probably stop by."

Christy's interest rose. If Tracy wasn't there, maybe she would have a better chance with Todd.

"I guess I'll go," Christy said. "I'll have my aunt drop me off."

"Oh, you don't want to do that," Alissa said with a light laugh. "Not for a party like this! It's only a few blocks. You can walk over with me if you want."

"That would be great." Christy cast a glance at Todd to see if he would offer to pick her up instead.

"We have to go," was all Todd said. "I'm taking Tracy to

work, and I told my dad I'd finish painting the front deck today."

"Bye!" Christy called out as Todd and Tracy left. "See you later!" She tried not to sound too disappointed that Todd wasn't going to spend the day with her.

Alissa and Shawn decided to leave too and walked off with their arms around each other. Alissa's bronzed body, like a magnet, drew glances from everyone she passed. Surely she knew everyone was watching, but she acted oblivious to the attention.

Christy pulled out her paperback and tried not to get too depressed about being left alone so suddenly. As the afternoon sun slowly beat down on her back, she kept looking up every few minutes, hoping Todd would return.

She couldn't figure him out. Yesterday he acted as if he really liked her, and then today he and Tracy acted like a married couple—arguing, him giving her a ride to work.

Where do I fit? she wondered. *At least he'll be at the party tomorrow night, and Tracy won't be there. I wish I could act the way Alissa does around guys. Then I would have a better chance at getting a guy like Todd to be interested in me.*

After several hours of making little progress in the book, she gathered up her belongings and hopped through the burning sand, wondering how Alissa could manage to walk so gracefully. Everything Alissa did was perfect. If only Christy could be like her.

The worst part about going back to her aunt and uncle's beach house was that she knew Aunt Marti would want a full report on the day, and there wasn't much to tell. Except about the party invitation. At least she had that to look forward to.

Marti lay stretched out in a lounge chair on the patio, a tall glass of iced tea in her hand. She had on a black bathing suit with a purple sash around the waist and an oversized straw hat with matching purple sash. Only her legs were exposed to the sun. She was studying a tabloid magazine. For just a moment, Christy thought her aunt looked a little like the movie star on the front of the magazine.

"Oh, Christy!" Her aunt looked up, startled. "I didn't see you there. Tell me all about your day, darling. Was it as wonderful as yesterday?"

Christy skimmed over the details, leaving out the part about being left alone, and told her aunt about the party invitation.

Aunt Marti cooed proudly, "I knew you could get in with the popular crowd if you tried. What time should I drop you off at the young man's house?"

"Actually, Alissa is going to pick me up." Christy hoped her aunt wouldn't object and insist on driving her, since Alissa made it sound immature to have an adult drop you off.

"Well, we'll see." Then with a look of terror she added, "Oh, dear! We'll have to go shopping to get you something nice to wear."

"But Aunt Marti, I got a whole new wardrobe just the other day, remember?"

"Yes, but we didn't get any real party dresses!" Aunt Marti seemed genuinely distressed.

"Party dresses? I don't think I should wear a dress, Aunt Marti. What if we play Twister, like we did at Paula's birthday party?"

"Twister?" Aunt Marti appeared unfamiliar with the game. "And who is Paula?"

"My best friend back home. I'm just going to wear jeans."

To Christy's relief her aunt backed off.

As Christy walked into the kitchen, Uncle Bob was taking a frozen package of hamburger out of the freezer.

"Holy mackerel!" he exclaimed when he saw Christy. "Are you ever sunburned!"

"Oh, really?" She seemed pleased. "I'm surprised I got any sun on my face. I think I was on my stomach almost all day."

"Here, little lobster." He handed her a tube of aloe vera gel. "Put this on after your shower, or you'll swell up like a tomato and scare all the guys away."

"I didn't scare them away at the beach today," Christy responded flippantly. "I even got invited to a party." She opened the refrigerator and scanned the shelves for anything edible.

"My, my," Uncle Bob retorted, "aren't we the little social butterfly all of a sudden! Will we have the honor of your presence at dinner tonight?"

"Yes, the party isn't until tomorrow night." Christy grabbed a spoon and started eating rocky road ice cream right from the nearly empty carton. Uncle Bob didn't seem to mind.

"Did Todd invite you to the party?"

"No, but he's going to be there," she told him as she finished off the ice cream. "The party is at Shawn's house, and I'm going with Alissa." Christy tossed the empty ice cream container into the trash and began going through the cupboards. "Is there anything to eat around here?"

"In a few hours there'll be a Mexican fiesta served on

the front patio," he said with a dramatic flair. "Shall I call you when it's ready?"

"*Si, si, señor!*" Christy called over her shoulder as she headed for the guest room.

Not until she looked in the bathroom mirror did she see what Uncle Bob meant about her face being sunburned. Even the tops of her ears were burned! As she washed her hair, the water from the showerhead felt like a thousand piercing needles jamming into her back. It took a major effort to get dressed. Even the aloe vera gel hurt as she gently applied it to her shoulders.

Later, as the three of them sat down for dinner, Aunt Marti got a good look at Christy's face. "Christy, darling! You're terribly sunburned. Didn't you take any sunscreen for your face today?"

"It's all right, Martha," Uncle Bob calmed her. "I gave her some aloe vera gel. She'll be fine."

"Now don't eat too much dinner, dear. You need to keep light on your feet for tomorrow night."

"Really, Martha!" Bob protested.

"Well, tomorrow night is going to be an important evening for Christy, and I only want to make sure she's at her best."

Christy didn't feel at her best when the important evening arrived. She had gotten so sunburned the day before that she spent the entire day lying around the house, moaning, drinking ice water, and tolerating Aunt Marti as she smeared a variety of home remedy concoctions on Christy's painful shoulders and back.

Christy wanted to go out on the beach to look for Todd, but her aunt wouldn't let her out of the house. So Christy spent the day thinking about him, imagining what it would be like the next time she saw him.

Around four o'clock she started going through her closet, trying to decide what to wear. Finally she settled on a new pair of jeans and a new T-shirt. It was the kind of outfit Paula would have worn, but Christy wished she had Alissa's phone number so she could call to see what she was going to wear. Alissa was so much more mature than Paula, and, having lived all over the world, she knew more about life than any of Christy's friends at home.

Brushing her short hair, Christy thought of Alissa's long, beautiful hair and decided to let hers grow out again. By the time she turned seventeen, it might be as long as Alissa's. She tilted her head back in front of the mirror, imitating Alissa's laugh, trying to swish her invisible long mane.

"Whatever are you doing, dear?" Aunt Marti had been watching from the bedroom doorway.

"Oh!" Christy spun around, startled. "Just...nothing."

"Well, it's really about time for you to get ready for the party. Have you decided what to wear yet?"

Christy looked down at her outfit. "This. I'm going to wear this. I'm almost all ready."

Aunt Marti scrutinized the outfit. "I suppose it is your decision. I was just trying to help." She turned to go, switching her guilty tone to an overly cheery announcement. "Dinner's ready."

I can't stand this! Christy inwardly screamed. *First, all I hear from adults is how to grow up and be true to myself and make my own decisions. Then, every time I turn around they remind me of how immature I am and how totally stupid my decisions are.*

Christy threw her hairbrush on the floor, swung the closet door open, grabbed her new sundress, and yanked the T-shirt off. *Ouch!* Her sunburned skin tugged and throbbed from all the violent action. She burst into tears and threw herself on the bed until the raging in her head subsided.

"I don't care what she thinks," Christy said, gathering her composure. "I'm going to wear what I want to wear. And I am *not* going to cry like a baby anymore!"

Christy put the T-shirt back on, brushed her hair, and calmly walked down the stairs.

6

What's a Girl Like Me...?

At the dinner table, Christy picked at her stir-fried vegetables quietly. Aunt Marti swung back into full control.

"I'm so anxious to meet your new friend, Alissa. I'm really very proud of you, Christy darling, for making friends so quickly and receiving an invitation to a party. It's absolutely marvelous!"

Christy didn't even feel like going to the party now. But she started to perk up as Uncle Bob told the humorous story of how his golf cart broke down on the fifteenth hole that afternoon. By the time Alissa rang the doorbell, Christy felt happy again and ready for a fun time.

Aunt Marti instantly took to Alissa. "She's the epitome of perfection," Marti whispered to Christy after they'd invited Alissa to come inside. "And she's a marvelous model for you to pattern yourself after."

Christy had had other thoughts about Alissa and the party as soon as she had opened the door. Alissa wore a dress—a stunning white, very fashionable dress that showed off her tan. The living room filled with the fragrance of gardenias as she made polite conversation with Bob and Marti. Christy studied her inch by inch. Her makeup was perfect, and her gorgeous long, blond hair was perfect— everything about Alissa was perfect! Christy hated her and, at the same time, would have given anything to be just like her.

As they walked the three blocks to Shawn's house, Alissa said, "I almost didn't come. Shawn! He's such a loser. So immature."

"I thought you guys were really starting to like each other."

"Is that what you thought?" Alissa seemed surprised. "He's a big baby. I've got better things to do than babysit little boys."

When they arrived, Alissa moved through the room with ballerina-like motions, first twirling to greet this person, then raising a slender arm to wave at that person.

Christy watched her in amazement as the throb of the blaring music made her heart pound. Neither Shawn nor Todd was around—just a sea of unfamiliar spectators casually observing Alissa's performance. Alissa carried out her well-rehearsed play until she floated to the couch, where the most gorgeous guy in the room sat. Christy guessed he must be at least twenty. With his bleached blond curls and scruffy goatee, he reminded Christy of a movie star Paula liked. She couldn't remember his name, but Paula had posters of him in her room.

Alissa obviously had zeroed in on this guy as the one she wanted to spend her time with. Christy knew that was the last she'd see of Alissa all night. As Christy watched Alissa smile and flirt with the guy, she felt intimidated, frightened, and painfully aware that she was the only one wearing jeans. All the other girls were dressed in stylish outfits. She felt like a three-year-old, quivering in the corner in her T-shirt. How could she ever admit that Aunt Marti had been right about the clothes?

Sure enough, Alissa and her new boyfriend were rising from the couch and heading for the front door, laughing, with their arms wrapped around each other.

Now Christy was mad—mad and frightened. Everything inside demanded she run out the door and keep running the three blocks back to Bob and Marti's house. But she couldn't make her feet move. She wasn't ready to face her aunt and explain why she was home so early. And what about Todd? He was the real reason she had come to this party.

People stood around with their backs to her, talking and holding beer cans; a few people were smoking. No one gave her a second glance. Trying to calm herself, Christy decided that maybe she would fit in better if she had something to hold in her hand like everyone else. Then she could stand there, holding a can of Coke, and wait for Todd to show up. With all the courage she could muster, Christy left her corner and found her way into the kitchen.

"Excuse me," she said to one of the surfers standing by the refrigerator. "Is this where you get stuff to drink?"

He didn't answer, just pointed to the ice chests on the kitchen floor and took another sip from his beer can. Christy stuck her hand into the ice and started scrounging around for a can of Coke. All she could find was beer. She went to the second ice chest and found the same thing. She didn't think she wanted beer. She had tried some once at Paula's house when she was ten and thought it tasted awful.

How could anyone drink the stuff?

Another guy came into the kitchen and yelled toward Christy, "Hey, grab me two cold ones."

It startled her. He was the first person who had spoken to her since she arrived.

"Do you know where Shawn is?" Christy asked.

He didn't seem to hear her over the music. She asked again, more loudly. "Do you know where Shawn is?"

The surfer helped himself to the drinks in the ice chest when Christy didn't respond to his request. He looked her over, as if he was trying to remember where he had seen her before.

"Shawn's upstairs," he answered. Then he made the connection. "Hey, did Alissa come?"

"Yes, but she already left." Christy had to shout the words as another song came on that was even louder. "Where upstairs?"

"Huh?"

"Where upstairs is Shawn?" She was yelling right into his ear.

"Huh?" He looked confused.

The music stopped suddenly, just as Christy was yelling, "I just want to ask Shawn if he has any Coke!"

The room fell completely silent. One of the guys said, "Whoa, baby. Party tonight!" The girl beside him laughed.

Why is everyone staring at me? Her heart pounded. *Do they think I'm a baby asking for Coke instead of beer?*

Hanging on to what little composure she had left, she headed up the stairs. She tapped on the first closed door, and a guy's voice hollered, "Go away!" A knock on the second door produced Shawn.

"Hi," she said, feeling totally stupid.

Shawn looked around behind her. "Where's Alissa?"

"She left with some guy." Christy's voice reflected her irritation at being left behind by Alissa. Shawn must also have felt irritated with Alissa because he let out a string of words that shocked Christy. How could they act so in love one day and despise each other the next?

"I really didn't mean to upset you, Shawn. I just wanted to find out if you had any Coke."

He gave her a startled look, just like the surfer downstairs had. Then, without saying anything, he motioned for her to step into the room. Christy thought it was a funny place to keep soft drinks. Six other people were sitting around on the bed and floor of what she guessed to be his parents' bedroom. Todd wasn't one of the six people.

Nobody said anything to her, yet they weren't completely ignoring her either. It was as if she had walked in on a private little clique, and for some reason she had been accepted without a word.

Shawn handed the guy by the nightstand a book of matches and then came over to Christy and in a rather low voice said, "The coke didn't come in. But this stuff is better than anything you usually get around here." Shawn held out a strange-smelling cigarette to Christy.

Everyone seemed to be looking at her. Beads of perspiration stung her sunburned forehead as the realization came over her, and she blurted out, "You mean, that's marijuana?"

"Yeah, I told you—the coke didn't come in."

"Oh!" Christy said, shocked. "I didn't mean...I was only...I was looking for something to drink!"

Shawn shook his head and turned away from her. The room suddenly felt very small, and the air was heavy with what smelled like thick incense. It made Christy feel lightheaded, and she couldn't think of what to do next. She hated feeling so immature and inexperienced. Yet there was no way she wanted to stay with this group, no matter how welcomed they made her feel.

What would Alissa do? The room spun around her. The music from downstairs pounded through the soles of her feet, reaching all the way to her temples.

Shawn turned back around and eyed her through the tendrils of smoke that rose from the joint in his mouth. Then he nodded, taking the joint and offering it to her. Christy closed her eyes. The smoke filled her nostrils. All of a sudden she heard a voice from across the room say, "Hey, how's it going?"

It was Todd.

Christy was flooded with embarrassment! Why did Todd have to walk in at that very moment? Without a word she rushed past Todd, fled from the room, and dashed down the stairs. Desperately she pushed her way through the crush of people who were drinking and laughing. The raging music taunted her all the way to the front door. Not until she'd run almost a block away did she let the tears fall.

I am just a big baby! she screamed to herself. Slowing to a walk, Christy tried to catch her breath.

Suddenly, someone from behind touched her sunburned shoulder. She turned with force, ready to swing at whoever it was.

"You going home now?" Todd asked gently.

She turned away and blinked back the tears. "I guess so."

"I'll walk with you." It was another one of his statements. Not a question or an invitation, just a fact. "Let's go this way," he added, heading toward the water.

Christy ran her finger under each eye, hoping to clear away any smudged mascara. Willingly she followed him, not sure of what might happen next and too unsure of herself to do anything else.

7

A Time to Cry

Christy and Todd walked through the soft, cool sand in silence. The sun had just set, smearing the sky with orange and pink swirls. Christy filled her lungs with the fresh sea air, anxious to cleanse the last hour from her mind. Todd kept his gaze fixed out at the ocean. Why had he come with her? She had been so naive about so many things at the party. Was being alone with Todd another unwise move? She didn't know who she could trust anymore.

Todd interrupted her jumbled thoughts. "You want to sit over there on the jetty for a while?"

"I–I don't know. I guess so." She felt guilty for not trusting Todd. But it was too hard to try to make any decisions at the moment.

They sat in silence for a long time, the waves crashing just below their feet, spraying a fine mist on Christy's jeans. The air felt warm, but the dampness of the ocean spray made Christy shiver, so she pulled her legs up and wrapped her arms around them, as if giving herself a comforting hug. The tranquility of the ocean sounds at night and the fresh, salt-laced air had a calming effect on Christy.

"So," Todd began. It was as if he had purposely allowed Christy time to clear her head, and now he was ready to talk. "Not your usual kind of party, was it?"

"No," Christy admitted.

She turned to him and noticed for the first time what a gentle face Todd had. His personality was strong and direct. But when she looked at him in the twilight haze, she could see something tender in his eyes. What had started as a crush was becoming something deeper than she had ever felt for any guy before. She really, really liked him.

"Can I tell you something?" she ventured. It was important that Todd knew what kind of girl she was. "I've never smoked any kind of cigarette before. I've never even seen or smelled marijuana! I thought the smell was nauseating."

"Is that why you turned it down?" asked Todd.

"No…" She hesitated a moment. "I mean, I thought about it for half a second because I thought that's what Alissa would do, and I felt so stupid just standing there. But then I guess I didn't because of my summer promise."

"Your summer promise?"

"Before I came here this summer, my parents made me promise I wouldn't do anything I'd regret later."

"Sounds wise." Todd's voice deepened as he added, "Promises can change your life, you know. Most people don't realize it, but a promise can last forever."

It was silent again for a few minutes as Christy reviewed the evening's events in her thoughts before asking, "Do you like it?"

"Like what?"

"Marijuana. Do you smoke it a lot?" Christy's boldness surprised even her, but Todd wasn't the kind of guy who played flirty games.

"No. I used to. Sometimes. But I don't anymore."

"Why?"

Todd looked right at Christy. "Because I'm a Christian now."

Christy was completely startled. She never expected such a statement from a California surfer. "What does that have to do with it?"

"Everything."

"Well, I'm a Christian too," Christy said, trying to recover from her surprise. "My whole family is. I was baptized when I was a baby."

"I was baptized right out there." Todd pointed to the ocean. "Last summer. July 27th."

"You're kidding!" Christy adjusted her position on the jagged rocks and sat up straight. "That's my birthday!"

Todd looked as though he was about to say something, but they were interrupted by a loud group of people coming toward them. It was the group from the party. Shawn was leading the way, whooping it up, making all kinds of loud noises with an echo of support from the others. The traveling party stopped on the beach a short distance from Todd and Christy. Shawn yelled something about surfing the jetty with his eyes closed.

"What's he doing?" Christy asked.

"He's stoned. I've seen him like this before. He totally goes into the ozone. Looks like he's going bodysurfing, which is really stupid. Wait here. I'll be right back."

Christy couldn't hear Todd as he confronted Shawn, but

she saw him pulling on Shawn's arm. Then Shawn jerked away from Todd and bellowed out a series of cuss words, ending with, "I don't need this from you! Get outta my face."

Shawn plunged into the water while a few of the guys in the crowd started pushing Todd around. He turned away from them and stalked through the sand back to Christy.

His voice filled with tension, Todd shouted at Christy, "Hanson's is still open. You want to go?"

"Sure. Where?" Christy couldn't remember where she had heard that name before.

"Get some ice cream."

"Okay." Christy hopped down and fell into step with his brisk march. "What about Shawn?"

"Hey, I tried, okay? He's responsible for his own actions."

His words brimmed with anger and frustration, which made Christy pull back. With all her heart she wanted to slip her hand into his and give it a comforting squeeze. But she was too shy. Instead she chattered away, trying to use her words to cheer him up as they walked the nine blocks to the ice cream parlor.

"My uncle played golf today, and the funniest thing happened! His golf cart broke down, and he walked all the way back to the clubhouse before he realized he had left his clubs back in the cart at the fifteenth hole."

Todd's response was minimal. Obviously it was much funnier when Uncle Bob told it. Todd remained solemn until they entered Hanson's Parlor. Suddenly he perked up, and Christy's heart sank when she realized why. Tracy worked here. And there she was, balancing a banana split in one hand and a malt in the other.

"Tracy! How's it going?" Todd ambled over to a table with Christy close behind.

"Hi, you guys! I'll be with you in just a second." Her hair, pulled up in a ponytail, was tied with a bright pink ribbon that matched the ruffled apron of her uniform. She looked too cute.

Christy sank into the chair and watched Tracy gingerly deliver two huge hot fudge sundaes to the table next to theirs. Then, wiping her hands on her apron, Tracy stepped over and said, "It's been so busy tonight! If you had come an hour earlier there wouldn't have been a place to sit."

"What do you want, Christy?" Todd asked, his steady manner returning.

Christy decided to play it coy in front of Tracy. "I don't know, Todd. I didn't bring any money with me."

"Don't worry, I've got enough. As long as you don't order the Hanson's Extravaganza."

"Oh, please!" Tracy moaned. "Making two of those in one night is more than I can handle, and I've already reached my quota!"

"Then I'll have a hot fudge sundae with chocolate chip ice cream and no nuts," Christy ordered.

"And I'll have my usual," Todd said, smiling at Tracy.

Christy tried to subdue her feeling of jealousy over Todd and Tracy's closeness because at this very moment, she realized, she was on what could actually be considered her first real date. She and Paula had a contest, now into its fourth month, to see who would be the first to go out on a real date. The rules were that the guy had to ask, he had to pay, and he had to be the one to take you home. Christy had two out of three so far. It looked as though

Paula would have to be the one to cough up the ten dollars.

Todd's "usual" turned out to be a mango shake with a pineapple wedge. Tracy placed the ice cream on the table with much more grace than Christy knew she could have managed and asked, "Weren't you going to Shawn's party, Christy?"

"I went, but there wasn't much going on, so, ah, I left." *Why did I make it sound like that? What if Todd tells her the real story of how I ran out of the house crying?*

"That's not exactly the whole story," Todd told Tracy.

Christy felt so foolish.

"It really ticks me off, Tracy. When we left, Shawn was totally stoned. I tried to stop him from going into the water, but he just blew me off like I was nothing to him." Todd took a chomp out of his pineapple wedge. "I almost slugged him, Trace. I almost bashed him right in the face. But I know it wouldn't have stopped him."

Christy felt excluded from the conversation as Tracy gave her advice to Todd. "I know it's hard, but you can't spend the rest of your life feeling responsible for Shawn. He's the one in the wrong. It's not your problem. Just turn it over to the Lord."

Todd's response held the same brother-sister argumentative spirit Christy had seen between the couple on the beach. "But he's my best friend! I can't just let it go like I don't care! You've never understood that about me, Tracy. I stick up for my friends, even when they're being jerks."

Tracy excused herself. "I have to go take some more orders."

"So..." Christy tried to break into the conversation. "You and Shawn are really close friends?"

"Yeah. We've known each other a long time, and we used to do everything together. I mean everything. But last summer when I became a Christian, we kind of went our separate ways. I wasn't into all the stuff he was into any- more. Except surfing."

Christy didn't understand why "becoming a Christian," as Todd said, would change anything between friends.

Todd remained withdrawn when he walked Christy home. She fought the sinking feeling that maybe he didn't like her the same way she liked him. But at the front door her spirits rose.

"I want to get your phone number," Todd said in his matter-of-fact way.

"7-9-4—" She stopped, realizing that was her home phone. She didn't know her aunt and uncle's number.

"Just a minute," she said, leaving Todd by the front door while she ran in to copy the number off the kitchen phone.

When she returned an ambulance siren blared a few blocks away. It was so loud that Christy could barely hear what Todd said as he waved good-bye. Did he say, "I'll see you tomorrow" or "I'll call you tomorrow"? Either way, Christy's excitement soared as she met Aunt Marti in the living room.

"Well, Christy my dear! I'm dying to hear all about your party. Did you and Alissa have a good time? What did you have to eat? Did you play Twister like you thought you would?"

Christy laughed and laughed.

"I don't understand. Why are you laughing, dear?"

Christy stretched out on the plush carpet and shook her

head. "Let me just say that it wasn't the kind of evening I thought it would be. But I ended up having a good time anyway, and Todd brought me home. He might call me tomorrow, so I better tell Uncle Bob not to give him a hard time."

"Whatever do you mean?" Aunt Marti asked, blinking her eyes. "Your uncle would never do anything to embarrass you!"

"Oh, right!" Christy laughed all the way up to her room. What a night! What a week! She felt as if she had grown up and changed more in the last few days than she had in the last three years.

When she woke up the next morning, Christy still felt exuberant. Cleansing her face and putting on her makeup, she thought about Todd. Should she go down to the beach or wait around for him to call? She curled her hair with special care and was nearly finished when Uncle Bob knocked on her door.

"Christy—telephone! Somebody named Rod or Claude or Schmod or something."

"Eeeeeeee!" Christy squealed. "I'll be right there!"

With one last look in the mirror she took the stairs two at a time and picked up the phone in the den.

"I've got it, Uncle Bob," she hollered and then heard a considerate click.

"Hello?" She tried to sound aloof yet interested and at the same time charming. Even though Todd didn't seem the type to play these kinds of games, why couldn't she?

"Christy. It's Todd. I'm at the hospital. Do you think your aunt or uncle could bring you over? It's Hoag Memorial."

Christy was so shocked she nearly dropped the receiver. "Todd! What—how—what happened? Are you all right?"

"It's not me. It's Shawn. He crashed into the jetty last night. Broke a lot of bones. Lost a lot of blood. He's still unconscious."

"When did you find out?"

"Last night when I left your house. There was an ambulance out on the beach. I had a feeling it must be Shawn, so I followed them to the hospital. I've been here all night. His parents are out of town. I thought I'd go back to his house and try to find some phone numbers of relatives or somebody who might know where they are." The weariness sounded in his voice.

"Well, what can I do?" Christy felt shocked and helpless but willing to do anything for Todd.

"I wondered if you could be with him in case he comes to. He might be able to tell you where his parents are. I wouldn't have called you except I couldn't get ahold of anybody else."

"Sure, Todd," Christy responded numbly. "I'll come right over."

Uncle Bob drove as Aunt Marti chattered nervously. Todd met them in the lobby and told them what room to go to and the phone number to Shawn's house. He looked pale and distraught. The expression looked out of place on his strong, gentle face. Christy wished she could throw her arms around him, hug him, and cry on his shoulder.

Todd left, and the three of them rode the elevator to Shawn's floor. Then so many things happened at once that it was hard to figure out what was going on. Shawn had stopped breathing and was taken immediately to the operating room. There was some kind of problem over Shawn's being under eighteen and his parents not being there to sign release papers for the surgery. Uncle Bob spoke in hushed tones with the doctor while Aunt Marti and Christy stood in the hallway. From out of nowhere a police officer appeared, and a nurse directed him to Christy.

"Excuse me, miss," he said, peering intently at her. He was a large man, and his mere presence startled Christy. "I'm Officer Martin. May I ask you a few questions?"

"Yes, sir."

"Were you with Shawn Russell last night at the time of the accident?"

"Yes. I mean no. I mean sort of," Christy floundered.

"I see." Officer Martin raised an eyebrow. "Perhaps we should sit down, and you should tell me what you know."

Aunt Marti was the first to sit down, nervously clicking her nails. "Now tell him everything, Christy darling." Her voice was higher and squeakier than usual.

"Well, there was a party at Shawn's house last night, and I got there about eight o'clock," Christy began.

"Were there drugs at this party?"

Aunt Marti gasped. "Heavens, no!"

The officer looked irritated. "Perhaps you can let the young lady answer for herself."

Aunt Marti recoiled in her seat.

Christy's heart pounded. "Yes, sir."

"There were drugs?"

"Yes, sir." Out of the corner of her eye she could see Aunt Marti turning pale. "I went upstairs," Christy told him, her voice shaking, "because one of the guys told me to go upstairs. See, I was trying to find something to drink besides beer, and I asked if they had any Coke, and they told me to go upstairs and ask Shawn. Shawn Russell. It was at his house. The party, I mean." She was shaking so badly she could hardly think straight.

"Go on," the officer instructed.

"Well, I went upstairs to the bedroom, and when I went in there were some people, and they were, well, I didn't know what they were doing at first. But then I figured out it was drugs. They were smoking marijuana."

"Oh!" Aunt Marti looked as if she might faint.

"Miss Miller," the officer bent down and looked forcefully at Christy, "did you participate in the use of any illegal drugs last night?"

"No!" The word jumped out of her throat like a scared cat. Then, pulling back, she said, "No, sir, I did not."

Never before in her life had she felt so good. So glad she had made the right decision.

Aunt Marti heaved a huge sigh of relief.

"Do you know the names of any of the other people at the party?" the officer asked.

"Just Todd. I think his last name is Spencer, but I'm not sure. He's the guy who is at Shawn's house trying to locate his parents."

"And you honestly did not know any of the other people in the bedroom last night?" He didn't seem convinced.

"No, sir."

"Okay, go on."

Christy gave him a few more details. Then he stopped her and questioned, "Now Todd was the one with you when you left the beach after Shawn headed for the water?"

Christy nodded.

"Did Todd try to stop Shawn from going into the water?"

"Yes, sir. But it was no use. He said Shawn was too stoned to know what was going on. Some of the other guys started pushing Todd around. I was afraid there might be a fight."

Christy noticed Uncle Bob walking back down the hall toward them, his face stone gray. He walked over to Christy and cupped her chin in his hand.

"I'm sorry, honey." Tears filled his eyes. "There was nothing the doctors could do."

"Oh, dear me!" gasped Aunt Marti.

"The patient expired?" asked the officer with no emotion in his voice.

Uncle Bob nodded.

"Well, thank you for your time, Miss Miller," the policeman said, briskly excusing himself.

Uncle Bob sat down and slipped his arm around Christy. She began to shake uncontrollably and cried into his light blue golf shirt, leaving streaks of mascara on the shoulder.

"Todd doesn't know!" she cried. "We've got to call him. Where's the number?"

Aunt Marti had regained her composure and was back in control of things. "Now, Christy, let your uncle call him. You stay here and calm yourself."

Christy's mind raced through its crazy maze while Uncle Bob stood at the phone booth a few yards away. How could Shawn be dead? She just met him a few days ago, and now he was gone. It couldn't be true. The tears flowed down her cheeks.

Uncle Bob returned and said softly, "I think we'd better go now."

"What about Todd?" Christy sobbed.

"I got ahold of him. He had tracked down Shawn's parents. They were staying with friends in Carmel but are taking the next flight back. Todd will pick them up at the airport." Then he added gently, "They don't know yet."

The drive home was uncomfortable. Except for Christy's sniffling and Aunt Marti's occasional deep sighs, all was quiet. Just as they pulled into the driveway, Aunt Marti broke the silence.

"Actually, Christina, I had no idea these were the kinds of friends you had been keeping company with! Why, if I thought for one minute that you were going to a drug party last night, I—"

Uncle Bob cut her off with a force Christy had never seen from him. "Martha, let it go! I mean it! Don't you dare say another word to her. Can't you see you're the one who pushed her into all this?"

"Me? How did I push her?"

"Yes, you! And you're too stubborn to admit it! You wouldn't let Christy stay innocent. You had to try to give her whole life a makeover, and the truth is she didn't need it!" With that he slammed the car door and stormed into the house.

"Well!" Aunt Marti was indignant. "I don't know where that came from."

Christy wasn't sure what she should do. She had never seen them fight like this before.

In the same way that a foaming wave recedes, Aunt Marti's anger disappeared, and her cool composure returned. "Christy dear, don't mind your uncle. I'm sure he didn't mean to hurt you. Why don't you and I go out for a salad over on Balboa Island? There's a marvelous little place I've been wanting to take you."

It seemed to Christy that the whole world was spinning around her. How could Aunt Marti talk about eating? She stared at her aunt. What a cold, insensitive woman! Did she think that ignoring reality would make it go away?

"Shall we go?" Aunt Marti prodded, fumbling for her keys.

Christy responded with all the graciousness she could find in her troubled spirit. "To be honest, Aunt Martha, I don't feel much like eating. I'd rather go lie down for a while—if that's okay with you." The ending came out as sarcastic as it was meant to.

Aunt Marti stiffened. "Fine. I'll just go by myself then."

Christy pulled herself out of the car and somberly opened the front door as the silver Mercedes lurched from the driveway and sped down the street. A pounding ache crashed against the insides of Christy's head. She retreated to her room, where she spent the rest of the day with the door closed. For a long while she lay on her bed, staring at nothing. Like a scratched CD that skipped back to the same place over and over again, Shawn's death would not stop playing itself over in her head.

So many thoughts pierced her. Why Shawn? He was only sixteen. Sure, he had been smoking dope, but it was still an accident. Couldn't God have kept it from happening? We all make mistakes. And where was Shawn now? Was he in heaven or... Was hell a real place? Do people really go there when they die? How could he have died, just like that? It didn't seem real. Nothing seemed real. Maybe if she could write everything out, take a look at all the events of the past few days on paper, they might make sense—or at least stop spinning around in her head.

She wrote everything out in a letter to Paula. It took hours, and her hand cramped from holding the pen so tightly.

"Christy?" her uncle called softly from the other side of her closed door.

She glanced up from her stationery pad.

"You want me to get you anything?" he asked.

"No, thanks."

"Anything to drink? Are you hungry at all?"

"No. I'd like to be alone, if that's okay."

"Sure," he said. "I won't bother you again. But be sure to holler if you want anything. Anything at all. Okay?"

"I will. Thanks."

She continued writing. It was the longest letter she had ever written. Twelve pages on both sides. Yet, as she reread it, the answers she was looking for weren't there.

The sun was starting to set when she looked out her window. Everything in the outside world went on. The waves kept coming in and rolling out. The seagulls kept circling the trash cans. The joggers arrived for their evening jogs, right on schedule. Nothing stopped. Life kept going for everyone else. It didn't seem right.

Finally the fatigue of the day overtook her. She went into the bathroom, soaked a washcloth with warm water, and held it against her face, breathing in the steam. Everything seemed harsh and severe. Even the washcloth felt coarse and prickly.

She barely knew Shawn, and yet she was overwhelmed with emotion. *What would it be like if the death had happened to someone I was really close to?*

She stumbled into bed, pulled the comforter tightly around her shoulders, and fell into a deep, deep sleep.

Questions and Answers

The next few days passed like a mist over the ocean. It was as if Christy knew things were happening, but all she could see were faint outlines, distorting the true forms of things. Nothing was clear or in focus.

Uncle Bob and Aunt Marti had reconciled after their tiff and had both come to Christy with their apologies. Aunt Marti laughed it off, while Uncle Bob's words flowed with genuine concern for Christy's feelings.

Aunt Marti suggested they fly to San Francisco for a few days. She wanted to leave the next day and had already made airline arrangements. But, with Uncle Bob's help, Christy persuaded her to take a later flight so Christy could go to Shawn's funeral.

On the day of the funeral she stood in front of her closet for the longest time, trying to decide what to wear. She had only been to two funerals before, but they were for old people and were too long ago for her to remember what she wore. She didn't have any idea what would be appropriate. She finally decided on the old skirt and long top she wore the day she and Aunt Marti had gone shopping. Maybe it wasn't stylish, but it was familiar and felt more secure than her new clothes.

Meeting Uncle Bob in the kitchen, Christy discovered that Aunt Marti had prepared her a protein drink for breakfast and was busy packing for their trip. Only Uncle Bob accompanied her to the funeral. Neither of them said much in the car. When Bob parked in front of the stark white, colonial-style mortuary, Christy had a strong desire to ask her uncle to turn the car around and go home. But there on the front steps stood Todd and Tracy. Christy hadn't seen Todd since that morning in the hospital, and he had called only once to tell her the time and place of the funeral. She sucked in a deep breath and headed for the steps.

Todd smiled when he saw her. "I'm really glad you came, Christy."

He looked exhausted. Christy wanted to cry, but instead she boldly held out her arms and let Todd fall into her embrace. They held each other for a long time. Then, without words, they pulled apart, and Tracy gave her a strong hug while Bob and Todd shook hands.

They shuffled into a small room glutted with monstrous flower arrangements. The air seemed to push against Christy's chest, choking her with its pungent sweetness. Organ music, slow and monotonous, pounded the insides of her head. She wanted to throw up.

A bald clergyman wearing a black robe delivered a short message. Shawn's mother sat in the front row, sobbing all the way through. Then a large, red-haired lady in a dark gray dress sang a morose song, clasping her hands together as if this were an opera rather than a funeral.

The clergyman stepped back onto the podium, announcing that one of Shawn's closest friends had asked to say a few words. With his firm, sure manner, Todd walked to the front. He looked confident, but Christy noticed his hands were shaking.

"I've been friends with Shawn for a long time," he began and then paused to clear his throat. "I was there the night he died, and I'll probably never forgive myself for not doing more to stop him." His voice cracked. "We were really tight. We did everything together until last summer, when I became a Christian. I really wanted Shawn to become a Christian too. I don't know if he ever did."

That's when Todd broke. He let out a deep, choking sob and quickly wiped his eyes with the palms of his hands. Christy blinked away her own tears and looked over at Tracy. Tears streamed down Tracy's face. She didn't even try to stop them.

Uncle Bob touched Christy's arm gently, offering her his handkerchief. She looked up at his face to signal her thanks and was startled to see how controlled he seemed. None of the emotion Bob had expressed at the hospital now showed on his face.

Todd was standing still, his head down, his jaw clenched, trying hard to get back in control. The clergyman had stepped back onto the podium and was motioning for Todd to sit down. Todd wiped his tears away and held up a moist palm as if to say, "Just a minute." He drew in a deep breath and said, "I want to read something. I..." He cleared his throat. "I found a verse in the Gospel of John that has helped me."

With trembling hands, Todd leafed through his Bible. When he found the verse he placed the Bible on the podium and looked up. His eyes misted with tears all over again.

"It's in chapter eleven. One of Jesus' closest friends died, and what blows me away is that Jesus cried. It says here that Jesus wept. It's okay for us to be upset when someone we love dies." Todd brushed away his trickling tears and kept going. "But the part I want to read is what Jesus said to His friend's family. He said, 'I am the resurrection and the life; he who believes in Me shall live even if he dies.'"

Closing his Bible, Todd looked over at Shawn's parents. His eyes were clearer, but Christy couldn't believe how pale he looked.

"What I want to say is that I wish I had this whole last week to live over again. I wish Shawn were still alive. I wish he'd believed in Jesus and turned his life over to Him."

Todd squeezed his eyes closed, as if trying hard to find the right words. "I'm not making this very clear, but I know that Jesus radically changed me. All I did was pray and ask Him to forgive my sins and take over my life. I just totally believed. And now I know I'm going to spend eternity with Him in heaven. I just wish..." He choked up again. "I wish Shawn...I wish all of you..."

Todd couldn't finish. He grabbed his Bible, stepped down from the podium, and shakily made his way back to the pew. Covering his eyes with his hands, Todd wept.

Christy thought she couldn't stand it another second. The clergyman stepped forward and, in a deep, controlled voice, offered a lofty-sounding benediction. The group dispersed. Many were sniffling, and most looked down rather than at the people around them.

Christy walked briskly to the car, swallowing back the tears. She wanted to leave—now. No way could she go to the gravesite. Bob didn't even ask. He drove home in silence.

Not until Christy was on the plane to San Francisco, looking out the window at the Pacific Ocean below, did she release the emotion she had choked down at the funeral. Turning her face to the window, she let the tears flow. Through bleary eyes she tried to focus on the miniaturized California coastline below. From up here the waves looked like a thin line of soap suds. Harmless. Soft and foamy. How could those same waves have taken Shawn's life? Is this how God sees everything? From such an exalted distance that it all looks insignificant? Unimportant? Did He really care about how people felt? Then she remembered what Todd had said: "Jesus wept." God must care.

"Christy—" Aunt Marti interrupted her thoughts as she tapped Christy on the shoulder. "I have something to say to you, dear. You mustn't get all worked up about this funeral. Your parents raised you to be a nice Christian girl, and you don't need to dwell on ugly things like death."

Christy glared at her aunt. *How can you simplify all of life like that to make it fit into your compact Gucci bag? There has to be more to life than money and clothes and being popular and all the other things you've drilled me on.* She reclined her seat with a jerk and put the headphones on, letting the beat of the music pound away her heavy thoughts.

Christy felt like a robot, moving through the San Francisco airport and into the taxi that took them to the St. Francis Hotel. Her head ached, and her jaw hurt from clenching her teeth. She should have been awed and impressed with the plush carpet, high, ornate ceiling, and tinkling chandeliers of the hotel lobby. She should have been taking mental notes so she could tell Paula all about it. But she didn't care. She dejectedly stood to the side, waiting for Aunt Marti to check them in. Christy fingered her purse strap and tried to close her ears to all the commotion around her. People spoke in foreign languages, bellhops bumped luggage onto wheeled carts, and at the other end of the lobby someone played a piano in one of the hotel restaurants.

As soon as they got to their suites, 1133 and 1134, Uncle Bob opened his bag and pulled out aspirin for Christy.

"These should help," he offered and then retreated to his and Marti's adjoining suite.

Christy unwrapped the glass in her bathroom and filled it with water. She swallowed the aspirin and looked herself over in the mirror. She didn't look too great. Swollen, red eyes. Downturned mouth. Even her hair looked droopy. She didn't feel too great, either.

Walking around her big room, Christy touched the glass doorknobs and smoothed her hand over the velvety, salmon-colored love seat. Then, pulling back the heavy drapes, she looked down on Union Square just as Bob knocked on the door.

"Ready to see the sights?" He walked in with Marti right behind him. Marti had changed clothes, and the room filled with the fragrance of her perfume.

"Are those all department stores out there?" Christy pointed out the window at the tall buildings that framed the park in the middle of Union Square.

"Yup," Bob said. "Why do you think we always stay at the St. Francis?"

"The Macy's over there is wonderful," Marti added, pointing to the right. "But we'll have to shop at Nordstrom and Saks as well."

"Wow!" Christy exclaimed. "I've never seen so many big stores—and all in one spot."

"Come on," Uncle Bob suggested. "Let's go for a cable car ride."

Even though it was mid-July and only four in the afternoon, they all took jackets. After a forty-minute wait they pushed their way through the crowd onto the cable car and headed for Fisherman's Wharf. Christy stood on the outside, her arm looped around the pole. The cable car jerked and swayed as the underground cables pulled it up the steep hill and pointed it toward the bright blue bay ahead. Breathless, Christy held on to the pole for dear life. What a ride! And what a festive feeling in the air! Did it come from all the tourists chatting with each other on the cable car? Or from the brisk wind chasing them down the hill? Perhaps it was the way all the houses they passed looked like something from a Victorian storybook, making the cable car ride seem even more enchanting and fanciful, as though it was taking them into a fairy tale. Whatever it was, Christy's exhilaration was quite evident to Aunt Marti.

"Didn't I tell you, Bob?" she whispered to her husband. They were seated on the wooden bench seat of the cable car directly behind Christy. "Poor thing merely needed to get away from all that stress. It's not good for a girl her age. Might cause premature wrinkles, you know!"

Uncle Bob smiled his agreement and then turned to the cable car driver, who was standing directly behind him, working the levers with his strong, gloved hands.

"You took that corner quite well," Bob noted. "You been doing this long?"

"Yes, sir," replied the large African-American man, who wore a jaunty beret and snappy brown uniform, "ever since 1985, when they opened the lines back up. They were closed down for refurbishing for two years, you know."

"Yeah, I remember hearing that." Bob seemed genuinely interested.

"We're pretty proud of our system. It's the only working cable car line in the world," the driver said.

"It sure is fun!" Christy yelled as the driver rang the brass bell. *Ding-ding-ding-ding*. Christy laughed.

"Hold yourself in there, young lady!" the driver warned. "We're passing another cable car."

Christy pulled her torso in until her stomach pressed hard against Aunt Marti's knees. The other car brushed past them, and Christy could feel the bump of a shoulder bag from someone hanging on to the passing car.

"That was close!" Christy exclaimed.

Uncle Bob squeezed her arm. "Glad to see the smile back on your face. What do you want to do? Eat first or browse through all the tourist traps?"

"Let's browse a bit first, don't you think, dear?" It was evident that Aunt Marti had already set an itinerary in her mind. "Bob, you can go check on your fishing boat, and then at, say, six-thirty, we'll meet you at Alioto's for dinner."

"Sounds good," Uncle Bob obliged, and as the cable car came to a stop they stepped off and went their separate ways.

"These little places are rather junky," Aunt Marti whispered to Christy as they entered a small souvenir shop. "But

I thought you might find a trinket to take home. Tomorrow we'll do some real shopping in the heart of the city. Now, when you see something you like, you let me know."

Christy picked up a small, brightly colored music box with a cable car that moved up and down a ceramic hill as it played "I Left My Heart in San Francisco."

"Look, how cute!" Christy exclaimed.

Aunt Marti caught the cashier's attention. "Do you have a box for this, and could you pad it well for us?"

The cashier carefully wrapped the music box as Christy softly hummed the familiar tune. *Actually, I left my heart in Newport Beach*. She dreamt of how wonderful it would have been to stand next to Todd on the cable car and to feel his arm around her as they rolled down the hills.

Aunt Marti brought her back to reality as they hailed a bicycle cab and rode in the rickshaw-type seat down to Pier 39. Bright, fluttering kites flew high in the summer evening sky while a variety of street performers gathered crowds. Christy found herself fascinated with a juggler who tossed meat cleavers into the air, but Aunt Marti was quite insistent about moving along.

They entered a shop specializing in every kind of Christmas ornament imaginable. Aunt Marti had a sudden inspiration to pick a theme for her Christmas tree and buy all the ornaments now. After much deliberation she chose lambs rather than angels and selected enough to fill an entire tree.

"I'll be at the register, Christy." She seemed quite pleased with herself. "Find anything you would like?"

"I'm not sure yet." Christy toyed with the ornament in her hand—a wooden teddy bear with the name *Todd* painted in fancy black letters. Except for her dad and brother, Christy had never bought anything for a guy before. She really wanted to get something for Todd. But a teddy bear ornament? What would Todd think of such a gift?

"Well, dear?" Aunt Marti called from the register, where she filed through her credit cards.

"No." Christy put the ornament back. "I didn't find anything here. Maybe at the next store."

The next store turned out to be a sweatshirt shop. Hanging from long wooden pegs on the walls was an incredible display of every color and size imaginable.

"This one's great!" Christy held up a black and white sweatshirt with bold letters across the front saying, "ESCAPED FROM ALCATRAZ."

"Well…" Aunt Marti wasn't convinced. "It's not very feminine, dear, but if that's what you want, I guess—"

"No," Christy said and laughed, "it's not for me! For Todd. Can I get it for him? Please?"

"I see." Aunt Marti surveyed the sweatshirt. "Yes, I suppose that would be all right. Why don't you pick one out for yourself too, dear. That blue one with the white sailboat is darling, don't you think?"

No, Christy didn't think the blue one was darling. She considered getting an Alcatraz sweatshirt for herself as well, so she and Todd could show up at the beach in matching shirts. But that seemed like something Paula would do and not what Christy could see herself doing.

Twenty minutes later they were sitting at a window booth in Alioto's, buttering warm sourdough bread and watching the misty fog creep in on the bay. Christy ordered crab legs, something she had never eaten before. She carefully cracked them and pulled the steaming, tender white meat from each leg, dipping it in the drawn butter. What a feast!

She was wiping her hands with the white cloth napkin when Uncle Bob interrupted Marti's chitchat to become philosophical with Christy.

"There are many things in this life to experience, Christy. It's okay to experience anything you want as long as you know when to pull back. Do you know what I'm saying?"

"I'm not sure." Actually, she was completely lost.

"It's like the cable car ride," Uncle Bob explained. "You were having a great time riding on the outside, hanging on and feeling the full force of the wind and the momentum of the cable car. But then you pulled yourself in, just in time, when we slid past the other car. And you were safe."

"What are you trying to tell me?" Christy popped the last bit of crab into her mouth.

"Just what I've told you before. Be true to yourself. Do what you want to do. Be your own person. Make the most of your life because it's your life. That's what I'm trying to say."

For once Aunt Marti remained silent as Christy bluntly replied, "But Uncle Bob, Shawn did what he wanted to do. He was his own person. And now he's dead."

It was silent for a moment, and then Bob answered. "That's exactly what I meant about the cable car." He leaned across the table to make his point. "You just have to pull yourself in at the right time, and you won't get hurt."

"I don't know," Christy countered. "I'm not sure I want to live on the edge like that. I mean, what about God?

Where does He fit in? Does He just let me go my own merry way, and if I don't happen to 'pull myself in' in time, then *splat, splat*, that's that, too bad, Christy?" She sat back in her seat.

Aunt Marti seemed embarrassed that they were discussing these things in a restaurant and tried to wrap up the conversation in her own compact way. "Of course not, dear. God is love. Everybody knows that. God helps those who help themselves. All you need to do is try to be a good person, just like Bob and I have always done."

"Yes, but Aunt Marti, are you sure that's all there is to it? For instance, how do you know for sure that you're going to heaven when you die?"

Aunt Marti bristled. "I don't think this is either the time or the place to get into a theological discussion, Christina." Then, turning to Bob, she added, "Pay the bill, will you, darling? I'm going to the ladies room."

It felt as if an icy wind had blown across the room as Marti left the table. Christy sensed the haze of the previous days closing in around her. She might be young, naive, and inexperienced, but she wasn't stupid. Why couldn't she figure this out?

Never before had she struggled with so many questions. Her aunt's and uncle's answers failed to satisfy her. She was determined to get a tighter grasp on what life was all about. And she would do it before she went back to Wisconsin.

9

The Boat or the Shore?

"Hurry, Uncle Bob! The phone is ringing!" Christy stood by the locked front door of the beach house with her arms full while her uncle lifted suitcases from the Mercedes' trunk. Aunt Marti was still in the car, checking her hair in the mirror. "Hurry, hurry!" Christy cried.

But, of course, by the time he dashed over and stuck the key in the door the phone had stopped.

"I'll check the answering machine," Christy offered as Bob returned to unload the car.

She listened carefully to the messages of the past three days and saved all of them. None of the calls were from Todd. With slow, dragging steps, Christy trudged upstairs to her room. Why didn't he call? Was it because he knew she was out of town?

Bob pushed the door open with her suitcase. "Oh, sorry! I didn't realize you were in here."

"That's okay. Could you lift it up on the bed for me?"

The first thing Christy took out was the bag with the sweatshirt in it. As she held Todd's up, a flood of second thoughts engulfed her. Would he think it was dumb? Should she really give it to him? Maybe it would be all right if she waited for the right moment—like when he came over to see her, or when he came to pick her up for their next date, or...

"Mail call!" Uncle Bob hollered just outside Christy's door.

Her heart jumped with farfetched hope. What if Todd had sent her a card? One of those cute, sweet, but not-too-mushy ones. She grabbed the four envelopes and quickly scanned the return addresses. One from her mom, one from Paula—no, two from Paula—and one from her little brother. Oh, well. So much for dreams.

"Don't get too excited now," Uncle Bob teased, watching disappointment overtake her.

Christy blushed, surprised that her thoughts showed so transparently on her face. She opened one of the letters from Paula first, and a ten-dollar bill floated to the floor.

"Money, money, money!" Uncle Bob sang out. "Boy, sure wish I got mail like that! What kind of sweepstakes did you win?"

Christy scanned the letter. "It's from Paula. See, we had this contest, and I kind of won. Sort of."

"I see." He raised his eyebrow speculatively.

"Well, I did win, really, but I guess I just don't feel like I thought I would. Oh, never mind."

"So, here you two are." Aunt Marti joined them.

"Hey, listen to this." Christy read the letter from her eight-year-old brother, David.

Dear Christy,

I miss you. I hope you are having a nice time at Uncle Bob and Aunt Martha's house. I hope you have fun when you go to Disneyland. Don't forget to buy something for me at Disneyland. I want a hat. Have fun.

Love,

David Miller

"Isn't that cute? 'David Miller.' Like I don't know his last name. Too bad he's not that cute in real life." Christy stuffed the letter back into the envelope. "When are we going to Disneyland, anyway? Sure would be fun to go on my birthday, which is only a few weeks away, hint, hint!"

Aunt Marti looked to Bob for an answer. He didn't say anything, so she spoke up. "I'm not exactly a Disneyland kind of person. That's more in your uncle's line of activities. You'll take her for her birthday, won't you, dear?"

Uncle Bob smiled one of his sly grins. "I don't think I'm exactly the guy Christy wants to go to Disneyland with, if she had her choice."

Uncle Bob winked, Christy blushed, and Aunt Marti suddenly caught on.

"Oh! I imagine you'd like to have Todd take you on your birthday! Wouldn't that be marvelous? Well, you just never can tell what might happen between now and July 27th. Think positively, Christy! Your dreams can come true." Aunt Marti swished out of the room, leaving the fragrance of her perfume behind her.

Christy read her other two letters. Things at home hadn't changed much. Paula sounded the same. Her mother sounded the same. How could they stay the same when so much had changed for her? She lifted her new blue dress from the suitcase and held it up, studying her reflection in the mirror. She hardly seemed like the same girl who had cried over her image in this mirror a few weeks ago.

Her short hair now fell into its own natural wave, and although it wasn't as stunning as when Maurice had fixed it, it still looked pretty on her. At that very moment she didn't regret having it cut. Her sunburned shoulders had peeled, but her face had stayed tanned and freckled, giving her a sporty appearance. She liked how she looked. And now she had this gorgeous little blue dress that Uncle Bob said made her eyes light up like "two limpid pools," whatever that meant.

Marti was the one who had an eye for clothes. She had picked this outfit, complete with new shoes, with special care at the Macy's across from their hotel. At Ghirardelli Square they found silver earrings that were dangly and daring. It was the kind of outfit that should be worn someplace special. Like maybe on a date? With Todd? All she could do was hope.

Christy was anxious to get down to the beach the next day. Anxious to see if Todd would be there, anxious to see if he would ask her out. She was so anxious that she was out on the beach before anyone else that morning—that is, almost anyone else. One person sat in a beach chair near the shore: Alissa.

All kinds of mixed feelings swarmed over Christy. Alissa hadn't gone to Shawn's funeral. She might not even know. Christy considered turning around and running in the other direction, but Alissa had already seen her and was waving for her to come over.

"The weather is perfect today!" Alissa greeted Christy,

acting genuinely glad to see her.

"Hi," Christy responded. "How was your date at the party last week?" What she really wanted to say was, "Why did you leave me, you traitor? Why are you so perfect and so horrible at the same time?"

"Wonderful!" Alissa bubbled. "His name is Erik, and he drives a Porsche, and we've been together every day since the party. This is the first time I've been down to the beach in almost a week."

"Alissa," Christy said cautiously. "Did you hear about Shawn?"

"Hear what?"

Christy gulped. "He went bodysurfing off the jetty the night of the party. Well, during the party, actually, but after you left with Erik."

"So?"

"So, I don't know how to tell you, but he crashed into the jetty, and they took him to the hospital."

"Probably serves him right," Alissa said, pouring coconut-scented suntan oil on her long legs.

"Alissa, he didn't make it. He died."

Alissa's jaw twitched slightly. Christy couldn't read her expression under her sunglasses.

"Shawn's dead," Christy said in barely a whisper.

"That's too bad," Alissa remarked, looking out at the ocean. "Did I tell you that Erik has a Porsche? It's black with black interior."

Christy couldn't believe her ears. "Alissa! I just told you Shawn died, and all you can talk about is a dumb car? Didn't you hear what I said?"

"Yes, I heard you."

"Aren't you shocked or anything?"

"Listen." Alissa flipped off her sunglasses. Her eyes bore into Christy's. "Maybe you're too young to know what life is all about, so let me tell you. Life is hard, little girl, and the sooner you figure that out, the better off you'll be."

Christy pulled back as Alissa continued her venomous speech. "Shawn died, okay? He's dead. People die, you know. They leave you, and you can't get all depressed about it. They're gone. There's nothing you can do to change that. You've got your life to live, so do what you want and let everybody else burn. If you want any happiness, you have to make your own, because when it's over, it's over."

"But—" Christy began.

"But nothing, girl!" Alissa interrupted. Her face burned fiery red, but her eyes remained like ice. "You're on your own. Nobody is out there waiting to answer your prayers or make your dreams come true!"

Christy released her breath and tried to think of something to say, but nothing came to her.

Alissa lay down on her towel with her eyes closed and her face toward the sun, dismissing Christy now that her speech was over.

Christy wasn't sure what to do. Inwardly she churned with anger. How could anyone be so cruel and coldhearted? The more she thought about it the more she wanted to yell back at Alissa and tell her she was wrong. There *was* more to life than living it up and then dying! But that's as far as she could get in her mental argument. She couldn't refute any of the things Alissa said by offering a better solution.

Completely exasperated, Christy jumped up and headed for the water. She went in only ankle deep, sloshing along the shoreline. After the water had cooled off her feet and time had cooled off her anger, she headed back to her towel. She had decided to face Alissa calmly, saying whatever came to her.

To her relief, Alissa was gone. Christy stretched out on her towel, letting the sun comfort her with its soothing rays. About half an hour later someone came up beside her.

"Hey! How's it goin'?" It was Todd.

"Hi!" Christy quickly sat up. Seeing Todd left her at a loss for words. "Hi!" she said again.

"Do you want to go to a concert tonight?" Todd sure had a way of getting to the point.

"A concert?" Christy's heart raced. "Sure!"

"How was your trip?"

Christy tried to calm down and sound a bit more mature. "We had a really good time."

Todd smiled his wonderful, wide smile. "Come on. Let's go in the water."

For the next few hours, Christy felt more alive than she ever had before. The water sparkled like a field of diamonds in the midday sun, and the waves came at them gently and calmly.

At one point, when a bigger than usual wave surged above them, Todd grabbed her hand and yelled, "Dive under!" His touch seemed so strong, yet tender in a way that warmed Christy even in the cool water. He held on until they came up on the other side of the wave, and then he was the one who let go. Christy wanted to feel that surge of excitement from his touch again, and her mind played with how wonderful it would be to hold hands with him that night at the concert.

"I'm ready to go in," he said after some time. "How

about you?"

"Sure. I'm ready for something to eat too."

"I brought some pretzels," Todd offered back on the beach as they dried off.

"Good!" responded Christy. "All I've got is some sparkling mineral water my aunt stuck in my bag. But at least she gave me two bottles!"

As they munched pretzels, Christy told Todd all about her trip to San Francisco: about riding the cable cars, tossing quarters into the guitar cases of street musicians, eating the best chocolate in the world at Ghirardelli Square, stuffing herself with crab at Alioto's. She even told him about the heated conversation about God that she had had with her aunt and uncle.

Todd listened attentively and then asked, "What did they say when you challenged them on their ideas about God?"

"The whole subject was dropped," Christy told him. "That's how it is with my aunt and uncle. They act like they have all the answers, but when I try to get something specific out of them, they change the subject."

"Yeah, my parents do the same thing."

Two small boys chasing each other to the water ran across Todd's towel, kicking sand into the bag of pretzels.

"Oh, well!" Todd grabbed the bag and peered inside. "Now we won't be able to tell if we're eating salt or sand on the pretzels." Todd tried to laugh at his own joke, but Christy thought his laugh seemed forced.

"Todd, how have you been doing since...since, you know, the funeral?"

"I haven't slept much. I keep thinking about that night

over and over again, trying to figure out what I could have done to stop him."

"That must be awful for you."

"It is."

Christy looked around. The beach was full of people today, but she didn't see any of the other surfers.

"Todd?" Christy's voice was low, her tone direct. "I feel as though I have a lot of unanswered questions since Shawn died, and I think you're about the only one who might understand what I'm trying to figure out. Can I ask you some questions?"

"Sure."

"Okay," she began. "First, how do you know you're going to heaven when you die?"

"Because I accepted Christ last summer."

"But what does that mean—'accept Christ'? I mean, I accept Him—I accept that He's God's Son and all that. I've never rejected Him or anything."

Todd looked out at the ocean. He seemed to be thinking hard. "It's so simple that it's hard to explain," he finally said. "People have a free choice to either live life their own way or live it God's way."

"But what *is* God's way?" Christy practically shouted. "My uncle keeps telling me to be true to myself, and Alissa was telling me that I've got to make my own way, and all my aunt does is avoid reality and try to think positively. I'm so mixed up!"

"I can see how you would be."

"At home it was easy. We all went to the same church, and everyone believed in God. Now you're telling me I have to live my life God's way if I want to go to heaven. What is

God's way?"

Christy took her eyes off Todd and looked out at the ocean. She didn't like it when she came across so dumb.

"It's like this," Todd explained. "You're looking out at the Pacific Ocean, right? Somewhere out there is Hawaii. Imagine that Hawaii is heaven. You'd never make it there swimming all by yourself. You need a boat. Jesus is like that boat. Do you follow me?"

"Sort of."

"Well, it's up to us to make the choice. We can reject a free ride on the boat to Hawaii, or we can sit here and say, 'Yes, I believe in that boat, and I believe in Hawaii.' But unless we actually get on the boat, we're never going to make it to Hawaii." Todd seemed pretty pleased with his illustration, but Christy was only slightly less confused.

"I believe all that," Christy agreed. There seemed to be something deeper to what he was saying, but she just didn't get it.

"Yes," Todd challenged, "but have you turned your life over to Jesus? Or are you sitting on the shore saying, 'I believe in the boat, and I believe in Hawaii,' but you haven't actually gotten into the boat yet?"

Todd had touched an area she wasn't quite ready to wrestle with. She pictured herself getting into a boat headed for Hawaii. It seemed risky—giving up the safety of being on shore, riding a boat through the wild waves.

"Oh, well." She smiled at Todd. "That gives me something to think about. I'll let it settle in for a while. I need to get back to the house pretty soon."

"I'll pick you up for the concert at about six-thirty?" Todd asked.

"Okay. I'll see you then!" Christy grabbed her stuff and headed for the house.

Life was really looking up. This was too good to be true! Christy thought about how she had accomplished so much by taking her aunt's advice. She really was becoming her own person.

"Aunt Marti!" she called, throwing open the screen door. "Uncle Bob!" She found them in the living room looking at a book of wallpaper samples.

"Guess what! Todd asked me out for tonight! Can you believe it? A concert! And he's going to pick me up at six-thirty! That means I only have three hours to get ready! I'd better get in the shower! I'm so excited!"

"Wonderful!" exclaimed Marti. "What are you going to wear, dear? Don't you think the new dress from San Francisco will be perfect?"

"I guess so. I hadn't really thought about what to wear. I'm just worried that my nose is starting to peel. Look at it."

"Haven't you been using the sunscreen I got you?" Marti scolded as the two of them headed up the stairs. Then, turning to her husband, she added, "Robert, be a dear and call Maurice to cancel my nail appointment this afternoon. I need to help Christy get ready!"

Standing alone with the book of wallpaper, Uncle Bob called up the stairs to his two elated women, "Noooooo problem!"

10

Big Night Out

At six o'clock sharp, Uncle Bob placed the platter of grilled chicken, potatoes, and salad on the dining room table. Aunt Marti was finishing filling the crystal goblets with water when Christy appeared in the doorway, wearing her new blue dress with silver accessories.

"You look absolutely stunning, dear! Don't you think her hair turned out nicely, Bob?"

"You look beautiful, honey. You ought to knock this guy right off his feet."

"Thanks," Christy said with a confident smile. "I really like this dress, Aunt Marti. Thank you for getting it for me."

"You know," Christy commented as they sat down to dinner, "people were actually dressed like this at that party I went to, and I felt so dumb wearing jeans. I'm glad to have something nice to wear tonight."

Aunt Marti smiled and looked pleased with herself.

"What concert are you going to?" Bob asked, offering Christy the platter of chicken.

"I don't know. But you don't have to worry about Todd. He's a great guy, and I'm sure he wouldn't take me to anything raunchy."

At 6:25 they all went into the living room to wait for the doorbell to ring. Christy carried in a gift-wrapped box and propped it by the front door.

"What's that?" Bob questioned.

"It's the sweatshirt I got Todd in San Francisco. Tonight should be a perfect time to give it to him. I hope he likes it!"

"He will, darling," Aunt Marti assured her. "He should be here any minute."

They waited and waited. Finally, at seven, Uncle Bob started suggesting why Todd might be late.

"Maybe he stopped to get you flowers."

"Oh, Uncle Bob! Guys don't do that kind of thing anymore."

"Then maybe he chickened out!"

"Robert! What a horrible thing to say!"

Tears filled Christy's eyes.

"Well," he defended, "I was only trying—"

Just then the doorbell rang. Christy blinked to keep her mascara from streaking. As she hurried to the door, she quickly grabbed the gift and concentrated on looking bright and cheerful. After all, Todd was bound to have some good reason for being so late.

Opening the door, she put on her sweetest smile and greeted Todd with an enthusiastic, "Hi there!"

Then she froze. He was wearing shorts! Shorts and a T-shirt! Why, oh why, had she worn a dress?

Todd didn't seem to notice that she was overdressed. Nor did he apologize for being half an hour late. His voice came out smooth and casual. "Hey, how's it going? You ready?"

Christy called out "Good-bye" over her shoulder and hurried to close the door before Aunt Marti could see what Todd had on. Too late. Bob and Marti had stepped into the entryway, and Bob was stretching out a hand to Todd.

"Good to see you, Todd. You remember my wife, Marti."

"Todd," Marti said with a smile, then calmly added, "so nice to see you again." She turned her back to him slightly and gave Christy a panicked look. "Are you sure you're ready to go, dear?"

Christy read the clue. She knew it was her opportunity to change clothes, but she really didn't know what to change into. She just wanted to leave with Todd. Now. Before anything could stop or change this opportunity.

"I think I'm all ready," Christy answered.

"You're sure, dear?" Marti gave her another piercing look.

"Yes, I'm sure. Let's go, Todd."

"Good night, then," Todd said to Marti. Turning to Bob he added, "We'll be back before eleven, sir."

"That's fine. Have a good time."

Christy and Todd headed toward the car.

"What's that?" Todd asked, looking at the box.

"I almost forgot! It's for you." Her voice came out shaky.

"For me? What is it?"

"Something I got you in San Francisco. If you don't like it, that's okay." Why had she bought him anything? Why was she dressed up? Why did she always feel so dumb? For a split second she considered telling him she didn't feel well and couldn't go. But then they were at the door of his old Volkswagen van, which he affectionately called Gus the Bus.

Todd slid the door open, and Christy nearly let out a scream. The van was full of people! And another girl—Tracy—was already sitting in the front passenger seat!

Todd made quick introductions. "You know Tracy and Doug. This is Brian, Heather, Leslie, and Michelle."

The only open seat was way in the back of the van. Christy retreated to the seat as fast as she could, her face hot with anger and embarrassment. And what was worst of all was that everyone had on jeans! She felt ridiculous in her fancy outfit. What were all these other people doing here, anyway? Hadn't Todd asked her for a date? What was Tracy doing here? Christy felt sick to her stomach.

"What's that?" Doug asked as Todd pulled out of the driveway.

"Something Christy got me in San Francisco."

"Here, I'll open it!" Tracy offered from the passenger seat.

Before Todd could answer she tore off the wrapping and held the sweatshirt up so everyone in the van could see. The remarks stung like saltwater. "Just what you need, Todd!" and "Guess she figured you out, convict!"

Christy didn't say a word all the way to the concert. Everyone else talked and laughed but didn't include her. They pulled into the parking lot of what looked like a community center, and the gang headed for the front door, where a crowd funneled its way into the auditorium.

"Come on!" Tracy called, pulling at Todd's arm. "If we hurry we can still get seats near the front!"

The others whooshed off with Tracy, but Christy lagged behind, desperately wishing that Todd would notice and come back to walk with her or at least pay some attention to her. But he didn't.

The fantasy balloon she had filled all afternoon completely deflated as she entered the large auditorium and sank down into a seat between Michelle and Heather. Tracy positioned herself between Todd and Doug at the end of the aisle and leaned forward to give a cute little wave to Michelle.

"That's it!" Christy growled under her breath. "I'm leaving."

"Did you say something?" Michelle asked.

"I'm not feeling real great," Christy said, startled that Michelle had heard her and even more startled that Michelle had talked to her. "I think I'll go call my uncle and ask him to come get me."

"You can't go now!" Michelle said. "The concert is ready to start. You won't want to miss it."

Just then the lights dimmed, and a young man walked onto the stage to announce the performer.

Michelle turned to Christy and asked enthusiastically, "Do you have any of her CDs?"

"Who?" Christy shouted over the clapping as everyone else rose to their feet.

"Debbie Stevens," Michelle hollered and pointed to the energetic young performer who appeared on stage, dazzling the crowd with her vibrant appearance.

"No! This is the first time I've heard her," Christy answered, stunned by the loud music and the crowd's excitement.

Clear and strong, Debbie's energetic voice filled the auditorium:

Everyone is telling me
Which way I should go,
But no one has the answers.
Don't you know?
I'm no fool. I look at you.
You're not living what you say.
Can anybody show me?
There's got to be a better way.

Christy listened carefully to the words. Surprisingly, she could understand most of them as the music loosened the self-pity knots that had tightened around her throat and stomach. Out of the corner of her eye, she could see Tracy swaying and clapping with the beat, laughing and moving free as a breeze. Todd and Doug followed Tracy's lead, and when Debbie announced the next song they whistled and clapped with their arms over their heads.

Great! This is everybody's favorite song, and I've never heard it, Christy thought.

You won't find it at the mall.
It never goes on sale.
You can't put it on your credit card
Or order through the mail.
Its value is priceless,
But for you, today, it's free.
Just give your heart to Jesus
And get life eternally.
You can't buy it,

The price already's been paid.
Jesus bought it for ya
When He raised up from the grave.

"Is this a religious kind of concert?" Christy asked Michelle.

"Yes! This is the church we all go to."

"This is a church?" Christy scanned the large room. It looked like any huge, windowed auditorium. The only hint that it might be a church was the long, padded benches they sat on.

As the concert continued, Christy listened with a discerning ear. The songs all had hidden messages, she realized, and since this was the kind of thing Todd liked, she wanted to try to get into it too. Maybe he would be more interested in her if she could talk to him about "the Lord" the way Tracy did.

She looked down the aisle at Todd. *He's so cute! I wish he liked me!*

Debbie sang for nearly forty minutes before introducing her final song. She asked everyone to sit down. "I want to tell you a story about something that happened to me a few years ago."

The group respectfully quieted down.

"I came to this same auditorium four summers ago with some friends and listened to a band play. At the end the drummer talked about how he had surrendered his life to Jesus and that he and all the other guys in the band were now Christians."

Debbie walked to the edge of the stage and continued to talk while she gestured with her hands. As she spoke in her animated fashion, she shook her head, causing the little curls around her face to shiver. "I couldn't figure out what they were talking about, because I grew up in a family that went to church all the time, and I thought I automatically was a Christian."

Debbie's words penetrated Christy.

"Then the lead singer told how to become a Christian, and a lot of people prayed with him that day. But I didn't. I didn't see why I needed to ask forgiveness for my sins. I mean, I was a pretty good person. I hadn't killed anybody, I never cheated on tests, and I tried to obey my parents. I didn't see what Jesus needed to 'save' me from, like these guys were talking about."

Christy glanced down the aisle, and Todd caught her gaze and smiled back. Her cheeks warmed as she focused back on the stage.

"Well," Debbie continued, "the next evening I rode my bike down to the beach and sat on a bench for a long time, just thinking. One of the guys had quoted a verse from the Bible that went like this: 'For all have sinned and fall short of the glory of God.'

"As I sat there looking out at the roaring ocean and watching the sky turn all the colors of a rose garden, I realized I had come short of the glory of God. It suddenly became so clear! No matter how good I tried to be or how many self-improvement plans I tried, I could never be good enough to stand before God, because He is perfect and holy. I needed Jesus to open a way for me to get to God.

"Right then and there I prayed a prayer that went something like this: 'Lord Jesus, I need You. Please forgive my sins and come into my life. Make me the woman You want me to be. Amen.'

"This next song I'm going to sing is one I wrote that night when I returned from my bike ride. That was probably one of the happiest nights of my life, because even though for so long I didn't think I needed Jesus, He knew I needed Him, and He never gave up on me."

The music began soft and slow, and Debbie sang,

I didn't think I needed You in my life
Until today.
When in Your very special way
You showed me
How You wanted me,
Showed me how You cared for me
Even when I didn't care.
Now I surrender my life to You
Give You all of my heart
You're the one I've waited for
Even though I didn't know.
Oh, Lord,
It was You who loved me first.

"What a pretty song," Christy whispered to Michelle.

Debbie closed her eyes and held the microphone close to her mouth as she repeated the final line, "Oh, Lord, it was You who loved me first."

The auditorium fell completely still. As the last strains of music faded, Debbie opened her eyes and said in a gentle voice, "If you haven't yet surrendered your life to Jesus, I'm praying you will tonight. He's there waiting. Lord bless you! Thanks for coming!"

The houselights came on, and people started chattering as they moved down the aisles to the back doors. Todd's group stuck together in their row, waiting for the crowd to subside.

"Hey, you guys! Let's try to go backstage and meet Debbie!" Doug suggested.

"Yeah, right!" said Heather.

"Come on!" he urged, leading the group up to the stage and looking for a way to get to the back.

"Can I help you guys?" asked one of Debbie's band members.

"We want to meet Debbie," Doug said confidently. "Do you think she would have time for some fans?"

"Sure, I don't see why not," the guy said. "Follow me."

He led them to a side door and down a short hallway to a small room, where he knocked on the door. "Debbie? You've got some fans here who want to meet you."

Debbie opened the door wide and blurted out, "Hi, fans!" Then she immediately flushed a deep red and turned to the guy in the band, slugging him in the arm. "Mark! I thought you were kidding. I didn't know anyone was really here!"

They all laughed, which helped everyone relax, and Debbie regained her composure, shaking hands with each of them and asking their names. When she came to Christy she said, "I'm so glad you came tonight!"

"I am too," Christy said.

"You know," Debbie told her, "I've always liked the name Christy. It means 'follower of Christ.' Did you know that?"

"No," Christy answered, surprised at Debbie's friendliness. Weren't singers supposed to be aloof, temperamental, and very protective of their backstage lives? Debbie sparkled with her genuineness.

"Your concert was awesome!" Doug said.

"I have all three of your CDs," Michelle said. "Do you have another one coming out soon?"

"Hopefully by December." Debbie flashed a bright smile.

Her shiny black hair curled in little ringlets across her forehead, and Christy thought she looked quite pretty. It wasn't necessarily her makeup, because she didn't have much on. But there was something about the way her eyes glistened that made her beautiful.

"I really liked your last song," Christy told her rather shyly. "It made me feel something."

"Oh? What did you feel?" Debbie asked.

"It's hard to explain." Christy wished everyone wasn't standing there, staring at her.

Todd may have sensed her uneasiness because he cut in and said, "We want to go buy some of your CDs, Debbie. Do you have a table at the back?"

"Yes."

Tracy piped up, "Will you autograph them for us?"

"Sure." Then reaching over and touching Christy on the arm, Debbie said, "Do you want to stay here and visit for another minute?"

"Me?" She didn't really, but she felt put on the spot and didn't know how to say no.

"We'll be back in just a minute," Todd told her and followed Tracy and the others out the door.

"So, tell me. What did my song make you feel?" Debbie asked, offering Christy a chair.

It took Christy a few seconds to clear her thoughts. Here she was, alone with a complete stranger who was asking her about her innermost feelings. All she could think of was that Todd probably wanted to get rid of her so he could put his arm around Tracy or something. What if they left without her?

"I...I don't remember," Christy stammered.

"That's okay," Debbie assured her. "I didn't mean to make you feel uncomfortable. I like talking to people after concerts to see how the Lord spoke to them through the music."

"Well, I really just came with some of my friends who come to a lot of these concerts. Maybe you should ask one of them, because they talk about the Lord all the time."

"Can I ask you something?" Debbie's eyes flashed their sparkles.

"I guess so."

"Christy, if you were to die tonight, do you know for certain that you would go to heaven?"

Christy's heart pounded. She had gone over and over that question when Shawn died. She had challenged her aunt and uncle on it, but nobody had ever asked her. "I'm pretty sure I would."

"There's a way you can be absolutely sure," Debbie said. "By asking Jesus to forgive your sins and come into your heart."

Why did they leave me here for Debbie to pin me down like this? Christy's heart raced.

"Yes, I know all that. I've gone to church since I was a baby."

"That's good," Debbie said. "But it's not enough. See, everyone has sinned, which makes us unable to come before

God, who is holy. The penalty for sin is death, and that's why Jesus died. To pay the price for our sins. Only through Jesus can we be saved."

Why is she preaching at me like this? Christy thought, feeling more and more angry at the group for leaving her.

"Thanks for your time," Christy said, trying to be polite. "But I'd really better go try to find my friends before they leave without me."

"Okay. Here," Debbie offered, "I'd like to give you one of my CDs. Everything I've been saying is in the words of the songs." She handed Christy a CD from out of a gym bag on the floor. Her photo and the words "Be Real" were printed on the front.

"Thanks," Christy mumbled. Then, feeling she had been rude to cut Debbie off so fast, she told Debbie, "I'll listen to it. I promise I will."

Debbie touched Christy's shoulder and looked gently into her eyes. "Just promise you'll listen to the Lord when He speaks to your heart."

Christy looked away. "Okay. Thank you again. This is really nice of you. I'd better go. Thanks."

The ride home proved to be as exasperating as the ride to the concert. Todd asked if anyone wanted to get something to eat.

"Sure!" exclaimed Tracy. "As long as we don't go to Hanson's Parlor!" She suggested they go to her house, because her mom had made cookies that afternoon, and unless her three brothers had gotten to them, plenty should be left.

The last thing Christy felt like doing was spending another hour or so around Tracy, on her territory.

"I think I'd better go home," Christy piped up from

her backseat prison, adding, "if that's okay with you, Todd." She hoped he would object and beg her to come along.

"Sure, if that's what you want."

Why did he have to be so easygoing and agreeable all the time?

"Your house is on the way to Tracy's anyhow," he added.

To Christy's surprise, instead of just dropping her off at the curb, Todd got out and walked her to the door.

"I'm glad you came tonight," he told her as they stood under the front light.

"You are? I didn't think you even noticed I was there with all your other friends."

Todd gave her a puzzled look. "Of course I noticed you. I hope you can come with us again sometime. When do you go back to Wisconsin?"

"The end of August. I don't remember the exact day."

"Well, good night," he said, giving her a quick hug. His tanned face was only inches from hers. "See you tomorrow?"

"Okay." Her heart melted. "See you!"

How could Todd do this to her? Up and down. Up and down. Did he have any idea what an emotional roller coaster he kept sending her on? She watched him walk to the van and gave a halfhearted wave to the others waiting for him.

"Hey," Todd called from the sidewalk, "I like your dress!" Then he sprinted to the driver's side, and, with a pop and sputter, Gus the Bus chugged down the street.

Bob and Marti were in the den. Uncle Bob was watching TV with the sound turned down, and Marti was talking on the phone. She hung up immediately, anxious to hear all about the big date.

Christy gave a brief rundown of the disappointing evening, leaving out the part about it being a Christian concert. She did tell them how everyone went to Tracy's house, but how she had no desire to go.

"Why, that horrid girl!" Marti exclaimed. "How dare she weasel in on your boyfriend like that!"

"She's really not horrid," Christy admitted, "and Todd isn't exactly my boyfriend. I mean, he obviously invited her to the concert too. He invited all of them. But," Christy added with a smile, "he did like my dress, and he did say he would see me tomorrow."

"That's my man!" said Uncle Bob, his eyes still fixed on the television. "Give him time. He'll come around."

"That's the problem!" Christy wailed. "I haven't got a whole lot of time. I'm going home in a few weeks!"

"Hang in there. Hang in there!" Bob muttered.

"How am I supposed to hang in there?" Christy asked, trying to get him to take his eyes off the TV and look at her. "How do I get him to like me?"

"Slam him! That's the way! Down on the floor. Now's your chance. Go for it!"

Christy glared at her uncle and then at the TV. "Wrestling!" she squawked. "I'm asking you for advice, and I think you're listening, but you're talking to some fake wrestler in a cape and mask."

"Oh, Robert!" scolded Aunt Marti.

"What?" He looked up, startled. "Did you say something?"

"Men!" sputtered Christy. "You're all weird! Weird! Weird! Weird!"

Everything a Girl
Could Ever Want

Christy walked the four blocks to Alissa's house slowly. An hour earlier Alissa had called, asking Christy to come over. She had reluctantly agreed, but the closer she got to Alissa's house, the more timid and uncertain she felt.

Alissa had sounded upset on the phone, and Aunt Marti said she had called the night before while Christy was at the concert. What did she want? And why had she called Christy instead of Erik?

Alissa answered the door with her usually perfect hair covering her right eye. Her shirt and shorts were wrinkled. "Come on in," she offered in an emotionless voice and showed Christy to the living room. They stepped around half-packed suitcases, and Alissa lifted a box off the couch so they could sit down.

"Are you leaving already?" Christy asked. "I thought your family was staying till the end of August."

"We were, but now we're not," Alissa replied softly. "I'm leaving to go back to my grandmother's in Boston."

"What about the rest of your family?"

"The rest of my family?" Alissa laughed. "What about the rest of my family?" Her eyes flashed their familiar fury. "I'll tell you about the rest of my family! This is it—me! That's my family."

"What do you mean?" Christy feared that Alissa might go into one of her rages, but she saw something different on Alissa's face that caused Christy to pity her.

"It's like this. I'm an only child, and my dad died three months ago of lung cancer," Alissa stated, the anger subsiding.

"Oh, I'm sorry. I didn't know," Christy said.

"I didn't tell you. So, my mom and I came here to rest and regroup for the summer. Except my mom brought an old friend with her. Her bottle."

"What do you mean?"

"I mean," Alissa squeezed out, "my mom is an alcoholic. She supposedly got help from a treatment center a few years ago, but as soon as my dad died she started to drink again. She stayed inside this house since the day we arrived and drank and drank until she didn't know where we were or how long we'd been here."

Alissa turned her head to look out the window, and Christy noticed her right eye was bruised and swollen. "How awful, Alissa! Are you okay? What happened to your eye?"

"My mom threw a punch at me when I tried to get her to go to bed last night. Erik was supposed to come pick me up, and my mom was lying on the living room floor. Erik hadn't met my mom, and I didn't want him to see her like that, so I tried to drag her to the bedroom. She got furious. She hit me and threw a bottle of vodka at me. She went crazy, screaming that she'd kill me. I got really scared and ran down the street to a pay phone. I called the police. They took my mom away. I'm pretty sure they'll put her back in a rehabilitation center of some sort."

"That's terrible! Is there anything I can do?"

Alissa switched back to her cool, matter-of-fact self and said, "I was hoping you could help me pack this stuff. I didn't know who else to ask. I've got so many phone calls to make, I'll never get this all done before my plane takes off at four o'clock."

For the next hour, Christy numbly packed Alissa's abundant wardrobe. Her clothes were in three different closets. She had many gorgeous outfits, expensive jeans, and more shoes than Christy could count. Alissa finished her phone calls while Christy jammed cosmetics into a small suitcase for her. Opening the last drawer, she pulled out a handful of eyeliners, a mirror, and a round, plastic compact.

Wonder what this is? Christy thought, popping the top open. A circle of little white pills curved around the inside with a number underneath each one.

"Everything is set." Alissa walked into the bedroom. "My mom sobered up this morning and agreed to sign her admission papers. If all goes well with the program they'll let her come back to Boston at the end of September. I packed her stuff this morning so I could drop it by the hospital on my way to the airport."

"How are you getting to the airport?"

"Erik said he'd take me."

"You're so lucky to have him," Christy said. "He must really love you. It's going to be awful leaving him, isn't it?"

"Oh! Where did you find those?" Alissa reached for the pink compact. "I've been looking for those for days."

The doorbell rang before Christy could respond.

"That's probably Erik," Alissa said, leaving Christy in the bedroom while she answered the door.

Christy heard Erik's voice echo down the hall, "You know I'm going to miss you."

Christy sat on the bed, thinking, *How sweet! I wonder if Todd will say anything like that to me when I go back home?*

"I'm glad you came, Erik." Alissa's voice was soft. "I'm not sure what I would have done if you hadn't come."

"I even came early," he pointed out. "Did you notice?"

"I'm glad, because I've got to take my mom her stuff."

"That shouldn't take too long." Erik's voice got lower. "There's still enough time for you to tell me good-bye."

"Stop it, Erik! Not now. I mean it!" Alissa's voice became muffled, and all Christy could hear were footsteps in the hall, coming toward the bedroom.

"Somebody is—" Alissa's voice came from the other side of the door.

Before she could finish the sentence the bedroom door swung open. Christy jumped to her feet, her eyes wide. There stood Erik with his arm around Alissa. Christy panicked. What should she do?

"Hey!" he shouted. "What are you doing here?"

"I–I was just leaving!" Christy stammered.

"Don't bother!" Erik stomped down the hall.

"Erik!" Alissa cried, stumbling after him. "I need you! Don't go now!"

He yanked open the front door. "Hey! I needed you too, but you didn't give a rip about me! I'm sick of your excuses and your little crybaby games. Grow up!"

He slammed the door, and Christy could hear his Porsche screech out of the driveway. She waited in the bedroom, not sure what to do next. She slowly made her way down the hall.

"Alissa? Are you okay?"

"What a jerk! I never liked him anyway." Alissa's eyes brimmed with tears as Christy sat down beside her on the couch.

"I'm sorry I messed things up for you."

"It wasn't you." Alissa let the tears flow. "He's just a big baby who can't handle it when he doesn't get his way. I've got better things to do than waste my time on him."

Apparently she hadn't convinced herself. She buried her face in her hands and cried until the tears ran down her arms.

"It's okay." Christy looked around for some tissue. "You're going to be okay. You've got everything any girl could ever want."

Alissa lifted icy, bloodshot eyes to meet Christy's gaze. "Everything any girl could ever want?" she asked sarcastically. "Then why am I so lonely all the time, Miss Know-It-All? Can you tell me that? And why am I so miserable that..." She hesitated and then blurted out, "That I tried to kill myself last December?" Her voice rose. "Can you answer me that?"

"No. I mean, I don't know." Christy felt the tears coming to her own eyes. "I can't believe you're telling me this, Alissa! You have everything. You're everything I want to be."

"No, I'm not." Alissa dried her eyes and smoothed her long, blond hair. "You just don't realize how good you have it. Stay innocent, Christy. Stay innocent."

For a moment they both were silent. Christy ached inside; she desperately wanted to help Alissa, to offer her some answers. If only there were some way she could help her. Then she had an idea.

"Let me call my uncle and ask him to take you to the airport, okay?" It wasn't much, but she knew it was a start.

While they waited for Bob to arrive, Alissa pulled herself together and appeared to have recovered from the blowout with Erik. Within twenty minutes, Uncle Bob pulled into the driveway and loaded the car with Alissa's belongings. They stopped at the hospital, and Christy waited while Uncle Bob helped Alissa take her mother's suitcases inside.

During the trip to the airport, Christy wondered how much she should try to explain to Uncle Bob. But he rolled through the afternoon with graciousness, and it wasn't until the two of them were driving home that he asked Christy if there was anything she wanted to talk about.

"Men are weird," Christy said. "I can't believe the way Erik treated Alissa and the way he walked out of her life as though he didn't care anything about her."

"I imagine Alissa has had lots of boyfriends like Erik," Bob contemplated. "She seems like a girl who has been around. That's not the best way to be."

"I'm beginning to see that. When I first met her I thought she was perfect. I wanted to be just like her in every way. I couldn't believe it this morning when she said she was so miserable. Thanks for coming and helping her out when I called you. That's the second time this summer you've been there for me when my new friends were in trouble. Thanks."

"Anytime. You want to stop somewhere for dinner?"

"Sure. I'm starved," Christy replied. "Just as long as it isn't Hanson's Parlor."

"What?"

"Never mind. That's another problem I've got to work on."

12

Hopes and Heartaches

"Christy? Bob? Are you home?" Aunt Marti called from her bedroom. It was after ten, and they were just returning from dinner after taking Alissa to the airport.

"Yes, my little peach fuzz," Bob called up the stairs.

Marti hopped down the stairs in a long, floral-print silk robe. "Christy, I've the most marvelous news to tell you! Your boyfriend came by while you were gone and asked why you weren't at the beach today." She settled herself on the couch and continued. "I told him you were over at Alissa's, goofing off."

Christy shook her head. "We weren't exactly goofing off!"

"No matter," Marti continued. "Todd and I had a nice little chat, and he said he would call you this evening. Well, the poor guy has called twice, and I guess he gave up because he said he would talk to you tomorrow. He certainly is a charming young man, Christy."

"If only he thought I was a charming young woman!"

"Oh! I nearly forgot. It was the most darling thing

you've ever seen. He was wearing the sweatshirt we got for him in San Francisco. It looked so adorable on him."

"Was he really? I can't believe it!"

"That's my man," said Uncle Bob with a twinkle in his eye. "Give him time. He'll come around."

"You flake!" Christy yelled and bopped him on the head with a pillow from the couch before heading up to her room. She decided to start a letter to Paula after getting ready for bed, but she kept falling asleep. Finally she gave in to the exhaustion and crawled between the covers with a yawn.

The next morning she lingered in bed for more than an hour finishing the letter to Paula and writing a short note to her parents. She probably would have stayed between the covers and dozed off again if she weren't so anxious to see Todd.

Should I go down to the beach, or will he come by again? I think I'll wait—at least till noon, and then, if he doesn't call or come over, I'll go down to the beach.

With special care, Christy showered, did her hair, and put on her makeup, thinking of Alissa the whole time.

I wonder how Alissa is doing at her grandmother's? I hope things turn out better for her. I can't believe Erik dropped her like that. I thought he really liked her. I thought she had her life so together.

Pushing thoughts of Alissa from her mind, Christy surveyed her wardrobe. She had some new clothes she hadn't worn yet. But the longer she looked, the more discouraged she became. Nothing seemed right for today.

"I don't have anything to wear!" she moaned, flopping onto the bed. "Guess I'll wear my bathing suit, a pair of shorts, and a T-shirt again. I sure am getting tired of wearing the same thing all the time."

"Christy?" The tap of acrylic nails had become familiar. "Christy darling!"

"Come on in, Aunt Marti."

"Who were you talking to, dear?"

"Myself."

"You're still in your nightshirt!"

"Yeah. I can't find anything to wear," Christy sighed.

"Maybe we should go shopping again. But not this morning. I've got a meeting. Why don't we go later this afternoon to South Coast Plaza? Bob could meet us there for dinner. Besides, I did want to find something for your birthday outing to—" She caught herself. "Well, to wherever you might go for your birthday."

"What are you trying to tell me, Aunt Marti?"

With a forced little laugh she responded, "Absolutely nothing, dear. I simply thought it would be nice to do some birthday shopping for you." Marti glanced at her watch. "Oh, dear! I really must be going. I'll be home around two-thirty, and we can leave soon after that."

She turned her head back toward Christy. "You really should hurry and get dressed. It's not polite to keep him waiting."

"Keep who waiting?"

Marti gave her a puzzled look. "You mean I didn't tell you?" She tilted her head back and laughed at a joke only she was in on. "Oh, dear me. Where is my mind today? I came up to tell you that Todd is waiting in the den."

"He is?" Christy suppressed a shriek. "Why didn't you tell me? What am I going to wear?"

"I must go, dear. You have a good time today, and I'll see you around two-thirty." She walked out the door, shaking her head and chuckling to herself.

Christy called out after her, "Tell him I'll be right down!" She scrambled to pull on a pair of shorts and a shirt and gave herself a quick glance in the mirror before bounding down the stairs.

"Hi, Todd! I'm sorry I left you waiting so long. My aunt didn't tell me you were here. I mean, she told me, but not right away. Otherwise, I wouldn't have left you here so long by yourself."

"It's all right. Do you want to go to Disneyland?" Todd sure had a way with words.

"You mean now?" Christy almost squealed.

"No. Next Friday. For your birthday."

"Are you kidding? Yes! How fun! I'd love to go!" Then Christy paused, her enthusiasm visibly diminishing. "Who else is going?"

"Just you and me," Todd said. "Unless you want to take somebody else. It's your birthday."

Christy blushed, ashamed for thinking Todd planned to take another Gus the Bus full of people to Disneyland with them. This was special. Her birthday. He must have thought of that.

"No," she replied softly, "I don't want to invite anyone else. Unless you do."

"Nope. We can celebrate our birthdays together. You'll be fifteen, and I'll be one year old in the Lord."

"What?" Christy asked.

"Remember that night on the beach after Shawn's party? I told you I became a Christian last summer on July 27th, and that's when you told me that's your birthday. So, you'll be fifteen, and I'll be one."

Todd stuck out his square jaw and casually folded his arms across his chest. Christy thought he looked a little bit like Uncle Bob when he was about to tease her.

"Are you hungry or anything?" Christy asked. "I haven't eaten breakfast yet, and I think my uncle is still in the kitchen. Maybe we can get something to eat."

They found Bob in his usual chair at the kitchen table, dunking a donut into a cup of fresh coffee. "Morning! You kids want some donuts?"

"Where did these come from?" Christy asked.

"When your aunt went out this morning she told me I needed some exercise. So, I briskly walked right down to the donut shop." He winked at Christy. "I could use some help destroying the evidence, if you know what I mean."

Todd and Christy laughed, and both pulled up chairs.

"What's the plan for today?" Bob asked.

"Marti and I are supposed to go to South Coast Plaza around two-thirty. You're supposed to meet us there for dinner."

"Good thing I asked you. My 'social director' hadn't filled me in on the plans for the evening yet. Must have just been one of those things that slipped her mind," he said good-naturedly.

"Right," Christy agreed, remembering the incident in her room that morning. "Her mind has been slipping a bit lately."

"You know, it's only eleven now. If you two want something to do, you could take the tandem out for a spin. We bought that bike last summer thinking we would get some exercise, but we've only used it twice."

"That would be fun! You want to, Todd?"

"Sure. Let's take it over to Balboa Island."

Bob helped them pull the bicycle from the garage and gave them a push into the street. Christy waved quickly and put her hand back on the handlebar to help steady the wobbly monster.

"I'm glad you're the one in front," Christy told Todd. "I'm not real coordinated on things like this."

Todd steered through the intersection; Christy did her best to keep her balance and not look at the cars roaring past them. They pedaled to the Balboa Island ferry. The ferry took on only a few cars at a time, but since they were the only ones with a bike they got right on. Todd pulled out a handful of change and paid their fare. The ferry lurched forward, chugging loudly on its short trip to the island.

"Look at all the sailboats!" Christy moved closer to Todd.

"Now there's a hot catamaran," Todd said.

"Where?"

"See, over there." Todd pointed, and Christy moved even closer so that her shoulder briefly pressed against his. She didn't know what a catamaran was, and she really didn't want to ask in case she sounded dumb. She just liked having an excuse to be close to Todd.

If only he would put his arm around me.

Before Todd could make a move the ferry pulled into its dock, and they hopped on the bike. They rode up the narrow streets lined with little beach houses. Cottages, really. Christy liked all the stained-glass windows and bright flowers in the tiny front yards.

"Do you want a Balboa Bar?" Todd called over his shoulder.

"I've never had one."

They stopped at the ice cream stand, and Todd said, "You can't go to Balboa and not eat a Balboa Bar. What do you want on yours? Chips? Nuts? Sprinkles?"

Christy looked at the pictures of the varieties of the ice cream bar to choose from. People were waiting in line behind them, and the girl at the window peered at her impatiently.

"I don't know." She hated it when she lost all her confidence like this. She put the decision back on Todd. "I'll have whatever you do."

Todd ordered two of the chocolate-dipped ice cream bars with nuts. Christy hated nuts, but she didn't say anything.

They walked past the specialty boutiques along the main street, enjoying the treat. Christy tried to casually pick off the nuts as she ate her ice cream and barely paid attention to what they saw in the shop windows. Her mind felt bogged down with the frustration she had experienced a few minutes earlier.

Why do I have such a hard time making simple decisions? Why do I always lose my confidence at key moments and act like a total idiot? Does Todd notice my insecurities? Does he like me? What about Tracy? Why is Tracy so much more self-confident and bubbly? Why can't I be more like her? Then a strange thought hit her: *How can I be true to myself, like Uncle Bob keeps saying, when I really don't like who I am?* Christy realized she kept wanting to be like somebody else. First Alissa, now Tracy. And at home she had always imitated Paula. *Paula,* she thought. *If Paula could see me now! It's a good thing I didn't mail her letter yet. I've got lots more to tell her!*

"How do you like it?" Todd asked, indicating her ice cream bar.

"I like it." Actually, she had eaten almost the whole thing and hadn't even noticed how it tasted. The sun was melting the chocolate, and she tried to lick the drips off the bar before they landed on her clothes. *What a jerk I've been. I've hardly talked at all. I hope Todd doesn't think I don't like him.*

"So," she began, realizing they had circled back to the bike, "what's new with you?"

"Not much," he said as they straddled the bike and pushed off. "What's new with you?" Then he smiled, and from the angle of his turned head, Christy thought she could see faint dimples in his bronzed skin. She hadn't noticed them before.

"This is fun," she said. "Thanks for coming." She leaned close to his broad shoulders so he could hear her.

"Sure," he replied, turning his head again. "We're going to ride the long way back, over the bridge instead of taking the ferry. Is that okay?"

"Sure." Christy leaned forward to check for his dimples. She wondered what it would be like to feel his cheek against hers. Her imagination sprinted. *What if Todd really starts to like me, and we start going together? Would he treat me the way Erik treated Alissa? What's going to happen in the weeks before I go home? Will I break my promise to my parents and end up doing something I'll regret later?*

Todd said something, but all she heard was the name *Tracy.* She clenched her teeth and said, "What? I didn't hear what you said."

"I wondered if you knew what time it is. I told Tracy I would give her a ride home from work at two."

Tracy! Why did he have to bring her up? Christy felt foolish for thinking about getting closer with Todd when he was far from having intimate thoughts about her. Christy pouted for the rest of the bike ride home. Todd didn't seem to think anything of her silence.

When they got to the house he helped her put the bike back in the garage. He smiled as if he were about to say something funny, but all he said was, "Later," and sprinted to Gus.

Christy watched Gus the Bus cruise down the street. As its faded tan backside disappeared through the intersection, she muttered, "Later."

Going through the back door of the house, Christy called out. Nobody was home. She scanned the refrigerator for something to eat and settled on a piece of barbecued chicken and a glass of milk.

For a long time she sat with her elbow on the kitchen table, her head resting in her palm. A familiar wave of depression came over her. Up and down. Down and up. Her whole life was a series of waves rushing in and pulling back. She wished she could somehow even out...find something stable to latch on to.

Having just spent the last two and a half hours with Todd, she should have been happy. Plus, she was going to Disneyland with him next week for her birthday. But she was miserable. All summer she had gotten everything she wanted and more. More clothes than she could wear—and she was going shopping again this afternoon. More opportunities to go places and do things than she had ever had at home. She had been spoiled rotten by her aunt and uncle for weeks, but she just didn't feel happy, and she couldn't figure out why.

She glanced at the clock. A quarter till three, and Aunt Marti still wasn't home. Typical.

Christy wandered aimlessly through the house for a while, looking at all the expensive things that adorned it. *The buying never ends for my aunt,* she thought, and suddenly the words to the Debbie Stevens song "You Can't Find It at the Mall" popped into her head. *Hmmm.* Christy was struck by a brief revelation. *Maybe Debbie was right. Maybe I do need Jesus in my life.* But that wasn't something she wanted to deal with at the moment. She needed to pull herself out of this emotional slump, and thinking about Jesus Christ dying on the cross and about her being a sinner was certainly not going to cheer her up.

She meandered up the stairs, trying to decide what to change into when the front door burst open. "Christy dear! Are you ready to go?"

Christy snapped out of her fog and called down from the top of the stairs, "I'll be there in a second." She ran into her room and in record time changed into a denim skirt and one of the shirts she hadn't worn yet. She didn't even take time to look in the mirror but galloped down the stairs calling, "I'm ready!"

Aunt Marti stood by the door with a stack of mail in her hand. She looked up at Christy and then frowned disapprovingly.

"What in the world is on your face, dear girl?"

"My face? I don't know."

Christy scurried to the downstairs bathroom with Aunt Marti on her heels. There in the bathroom mirror she saw it. A big glob of chocolate from the Balboa Bar had streaked across her cheek and dried, leaving a skid mark that stretched from her upper lip almost all the way to her ear!

Christy burst into tears. "No!" she sobbed. "No! No!

No! Why am I such a klutz! Todd must have seen me like this; why didn't he say anything?"

Aunt Marti, apparently thinking Christy's outburst was overdone, scolded, "This is no way for a young lady to act. Calm yourself. Here I thought you were all ready to go shopping, but you haven't even washed your face. Now, go upstairs and do something about your eye makeup too. And that shirt doesn't really go with that skirt, you know."

Christy stomped upstairs to redo herself according to Aunt Marti's directions, muttering and sniffing all the way.

Despite all the trauma they actually made it to South Coast Plaza by four o'clock. But Christy had a hard time getting into the mood to shop after all her aunt's reprimands.

"Christy, this is a cute skirt, don't you think?" Her aunt held up a short green one.

"No. That shade of green isn't one of my colors, remember?" Christy jabbed. "But I like this." She held up a pleated plaid skirt. "This is perfect, don't you think?" It wasn't even that cute, but it was something Marti would never select.

After several encounters, Marti lowered herself into a chair and said with resignation, "It's up to you, Christy. Whatever you want. You know what you like."

Christy did something she had never done before. She went through the racks, randomly picking whatever appealed to her and trying it on. If it fit she asked her aunt to buy it. She never looked at a price tag. Maybe the stack of new clothes would add up to more than five hundred dollars. It was stupid, she knew, but it was the only way she could think of to get back at her aunt.

The total came to more than seven hundred dollars, but

Aunt Marti put it all on her credit card without batting an eyelash. Suddenly, Christy felt sick to her stomach. Seven hundred dollars? She couldn't do it. She just couldn't do it. Besides, wasn't it Uncle Bob who really paid the bills?

"Wait," Christy said to the salesclerk. "I, um, I think I may have gotten some of the sizes wrong. Could you cancel that? I need to go try some of these on. I'd hate to get home and find out some things didn't fit."

Aunt Marti looked thoroughly annoyed. "Well, hurry along, dear. We're to meet your uncle in half an hour."

Christy slipped into the dressing room, the clerk following her with the stack of clothes. She peeled through the pile behind the closed door and settled on five items. They all sort of matched, and they were the things she liked best. One T-shirt was even on sale.

"Here." Christy handed the diminished stack to the clerk. "This is all."

"You're sure?" the clerk questioned.

"Yes."

Marti didn't say a word. She kept silent until they met Bob at the restaurant.

"Well, well!" he said, eyeing their bags. "Looks like you've met with some success."

"Yes," Marti said coolly. "If only your niece's taste in clothes were as strong as her impulsiveness, we would be doing quite well!"

Her comment hit Christy like a gale-force wind. That was it! Something snapped. In Christy's mind, Marti instantly transformed from a sophisticated, rich aunt to a snooty, self-centered peacock. So what if she had enough money to buy whatever she wanted? She didn't have much of a heart. Her lack of consideration for other people's time and feelings had showed itself over and over again.

Christy wanted to snap back, "I'm tired of you trying to make me into the perfect little daughter you never had. I don't need your money or your lectures anymore. I don't want to be the person you want me to be. I just want to be Christina Juliet Miller from Wisconsin. And if that's not good enough for you, then that's too bad." But all she said was, "I'd like to have steak for dinner. Is that okay with you, Uncle Bob?"

"Sure, honey. Whatever you would like."

Aunt Marti gave her a look of disdain and ordered the mini chef's salad.

Although Christy wasn't really hungry, she ate all her dinner, including a baked potato with gobs of butter and sour cream and a butterscotch sundae for dessert—just to prove to Marti that she was her own person. That night when she couldn't sleep because her stomach hurt, she wasn't sure exactly what she had proved.

Over the next few days Christy found more opportunities to silently rebel against her aunt's manipulations. They were subtle little things that she was sure Marti didn't even notice at first. But, for her, every act of insolence fanned the inner flame of dislike for her aunt.

One afternoon when she came in from the beach she answered the phone and took a message for Marti about a special meeting at the community center that evening at seven. Christy purposely left the message hidden under the pad of paper until six-thirty that evening. Then she slyly put the note on top of the desk and said, "You did get the message by the phone, didn't you?"

It wasn't like her to be vengeful like this, but the more

she held her frustrations inside, the more her bitter little darts flew. She had been around Marti enough to know what bothered her, and Christy purposefully did whatever she could to prompt the aggravation, like eating in front of the TV or leaving her sandy beach towel on her bedroom floor. Then there were the two killer pet peeves: slouching and nail biting. Christy did both, whenever possible, just to perturb her aunt.

Like a wounded animal, Marti backed off. Her aggressive attacks digressed into a timid routine of gentle reminders.

Coming in from the beach one afternoon, Christy met her aunt in the kitchen.

"A letter came for you," Marti said. "It's on your bed."

"Okay." Christy grabbed a handful of her uncle's secret recipe chocolate chip cookies and headed for her room.

"Say, Christy," her aunt called after her, "why don't you leave your towel here? I'll throw it in the wash for you. And perhaps you'd like to take a napkin with you. Just in case," she weakly added.

Christy stuffed a cookie into her mouth, ignoring the suggestions and fighting back the guilt she felt over acting like such a brat. She didn't like being this way, but once she started it was easier to keep up the antics than to stop. She had never been good at apologizing. Especially when the other person deserved what she was getting.

Her room, bright and refreshing, looked tremendously inviting this afternoon. She found the letter on her bed, as Marti had said. To her surprise she saw it was from Alissa. Christy read it over and over, realizing how good she really had it. Alissa's life sounded so sad and hopeless.

Dear Christy,

I arrived at my grandmother's with very few problems. I would like to thank you and your uncle for the ride to the airport and for your help in getting me packed.

My mother is keeping up with her alcohol control program, and the director of the center called yesterday to say that if she keeps improving, she will be released within a few weeks.

I'm staying with my grandmother until school starts, and then she is sending me to boarding school. My address is on the envelope. It would be nice to hear from you if you have a chance to write.

I think about you and Todd and Shawn and Erik a lot. I regret how my time in Newport went, especially since it was so short. I know I said some cruel things to you on the beach that one day, about Shawn. All I can say is that I don't know why people die, and I don't know how to deal with it. I wish I could find some peace to ease to all the pain in my life. My grandmother is sending me to a psychiatrist three days a week to work through some of these things, and she forbids me to go anywhere by myself.

Well, I didn't intend for this to be a sad story about my horrid life. I wanted to let you know I appreciated your support, and I'd like to keep in touch with you. I wish my life were like yours—innocent and free, with a real family on a Wisconsin farm. Sounds pretend.

Well, please say hi to Todd for me. You are so lucky to have him.

Yours,
Alissa

Christy cried over the letter more than once. Being so far away from Alissa, all she could do was write her back. But she ended up throwing away every letter she started. She wanted to encourage Alissa somehow, to give her some hope. But she couldn't find the right words. Everything sounded so phony.

Then there was the part about being so lucky to have Todd. That was a laugh! Christy didn't have Todd. Nobody had Todd. Things with him were as up and down as ever. They saw each other all the time at the beach, but when things started looking up, Tracy would appear and Christy would take the backseat again. Plus, Todd had all his surfer friends, with whom Christy never managed to quite fit in. Some of them were pretty weird. A few too many conks on the head by a surfboard or something.

That very morning one of the guys had said, "Totally wasted!" when he came up from the water. He shook his head full of blond, curly hair so that the spray fell all over Christy. "Thrashin', man! I was, like, totally eating blue chunks." Then he stuck his board under his arm, mumbled, "Trash this," and walked away.

Christy had turned to Tracy. "Was I having a conversation with him? I think I need an interpreter."

"The waves aren't any good. He's going home," Tracy said.

"Oh. I'm glad Todd doesn't talk like that." Christy looked out at the water, watching Todd skim the waves on his familiar orange surfboard.

"Todd kind of talks everybody's language. He has his surfer friends, but then he hangs out with all the straight kids, too."

"You know him pretty well, don't you?" Christy ventured.

"I guess."

It seemed strange to Christy that Tracy was always friendly. Christy had to work hard at maintaining her coolness toward Tracy because she was such a free spirit and so likable. Why didn't Tracy fight harder for Todd's attention?

Finally, Christy came right out and asked her, "Tracy, do you like Todd?"

"Todd? I love Todd."

"Then why don't you get jealous when he does things with other girls?" For good measure, Christy threw in, "Like tomorrow, for instance, he's taking me to Disneyland for my birthday."

"Oh, really?" Tracy remarked without a hint of envy. "I hope you have fun! Happy birthday, too, if I don't see you tomorrow."

"Thanks," muttered Christy, not content to let her question go unanswered. "Doesn't that bother you or anything?"

"No, not a bit. Todd and I have been friends since last summer. The same guy led us both to the Lord here on the beach."

"What do you mean he 'led' you to the Lord?"

"I mean, he told us how to become Christians."

"You mean how you're supposed to ask forgiveness for your sins and ask Christ to come into your heart?" Christy asked.

"Exactly. Have you done that too?"

"No, I haven't done that exactly, but I'm still a Christian," Christy said.

"Well, I know this could sound harsh," Tracy said, "but nobody can become a Christian by just being good. That's why Christ died on—"

"I know all that!" Christy cut her off. "I don't know why everyone has to talk about sin so much."

"Because that's what separates us from God. As long as we're separated from Him, we'll never be able to become the people He wants us to be."

"I don't know what you mean."

"Haven't you ever felt guilty for stuff and wished you could unload it all and start fresh?"

Christy flashed back over the past week and all the guilt she felt over her behavior toward her aunt. "Yes. Of course." Then she thought of Alissa's letter.

"You don't have to live with that. You can be free from all that junk if you ask forgiveness from God and ask Jesus to come into your life and be your Lord."

Christy felt uncomfortable. She envied Tracy's openness and the way she talked about God as though He were a close friend, not a distant, almighty power ready to strike whenever someone did something He didn't like.

"You make it sound as though you and God are friends," Christy said, beginning to let down her guard.

"We are. Best friends."

"I don't know. I always thought God was way up there, and I was way down here, and it was up to me to be a good person."

While they talked, Todd came in from surfing. Playfully shaking himself like a wet dog, he sprayed water all over the girls, who squealed and laughed.

"Watch it! You're dripping on my legs!" Christy protested. "It'll leave those salt dots."

"Salt dots, huh? There's only one way to get rid of salt dots." Todd got a mischievous gleam in his eye.

Christy shot a glance at Tracy, who nodded a quick yes to Todd. Before Christy realized what was happening, Todd grabbed her by both wrists, pulled her up, and started dragging her toward the water.

"No, no! I'll go in by myself."

As soon as Todd let go of her wrists, she ran in the other direction, laughing and looking behind to see if Todd was chasing her. Doug saw all the action and blocked Christy's escape, grabbing her arm.

"Hold her!" Todd yelled.

Christy squealed, "No, no! Let me go!"

"Ready for a dip?" Todd asked, taking hold of her ankles.

"No! Stop, you guys!" Christy struggled, but with Doug holding her wrists and Todd holding her ankles, she couldn't wiggle free. They lifted her and trotted down to the water's edge.

"On three," Todd commanded as they swung her over the foamy waves. "One, two, three!"

They let go, and Christy landed in about four feet of water with a mighty splash. Completely drenched, she rose to her feet and shouted, "I'm going to get you guys back! Just wait!"

Doug had jogged up to the dry sand. Todd remained at the shoreline.

"What's that?" Todd said. "You want to go bodysurfing?" He high-stepped through the water to where Christy stood with her hands on her hips.

"Come on," he shouted. "Dive under."

Together they plunged beneath the oncoming wave. They swam out to where the waves were building, and for more than an hour they rode the surging water together.

Don't let this day ever end, Christy thought as another wave lifted her, carried her, and exhilarated her. *Please don't let this feeling go away. Ever!*

As Christy lay on her bed later, with Alissa's letter still in her hand and the light fading in the room, she could feel the churning force of the ocean once more. And the exhilaration of not only riding the waves, but also of being with Todd. That was today. Who knew what tomorrow would be like with on-again-off-again Todd? Tomorrow. A day at Disneyland. With Todd. Would it be awful, like the concert, or wonderful, like the bodysurfing? Her thoughts were interrupted by a knock at the door.

"Christy?" came Uncle Bob's voice. "Telephone, hon. It's your mom and dad."

"Thanks, Uncle Bob," she said as he handed her the cordless phone. It was a typical conversation with her parents. Her mom tried to slowly bring the topic around to the point she wanted to make, but her dad cut in and jabbed the sharp words at Christy; "You need to come home Sunday."

"Sunday!" she squawked. "You mean this Sunday?"

"Yes, this Sunday."

"That's only three days away! I'm supposed to stay here till the end of August."

"Don't make this any harder than it already is," he barked gruffly. "Your vacation is over. Now. Don't miss your plane."

"But, Dad—" she began, but then she heard the click on the other end, indicating that he had hung up.

Her mom was still on the line, though. "I gave Bob all the flight information, honey. He said you've been having a wonderful time."

"Mom, why do I have to come home?" Christy fought the tears with all her might.

"You just do, Christy. We'll explain everything when you get here Sunday."

Christy hung up the phone and slid under the covers on her bed, feeling cold all of a sudden. She wanted to cry, but the tears didn't come. Everything seemed so pointless. She had to go home in three days, and she didn't know why. Was it her dad's farm? Were things going worse for them financially? Or was she the problem? Were her parents punishing her for something? What had she done? She had kept her promise; she hadn't done anything she regretted. At least not yet. But she still had three more days, starting with her birthday tomorrow with Todd.

Her birthday. Neither of her parents had even said, "Happy birthday." With that sharp realization came the tears. Bitter, salty, angry tears.

13

The Magic Kingdom

Todd showed up right at nine o'clock the next morning. Christy fumbled for her sandals.

"I can't believe he's on time!" she said in a panic to her aunt.

"I'll go chat with him," Marti offered. "Hurry along."

Christy took one last look in the closet mirror. She loved this outfit. The denim shorts and peach-colored T-shirt were some of the new clothes from Aunt Marti, but she'd tried them on together only two days ago and decided they were the most comfortable of all her new clothes. If she was going to be shipwrecked on a tropical island, this is the outfit she'd want to be wearing.

Disneyland may not exactly be the same as a tropical adventure, but Christy felt as if she were going into parts unknown. She would never again have this kind of freedom. When she returned to Wisconsin her parents would clamp down on everything—makeup, dating, clothes, curfews. She had better enjoy it all now, while she had the chance.

She took the stairs lightly and greeted Todd with a confident "Hi!" Todd looked like his usual casual self in his shorts and white T-shirt.

"You two have a marvelous time!" Aunt Marti grinned approvingly.

"When do you think you'll be home?" Bob asked.

"When do you want Christy back, sir?" Todd asked.

"Make a day of it, kids." Bob waved his hand in the air. "We won't be worried unless it's midnight and we haven't heard from you."

"Bye," they both called out and walked toward Gus. Christy thought she was going to burst with excitement and anticipation. Then Todd opened the front door of the van, and there sat Tracy, like a rock.

"Hi!" Tracy greeted her. "Happy birthday!"

Christy lost it right then and there. "Is this your idea of a surprise present?" she snarled at Todd. "I didn't think anybody else was going to Disneyland with us."

"I'm just dropping her off at work," Todd said calmly.

"Oh. I'm sorry," Christy whispered, completely ashamed.

"That's okay," Tracy said reluctantly, then handed her a box. "Here. This is for you. Happy birthday."

Todd drove to Hanson's Parlor in silence.

Christy felt awful. *Why did I have to go and ruin the whole day like that?*

"You can open it whenever you want," Tracy said, jumping out of the van. "I'm sorry I upset you. I wasn't trying to."

"I know, Tracy," Christy said, moving up to the front passenger seat. "I was just being a jerk. I'm sorry."

"Don't worry about it." Tracy's bounce returned. "I hope you guys have a really fun time! Think of me as I slave over gallons of ice cream all day."

They drove in silence for a few miles before Christy looked over at Todd. His teeth were clenched, which made his jaw look even more solid and manly.

"You okay?" she asked quietly.

"Not really."

"Is it because of how I acted with Tracy?"

"No, that's something between the two of you. Tracy doesn't have a problem with me spending the day with you. I'm not sure why you have a problem with me taking her to work."

"I don't. I guess I'm jealous of her in some ways."

"There's no reason to be. She's about the most loving, caring person you'll ever meet."

She looked at Tracy's gift, which she still held in her lap. "I wonder if I should open this now."

"Sure. Go ahead. I already know what it is. I hope you like it."

Christy read the card written in Tracy's handwriting:

For Christy,
We hope this will help you understand everything we've been saying about the Lord. Happy Birthday!
Love,
Tracy and Todd

"This is from you, too?" Christy asked Todd, tearing off the paper.

"Yeah. I picked it out, but Tracy made the cover and wrapped it and everything."

Christy pulled back the paper and lifted up a Bible. The cover was made from pink quilted fabric with tiny white flowers around the edges. Two white satin ribbons were attached as book markers.

"This is really nice, Todd. Thanks!" She secretly wished it had been something more personal. A Bible was something she imagined her Sunday school teacher giving her.

"Glad you like it," he said, his smile returning. He stuck a Debbie Stevens tape in the tape deck, rolled down the window, and cranked up the volume.

Christy rolled her window down too, welcoming the breeze. She wanted to start this day all over and concentrate on the time she had with Todd. She wasn't going to let today slip through her fingers the way their bike ride to Balboa Island had.

"Did I tell you I went surfing this morning?" Todd asked.

"This morning? You're kidding! When?"

"About six-thirty. My dad woke me up when he left for work."

"Were the waves any good?"

"Naw. Just ankle slappers. I hung out on my board for a while, but this whole thing with Shawn is really tearing me up. We used to get up early and go surfing."

"Really? I never would have guessed. You guys are so different. Or, I mean were so different. Or whatever you're supposed to say."

"It's okay; I know what you mean."

They chatted easily, and within a short time, Todd pulled Gus into the Disneyland parking lot entrance and handed the parking lot attendant a fifty-dollar bill for the parking.

"Do you have anything smaller?" the attendant asked.

"Let me check."

Christy watched as Todd peeled through a huge wad of bills until he came to a bunch of twenties.

Where did he get all the money? Maybe Disneyland is more expensive than I realized.

"Well, you ready for the Magic Kingdom?" Todd asked, locking up Gus.

Christy smiled.

"Good." He stuffed his keys into his pocket. "I think it's ready for you."

Todd paid for their all-day passes at the front gate, and as they entered, Christy pointed to the flower garden that formed a picture of Mickey Mouse. "When I was little, I saw that on TV, and I tried to get my mom to plant our flowers to look like that!"

Todd laughed. "Did she?"

"No. I tried to do it myself with rocks and dirt clods, though. Didn't turn out very well. I wish I had a camera with me. I'd take a picture of it."

"I don't think so, Christy," Todd said, shaking his head and grinning. "You don't take a camera to Disneyland. Makes you look like those people over there—tourists."

Todd pointed to a family on Main Street. The large mother and three pudgy kids were standing in front of a barber shop quartet, which was riding a bicycle built for four. The family members nearly hid the quartet. The father was bending backward in a hilarious position, apparently trying to get it all in his viewfinder. Todd and Christy looked at each other and muffled their laughter.

"Must be from the Midwest," Todd teased.

"Hey!" Christy socked him in the arm. "Watch it. I'm from the Midwest."

Todd shot her a sideways glance, his dimples showing as he suppressed a laugh. "I know."

Then he held out his hand for Christy to take. "Come on. Let's get on some rides."

Christy slid her hand into his and felt a warm rush spread through her fingers, up her arm, and through her whole body. *Don't let go! Don't ever, ever let go!*

They waited in line for half an hour to go on the bobsleds. Todd said this was his favorite ride and they had to go on this one first. They talked and laughed and even struck up a conversation with the people in line behind them.

Todd stepped into the shiny, red bobsled first and slid all the way back, his legs pressed against the sides.

"Step in, please," the ride attendant directed. He was dressed in green knickers and kneesocks. He looked like a goatherd.

"Where do I sit?" Christy asked.

"Here." Todd patted the slice of seat right in front of him.

For a moment Christy thought she would never fit there. Then the attendant took her elbow and hurried her. She stepped in cautiously and wedged her body in.

"Am I squishing you?" she asked.

Suddenly the bobsled lurched forward and began its steep climb to the top of the Matterhorn.

"Relax," Todd said. "It's okay. You look like you're about to jump out."

"I'm thinking about it," Christy admitted, cautiously leaning against Todd's chest. He felt solid and warm and, oh, how she wished he would wrap his arms around her!

The clinking sound of the rails beneath them slowed to almost a stop at the crest of the Matterhorn. Christy looked straight ahead, and all she saw was sky. Fear gripped her. She grabbed the handrails inside the bobsled, squeezed her eyes shut, and let out a wild shriek of sheer terror as the sled plummeted down the other side of the mountain. Forget snuggling! Forget the tender moment! Hanging on was all that counted.

Several sharp turns and dips later the racing bobsled splashed through the water and jerked to a stop. Another attendant offered his hand to help her out.

"You okay?" Todd asked, directing her to the exit.

"Yes." Her whole body trembled, and she felt silly for screaming.

"That was just our appetizer ride. Now I think you're ready for Space Mountain." Todd had a look of boyish excitement in his eyes.

"How about something to drink first? I think I need a few minutes to recover."

All day long they went on rides and ate and went on rides. After buying something to eat from every snack cart and experiencing every attraction in Tomorrowland, they headed for Adventureland.

Climbing atop the Swiss Family Robinson tree house, they looked out over the amusement park. Todd talked about his dream to someday live on a tropical island.

"I'm going to surf all day, eat papayas and mangos, and sip coconut juice right from the coconut."

"Sounds exotic," Christy said. "Are you going to live in a tree house like this one?"

"Yup. I'm going to sleep in a hammock, too."

"And what are you going to do for money?"

"Oh, I'll just trade beads with the natives and live off the land."

"You know, you would have made a great hippie."

"I probably would have. My dad always says he was the last hippie."

"You're kidding."

"Nope. He met my mom at Berkeley during a protest march, and they moved in together the next morning—after they got out of jail, that is."

"I don't believe it," Christy scoffed.

"It's true!"

After the tree house they waited in line for almost an hour for the Pirates of the Caribbean ride. When they got off, they decided to wait in line to eat dinner at the Blue Bayou Restaurant. About half an hour later they were seated. Neither of them was very hungry, but they were glad for a cool, quiet place to sit. Their table was only a few feet from where the Pirates of the Caribbean boats launched for their journey. The fake, twinkling fireflies were what Christy liked best.

"Isn't this relaxing? I feel like I've been transported to another time and place. I can't believe how real these little fireflies look. They are pretend, aren't they?"

"Of course," Todd said with a laugh. "Amazing how real they can make stuff look now, huh? Do you know what you want yet?"

The panic that usually seized her at a time like this didn't appear. "The chicken sounds good. Although, to be honest, I'm not real hungry."

They took their time eating, and when the waiter brought the check, Todd laid down a fifty-dollar bill. Christy thought back over the day. Todd had tossed around cash like it was play money. He had paid for everything, including a sweatshirt and a little Winnie the Pooh stuffed toy.

Todd crammed the change into his pocket and asked, "Well, what do you want to do now?"

"Let's go on some more rides. And then I need to find a souvenir for my little brother back home."

Todd took her hand as they left the Blue Bayou and held it as they strolled through New Orleans Square. Oh, how she wished her hands weren't so sweaty! Would Todd notice? His hand felt so strong and sure. She loved feeling close to him and secure as they slid through the crowds.

"Hey, how 'bout one of those for your brother?" Todd pointed to a mound of Mickey Mouse hats in a shop window. They darted in, laughing at each other as they tried on all the different hats. Finally they agreed on a black pirate's hat with a long, blue feather.

"David will love this! I just hope I can get it home in decent shape."

"When are you going back?" Todd asked as they got in line for the Jungle Cruise.

"That's something I wanted to tell you." Christy held his hand a little tighter. "My parents called last night and told me I had to come home right away. I'm leaving Sunday."

"This Sunday? The day after tomorrow?"

"Yes."

"Why?" Todd asked. Christy thought she could read a

look of disappointment on his face. "School doesn't start for five more weeks. I don't even leave for my mom's until the first of September."

"I know, but I guess things aren't going so great, and my parents want me home so we can go through it together."

"Go through what?"

"Well, the only thing I can figure out is that it must be the farm. I think I told you that my dad's a farmer. Not as exciting as a reformed hippie, I know. But we haven't really made it financially for the past three or four years, and my dad has sold off a lot of our land. I guess a bunch of stuff has happened since I left. I'm not sure what's going on. All I know is that they want me home right away."

"That's really too bad." Todd squeezed her hand.

"I'm going to miss you, Todd. We'll have to write or something."

"I'm not much of a writer, to be honest."

"Well, Tallahassee's not as far away from Wisconsin as California is. Is it?"

Todd laughed at her logic. "I don't know."

They had made it to the front of the line and stepped down into the boat. The ride operator, dressed in safari gear, advised the passengers to keep their hands and arms inside the moving vehicle at all times, warning them of the untamed animals they would encounter ahead.

Todd slipped his arm around the back of the seat. "This used to be my favorite ride when I was a kid."

"I thought the bobsleds were."

"Well, okay, this one and the bobsleds."

He looked like a kid now, eagerly taking in all the fake jungle bird sounds. She could almost imagine him swinging on one of those jungle vines. *You Tarzan, me Jane.* Her mind drifted, creating a jungle romance.

"Just ahead," the driver spoke into his microphone, "are the wild hippos. But have no fear, folks. They're only dangerous when they wiggle their ears!"

Christy looked over her shoulder at the wild hippos rising out of the water only a few feet away from her. The largest one opened its jaws and, to her surprise, began to wiggle its ears.

"Oh, no, folks! Look out! He's wiggling his ears!" The driver grabbed his cap gun and shot rapidly at the beast.

Completely startled, Christy let out a scream and threw herself onto Todd's chest. The elderly couple next to them started laughing, and their small grandson patted Christy on the leg, saying, "Don't cry, lady. Monster all gone!"

Everyone on the boat watched as Christy peeled herself off of an embarrassed Todd. The driver made the most of the situation.

"It's okay, folks, the young lady will be all right. Actually, we hired her to come along and add some excitement to Disneyland's own version of the Love Boat."

Everyone laughed. Christy was totally embarrassed, but she laughed too. Todd slipped his arm around her and smiled an easy smile that said a thousand things to Christy. She read something deep and wonderful in his silver-blue eyes—or did she?

That's when Christy began to wonder if he would kiss her good night when they got home. It flooded her thoughts so much that she barely paid attention to what they did the rest of the night. She didn't listen to what Todd said. Instead, she drew inward, self-conscious about how she looked, wondering if she would bump into his nose when they kissed, how she should hold her mouth.... It was torture!

Around nine o'clock they stopped outside of Bear Country and watched the nightly fireworks display. Todd put his arm around her, and she rested her head on his shoulder, feeling the same bright explosions inside as each fireworks burst in the night sky. In the distance they watched as a real live Tinkerbell, hooked on a cable, "flew" from the top of the Matterhorn and across the Magic Kingdom to Fantasyland.

As they were leaving the park, they made one last stop at the Emporium and watched the glassblower make a tiny Tinkerbell figurine. The liquid-hot glass looked like clear bubblegum as the craftsman pulled and pinched and twisted it about his blue-flamed blowtorch.

"That's so amazing," Christy said when the craftsman had finished and held up the figurine.

"You want it?" Todd asked.

"Well, I don't know." Every time she had looked at something twice or said she liked it, Todd had pulled out his bank roll and bought it for her.

"Excuse me," Todd said to the salesclerk in a long dress and white pinafore. "Could we get that glass Tinkerbell he just made?"

"Certainly," she said and gently wrapped the tiny fairy in tissue paper and placed it in a box.

"Thanks, Todd." Christy squeezed his arm. "I really appreciate your getting me all these things. Thanks."

"It's all right," Todd said casually. "Want anything else to eat?"

"Are you kidding? I don't think I can eat another bite for a week!"

They walked out on Main Street, and Christy noticed all the little white twinkling lights strung on the trees. *It really is a fairy-tale land.*

Juggling all her shopping bags, she realized Todd had his hands full of bags too. She hadn't remembered buying this much, but now the bags felt heavy and burdensome. Her feet ached, her throat ached, her arms ached. If she went on one more ride she would be too tired to scream.

"Anything else you want to see?" Todd asked.

"Just a nice place to sit down."

"How about Gus?"

"Sounds good."

They rode the shuttle through the parking lot, balancing all the bags on their laps. Most of the cars had disappeared from the lot that was several times bigger than her hometown park.

It was a mellow ride home in Gus, both of them too tired to say much. Christy probably would have fallen asleep except her mind kept torturing her about the moment when their date would end. She played the scene over and over in her imagination. Would he kiss her? What would it be like? Should she close her eyes? What if she had bad breath? She could hardly stand the suspense.

Finally the moment arrived when Todd walked her to the front door. It was almost midnight. Her heart pounded wildly. She swallowed hard.

"Thanks, Todd. This was the best birthday I ever, ever had." She looked up at him shyly, expectantly.

He put his arms around her and hugged her tightly.

"Good night, Christy," he said softly. And then he pulled away without kissing her.

"Good night," Christy echoed, hiding her disappointment.

Todd stuck his hands into his pockets and headed toward Gus. Then, as if he had forgotten something, he turned around. Christy's heart froze.

He's coming back! Now what should I do? Is he going to kiss me now?

"I almost forgot," Todd said with a laugh. "Here." He pulled a wad of money from his pocket and handed it to Christy.

"What's this for?"

"Your aunt. It's what's left over."

"What do you mean? I don't get it."

"It's left over from the money your aunt gave me to take you to Disneyland. We didn't spend it all, so I thought you should give her the rest back."

The blood drained from Christy's face. "You mean my aunt asked you to take me today, and she even gave you the money?"

"Hey! It's cool. We had a great time. I'm glad she talked me into it."

"Talked you into it!"

Christy turned on her heels and jerked the front door open, catapulting up the stairs. In her fury she stumbled on the third step and lost her sandal. With the rage of a wild warrior she grabbed her sandal, heaved it toward Todd, and fled to her room. Some day in the Magic Kingdom! So much for happily ever after! Her "fairy godmother" was only her aggravating aunt, and her handsome prince had just turned into a toad!

14

The Promise

The digital clock on the nightstand read 12:04. The sun shining in through Christy's bedroom window was so bright it seemed to shout at her. She didn't feel much better than she had twelve hours earlier when she had thrown her shoe at Todd, flung the money in her aunt's face, and screamed, "Get out of my life!" As a grand finale she had heaved a pillow at her uncle when he followed her into her room to try to talk to her.

They were wise to let her sleep, to leave her alone for the last twelve hours. Christy knew she couldn't burrow in her bed any longer; she had to rise and face the inevitable. Things needed to be settled with her aunt, and she had to pack before her plane left tomorrow morning.

Thinking about all those hard issues only pressed her deeper into her pillow. She felt gunky. Her top eyelashes stuck to the bottom lashes, her teeth seemed encased in caramel corn, her eyes were puffy from crying, and she was all tangled up in her Disneyland clothes.

Strewn across the floor were the shopping bags she had

thrown hither and yon in her fury. Bags filled with all the souvenirs Todd had bought for her. Or rather, bags that her aunt had financed Todd to get for her. Her room was a mess, she was a mess, her life was a mess.

"That's the problem with hissy fits," Paula had said once. "You always have to clean up after yourself, and it's very humbling."

What humbled Christy at that moment was seeing her new Bible fanned out on the floor where it had landed after being ejected from a flying bag. Meekly, she slithered out of bed and retrieved it, smoothing down the wrinkled pages.

"I'm sorry," she whispered. "It's just that I don't think any of this is fair. Why did my aunt make such a fool out of me? Why did Todd go along with her? And why do I have to go home tomorrow? Now things will never work out between Todd and me!"

Christy realized she was talking to God as if it were the most natural thing for her to do, just like her new friends talked to Him. "I don't know what my problem is. I just feel like I'm losing it. Like everything around me is going under. What am I doing wrong, God?"

In the silence that followed a piercing thought came to Christy: the nightmare she had had weeks ago. The memory so filled her mind that the feelings all came back, rushing toward her with urgent freshness. It was as if she were, once again, barely hanging on to the side of the boat. The tentacles of seaweed were wrapping themselves tighter and tighter around her legs. She was facing that terrifying moment all over again, the moment when she had to decide whether to get into the boat or let the seaweed pull her under. Only this time she was wide awake, and the dream paralleled reality too strongly for her to ignore it. Jesus was that boat, like Todd had said. And if she ever wanted to get to heaven (or Hawaii, as Todd had called it), she had to get in the boat.

She knew what she had to do, and she knew she had to do it now. Christy knelt beside her bed, bowed her head, and closed her eyes. Then she spoke aloud in a soft voice.

"God, I realize that what's missing in my life is You. I mean, I've known about You my whole life, but I don't know You the same way Todd and Tracy do. And I want to know You personally, like they said. I really want You to come into my life. So, Lord, please forgive all my sins and come into my life right now. I promise my whole heart to You forever. Amen."

She opened her eyes and turned to study her reflection in the mirror. She looked the same as when she had pulled herself out of bed—hair a mess, clothes wrinkled, raccoon eyes from smeared mascara. But inside she knew she was different. Not wildly emotional or anything, just clean. Secure. Happy. She smiled and hugged her Bible close to her. She was in the boat, and the adventure was just beginning.

The first big wave ahead would be facing Aunt Marti.

Christy showered and dressed quickly. She found her aunt and uncle sitting on the patio, sipping iced tea. Christy quietly slid past her aunt and settled on the chaise lounge next to her uncle's chair. They both acted as though she weren't there, waiting for her to make the first move.

"About last night..." Christy began, rubbing her hands together, "I think I owe you an apology."

"No, darling." Aunt Marti turned to face her. "I realize that it is I who owes you an apology."

Uncle Bob remained quiet with a furrowed brow, as if

he were unsure where this conversation would lead.

"I was terribly at fault, and I'm not sure I can ever forgive myself for not preparing you for your first experience."

"Well," Christy fumbled, "it's not that you didn't...I mean, I really shouldn't have expected anything more, I guess. It's just that I really thought Todd wanted to be with me just because he liked me, but..."

"No, Christy, don't blame yourself. And don't blame Todd. It's my fault. I really should have seen it coming and done more to prepare you."

"It just hurts, that's all. And I felt so stupid. So used."

"Yes," Aunt Marti agreed, "men can make you feel that way—especially the first time."

"What do you mean, 'Men can make you feel that way'?" Christy asked belligerently. "You made me feel that way, Aunt Martha!"

"*I* made you feel that way? How could I possibly make you feel used?"

"By giving Todd all that money and bribing him into taking me to Disneyland!"

Aunt Marti stared at her in disbelief. "You mean that's what all the tears were about last night? The screaming and the turmoil were simply over my helping to finance your birthday excursion?"

"Yes." Christy stared back. "What did you think I was so upset about?"

Bob interjected, "You don't want to know what she thinks you were upset about. She's lost all comprehension of youthful innocence. Too many soap operas. It's warped her mind."

"It has not, Robert! I resent you saying such a thing!

Here I was, honestly concerned that Christy had her first intimate encounter with a young man and feeling guilty for not doing more to prepare her!"

Christy was stunned. She had been worried about whether or not Todd would kiss her, and her aunt was imagining much more.

"Why, I have done nothing but lavish my love on you all summer long," her aunt continued. "I've given you everything a young girl could dream of. Your uncle and I have made a great number of sacrifices for you, and if this is all the thanks we get, then perhaps it's for the best that you're leaving tomorrow. Maybe once you're gone you'll appreciate all we've bought for you."

Christy wanted to rush over to her aunt, first to hug her and then slug her. How could she think in such a twisted way? How could she take a situation and bend it so that Christy came out the guilty party? Yet, she was right too. Christy had taken all the clothes and dinners out and excursions for granted.

"Aunt Marti," Christy began cautiously, hoping to melt her aunt's frosty stare, "it's just that there are some things you can't buy with money."

As soon as she said it, Christy thought of the Debbie Stevens song "You Won't Find It at the Mall." Now she really knew what that song meant.

"But," she added quickly, "I appreciate all that you have done for me. I really do. I'll never forget this summer. It's been the best summer of my whole life!"

Aunt Marti didn't respond. She stared out at the ocean, her lips pulled tight with anger. "I have nothing more to say, Christina."

"I'm sorry," Christy said with tears in her eyes. "I'm sorry for being such a problem to both of you."

"You know we loved having you here." Uncle Bob reached over and gave Christy's shoulder a squeeze. "Why don't you enjoy your last afternoon and go join your friends down on the beach?"

"I don't know if I ever want to see Todd again. Or what I'd say if I did."

"Sure you do. Besides, this is your last chance. Make the most of it, honey. And by the way, would this, by any chance, be yours?" He held up the sandal she had hurled at Todd.

"Yes," she said sheepishly and took it from him.

"Go ahead," Aunt Marti obliged. "You need to make up with Todd before you go home."

"I need to make up with you, too," Christy gently pointed out.

"All is forgiven," Aunt Marti said with a little smile.

Christy rushed over to her aunt and bent down to hug her. Laughing uncomfortably, as though she wasn't used to such affectionate displays, her aunt returned the hug.

"Now get going," she said, releasing Christy and smoothing her own slightly rumpled hair.

Twenty minutes later, Christy shuffled through the sand, wondering whom she would find down by the jetty. Alissa was back in Boston. Tracy was probably at work. Todd...who knew what Todd was doing?

After all, nobody paid Todd to spend time with me this afternoon, so why would he be hanging around?

She scanned the surfboards out in the water, but Todd's orange board wasn't among them. She approached the group that Todd tended to hang around with, but the only ones she knew were Heather, Doug, and Leslie. Remembering how she had felt like an outcast the night of the concert, Christy hesitated, not sure she wanted to face the group. But it was too late. They had already seen her and were motioning for her to join them.

"Hey, Christy," Doug greeted her, "you just missed Todd. He was here all morning. Said you guys had an awesome time at Disneyland!"

"Awesome?" teased Leslie. "Nobody uses that word anymore."

"Doug does!" Heather said with a giggle. "Tracy said she and Todd gave you a Bible. That was so cool of them."

"Oh, *cool*," Doug teased. "Now that's a real groovy word."

Heather wadded up a T-shirt and threw it at him.

"Yes," Christy said, trying to appear relaxed. "It's a really nice Bible." She wanted to tell them of her decision that morning to give her life to Jesus, but she didn't know how.

"We're all going to have a barbecue here tonight," Doug announced to her. "You should come."

"Where's it going to be?"

"Over there at the fire pits." Heather pointed. "Everybody just brings food, and we sit around and talk and sing and stuff. It's kind of our church group, but we try not to be cliquey. Michelle, Doug, and I are coming, and Todd said he might come and bring his guitar."

"Todd plays a guitar?" Christy asked.

"You didn't know that? He's really good."

For the next couple of hours, Christy talked to Heather while Doug rode his body board. She lay on her back the whole time to get as much sun on her face as possible, so that when she got off the plane the next day everyone would know she had been to California.

Around five o'clock, Christy headed back to the house to get some hotdogs for the barbecue and to grab her new Disneyland sweatshirt.

On the side table by the front door was a letter for her. She thought it was Paula's writing at first but then realized it was Alissa's. Come to think of it, Paula hadn't written her in a long time. Oh, well. Tomorrow she would be home and could tell Paula all about Disneyland, the catastrophe with Todd, and opening her heart to the Lord. So much had happened in such a short time.

Christy sat on the bottom step and skimmed the letter from Alissa. She sounded a little better than she had in her last letter, but maybe that was because of the new boyfriend she mentioned. Her grandmother even approved of him. He was a college sophomore named Everett, but everyone called him Bret. She sounded pretty happy with him, but Christy wondered how long that would last.

Christy stuck the letter back in the envelope and decided she would write Alissa on the plane. She felt she now had some answers to offer. Having Jesus in her heart made her feel as though she weren't all alone anymore, trying to figure things out on her own. *Alissa needs that kind of friend. Somebody who isn't going to leave her.*

Christy pushed her bedroom door open and found Uncle Bob folding a pair of her jeans into a suitcase.

"I hope you don't mind," he said. "I think we'll need to get a few boxes or another suitcase. Seems you're going home with more than you brought!"

"You don't have to do that. I can do it later."

"Well, your aunt's made reservations for six-thirty at the Five Crowns Restaurant, so I thought I'd get a head start for you."

"Oh, no!" Christy moaned. "I was going to go cook hotdogs on the beach with everybody. We don't have to go out to eat, do we?"

"I think she wanted to make your last night here special."

"It will be special if I can spend it with my friends," Christy pleaded.

"Well," he said, his eyes twinkling, "tell you what. You go have your cookout with your friends. Don't worry about your aunt. I'll take care of her."

"You are so awesome!" Christy threw her arms around his neck and hugged him.

Christy spent a few minutes in front of the mirror, fixing her hair. Then she splashed her face with cool water and smoothed some aloe gel over her sunburned cheeks. She looked like a true California girl: dark tan, sun-streaked hair.

I'm going to move to California as soon as I'm old enough. Maybe I'll go to college out here. This was her real home now. She felt no connection with cows and snowdrifts and all that went with Wisconsin living. Palm trees and surfboards—that was more her real self now.

Christy dabbed on some mascara, grabbed her sweat-shirt, and slipped downstairs to the kitchen, where Bob, with a wink, handed her a bag of cookout food. Christy rushed to the fire ring, where some of the guys had already started a fire. Tracy stood there, straightening out coat hangers to cook the hotdogs on. Cute, petite Tracy with her quick smile and big brown eyes. Christy had tried so hard not to like her, but now she realized how much she was going to miss her.

"Christy! Todd told me you're going home tomorrow. I can't believe it!" She tossed the coat hangers down and gave Christy a friendly hug. "We're going to miss you so much."

Christy quickly looked around. Todd wasn't there. She was disappointed and relieved at the same time,

"Thanks," she said as she hugged Tracy back. "And thanks, too, for the Bible and the cover you made. I really like it."

"I'm so glad. After our little encounter yesterday morning I wasn't sure if I should give it to you or not," Tracy said.

"Well, I'm glad you did. Do you know if Todd is going to come tonight?"

"I don't know. Hey, Brian, do you know if Todd's coming?"

"He was out here this morning when we were talking about it, but he didn't say."

"Who knows with Mr. Unpredictable," chimed in Michelle.

Well said, Christy thought.

For the next hour or so she kept looking, hoping that Todd would show up and yet wondering what she would say to him if he did—or what he would say to her. After a while she quit watching for him and tried to push him out of her mind. Everyone else was being so nice to her that it made it easy to have a fun time. Christy quietly thought about how much she was going to miss this new group of friends. She watched as the sun slipped into the ocean like a huge orange beach ball and wished she'd gotten to know all of them better. She also wished again that she didn't have to go home.

"So what if Todd isn't here with his guitar?" Tracy said as the sky began to darken. "Let's sing anyway."

The group, eleven of them, gathered around the fire and began singing choruses that Christy had never heard before. Some of them were soft and gentle, others loud and spirited. But they were all about the Lord, or rather songs that they sang to the Lord. She recognized some of the songs as verses she'd learned in Sunday school.

This is the most beautiful place in the world. What a perfect night! If only Todd were here. If only we hadn't ended last night in such an awful way. This clear night sky, these gentle breezes, and these songs are all so wonderful. I don't want to go home. I want to stay here forever!

Michelle must have noticed Christy's tears glistening in the firelight, because she leaned over and said, "It's probably going to be really hard for you to go home."

Christy's cheeks stung from salty tears on her sunburn. "I don't want to go."

"It'll turn out all right. You'll see."

The next song they sang was another Bible verse:

Trust in the Lord
With all your heart
And lean not on
Your own understanding.
In all your ways acknowledge Him
And He will direct your paths.

Christy had never felt her heart so full. The group huddled around the fire until the last log snapped and fell into a mound of red-hot embers. Then they went around the circle, and everyone prayed. Some prayed for their families; some prayed for their friends—that they would become Christians. Others thanked God for things He had done for them. Christy was the second to the last one to pray. Surprisingly, the words came easily.

"Dear Lord, I want to thank You for coming into my life this morning. Please be with my family and the problems we're having now, and please be with me when I go home tomorrow. Amen."

The next person, Doug, didn't pray. Instead he put his arm around Christy and pulled her close. "Did you really?" he asked.

"What?" Christy looked up, startled.

Everyone was looking at her.

"Did you really ask Christ into your heart this morning?"

"Yes," Christy answered, surprised at the reaction of everyone around her.

They all spoke at once: "That's great!" "Wow!" "You're kidding!" "I can't believe it!" "We've been praying for you!"

Everyone gathered around her in a big group hug, and Christy was amazed at how excited they all were. She never felt so loved and accepted. Doug gave her the biggest hug of all of them.

If only Todd had been there! It killed her, not knowing if she would ever see him again, especially after their closing scene at the door last night. She wasn't sure how they would have worked it out, but she was sure they could have if they tried.

The group hung around the fire pit until everyone felt

chilled from the night wind. At about eleven o'clock Doug walked her home.

"So, did you have a good summer?" he asked, stroking his fingers through his short hair.

"It went too fast."

"I'm so glad I got to know you," he said. "You can't believe how excited I am that you became a Christian. You'll never be sorry."

"Does the Lord really help you when things are tough?" Christy asked.

"Of course. But you know He doesn't take away the rough times. He helps you through them. Besides, all the difficult stuff makes you grow. It helps you depend on Him and not on yourself."

They were at Bob and Marti's front steps, and Doug added. "At least that's what happens to me when I go through hard stuff."

"You know what I'm going to miss?" Christy asked, standing with her back to the front door. "I'm going to miss listening to people talk about God so easily and naturally. I've learned a lot from you guys this summer. I don't have any friends at home who love God the way you do."

"Well," Doug challenged, "you'll have to tell them. Start your own group of God-lovers."

"God-lovers?" she repeated.

"Or whatever you want to call them. It takes only one person."

Doug was so easy to talk to. Why didn't she like him the way she liked Todd? He was cute, nice, and caring, but there was just something about Todd.

Todd. Why wasn't Todd standing by the front door with me tonight instead of Doug? She knew she had ruined everything when she threw her shoe at him.

"I'd better go in," she told Doug, shivering a little in the damp air. "Good-bye! I hope I see you again sometime."

"Here." Doug gave her a big hug. "I'll see you in heaven, if not before."

Christy gave a little laugh and went inside. She found her room completely cleaned, and on the floor were three new leather suitcases, all packed but still open. A note from her uncle was pinned to her pillow: *Hope you had a good time. You'll need to get something out of your suitcase to wear tomorrow on the plane. I'll wake you up at six o'clock so you'll have time to get ready.*

Christy couldn't sleep. She had so much floating around in her mind. *Why didn't Todd show up tonight at the barbecue? Will I ever see him again? Why do I have to go home tomorrow? Why is life always so complicated?* She wore herself out trying to come up with the answers.

Finally she released it all, thinking about Doug's statement that God would help her through the rough times instead of taking them away.

"Okay," Christy prayed, "I guess I'd better depend on You to help me through all these frustrating things, because I'm going to go crazy trying to figure them all out."

She snuggled under the warm covers, and then she softly sang, "Trust in the Lord with all your heart..."

She fell asleep before she finished.

The next morning Uncle Bob tapped on her door at 6:02. "We need to leave in an hour for the airport, Christy. Let me know if you need help with anything."

She showered and dressed in a daze. Her ears buzzed as if a

toy airplane were circling round and round in her head. After curling her hair, she crammed the last bag of cosmetics into the last suitcase. Opening her door, she hollered, "I'm ready!"

Aunt Marti appeared in the hallway. "Are you sure you have everything, dear?"

Marti looked stunning in a bright yellow and navy blue outfit. Her cool composure reigned; nothing of their conflict from the day before remained. Apparently Bob had smoothed over the restaurant situation, but Christy wisely thought she had better not bring it up.

"Yes, but I can't carry these suitcases. They're way too heavy."

Uncle Bob had to make a separate trip for each suitcase, throwing the leather monsters into the trunk. They pulled out of the driveway, and Christy tearfully took one last look at the house, one last gaze out at the beach, and allowed herself one last thought centered on Todd. It was all over. Her summer. Her first love...

The car stopped at a red light. This was the same intersection she and Todd had crossed on their bike ride. *Todd.* Just thinking about him caused a painful ache deep inside her. She swallowed the swelling wad of agony in her throat.

"Are my lights on?" Bob asked Marti.

"No."

"Then why is the guy in the car behind me flashing his lights and waving?"

Christy turned around. "It's Todd! Don't go yet!"

"But, Christy darling, the light's turned green!" Marti protested.

Christy jumped out of the car and bounded toward Gus. Todd stepped out of the van, with the engine still running, and handed Christy a small bouquet of white carnations. Her favorite! How did he know? Had her aunt set him up again? At this point she didn't care.

"I'm glad you stopped!" Todd said with a smile that showed his dimples. "The horn's not working in ol' Gus this morning."

"Thanks for the flowers."

"That's okay. Hey, Tracy called me last night after she left the beach and told me about your decision to turn your life over to the Lord."

"Yes," Christy said shyly. "It all made sense finally, and I knew it was time to get in the boat, like you told me."

"Christy," Todd said, tentatively reaching over and touching her shoulder. "You have no idea how happy I am for you. I've been so bummed out about Shawn. But knowing that you've become a Christian..." He began to choke up. "It's just the best thing that could've ever happened."

"I know," Christy whispered. She quickly searched Todd's bronzed face for one last time, desperately trying to remember everything about him—his strong jaw, those faint dimples when he smiled, his sun-washed blond hair, and those screaming silver-blue eyes, which were now staring deeply into her eyes.

The driver in the car behind Todd, exasperated from waiting, pulled out around them and laid on the horn as he sped through the yellow light.

"I guess I'd better let you go." Todd's mouth turned up in one of his wonderful, confident grins. "I wrote down my address in Florida. It's on a card inside the flowers. I'm not promising I'll write a lot, but if you want to write me, I promise I'll write back."

"Okay," she agreed. Forcing back the tears, she whispered, "Bye, Todd."

He leaned down, right in the middle of the street, in front of the whole world, and gently pressed his lips against hers. A brief, tender kiss. The kind that only comes from innocent love and whose memory lasts a lifetime.

"I'm going to miss you," he whispered.

"I'm going to miss you too!"

Todd glanced up and changed his tone. "Light's green again. You'd better go."

"Bye!" she called, dashing to the car. "I'll write you, I promise!"

Uncle Bob sped through the intersection, leaving Gus the Bus behind at the red light.

It was blissfully quiet for a few minutes as Christy pressed her lips against the bouquet of carnations, reliving the memory of her first kiss.

"Well," Aunt Marti clucked. "Just for the record, I had nothing to do with that rendezvous."

"You didn't? Really?" Christy's voice floated light and dreamy. "How did he know carnations were my favorite? And white carnations, too?"

"Kismet," Uncle Bob stated.

"What's that?"

"Some things you just can't explain. You have to figure a higher source is orchestrating the whole program."

"There is!" Christy agreed. "And I know Him personally."

"Well, that's nice, Christy dear. That's a very sweet way to think of God." Aunt Marti pulled down the visor to check her lipstick in the mirror.

"It's more than that. I made a promise this summer. To the Lord. I promised to give Him my whole heart. Now I'm trusting Him to work out whatever He thinks is best for my life."

"That's fine, dear." Aunt Marti pursed her lips together. "But my advice would be, don't overdo this religious approach to life. You control your own destiny, really, and there's no use waiting on God when you're perfectly capable of taking care of things yourself."

"Your aunt's right," Uncle Bob concurred. "As I told you weeks ago, 'To thine own self be true.'"

Christy laughed quietly and brushed the carnations against her cheek. "Nobody can control their own destiny, and I tried being true to myself, but I started going under. I'd rather be true to the Lord. It's way more fun! Besides, I know for sure that I'm going to make it to Hawaii now."

Marti cast a sideways glance at Bob and whispered, "What do you suppose she means by that?"

Bob gave her a look that said, "Who knows?"

Christy smiled, brushing the carnations back and forth underneath her nose, breathing in the spicy-sweet fragrance. Inside she glowed with an unspeakable joy as her summer in California rolled out like the tide, leaving treasures on the shore of her heart, changing her life forever.

BOOK TWO

A Whisper and a Wish

To the youth group at Fremont Community Church:
May each of you continue to listen for His still,
small whisper as you grow in Him.
To Janet Kobobel, my editor, my friend:
Thanks for patiently teaching me what happens
after a wish comes true.
To my First Love, my Best Friend, the Author and
Finisher of my faith:
Thank You for keeping all Your promises.

Paula, My Friend

Tall, slim Christy Miller eagerly tapped on the front door of her best friend's house. "Come on, Paula, answer the door!" she mumbled, clenching the crumpled Disneyland shopping bag in her hand. Her denim shorts and bright yellow T-shirt, bought while in California, made her feel as though she were still on the beach, not back home in Wisconsin.

The door opened, and Christy shouted, "Surprise!"

But it was Paula's mom who stood behind the screen door. "Christy?" she said with some hesitation.

"Hi! Is Paula home?"

"Well, come in! I almost didn't recognize you with your hair cut short. When did you get back?"

"Last night."

"I thought you were staying with your aunt and uncle until the end of the summer."

"I was, but my parents had me come home early so I could help with the move and everything."

Paula's mom shook her head. "We still can't believe your

folks decided to sell the farm. Not that we blame them. It's been tough financially for all of us."

"Did they tell you we're moving to California?" Christy asked excitedly.

"Yes. Paula's already asked if she can stay with you next summer."

"Can she?"

"She's in her room. Why don't you go ask her?"

Christy slipped down the hallway, her heart pounding. She had been gone for almost two months and had changed so much. Had Paula changed? Should she knock or walk in?

Christy chose the sneak approach. She slowly inched the door open. Paula sat on her bed with her back to the door and the radio on loud enough to cover Christy's footsteps as she tiptoed in. Sneaking up to the edge of the bed, Christy leaned over so her face was right against the back of Paula's head. "Boo!" she shouted.

Paula shrieked, fell off the bed, and knocked the phone off the nightstand.

"Christy!" she screamed. Then she jumped up, snatched a pillow off her bed, and heaved it at Christy. "Give me a heart attack, why don't you!"

Paula's long, straight, blond hair fell in front of her face as she grabbed another pillow. An all-out pillow fight ensued until Paula shouted over Christy's laughter, "Wait a minute! Wait a minute!" She picked up her phone.

"Hello? Hello? Oh, well," Paula said with a laugh, "I guess she'll call back."

The two friends flopped onto the bed, caught their breath, and looked each other over. Paula still had a baby-doll face and round, flushed cheeks. But something in her eyes made her seem older than when Christy had seen her last.

"Christy!" Paula squealed. "Look at you! You're so tan, and your hair—I can't believe it! You said it was short, but it's so light. Did the sun do that?"

"I guess so. Or maybe it was the salt water. I don't know. So? Did you miss me?"

"Did I miss you? Are you kidding? I can't believe how different you look." Suddenly Paula's expression got serious. "Is it true your parents sold the farm and you're moving to California?"

"Yes!" Christy bubbled. "Isn't that too good to be true? When my parents called and said I had to come home early, I thought something terrible must have happened. I never dreamed they would tell me we were all moving to California!"

Paula tugged on the frayed edges of her cutoff shorts.

"Start saving your money for next summer, Paula, because when you come stay with me we're going to have such a great time! I'll get my aunt to take us shopping, and we'll have barbecues on the beach with all my new friends, and, Paula, you are going to love Todd. He's the most fantastic guy in the world!"

Paula smiled a still, polite smile.

Christy stopped. "What? What's wrong?"

"Nothing. Go on. You were saying how you're in love with Todd."

Christy giggled. "He gave me flowers, Paula! When I left yesterday he surprised me with a big bouquet of white carnations, and then..." Christy paused. "Paula, what's wrong? Tell me."

"Well, it's just that you're leaving," Paula said with a sniffle, "and it doesn't seem to bother you a bit."

"What do you mean?" Christy slipped off her sandals and listened closely to her friend.

"All your letters from California this summer sounded so wonderful, bragging about all those exciting places you went to and all the stuff your aunt bought you—like all your dreams were coming true. And here I sat, day after day, bored out of my brain."

"But, Paula, it wasn't perfect like you think. Some really hard things happened this summer too. It wasn't all fancy restaurants and adventures." Christy paused and remembered Shawn's death, all the times she felt she didn't belong, and the insecurities she experienced with Todd. "I had to grow up a lot."

"Still, Christy, you had a dream summer. Admit it! And now you're moving back there, and you don't even act sad about it."

"Well, I'm sad about leaving you, but you're going to come stay with me next summer. Can't you see why I'd be excited to move back there?"

"I guess, but still—"

The phone rang and Paula answered with a sulky "Hello."

"Oh, hi! It's you," she said brightly. "Yes, I'm sorry. My phone got knocked over. What? Really? Tonight? Yeah, I'm sure I can. Who? You're kidding! He's such a TWH! I'm definitely coming. I'd better go. There's somebody here. Okay. Bye."

Christy smiled but felt tense inside. *Who's on the phone who can make Paula change from glum to sunshine so instantly?*

"Who was that?" Christy asked.

"Melissa. You don't know her. She works at Dairy Queen. Her brother is a TWH, if you know what I mean." Paula's blue eyes looked like the big, round eyes of a baby doll.

"No, I don't know what you mean." Christy tried to hide her hurt feelings.

"Oh," Paula said flippantly, "it's this little code Melissa and I made up. It stands for Total Whompin' Hottie. He's going to be at Melissa's party tonight. Look, I've got a picture of him. Is he a TWH, or what?" She held out a photo of a tall guy dressed in a black leather jacket, standing next to a motorcycle with his arms folded in front of him.

"How old is he?" Christy asked, sounding motherly.

"He's only eighteen," Paula said, flipping her hair back.

"Paula!"

"What?"

"You're only fourteen."

"I'll be fifteen in seven weeks and two days," Paula said, snatching the picture.

"Well, still, Paula!"

"What?" She looked at Christy with her lips pressed together.

"I think there might be some other guy out there who you could go after."

"Like who?"

"Like, well...I don't know! But you and an eighteen-year-old doesn't sound real good."

"It doesn't, huh? What about Todd? Did I start questioning you when you wrote and said you were going out with a sixteen-year-old California surfer whose best friend died from a drug overdose?"

"It wasn't a drug overdose, Paula. Shawn crashed into the jetty while he was body surfing."

"Right. Body surfing at night, and so stoned he didn't know what he was doing. Tell me how great that sounds, Christy."

"Paula! That was Shawn. Todd isn't like that. He's a Christian. And I'm a Christian now too." She spit the words out, angry and hurt yet feeling foolish for arguing this way with her lifelong friend.

"What's that supposed to mean? 'I'm a Christian now too,'" Paula mimicked.

Christy pulled back, fumbling for some kind of answer while her heart pounded accusations through her veins. *Some Christian you are! Yelling at your best friend. Real Christians don't yell at their best friends.*

"Paula," Christy began slowly, "I'm sorry. Let me try to start again. When I say I'm a Christian now, what I mean is that I gave my heart and my life to Jesus Christ."

Christy and Paula had always been able to talk about anything, but now she felt frustrated and unsure of how to explain something she barely understood herself. "My whole life I've felt as though God was all around me, you know what I mean?"

Paula nodded slightly.

"My beach friends explained that that's not enough. I needed to surrender my life to the Lord—to open the door and let Him in. So I asked God to forgive me for all the wrong stuff I've done, and I invited Jesus to come into my life. Then I promised Him my whole heart. Forever."

Paula squinted her big, blue eyes. "So what does that mean? Are you going to become a nun or something?"

"No!" Christy playfully tossed a pillow at Paula. "I don't really know how to explain it. It's as if God isn't just all around me anymore; now He's inside me."

"Well, good," Paula said, suddenly sounding sweet but distant. "I'm happy for you, Chris, really. Sounds like everything in your life is going the way you want it to."

"I guess it kind of is," Christy said. "I still have so much to learn. All my beach friends are really super close to the Lord, and they talk to Him like He's their best friend. I don't feel that close yet. But then," Christy said with a smile, "I only started this relationship with Him a couple of days ago."

Paula's phone rang, and she grabbed it on the first ring. "Hello? Hi, Melissa. What? Oh, please. Not that song again!" Paula handed the phone to Christy. "Here, listen." Christy could hear the beat of an unfamiliar song as it pounded through the receiver.

Paula pulled the phone back and sang along in a whining voice, making fun of the song. Then she said, "I'm sick of that old song, Melissa. Aren't you? What? No, she's still here. Okay. I'll call you when she leaves. When? I don't know. Pretty soon. Okay. Bye."

The remarks stabbed Christy's heart. She realized Paula had made friends this summer too. They had both changed. Things weren't the same between them anymore.

Paula eyed the Disneyland bag Christy had dropped on the floor when she came in. "So, are you going to show me all your souvenirs from Disneyland?" Paula asked.

"Oh, yeah. Here," Christy said. "This is for you."

"Really?" Paula jumped from the bed and scooped up the bag. "I can't believe that on your big date to Disneyland with Todd you actually thought of me!"

"Of course I thought of you. I thought of you all summer, Paula. You're my best friend."

Paula looked directly at Christy before opening the bag and said softly, "I honestly thought you had totally forgotten about me."

"How can you say that?" Christy wanted to add, "Did you think at all about me, Paula? Or were you too busy with Melissa at the Dairy Queen?"

"I love it!" Paula squealed, pulling the Minnie Mouse sweatshirt from the bag and holding it up. "How adorable! This is just what I asked you to get. Thanks, Chris!" Paula quickly slipped it on over her clothes. The oversized sweatshirt completely covered her shorts.

"What do you think?" Paula asked, modeling in front of her full-length mirror. "I'm going to wear it tonight to the party. Melissa is going to love it! If I would have thought of it, I would have asked you to get a matching one for her."

A matching one for her! The thought jabbed Christy and kept jabbing her as she shuffled home in the mucky heat of the late July afternoon. The smell of cows permeated the air, and a swarm of annoying little gnats buzzed around her head. Christy kicked at the pebbles in the dirt and muttered, "You should have gotten a matching one for Melissa."

Great, Paula. Just great. Go to your stupid party. Let Melissa be your best friend instead of me. Doesn't bother me a bit. I'm moving to California.

Then it hit her. Like a cruel slap in the face, Christy realized why her parents had been so tense last night when they picked her up from the airport and told her they had sold the farm. They really were leaving everything. Their lives would never be the same. She would no longer live close to Paula, and they'd never again go to the same school. She was leaving for good. Everything was about to change.

Then the final blow, the stunning realization, hit her full on: *Even if we weren't moving to California, even if everything were the same and we were still living here, I still just lost my best friend.*

2

The Land of If Only

Miserable. It's the only word that described how Christy felt when they pulled into her Aunt Marti and Uncle Bob's driveway in Newport Beach, California. Here she was, in her wonderful, California dream locale, and she hated everything and everybody. The whole family seemed to feel the same way.

They had been traveling cross-country for seven horrible, miserable days. And now, stumbling into Bob and Marti's luxurious beachfront home, they continued to gripe and complain, as if being there were some kind of disease inflicted on them.

"Anyone hungry? Sleepy? Ready for a shower?" Uncle Bob, a handsome, easygoing man in his early fifties, offered his usual hospitality and received only grunts in return.

Christy's dad, a large man with bushy eyebrows and thick, reddish brown hair, carried in the last of the luggage. Her eight-year-old brother, David, planted himself cross-legged in front of the TV. He was a smaller version of their dad and was, in Christy's opinion, annoying in every way.

Christy went to the open sliding glass door that looked out onto the wide, sandy beach and, beyond that, the Pacific Ocean. The sun had set, but the sky retained a streak of gold clouds, with enough light to see the silhouettes of a few surfers catching a final wave.

Down the beach to the left, Christy spotted a campfire starting up and the outline of a small group standing around the fire ring, probably roasting hotdogs.

She drew in the damp, salty evening air, and for the first time in days something besides anger and frustration stirred inside her. Little bits of memories ignited, like kindling in the campfire.

Her heart warmed, her spirits rose, and she felt drawn to the small group down at the beach. It might be her friends from this summer. They would be so surprised to see her! *Todd! Todd might be there*, Christy thought. *Oh, I can't wait to see him again. Maybe he brought his guitar, and I can hear him sing.*

"Dad?" Christy called out, gliding into the kitchen with renewed hope. "Mom? Could I go out on the beach for a little while?"

Her parents slumped at the kitchen table, looking drained and aggravated. Marti, a petite woman with short, dark hair and a striking, polished appearance, stood in front of the open refrigerator. Bob was pushing the buttons on the microwave, warming up some food for them. It was obvious by the expressions on their faces that no invigorating sea breeze had stirred their souls the way it had revived Christy's. Still, she had to ask.

"I just want to go down to the fire pits and see if my friends are there. Could I? Please?"

"'Course not!" Dad snapped. "It's the middle of the

night. You didn't let Christy go out alone after dark when she stayed with you, did you?"

"Well, actually," Aunt Marti began, "there were other young people, and—"

Bob cut in. "You like drumsticks or thighs, Norm?"

"Whatever you've got left. Either one is fine."

"Christy," Bob continued, "did you notice the new wallpaper in the den? We got it up just last week."

"Christy was here when we were trying to decide," Marti added, reaching for a bottle of flavored mineral water. "Do you two like orange and passion fruit?"

"Doesn't matter. Whatever you have." Mom's voice sounded beyond weary. Her short, brown hair lay flat against her head, and her round figure fit snugly in the kitchen chair.

Christy realized it was hopeless. If she asked again to go out on the beach she would only cause a problem. Her uncle had conveniently helped her avoid what could have been a major confrontation. She better not press it.

Squelching all her hopes and anxious feelings deep inside, she sat with the adults, silently nibbling on a chicken drumstick. She told herself that tomorrow she could walk barefooted in the sand, and she would see all her friends; then she would feel alive again.

The next morning, Uncle Bob, wearing a Hawaiian print shirt and gray shorts, greeted her in the kitchen. "Good morning, Bright Eyes!"

"Morning!" Already dressed in her bathing suit and a big T-shirt, Christy slid into an oak chair at the table, where the sun streamed through the window like golden syrup.

"Ready for an omelette and raisin toast?" Bob asked.

"Sure!"

"It's absolutely terrific having all of you out here. Marti and I have wanted this for years," Bob said as he expertly flipped an omelette onto a plate.

"I don't know if my family feels the same way," Christy said quietly, pouring herself some orange juice from the pitcher on the table.

"Why do you say that?"

"Well, my mom has acted super strange ever since we left Wisconsin. And my dad, well, I don't know. The trip out here was horrible, and we all said some pretty mean things. But a couple of days ago my dad said this whole move was a big mistake."

Bob set the steaming omelette in front of Christy and said, "Don't worry about it. He'll change his mind after the interview today at Hollandale Dairy. You'll see."

"I hope so." Christy smeared butter on her raisin toast and said in a low voice, "I kind of feel as though this is all my fault."

"Your fault? How could other people's moods be your fault?"

"I don't know. Because everything is turning out so awful, and I wanted them to like California as much as I do."

"Give them some time, Christy. Are you writing all these things down in your diary?"

"What diary?"

"I thought all teenage girls kept diaries," Bob said.

"I don't have one."

"I'll get you a diary today," Bob promised. "You should try to write in it whenever you can. It'll help you figure out yourself while you're going through all these changes."

Christy ate a few bites in silence. *Why is it that I can talk to my uncle so easily, but I can't talk to my parents? I wish I could talk to them about stuff the way I talk to Uncle Bob.*

"Thanks for the omelette. I don't think I can eat any more, though. We kind of didn't eat a lot on our trip out here, and I think my stomach shrunk or something."

"No problem."

"Uncle Bob, do you mind if I take some drinks and stuff down to the beach?"

"Of course not. Help yourself."

"I wanted to be the first one down there and surprise my old friends, if any of them are around," Christy said, clearing her dishes.

"I meant to ask you about Todd. Did he write or call much?"

"No," Christy said flatly. "That turkey! I wrote him three times, but I had to send the letters to his mom's in Florida because I didn't have the address here."

Christy pulled a beach towel off the shelf in the laundry room and grabbed a drink and some grapes from the refrigerator. "Do you think my parents will mind if I go out on the beach? They're still asleep, and I don't want to wake them."

"I'll handle your folks. Piece of cake." Bob winked at her, and she smiled back.

"Thanks, Uncle Bob."

"Listen, why don't you plan on checking back in at lunchtime. The rest of the household should be up and at 'em by then."

"Okay," Christy agreed and headed for the sliding glass

door, eager to slip out before anyone else woke up.

"Have a good time with your friends!" Bob called after her.

Christy eased her bare feet into the golden sand and hurried toward the ocean, drawn by the endless waves rolling in and out with their crashing, foaming majesty. The sky seemed to blend right into the horizon like a seamless blue robe gently draped over the world and propped up by the wild ocean breezes.

I'm here. I've come back, she called out silently to the clear morning sky. Then, prancing along the shoreline, she played tag with the waves, daring them to erase her footprints.

So, this is going to be my new home. Of course I'll adjust. I'll love going to school with all the friends I made this summer. The frustrations and agony of being uprooted and moving out here began to wear away, washed by the morning tide.

I'm here! Todd! I'm back.

Christy excitedly scanned the water for Todd's familiar orange surfboard. Five surfers bobbed over the morning waves, but Todd wasn't one of them. All she could do was wait. She spread out her towel, dug her toes in the sand, and settled in.

Soon a girl's voice behind her called out, "Christy?"

She turned to see one of her summer friends, Leslie, tanned and smiling, her long, wavy hair flipping behind her in the wind.

Christy jumped up. "Hi!"

"Christy! I can't believe it's you!" Leslie said, giving her a hug. She propped her beach chair next to Christy's towel and said, "So what are you doing here? This is such a surprise."

Christy sat down and explained that her family had moved out here for good.

"I don't believe it! When did you get here?"

"Last night. Around eight."

"You're kidding!" Leslie's gray eyes grew wide. She leaned back in her low beach chair.

"No. Why?"

"Oh, you're not going to believe this, Christy! You could've come to our barbecue last night. We didn't know you were here."

"That's okay," Christy said.

"No, Christy, it's not okay. You're going to die when I tell you!"

"What?"

"The barbecue last night was a big going-away party for Todd. He left early this morning for his mom's in Florida!"

"No!" Christy wailed. Inside, all the dreams she had of seeing Todd again instantly shriveled up.

"If you would've shown up last night at the fire pit..." Leslie shook her head, and Christy forced herself to hold back the tears that begged to pour themselves out.

"I can't believe you were here the whole time! To think that you were only a few blocks away from where we were all sitting around the campfire..." Leslie must have noticed Christy's tears and suddenly tried to change the direction of their conversation. "You know, Todd really missed you after you left."

Christy blinked and swallowed and blinked some more.

Leslie seemed to be searching frantically for the right thing to say. "You know, Todd told me you were the best thing that had happened to him this summer."

"Did he really?" Christy asked in a whisper.

"Yes, he really did." Leslie smiled and spoke more calmly. "I don't know why it didn't work out for you two to see each other last night, but don't let it destroy you. You can drive yourself crazy living in the 'Land of If Only.'"

"The what?" Christy asked, blinking and sniffing quietly.

"I heard this lady talk once about how you could spend your whole life in the 'Land of If Only' by always looking back and saying, 'If only I'd done this' or 'If only I hadn't done that.' It can really mess you up if you're always wishing things were different than they are. She said that when things happen that you don't understand, you have to believe God is still in control and nothing happens by mistake."

Christy looked out at the ocean and shook her head. "You make it sound so easy to trust God for everything, Leslie. I'm not sure it's going to be that easy for me."

"It'll get easier the more you do it."

Just then a voice behind them called out, "Hey! Leslie!"

They turned to see Tracy and Heather. Both girls looked the same as they had during the summer: petite Tracy with her heart-shaped face and skinny Heather with her wispy, blond hair that danced around her face.

"It *is* Christy!" Tracy said to Heather. "What are you doing here?"

They all hugged and began to tell Christy that she should have come to Todd's going-away barbecue the night before.

"Save your breath," Leslie said. "We've already been through all that."

"Did you see Doug already?" Heather asked, then zipped down to the water, waving for Doug to come in from surfing.

"I wondered if that was him," Christy said, watching the tall, broad-shouldered surfer emerge from the water. His short, sun-bleached hair stood straight up in the front. To Christy's surprise, when Doug recognized her he ran to greet her, dropped his board, and gave her a big, saltwatery hug.

"Christy! Man, what a surprise! How are you? Wow, this is totally awesome!" Suddenly his exuberance turned to a look of disappointment. "Oh, man! You should've been here last night when we had the—"

A chorus of female voices cut him off. "She knows!"

"Whoa! Excu-u-use me!"

"So, tell us what's happening, Christy. How come you're back?" Heather asked.

For the next few hours they all sat around talking and laughing. The sun pounded their shoulders with its late summer fierceness, and the waves, like an uneven metronome, beat the shore in time with their conversation. It felt indescribably wonderful to be here. Another one of their friends, Brian, snuck up behind Heather and shook his wet hair all over her back.

"You gweek!" Heather shouted.

"Gweek?" Brian questioned.

Christy could see shy Heather beginning to blush. "Yeah, gweek!" she lashed back.

"Now there's a new word. Did you go to the library to look up that one?"

"As a matter of fact," Heather said slowly, obviously trying to think fast, "I went to the library and looked up *gweek*. It said, 'prehistoric, total nerd-ball,' and then it had a picture of you, Brian!"

They all burst into laughter except Brian, who said, "Okay, Heather. You asked for it!" He pulled her up by the wrists and hollered for Doug to grab her ankles. In an instant the two guys had hustled the screaming, kicking Heather down to the water and, on the count of three, tossed her in.

"Do they like each other?" Christy asked Tracy.

"Who? Brian and Heather? Who knows? They have a great time like this, but if they tried to go out it would probably be a disaster. I don't think Brian will ever ask her out. Why ruin such a great friendship?"

"Kind of a strange way of looking at things," Christy said.

"I don't know. Sometimes I think dating is a strange way of looking at things. It's so much more fun being friends with a bunch of people and all going places together," Tracy answered matter-of-factly.

Leslie leaned over from her beach chair and said, "Tracy hasn't fallen in love yet. Wait until she meets a guy she's gaga over. She won't be so crazy about group dating then."

Heather scampered up from the beach, drenched but glowing. "I can't believe he did that!" she stammered.

Leslie, Tracy, and Christy exchanged glances that said, "Oh, sure!"

"Come on, you guys!" Heather said. "Let's go in the water! The guys are already out there."

The four of them clumped together and laughed all the

way to the shoreline. When Christy first encountered the Newport Beach waves at the beginning of the summer, they had intimidated her—overwhelmed her. The day she met Todd, an angry wave had rolled Christy up into a little ball and literally pitched her at Todd's feet.

Today she faced the waves with boldness. Her tall, slender frame ran toward them, slicing into their fury with the grace and agility of a young dolphin. Bobbing above the foam on the other side of the crest, she felt as if her face and hair shimmered in the sparkling field of water diamonds.

"I love this!" She flung the words into the air.

Tracy and Heather laughed as they bobbed beside her.

"You've been away too long," Tracy said.

"Come on," yelled Heather. "Let's catch this wave. Look at it!"

They kicked and thrashed through the water that swelled behind and before them until the mighty wave lifted them like a handful of arrows, shooting them toward the shore. Heather and Leslie rode it nearly all the way, but Christy and Tracy collided with each other, tumbling to shore like a pair of tennis shoes in the dryer. When they all caught their breath, they laughed hysterically at how the wave had pulled and twisted their hair into wild, wet, sandy styles.

"You should see your hair, Christy!" Heather squeaked like a toy mouse. "If you sprayed it purple right now, you'd have the perfect punker look!"

Christy laughed with them, patting down the stiff rooster's comb on top of her head. Then she turned around and went back for more tumbling and bodysurfing, while the guys raced them on their body boards.

Sometime later, breathless and with their bathing suits

filled with sand, they retreated to their towels. Christy reluctantly asked the time.

"Probably close to two," Tracy said.

"Yikes! I'd better go up to the house and check in. I'll be back later, if I can." Christy gathered up her things and said good-bye to her friends.

Oh, how she wished Todd were with them today! Would he read her letters when he got to Florida? Would he ever write her back? Most of all, she wondered if what Leslie said was true. Did Todd really think she was the best thing that had happened to him this summer?

3

Dear Diary

Christy's mom and Aunt Marti were stretched out in lounge chairs on the front patio, shaded by a big yellow and white umbrella. Both looked up when Christy came in from the beach.

"Good morning!" Christy greeted them brightly.

"Try 'Good afternoon,'" Marti said, spreading her full lips to reveal a contented smile. She looked young in her crisp white shorts and black knit top. Never before had Christy realized how much the two sisters, her mom and Aunt Marti, were worlds apart. Seeing them side by side in Marti's domain made her mother look like the frumpiest, plainest, dullest woman in the world.

Her mother's graying dark hair lay flat against her head, whereas Marti's dark, full hair framed her face perfectly. Christy's mom's face looked wrinkled and bland, without a spot of makeup. Marti's smooth skin was enhanced by bright lipstick and dramatic eye makeup.

Now that we're in California, maybe Mom will let Marti change her from a farmer's wife to a socialite, Christy thought.

Christy smoothed her towel over a patio chair and sat eye-level with her mom and aunt.

"Christy!" Mom yelped, getting a good look at her face. "Look at you! You're burned to a crisp!"

Christy touched her cheeks. "It's not that bad."

"Dear, you should always use sunscreen on your face, remember?" Marti said sweetly.

"I did," Christy said.

"Do you need some more of the sunscreen I bought you?" Marti asked.

"Did it come off when you went in the water?" Mom said.

"Oh, this is great!" Christy teased. "Now I have two mothers telling me what to do all the time!"

"Every girl on this planet should be so fortunate," Marti returned with her self-confident grin. "Did you have a nice time with the other young people on the beach?"

"Yes." Christy settled back in her chair. "Some of my old friends were there, but not all of them." She didn't know if her aunt had said much about Todd to her mom, and she wasn't sure she wanted to bring up the subject. Her parents might really be upset if they knew that she had gone to Disneyland alone with Todd and that he had driven. With all the franticness of moving, Christy hadn't told her parents much about Todd.

"You should've met this one friend of Christy's," Marti said to her sister. "Absolutely a doll! The kind of teenager who makes you feel there's hope for our future."

That's sweet, Aunt Marti. I didn't know you felt that way about Todd.

"Her name was Alissa."

Oh...

Marti touched her sister's arm for added emphasis. "Gorgeous girl. Had a very refining effect on Christina, I'm sure."

All the aggravating feelings Christy ever had for her aunt returned like a monstrous wave, crashing her spirits with its force. *You are so clueless, Aunt Martha! Alissa has more problems than anyone I ever met! Todd and his friends were the ones who influenced me the most. Not Alissa!*

"Did you see her today?" Mom asked.

"Who?"

"Alissa, this nice girl Marti liked."

"No, she's back in Boston at her grandmother's."

"You know," Marti said, springing from her chair, "I think Bob said a letter came for you from Boston. Let me see if it's in the den."

Marti scampered off, and for just an instant Christy smiled at her mom. *Maybe I don't want Marti to remake you. Maybe I need you to be the plain, old mom that you are.*

"The men went to San Marcos to check out the dairy," Mom said. "I hope everything turns out okay."

"Where's San Marcos?" Christy asked, taking a sip of her mom's iced tea.

"I think Bob said it was about an hour and a half drive south of here, toward San Diego."

An hour and a half! Christy nearly spit out the tea. "You mean the dairy is more than an hour's drive from here? I thought it was right around here."

"Christy!" Mom looked surprised. "You knew we weren't going to live here."

"I knew we weren't going to live *here*, with Bob and Marti, but I thought we were going to live in Newport Beach."

Her mother shook her head. "Sometimes, Christina, I think you live in a dream world. You only hear the things you want to hear. We could never afford to live here. If the job works out for your father, Bob has a friend in real estate who will rent us a house in Escondido."

Christy couldn't believe what her mother was telling her. "Where's Escondido?"

"Near San Marcos, of course. The house is in the older section of town, and the rent is what we can afford."

"Where will I go to school?" Christy had pictured herself starting school next week with at least one of her beach friends in some of her classes. Now the thought of beginning a brand-new school without knowing a single person absolutely horrified her.

"We'll figure all that out once we get to Escondido."

No! No! No! No! Why can't we live here? Why didn't anyone tell me the dairy was so far away?

Like a complicated machine grinding to a halt, Christy's thoughts froze. *Maybe Dad's job will fall through, and we'll have to go back to Wisconsin.* Then, without warning, her thoughts spun forward. *What am I thinking? I want to live here, not Wisconsin!* Mentally, she scrambled to find the "off" switch.

"I was right!" Marti announced, swishing a letter in the air. "Here it is, Christy. Listen, your mother and I were just about to run some errands. I've got to go to Corona del Mar first, then we can browse through a few shops on the way back. Why don't you hurry and get cleaned up? I need to get to the dry cleaners before four."

"I don't know…" Christy fumbled with the words, knowing how her aunt didn't like others bucking her plans. "If it's okay with you, Mom, I'd kind of like to stay here instead."

"Why?" Marti demanded.

"Well, it was a long trip out here, and I'd like to unwind a bit." The words didn't even sound like hers. Christy had grabbed frantically for an explanation that would satisfy her "two moms" because she needed some time alone to think.

"Actually, that sounds sensible, Christy," Mom said, standing up. "I'm going to run a comb through my hair, Marti. Then I'll be ready to go."

"Why don't you change, too? We have time."

Christy's mom looked down at her slightly crumpled navy blue cotton skirt and her white cotton blouse. "This is all right, isn't it?"

Christy couldn't believe it! Marti had played the same game with her this summer, but Christy never thought Marti would torture her own sister with the "you don't look good enough to be seen with me" game.

"Suit yourself," Marti said briskly. "I'll grab my things and pull the car out."

"Have fun!" Christy called after them. She knew what their afternoon would be like with Marti at the control panel. She knew it would be an education for her mom. She also knew it probably wouldn't be fun.

Stretching out on the vacated lounge chair, Christy slit open the envelope with her thumbnail and pulled out a one-page letter from Alissa.

Dear Christy,

I received your letter today and was happy to hear from you. I'm still with Bret. He's a wonderful guy. Too good for me, really. My grandmother loves him and invites him over constantly. I'm almost afraid to break up with him because my grandmother would miss him too much! Just kidding. Part of your letter intrigued me. You said you'd "given your heart to Jesus" and that you felt that if I would do the same, my life would change.

What I don't understand is how you give your heart to someone who's dead. I believe Jesus was a good man, a good example—like Buddha and Mohammed. But why in the world would you make promises to a man who no longer exists? And how could that possibly change your life?

I'm not putting you down, Christy. If that's what you believe, it's your own choice. But it certainly doesn't make any sense to me. I can't understand why you would wish I would make the same choice. Maybe I don't understand what you mean.

Please write when you find time.

Peace,

Alissa

Christy leaned forward in the lounge chair, nibbling on her thumbnail, trying to think of how to answer Alissa. Her mind went blank. She felt numb. There was too much going on inside right now for her to think straight about anything.

"Just give me some time, Alissa," Christy whispered. "I'll figure this out." *If only we didn't have to live in Escondido. If only I could stay here with all my Christian friends. If only—* Christy caught herself. *Oh, man! It's just like Leslie said. The Land of If Only. I think she's right. I'd better stop it before I drive myself crazy.*

Christy pulled herself together and headed for the shower. With each step up the stairs she repeated Leslie's words: "God is in control. God is in control." At the top of the stairs she stopped and smiled. "Lord, having You at the control panel is going to be an education for me, isn't it? I just hope it's going to be fun."

Christy wrote those very words in her diary that night before going to bed. Bob had kept his promise and bought her a diary that day. He gave her the brown, leather-covered book after the whole family had walked along the beach.

"Try to write in this diary every day, okay?" he prompted her. "Write what you're feeling, what you're thinking; write down what happens to you. Write your dreams, write your sorrows. Don't neglect it. During these next few weeks this little book might become a real friend to you."

"Yeah," Christy had whispered, "it might be my only friend."

4

The Slumberless Party

Escondido, Christy found out from Uncle Bob, means "hidden" or "hiding" in Spanish.

It fits, Christy thought when the family pulled up in front of the house that would become their new "Home Sweet Home." *This place is so hidden I doubt anybody will ever find me here.*

The house was small with a red tile roof and was tucked between six towering eucalyptus trees. The grass in front, withered and brown, had splotches of tall weeds that were bent and yellowed from the hot September winds. The screen door in front had a big rip in it, and a smashed clay pot lay strewn across the narrow front porch.

Mom surveyed the pathetic scene and looked as if she might cry.

"Hank said he'd meet us here at eleven. We're a little early," Uncle Bob said, looking at his watch.

"You suppose this real estate tycoon would be willing to knock off a couple of bucks' rent if we agree to fix up this place?" Dad asked.

"Don't see why not. Let me talk to him," Bob said.

Someone in a bright red BMW honked and pulled into the driveway behind Bob's Mercedes. The car's door swung open, and a large man in a gray business suit hopped out. "Bobby-boy!" He greeted Christy's uncle and then quickly, vigorously, shook hands with all of them.

Christy noticed a girl with long, wavy blond hair sitting in the passenger seat of the BMW. She kept her back to the group of them standing on the dead lawn. A few minutes later Christy noticed that the girl had opened the sunroof so that the loud music from the radio poured out.

"Come on over and meet my little girl," the realtor said loudly. They all followed him to the car, where he tapped on the window. The thin, nice-looking girl rolled it down and then lowered the radio's volume.

"Brit," her dad said, "this is the Miller family. That's Davey over there, and this is Crissy."

"Christy," she corrected him softly. Nobody, but nobody called her "Crissy." Ever! Who was this clown, anyway? And what kind of a daughter did he have?

"Hi," the girl said with little expression on her face.

Christy returned the same level of enthusiasm with an equally flat "Hi."

"You two get to be real good friends, now," the man said. "We'll go on inside. I've got the house keys right here, and I've got some rental papers for you folks to sign. This used to be a guest house, you know, for that large estate over there. Very historic area, this part of town."

They walked off and left Christy standing alone in the bright sun, feeling lost and humiliated.

The girl in the car turned the radio back up and tilted her seat back so her face was in the shade. She had a narrow face, high cheekbones, and deep gray eyes. Glancing up at Christy, she remained expressionless.

"Um..." Christy tried to find a starting point. "I don't think I got your name."

"It's Brittany," the girl said. "What was yours again?"

"Christy."

Silence hung between them as a hot wind made Christy's white T-shirt flap, drying some of the perspiration dripping down her back.

"Is it always hot here like this?" Christy asked.

"No. Only when we have the Santa Ana winds. Usually the first week of school is the hottest week of the whole year. It's really dumb. I don't know why they don't shut down and let everybody stay home till the end of the month when the weather is cooler."

"Where do you go to school?" Christy asked.

"Kelley High. You'll go there too. What year are you?"

"A sophomore," Christy said.

"Me too." Brittany looked a little more interested in Christy. "I wonder if we'll have any classes together."

"I'm not registered yet."

"Try to get Health with Ms. Archer. I was T.A. for her class last year. She's a modern teacher, if you know what I mean."

Christy didn't know what she meant. She didn't even know what "T.A." meant. She didn't want to ask. All she wanted was for Brittany to like her. To accept her. To be her friend.

That night Christy wrote about Brittany in her diary:

I think I've found my first friend. Her name is Brittany. She reminds me of Alissa in some ways—intriguing and intimidating at the same

time. She's the kind of girl I always think I want to be like, but when
I'm around her I feel as though I'm not on the same level.

I think I'd like to be like her because Brittany seems so mature
and experienced. Not clumsy, the way I am.

Still, I don't know. I liked having Paula for my best friend
because we seemed to be the same in so many ways. At least we used
to be. I think I'd like to be more sophisticated, like Brittany.

The next morning, Christy woke up early. Her room
felt unbearably hot. She pushed her window open all the
way, and the desert winds fluttered the thin, white curtains.
The overly spicy fragrance of eucalyptus filled her room,
smelling like the Aqua Velva aftershave her dad wore on
special occasions.

She slipped on a wrinkled pair of shorts and a sleeveless
red cotton shirt and then set to work, unpacking the last
four moving boxes in her room. By 8:30 everything had
been unpacked and arranged the way she liked it.

Her room didn't look too bad. It was much smaller than
her room on the farm, but the closet was bigger, which
meant she had no trouble getting all her clothes in.

On top of her antique dresser she had arranged all her
treasures. The glass-blown Tinkerbell from Disneyland, the
ceramic music box with the cable car that moved up and down
a little hill, a framed picture of Paula and her from their eighth
grade graduation, and, in a Folgers coffee tin, her dozen dried
carnations from Todd, which now smelled an awful lot like
coffee and not at all like spicy-sweet carnations.

Christy smoothed back the yellow patchwork quilt on
her bed and placed her Winnie the Pooh bear against the
pillow.

"There you go, Pooh," she said cheerfully. "Your new home. How do you like it? I know," Christy said, sitting on the bed and taking Pooh into her arms. "I'm pretty scared too. But we'll make it. You'll see. God is in control. We just need some friends."

Two days later, Christy started her first day at Kelley High. To her relief she and Brittany had algebra together for third period. They also had Ms. Archer's health class together for fourth period. At lunch, Brittany introduced Christy to two other girls.

"This is Christy Miller," Brittany said. "She's new. Just moved here from Iowa or something."

"Wisconsin," Christy said softly.

"Wisconsin," Brittany repeated. "And this is Janelle and Katie Cougar."

"Oh, thank you very much!" Katie said in a sarcastic voice. "I suppose I am now labeled for life: 'Katie, the Kelley High Cougar.'"

Katie, a lively, athletic girl, wore her straight, thin, copper-colored hair in a short, blunt cut so that it swished like an oriental fan every time she moved her head. Her eyes looked like cougar eyes, bright green and flashing.

"She's our school mascot," Brittany explained.

Janelle started talking in a breathless, flighty sort of way. "Come on, Katie! Do one of your little cheers for us!"

"That's okay, Janelle. I'll save it for the rally on Friday," Katie said.

The three girls joked and talked while Christy silently looked on, eating her peanut butter and honey sandwich. She liked Katie and Janelle instantly.

Janelle wore her jet black, curly hair loose around her

face, which made her look as if she'd just flown in from somewhere exotic. Her bright personality matched her carefree appearance. Christy decided she would try with all her might to be accepted by this group of girls, especially Janelle.

To Christy's delight, she and Janelle were in the same Spanish class after lunch. Christy took a seat behind her. Everyone in the class seemed to know Janelle, and Christy felt excited about the idea of being friends with someone so popular.

It seemed that everything was turning out just right as the week went on. The girls included her in their little lunch group every day, and on Thursday Brittany even complimented Christy on an outfit that her aunt had bought her last summer.

"It makes you look so thin," Brittany said.

Then, Friday at lunch, Christy knew her worries about making friends were over. Janelle announced that she was having some friends over to stay the night and she included Christy in the group of girls she invited. Inwardly Christy congratulated herself and thought how easy it had been to get in with a popular group of girls. Janelle enthusiastically told everyone, "Bring some t.p. with you!"

"Some what?" Christy asked Brittany.

"T.p. You know, toilet paper!" Brittany answered.

"Oh." Christy looked to the other girls for an indication of what they were talking about.

Janelle held their attention with her lighthearted giggle. "We're going to get his house better than last time!" she declared, and all the girls around her went on about some guy named Rick Doyle.

Oh, well, guess tonight I'll find out what all this is about.

That afternoon, Mom was hesitant about letting Christy go to the party until she found out that Brittany would be there. Mom insisted on talking to Janelle's mother on the phone to make sure the party would be supervised.

Then, that night, Mom actually walked Christy to the front door to check out the whole situation before completely agreeing that Christy could stay. It was so embarrassing.

The worst part was when Christy's mom said, loud enough for some of the other girls to hear, "Now, if you have any problems, Christy, you call me. Even if it's the middle of the night. Okay?"

Christy nodded and breathed a sigh of relief when Janelle's mom said, "They'll be fine," and shut the front door.

I can't stand being treated like a baby! I hope the other girls didn't hear all that, Christy thought. *When I'm a mother someday, I will never, ever treat my children that way!*

Christy's thoughts were interrupted by Janelle's contagious laugh. "How many did you bring, Christy?"

"How many what?"

"Rolls of t.p."

Christy was confused, but Brittany interrupted and said, "Look, you guys! I'm ready for Rick's house!" She pulled two jumbo packs of toilet paper from the center of her sleeping bag.

"That's great!" Janelle squealed. "How many did you bring, Christy?"

Christy meekly pulled her one roll of toilet paper from her overnight bag and said, "I don't mean to sound really dumb or anything, but what are we going to do with the toilet paper?"

"Go papering!" Janelle giggled. "Haven't you ever been papering before?"

"No."

"You only do it to people you like," Brittany explained. "Like really cute guys."

"Like Rick Doyle," Janelle added.

Brittany must have read the confused expression on Christy's face, because she continued her explanation. "See, in the middle of the night we'll all go to Rick's house and really quietly string toilet paper in the trees and around his car and around his bedroom window."

"Why?" Christy asked.

Janelle laughed and echoed Christy's why. "Because...I don't know! We just do it for fun and try not to get caught."

"Sounds like fun." Christy tried to get her spirits up and bouncy the way everyone else's seemed to be.

"Okay, you guys," Katie called from the crowded living room. "Everybody's here. Let's get the games going."

They all sat on the floor, and Janelle gave each of them a small piece of paper. She told them to write down their most embarrassing moment without writing their names and then put their folded pieces of paper into the bowl.

Janelle kept giggling as Christy tried hard to think. Finally she wrote about the time last summer when she was learning to body surf with Alissa, and a huge wave took her under and landed her on the shore, covered with seaweed, in front of Todd and a bunch of his surfer friends.

Once they had all put their papers into the bowl, Katie drew them out one by one and mercilessly read them aloud to the group. Everyone tried to guess to whom the incident happened.

Janelle laughed the longest and hardest of anyone, especially about her own. Hers was from junior high when she dressed in a hurry after P.E. one day and forgot to put on her skirt. She felt as though she were dressed because of her half-slip. Hurrying out of the girls' locker room, she ran past the entire guys' P.E. class, and got all the way to her English class and into her seat before the guy next to her said, "Hey, did you forget something?" Then she had to run all the way back to the girls' gym to get her skirt.

Christy turned several shades of red when hers came up. "It has to be Christy's," Brittany said. "Look how embarrassed she is just listening to Katie read it."

"That must've been awful," Katie said, "ending up on the beach in front of all those guys!"

"It was!" Christy agreed. "But the good part was that's how I met Todd."

"Ooooh!" the girls all teased. "Tell us about Todd!"

"First let's finish this game," one of the girls urged.

The next one Katie read was her own. Everyone guessed it before she finished reading. Her most embarrassing moment was when she tried out for mascot the year before. Her shorts ripped in the back, right in front of the judges. She didn't know it and kept right on going, finishing the whole routine with her bright pink underwear flapping in the breeze.

"I need a new most embarrassing moment," Katie moaned. "You guys already know my life story!"

Of all the stories, Christy thought Brittany's was the most embarrassing. She wrote that at a pool party last summer at her house she dove into the pool, and her bikini top came off. She treaded water in the corner of the deep end while

Janelle tried to get it. But the strings got tangled in the pool filter, and Brittany's dad had to retrieve the top.

"It was the worst!" Janelle said.

"Were there any guys at the party?" someone asked.

"Yes!" Brittany said. "Only about eight of the cutest guys in the whole world!"

"Was Kurt there?" Katie asked.

"Please don't ever mention that name around me again!" Brittany said dramatically.

"Kurt is a jerk," Janelle added.

"Wait a minute," Katie said. "I thought you two were still together."

"No way! We broke up before school even started."

"Okay, okay! So I'm a bit behind on the latest romance scandals around here. I'll have to renew my subscription to the *Kelley High Tattler*."

The girls all laughed, and the game seemed to have officially ended. For the next hour or so they munched on the snack food as half a dozen conversations whirled around Christy. She sat quietly sucking the sugar coating off the peanut M&M in her mouth.

Had these girls really accepted her? Was she part of their group now? She felt like it, even though the things they talked about were more intense than what she and Paula would talk about. A few of these girls dressed as though they were twenty instead of fifteen. Several of them had fashionable, mature-looking hairstyles and wore excessively wild makeup. Christy's parents had agreed to let Christy use some of the makeup Aunt Marti bought her last summer. Their only rule was, "If we can tell you have makeup on, you're wearing too much." So far there had been no problems.

"Come here, you guys," Katie called from the kitchen. "Janelle's calling Rick!"

"Is your refrigerator running?" Janelle disguised her voice over the phone. "Then you'd better go catch it!"

She clicked the receiver down and broke into a burst of her wild laughter. "He's home all right! He asked if I was on drugs."

"Janelle, you're so crazy," Katie said. "I can't believe you did that! That has to be the oldest phone prank around."

"Oh, come on, Katie. You just wish you were the one who called him instead of me."

Who is this Rick, and why are they so crazy about him? Christy thought.

Shortly after midnight, Janelle announced they were ready to go. Christy followed the others as they piled into the back of Janelle's parents' motor home.

"I can't believe your mom agreed to drive us," Christy whispered to Janelle.

"She loves this. My mom did much worse stuff when she was a teenager. She thinks this is great."

The motor home slowly drove past a big, Spanish-style house with a red tile roof and a long front yard with bushes to the side and two birch trees by the street.

"That's it," Janelle whispered. "Park down the street, Mom."

Christy followed the rest of the girls as they quietly hopped out of the side door of the motor home. They ran like timid deer to Rick's front yard, with the rolls of toilet paper stashed under their shirts. She watched the other girls unwind their t.p., draping it over the bushes, throwing it into the big tree, and waiting for it to come down on the other side.

Slowly, cautiously, Christy unrolled her t.p. in a long line over the top of the bushes along the side of the yard. She spotted Janelle in the shadows, tiptoeing to the front of the house, where she bravely zigzagged the paper across the front door.

Another girl tied a precarious bow onto the mailbox. With hushed whispers the girls completed their task. Then Katie and Janelle slipped around the side of the house to what Janelle insisted was Rick's bedroom window. They tried to weave the t.p. across his window. It wasn't working very well, and they hoarsely squabbled over what they were doing wrong.

All of a sudden the bedroom light flicked on. Katie screamed. Then Janelle screamed. Then they ran. Their terror set off a chain reaction among the group waiting in the front yard. Girls started running in every direction. In her panic, Christy ran behind some bushes and hid.

Then two things happened. First, the porch light snapped on, and a tall man in pajamas swung the door open, sliced through a spider web of toilet paper, and charged into the darkness with a baseball bat.

At the same time, to Christy's horror, she saw the motor home zooming past the house with all the shrieking girls inside.

They left me! No one told me to run instead of hide. What am I going to do? Christy thought hysterically.

"Rick!" the tall man bellowed from the front door. "Come see what your fan club left you."

A tall, broad-shouldered guy with thick, curly brown

hair appeared in the doorway wearing flannel shorts and a T-shirt.

"Not again!" he moaned.

"They're getting pretty brash, Rick. Your mother woke me up and said she heard a burglar outside our bedroom window."

"Can I clean it up in the morning, Dad?"

"Nope. Do it now," the man said.

Then they both disappeared into the house.

Nobody Told Me
to Run

What am I going to do? What am I going to do? Christy panted behind the bushes. *Should I run? Where would I go? I don't know where I am. Should I try to find a phone? Who would I call? I don't know Janelle's number. And right now I'd rather die than call my mother to come get me.*

Christy rose from her crouched position to see if the noise she heard could possibly be the motor home returning. It wasn't. It was the automatic garage door opener on Rick's garage door. He was coming out!

Christy ducked back in her hiding spot. *What am I going to do? What am I going to do?*

Rick began pulling the long strands of toilet paper from the tree and stuffing them into a garbage bag. He made his way all around the tree and then started for the bushes.

He's heading this way! What am I going to do? Christy's teeth chattered. She shivered uncontrollably, not from the cool night but from sheer terror. Rick now stood directly over her, briskly pulling the t.p. from the bushes.

She couldn't stand the suspense any longer. Without

thinking, she gave in to the adrenaline pumping through her veins and popped up like a jack-in-the-box.

"Hi!" she squeaked.

"Ahhhhhh!" Rick dropped the bag of trash and stumbled backward. Quickly gaining his composure, he strained to see Christy's face, "Hey, who are you? What are you doing in there?"

Christy felt numbed by the bizarreness of the situation.

"Bye!" she squealed and took off running. She ran and ran and kept on running as fast as she could, with absolutely no idea where she was or where she was going.

The worst part was, Rick ran after her. "Wait! Stop! Come back!" he called.

But Christy kept running down the middle of the dark street. A car turned the corner and headed toward her. She moved closer to the sidewalk and kept running.

"Stop, will you!" Rick yelled. But his voice was drowned by the persistent honking of the car coming toward them. The lights began to flash, and Christy realized it was the motor home.

It slowed down, and Katie threw open the front passenger door. "Get in!"

In one awkward, flying leap, Christy threw herself into the front seat. As the motor home sped up, all the girls in the back pressed their faces against the windows, yelling and whistling at Rick.

Katie and Janelle shrieked with laughter in the front seat. "What in the world happened, Christy? Why was he chasing you?"

"Are you all right?" Janelle's mom asked.

Christy panted and rolled down the window for some

air. The sweat dripped from her forehead and down the back of her neck. She had never felt so out of control. All she could do was laugh. A frantic, relieved, deep-chested laugh.

"Yes," she panted, "I'm all right."

The girls in the back all pushed into the opening to the cab and fired questions at her nonstop. "What happened?" "Why was Rick chasing you?" "What did you do?"

"I can't believe this!" Janelle squawked. "What happened, Christy? We didn't even know you were missing until we almost got all the way home. Everybody was talking and laughing, and then Katie said, 'Where's Christy?' and everybody freaked! Then, before we even got back to Rick's block..."

Katie finished the sentence. "...there you were running down the middle of the street at one o'clock in the morning with Rick Doyle chasing you!"

Christy took another gulp of air and began to explain. "I didn't know you were supposed to run! When the light went on, I hid in the bushes. Then you guys left, and I couldn't move because Rick and his dad were standing right there."

"You're kidding! Then what happened?"

"I was going to try to sneak away, but Rick started cleaning up the toilet paper. When he came over to the bushes where I was hiding, I panicked."

"What did you do?"

"I-I..." Christy paused. "I can't believe I did this! It was so stupid!"

"What?" they all yelled.

"I stood up and said, 'Hi!'"

The whole group broke into uncontrollable laughter.

"I really scared him too," Christy went on. "And then I got so scared I started to run. He ran after me, and that's when you guys showed up."

"Did he know who you were?"

"No, it was too dark. Besides, he's never seen me before. When he was running after me he kept yelling, 'Stop! Who are you?'"

"Does this sound like Cinderella or what?" Katie teased. They all fell into another round of riotous laughter.

"I can see him at school on Monday," Katie joked. "Rick will be trying the cardboard toilet paper tube on the foot of every maiden in the kingdom!"

Christy felt herself blushing as they teased. She wasn't used to being the center of attention, but she loved it. They treated her as though she were some kind of heroine. Her escapade served as the highlight for the rest of the night. Katie said it was a tale that would probably be passed on for generations.

By three o'clock in the morning all conversation had subsided on the living room floor. Katie and Janelle were stealing one of the girls' underwear from her overnight bag and giggling at their plans to freeze the bra.

In the darkness, Christy crept to the bathroom and opened the unlocked door. Only a night-light was on, but in the dim light, to her surprise, she saw Brittany kneeling over the toilet, throwing up.

"Brittany?" Christy whispered. "Are you okay?"

"Oh, yeah. I'm okay." Brittany rose to her feet and flushed the toilet, but the vile smell lingered in the air.

"Do you want me to see if Janelle has something for

upset stomachs?" Christy asked, holding her breath. It always made her feel like throwing up whenever she heard someone else doing it or when she smelled it.

"No! No!" Brittany whispered urgently. "I'm fine."

"I'll go use the other bathroom," Christy offered and slipped down the hallway to the kitchen, where Janelle and Katie stood by the freezer. "I think Brittany might need some 7-Up or something. She was throwing up in the bathroom."

"See! I told you," Katie whispered to Janelle. "She's anorexic."

"Anorexics starve themselves. I see her eating all the time. Didn't you see her eating all those brownies tonight?"

"Then she's the other thing," Katie accused. "Bohemia, or whatever—when they eat everything and then throw it all up."

"It's bulimia, Katie, and you can't prove that."

"I just think it's strange that she lost, like, twenty pounds this summer."

"She had a boyfriend," Janelle countered. "Kurt told her when they started going out that he liked skinny girls, so she shed a few pounds. What's strange about that? Now that they broke up, she'll probably gain it all back."

Christy felt completely left out of their conversation. When Katie and Janelle talked, their sentences almost overlapped each other because they were both so quick to answer the other.

"Well, I thought I should tell you in case she needs something later," Christy said.

"Okay, thanks," Janelle said.

Christy quickly used the other bathroom and returned

to her sleeping bag. Brittany had moved her bag next to Christy's and lay stretched out, still awake. "So, tell me about your boyfriend, Todd."

Christy slipped her legs into her sleeping bag and asked softly, "Are you okay?"

"Of course. I'm fine. Are you and Todd still going together?"

"We never were really going together or anything," Christy explained. "We just spent a lot of time together this summer and got to know each other pretty well."

"Were you guys, you know, really close?" Brittany asked.

"Yes," Christy said with a sigh. "I really miss him."

"How involved were you?"

"Involved? What do you mean?"

"You know, like kissing and stuff."

"Well, he kissed me good-bye the day I left and gave me a bouquet of carnations," Christy said proudly.

"That's it? One kiss? I thought you said you were really close." Brittany fluffed up her pillow and rolled onto her stomach.

"We were close. At least I felt close to him—sometimes." Christy thought back on their roller-coaster relationship. "I guess I felt so close to Todd because he's the one who really helped me become a Christian."

"You're a Christian?" Katie asked, overhearing them and pulling her sleeping bag over to join them.

"Yes," Christy said. "Are you?"

"Yes! So is Janelle." Katie called out softly across the room. "Hey, Janelle. You still awake?"

"Yeah." Janelle sat up in her sleeping bag across the living room floor. "What is it?"

"Christy just said she's a Christian! Isn't that great?"

Janelle flopped her head back down onto her pillow. "That's great," she mumbled.

Christy felt a little embarrassed that Katie had just announced to the whole room that she was a Christian.

"This summer I went to Hume Lake with Janelle and her church youth group," Katie said. "Hume is a fantastic camp. You'll have to go with us next summer. I loved it! On Wednesday night the speaker talked about how God loves us and wants us to be part of His family. I told my counselor that my life was too messed up, and I could never be good enough to be a Christian. She told me how it wasn't based on anything I could do; it was a matter of whether or not I wanted to accept God's free gift."

Christy enjoyed watching Katie's animation as she talked. It was as if her mouth wouldn't be able to move unless her hands were somehow in motion.

"That night I prayed and asked the Lord to come into my heart and make me into a brand-new person. And He did! I feel as though I've started my life all over again. I can't believe how great it is being a Christian!"

"It's pretty great," Christy agreed. "But I don't know if my life has really changed all that much."

"Oh, mine has. My life was a mess. It still is—I mean my family is all messed up. But I don't feel all that agony inside anymore. I feel as though I'm part of God's family. He really, truly is like a father to me. For me, it was as if my heart melted when I asked Christ to come inside and pick up the pieces. I don't think I'd want my life to continue if God wasn't in it."

"Wow," Christy said softly. "I wish I felt that close to

God. I know He's in my life, and I know He's interested and everything, but I don't really feel as if He's that involved. Do you know what I mean?"

"I'm not sure." Katie thought for a minute and then said, "You know, a couple of Sundays ago the pastor at church said that if you want to grow as a Christian, you have to let the Lord into every area of your life. Otherwise, it's like inviting someone into your house and making him stand in the corner the whole time. If you never invite him to sit down or eat with you or do any of the things you'd do with a real friend, then you'll never get to know him."

Hmm. I wonder if Jesus is just standing inside my life, or if He's really free to move into every area? Everything is going pretty well right now. I guess He must be in there doing something to make everything work out so well.

"Do you want to go to church with us sometime?" Katie asked. "I get a ride with Janelle every week. I'm sure her family could pick you up too."

"That'd be great!" Christy exclaimed. She noticed that Brittany was being awfully quiet, and she wondered if Brittany felt left out. Christy remembered how left out she felt last summer when her beach friends had talked about "the Lord" and she didn't know what they meant.

"Brittany?" Christy asked. "Do you want to go to church with us too?"

She didn't answer. She was already asleep—or at least pretending to be.

"Janelle invited her to go to Hume Lake last summer, but she didn't want to go because Kurt wasn't going. Maybe she'll come now that she's not with him anymore."

As their conversation wound down, Christy yawned and

stretched out in her sleeping bag. Within minutes she was asleep.

The next morning around nine-thirty Janelle's mom put out orange juice and donuts for the girls, but none of them was very hungry. They bumped around getting their sleeping bags rolled up and crabbed at each other about getting into the bathroom.

All Christy wanted to do when she got home was sleep. But, instead, she was handed a rake. All day the family worked in the yard. They didn't finish, so they spent Sunday doing the same.

Monday at school the girls were still talking about the slumber party and greeting Christy as if she were the life of the party. Brittany even invited Christy to come to her house after school. It was encouraging to be liked and included.

Christy called her mom from school at lunch to ask if she could go home with Brittany. To her surprise her mother said, "I suppose so. See if Brittany's mom can bring you home."

Brittany lived in a huge, ultramodern house with a swimming pool in the back, overlooking a lake.

"This is sure pretty," Christy said as she lay back in the padded lounge chair. "What lake is that down there?"

"Lake Hodges. It's not very exciting. You can't go water skiing or anything. Just fishing." Brittany pulled her hair back in a scrunchie and took a sip of her diet soda. "Sure is hot today."

"Is your mom at work?" Christy asked.

"Who knows," Brittany answered flatly.

"What does that mean?"

"My mom moved out last spring. Last my dad and I heard, she was living in Paris."

"In Paris? Why?"

"She just flipped out. Went to go find herself or something, I don't know. She and my dad haven't gotten along for years. But I keep thinking she'll show up someday." Brittany sat up. "Do you want to hear something totally off the wall?" She went on before Christy could answer. "I have this dream that I'll come home from school one day, and Mom will be in the kitchen, Dad will be in the den reading the paper, and my brother will be back from college. We'll all sit down together to eat dinner, and everybody will be happy. Is that *Leave It to Beaver*, or what?"

Christy offered Brittany an encouraging smile. Everything within her ached for her new friend. Over the weekend Christy had argued continually with her brother. Their dad had yelled at both of them the whole time they were doing yard work (not that they didn't deserve it), and their mom had floated around in her lethargic mood. Christy thought her family was a mess, but compared with Brittany's, she had it made.

Christy ended up calling her mom and asking her to pick her up, which didn't please her mother a whole lot. When Mom found out Brittany was alone every day after school, she insisted that Brittany come over to their house.

It seemed to work out well. The girls got together at Christy's every afternoon that week, and Christy benefited tremendously from Brittany's help on her algebra. Christy hated math, but when Brittany explained it, it made sense.

On Thursday afternoon, Mom and David went to pick up Dad while Christy and Brittany did homework at the kitchen table. Brittany got up to get a drink and bumped a butterfly magnet off the refrigerator. She picked it up and then told Christy, "My mom had a magnet like this on our refrigerator. She had all kinds of magnets. One of them was a little sign that said, 'One moment on the lips, forever wear it on the hips!'"

Christy laughed.

"One day," Brittany went on, warming up to the subject, "my dad gave my mom a magnet in the shape of a lamb that said, 'Ewe's not fat. Ewe's fluffy'; you know, 'e-w-e,' ewe."

"How cute!" Christy said.

"I thought so too, but my mom got really mad at him and smashed the poor little lamb into a thousand pieces."

"Was your mom..." Christy hesitated. "...'fluffy'?"

"No, not at all. She was super thin. She was always dieting, and she was always thin." Brittany paused for a moment and then added, "She had a little help."

"What do you mean?"

Brittany lowered her voice. "She took some diet pills that the doctor prescribed for her."

"Oh," Christy said, unimpressed.

"She left a bottle when she moved out."

Christy didn't understand why Brittany was looking at her so intently or why she was acting as though the diet pills were a big secret. She gave Brittany a look that said, "So?"

"Can you keep a secret?" Brittany asked.

"Yes."

"Don't tell anyone, but I took the bottle to the pharmacy, and they refilled it without even asking who I was or for a signature or anything."

Christy gave her another "So?" look.

"I've been taking the pills for a couple of months, and I've lost more than twenty pounds."

"I don't think you need to lose any more," Christy said.

"I'm not," Brittany said defensively. "I'm just telling you in case, well, if you might want to lose a few pounds. I could give you some of the pills. They're totally safe."

Christy sat still, her mind soaking up what Brittany was saying. For a long time Christy had been intrigued by those TV and magazine ads about losing weight. She thought she could stand to lose some weight, just around her stomach and her thighs. She never seriously considered taking anything to help her accomplish her goal, but the thought now made her heart race.

"I don't know," she stammered.

"If you don't like feeling hyper, there's something else you could take. That's what the diet pills do. They make you feel as if you have all this energy, and you only need about an hour's sleep every night. But when you crash, you really go out. Lately I've been taking laxatives. They work great. Make me feel healthy because they help clean out my system, especially when I've eaten a lot of junk food."

"You take laxatives?" Christy asked.

"Yes." Brittany tilted her chin down, turning her head and looking up at Christy like an innocent child.

"That sounds gross!"

"The kind I take are mild. You just swallow them like an aspirin. Here, I'll show you." Brittany opened her purse and lifted out a small box of laxatives along with a prescription bottle of diet pills.

"Why don't I give you some of these laxatives, and if you

feel like losing a few pounds, you can take them. Or if you want to try the diet pills, I'll give you what's left in this bottle." She handed the prescription bottle and box of laxatives to Christy. "There are only a few left in here, but I've got another whole bottle full if you want some more."

"I don't know," Christy said, scrunching up her nose. "I don't think I should."

Brittany gave her a motherly look. "They won't hurt you, Christy. It's not like taking drugs or anything. The best part is, since I've lost a few pounds, I've gotten more attention from guys than ever before in my life. Which reminds me of something. Did you see Janelle today after lunch?"

"No. Why?"

"She told me in English class that Rick Doyle found out she had the sleepover last Friday night. He came up to her in the hall and asked about you!"

"You're kidding!" Christy felt excited and nervous just hearing his name. "What did he say?"

"He said he wanted to find out who the girl was who ran away from him."

"What did Janelle say?"

"She had some fun teasing him. She didn't tell him your name. She said he'd have to find out on his own, and then she said, 'What's the matter, Rick? Are you so used to girls flocking in your direction that you can't handle it when one runs away from you?'"

"Oh, no!" Christy groaned, tilting her head down and staring at her algebra book. "I feel so stupid. I don't ever, ever, in my whole life want to meet him face-to-face."

"Oh, come on! You've got a wide-open invitation to catch the most desirable guy in school. And, Christy, if I can be honest with you, if you were to lose about five, maybe ten pounds, the guy wouldn't be able to take his eyes off you!"

"Brittany!" Christy said in a long, drawn-out wail. "He's not interested in me, okay?"

Brittany ignored her and went back to work on her algebra, humming to herself.

Christy's mind raced. *Could Rick actually be interested in me? What if I were a few pounds thinner? Or what if I started wearing more makeup, like Brittany and her friends?*

Somewhere deep inside of Christy the seeds were planted, and somehow she knew it was going to be very hard to ever be happy with herself the way she was.

If only I could lose some weight. Hmm...What would it be like to have a guy like Rick pay attention to me?

6

Just Say No

Christy ate dinner slowly, chewing every bite twenty times. She had read in a magazine at Brittany's house that counting her bites would help her eat less and lose weight.

David rattled on and on about his day at school and how some kid in his class got in trouble for cheating. Dad looked more tired than usual, but he wasn't grumpy, which was good. Mom looked as if she had something on her mind. After David excused himself from the table and planted himself in front of the TV, Mom asked Dad if he would like a cup of coffee.

Aha! Christy thought. *I knew you wanted to talk to Dad about something.*

Mom always used a cup of coffee as her buffer between herself and her husband when she had something to ask. Christy was still slowly chewing her twenty bites. Her mom didn't seem to mind if she stayed at the table. Maybe it would even give her mom more buffer.

"Norm, I've been thinking."

"Um-hmm," Dad answered, sipping his coffee.

"I think it would help out all around if I found a part-time job. Just while the kids are in school, of course. I could do some kind of secretarial work or maybe work at a fast-food restaurant."

"No wife of mine is going to wear a Burger King hat."

"Well, all right. I don't care what I do, but I need to find something. Yesterday I called our landlord to ask if we could put in a fall garden, now that the yard is all cleaned up, and he said no."

"Why?"

"I don't know. I think he was having a bad day. The phone rang at his office about fifteen times, and he was the one who finally picked it up."

"There's your answer," Dad said.

Mom looked at Christy; Christy looked at her dad. *Nineteen, twenty,* she counted, then swallowed and looked back at her mom.

"What?" Mom asked. "What answer?"

Dad slowly took a swig of coffee. "The man obviously needs office help if he can't get someone to answer the phone for him. Go see him tomorrow. Tell him you'll answer his phones. What's his name? Hank?"

"I have his card," Mom said, jumping up and rummaging through a basket by the phone. "Here it is. Hank Taylor. Taylor-Made Properties. I wonder if he does need office help? Part-time, of course. Norm, what do you think?"

"Like I said, there's your answer."

Her dad's bluntness made Christy smile. *I hope Mr. Taylor hires her. That would be perfect! Then Brittany and I would get to do things together all the time.*

Not until she was in bed and almost asleep did she

remember the laxatives and diet pills Brittany had given her. Brittany told her to take one or two before going to bed.

They were in her backpack, which she'd left in the living room. Of course, her parents were sitting on the couch, watching TV. They wouldn't go to bed until ten.

She tossed and turned. Brittany's voice echoed in her head: "Christy, if I can be honest with you, if you were to lose about five, maybe ten pounds, the guy would not be able to take his eyes off you."

Maybe if I take only one, Christy reasoned. *What harm can one do?*

Then she remembered last summer when she had said no to marijuana. This was different, but still, she never regretted saying no then. She knew she would have regretted it later if she'd tried even one puff. No, she didn't need to try diet pills or laxatives. Tomorrow she would throw them away.

She picked up Pooh Bear and whispered in his ear, "And if Rick Doyle is truly interested in me, he can be interested in me, five extra pounds and all!" Christy hoped she could always convince herself of the same thing so easily.

The next morning, right before first period, Brittany met Christy at her locker, her eyes full of anticipation. "Well, how are you doing?" she asked with hidden meaning.

"Fine," Christy said brightly.

"How many did you take?" Brittany asked.

"Oh!" Christy caught on. "Those! I didn't take any. I didn't want to. You can have them back. Here." Christy reached in her purse for the prescription bottle. Brittany stepped in front of her and grabbed Christy's wrist.

"Not here!" she said through her teeth, looking over her shoulder at the crowd of students in the hallway. "Give them to me later, okay?"

Christy didn't talk to Brittany again until after school, but Brittany was too busy sharing the latest news flash on the school's hottest couples to ask for her diet pills back. "Did you hear that Janelle likes Greg now? He's a senior! Can you believe it? And you'll never guess who was waiting for me at my locker after school. Give up? It was Kurt. He said he'd been thinking about me. He put his arm around my waist and said, 'I see you've lost your baby fat.' And I told him, 'Oh, yeah? Well, you wouldn't know, would you?' And then he said he wanted to take me out this Friday, and I said, 'Only a fool would go out with you, Kurt, and I'm no fool.'"

"That was kind of cruel, don't you think?" Christy asked.

"After the way he messed up my life? Are you kidding? I would never go out with him again. I can't stand him! Once it's over, it's over, as far as I'm concerned."

"Can't you still try to be friends with him?"

"Why? He used me, Christy. That's how most guys are. They use you, and then they drop you. You can't squeeze a friendship out of that kind of treatment."

"Not all guys are like that," Christy said sharply.

"Oh yeah? What about Todd? Did he ever write you, like he promised?"

"Well, no. Not yet." Christy felt a familiar throb pounding in her throat. It came every time she thought about Todd. Maybe Brittany was right. Maybe he never would write to her.

"Guys are famous for making promises they never keep, Christy. You need to get Todd out of your mind. Forget about him and start concentrating on Rick. I heard today that Rick is still trying to find out who you are."

"Oh, really? Did he mention the way I 'ran into' him this morning in the hall?"

"No!" Brittany's voice perked up. "Tell me what happened."

Christy proceeded to tell her about the incident in the hall—how she ran right into Rick on her way to her locker. He acted as though he recognized her, but he didn't say anything, and she kept going without looking back.

"This is too good to be true!" Brittany said triumphantly. "You've got the guy hooked! Just think, by the time you two actually meet, you're going to be so thin you'll be totally irresistible to him."

"Forget it, Brittany. It's never going to happen. Oh, and I just remembered something. My mom is thinking about getting a part-time job. Do you know if your dad needs anyone at his real estate office?"

"I don't know, but I'll ask him. He probably does."

That night after dinner Brittany's dad called and asked Mom to come in for an interview for a receptionist position the next day. Mom acted strangely after she hung up the phone. She hadn't been able to get ahold of Mr. Taylor that day, and she seemed pleased yet somehow irritated that Christy had managed to set up the interview through Brittany.

About twenty minutes later the phone rang again. This time it was Uncle Bob and Aunt Marti. Mom chatted excitedly about her upcoming interview, sounding confident and eager.

"Christy," her mom called out cheerfully, "come to the phone. Your uncle would like to speak to you."

"Hi, Bright Eyes. How's everything going for you?"

"Fine. How are you?"

"Good. We're doing real well. Listen, I've got a letter here that came for you."

"Really?" Christy felt her heart begin to race. "Who's it from?"

"I don't know; there's no return address."

Christy felt a burst of hope that the letter was from Todd. Then she remembered the last letter that had come for her at Uncle Bob's. "It's probably from Alissa," Christy said, feeling horribly guilty because she hadn't written Alissa back yet. She didn't have an answer to Alissa's questions about why Jesus was different than Mohammed or Buddha. She hadn't thought much about it, since she was so involved with her new friends.

"Could be," Bob said slowly. "I'll round up the carrier pigeon and shoot it off to you tomorrow. Hang on. Your aunt wants to talk to you."

"Christina dear, I just had a thought. Bob and I are going out to Palm Springs next weekend. Perhaps you and David would like to join us."

"Really?" Christy tried to think fast. She would love the chance to go to Palm Springs, but *not* with David! She lowered her voice and turned toward the wall so the others couldn't hear what she was saying.

"It's nice of you to ask, but it might not be much fun if you have to look out for both of us."

"Of course. How silly of me! You'd probably rather come with your friends. How much fun can you have with a little brother tagging along? Let's do this: You and some of your girlfriends come on this excursion, and then we'll take

David and some of his friends on another outing, another time. Now let me talk to your mother and fill her in on the details. You'll have to miss school on Friday because Bob's golf tournament begins that morning. We'll pick you and your friends up on Thursday right after school. Does that sound good to you, dear?"

"It sounds great, Aunt Marti. I hope my parents will let me go."

"Of course they'll let you go. Here, put your mother on the line."

"Okay, here she is."

Christy went back to the sink and began rinsing off the dinner dishes.

"Really, Marti," she heard her mom say, "I don't think you have to do this." She was quiet for a moment; then she handed the phone to Dad.

He listened to Aunt Marti and threw in a "Well, really" and then a "You folks don't need to."

But when he said, "All right, then," Christy knew she was going to Palm Springs. She felt like jumping up and down. *They're going to say yes! My parents are going to let me go.*

Suppressing her excitement, Christy wiped her hands off and tossed the dish towel on the counter. She turned to face her parents. They both looked the way they had months earlier when they said she could spend the summer with her aunt and uncle. That night they had made her promise that she wouldn't do anything that summer in California that she would regret telling them later.

Tonight their approach was a little different. "You can go," her dad said, "as long as you have all your homework done."

"No problem," Christy said lightheartedly. She felt as though they really trusted her, and it felt great.

"Now, Christy," her mom said, "this is awfully nice of them. I hope you realize that."

"I do," Christy said. "Thanks for letting me go."

"Marti said you could bring several friends. Why don't you invite Brittany?" her mom suggested.

"Okay. I thought I'd invite Janelle and Katie, too." Christy's imagination spun wildly as she pictured herself having an all-weekend slumber party with her new friends.

"Don't be disappointed if Janelle and Katie aren't able to go with you," her mom said.

"Why wouldn't they?"

Mom picked up the dish towel, folded it neatly, and placed it back on the counter. "Well, from what you've said about them, they seem to be very popular girls."

"They are."

"What I'm trying to say is that you don't have to try so hard to become friends with these popular girls. Sometimes the best friends can be the quiet, less popular ones. Do you understand what I'm saying?"

"I think so," Christy said.

"Give it some thought," her mom said.

Her mother's words rumbled around in Christy's mind. *Is Mom saying that I'm not popular or that I shouldn't try to be popular? These girls really like me. They want me to be part of their group. Of course they'll want to go to Palm Springs with me. Why can't my mom see how important this is?*

7

From Pity Party to Pizza Party

The next day at lunch, Christy waited for Katie and Janelle in the spot where they all usually ate together. But neither of them showed up. She spotted Brittany across the grass, surrounded by four guys and too absorbed in them to notice Christy standing off by herself.

I can't believe this. Was Mom right? Are Janelle and Katie snubbing me? Christy sat down alone and yanked a pear out of her lunch sack. The fruit had so many bruises on it she couldn't find a spot to bite into without hitting mush.

Around her clumps of people gathered. They were all talking and laughing, wrapped up in their private worlds. Christy felt like an alien. No, worse than that. She felt invisible. Like somebody could walk right through her and wouldn't even disrupt her molecules.

Why did Janelle and Katie leave me like this? What's wrong with me? I thought they liked me. I hate eating all by myself.

What made everything worse was that Christy could picture Paula, right now, eating lunch at their old high school. Paula would be sitting on the edge of the table, never on the bench, drinking her daily can of kiwi-strawberry juice and laughing. Except now it was Melissa, not Christy, who shared Paula's secrets and laughed at her antics.

Christy let herself drift off into the Land of If Only and for the rest of the lunchtime felt sorry for herself.

The shrill bell came as a welcome, nudging Christy to gather her things and wander off to Spanish class. She expected Janelle to come flying in and take the seat in front of her, but Janelle never showed up. She found out later from Brittany that both Katie and Janelle had gotten special permission to paint signs all afternoon for that night's football game.

They could've asked me to help, Christy thought. *I know how to paint.*

When Christy got home from school she hid out in her bedroom. She threw herself on her bed and mentally listed all the reasons nobody seemed to like her.

She decided to try something. Standing up straight, she peered into the oval mirror above her dresser and projected her best "I'm too good for the rest of you" look. No good. Her eyes had too much natural sparkle.

Next she tried a bright "Everybody look at me; I'm a fun person" look, but that didn't work either. When she smiled real big, all she saw were her large teeth. She didn't look full of carefree abandon, the way Janelle did when she smiled.

As she studied her next look, the "I'm so lonely; won't somebody please feel sorry for me and be my friend" one, David barged into her room without knocking.

"What do you want?" she hollered, spinning around. "Get out of my room!"

"Okay, okay," David said, stepping back two giant steps. He was officially "out" of her room.

"Would you close my door, please?" She preferred to have her pity parties in private.

"Okay. I guess you don't want to talk to the person on the phone. I'll go hang up for you."

"David!" Christy leaped across her room and elbowed her brother out of the way, managing to make it to the phone before he did. "Hello?" she answered breathlessly.

"Queen Christy doesn't want to talk to you!" David yelled toward the phone.

"David!" Christy covered the mouthpiece. "Get out of here!" She put the phone back to her mouth. "Hello?" she said sweetly.

"Hi, Christy!" Janelle said in her bouncy manner. "Are you going to the game tonight? I didn't see you today, so I didn't get to ask you. Katie needed help with some of her mascot duties, so I didn't go to Spanish. Did I miss anything?"

"Not really. We're suppose to work on the next dialogue for Monday." Christy felt a rush of joy. Her friends hadn't forgotten about her after all.

"Oh, yuck. I still haven't memorized the dialogue from last week," Janelle groaned. "Spanish is not my favorite subject, let me tell you. So, are you going to the game tonight?"

"I don't think so. I'm supposed to babysit my little brother."

"Well, try to get out of it. We could give you a ride."

"I'll have to ask. Could I call you back if it works out?"

"Sure. Wait a sec.... Oh, Katie just said that you wanted to go to church with us sometime. Do you want to go this Sunday?"

"Yes, I do, if that's not a problem."

"Of course not. We'll pick you up around 8:45."

"I really appreciate it," Christy said, feeling as though the whole world had changed from clouds to sunshine. Janelle actually included her in her evening plans for the football game! This would be an ideal time to invite her to Palm Springs.

"Janelle," Christy asked with a smile in her voice, "I was wondering if you'd like to go to Palm Springs next weekend."

"Are you kidding? Of course I would! Who's going?" Janelle answered without a moment's hesitation.

"My aunt and uncle are. They said I could bring a couple of friends with me."

"When are you going?"

"Next Thursday. You'd have to miss school on Friday."

"Oh, wouldn't that be too bad? Missing school?" Janelle laughed. "I'm sure my mom would let me. I've been extra good and helpful around the house because I was hoping Greg would ask me out, and I wanted to be on her good side when he did. I might as well use up my good credit now. Greg may never wake up and realize how ravishing I really am!"

Christy heard someone, probably Katie, laughing in the background. "I was going to invite Katie, too. Do you think she can go?"

"She's right here. I'll ask her."

Christy heard their muffled conversation in the background. When Janelle came back on the line, she said, "Katie can't go because of the game next Friday night."

"Oh, I forgot," Christy said. "That's too bad."

"But Brittany's here," Janelle added. "She said she'd love to go with us. Is that okay?"

"Sure," Christy said.

"Oh," Janelle cut back in. "Katie said we have to leave for the stadium in about half an hour, so hurry up and call me back if you want a ride."

"Okay. Thanks! Bye."

It was amazing how energetic Christy felt after that phone call, even though her mom said Christy couldn't go to the game. At this point it was that they had included her that mattered. She had so much to look forward to—church on Sunday, Palm Springs next weekend. Why did she doubt her new friends' loyalty? They invited her to the game, didn't they?

Christy woke up Sunday morning in a great mood. Slipping her best blue dress over her head and adjusting the top, she thought back to when Aunt Marti bought it for her last summer. She hadn't worn it since the night Todd took her to the Debbie Stevens concert. It made her feel pretty and sophisticated.

After carefully applying her makeup, she hung her head down and brushed her short, nutmeg-colored hair until it was full all around. Then, shielding her eyes, she quickly squirted on some spritz. One last look. One last dab of mascara.

She thought she heard a car pull in the driveway. Christy grabbed her purse and the Bible Todd and Tracy had given her and hurried to the front door.

"Be sure to take your key," Mom called through her parents' closed bedroom door. "We might run a few errands while you're gone."

"Okay. See you later. Bye."

David looked away from the TV as Christy swished past and said, "Where are you going?"

"Church. See you later."

Christy felt a little self-conscious on the way to church. Janelle and Katie kept commenting on her hair and her outfit and how nice she looked. The remarks made her feel uncomfortable in a good way. It was better than being ignored any day.

When they pulled into a huge parking lot, Christy asked in surprise, "Is this your church?"

"Yes. Why?" Janelle said.

"It's so huge!"

"Not really," Katie said. "What was your church like back in Ohio?"

"Wisconsin. And our church was, well, like a church. White with a steeple, and the little kids met in the basement. Our high school Sunday school class had about seven people in it—on a good Sunday."

"Get ready for a surprise, then!" Janelle said. "I think we have 250 in our high school group."

They walked briskly toward a building Janelle called the "youth facility." Christy held her breath as they entered a large room with seats set up like a movie theater. Four guys stood in the front of the room playing guitars while another played a keyboard. All the high-schoolers were sitting or standing around, talking above the volume of the upbeat music.

"You okay?" Janelle asked, looking at Christy's face.

"I've never been to a Sunday school like this before!" Christy said over the loud music.

"Come on, let's find a seat."

They found three seats together, and Christy sat on the end, looking around her blankly as Janelle and Katie continued their nonstop conversation. A pretty girl with flawless skin and perfect white teeth tapped Christy on the shoulder.

"Hi. Welcome!" she said brightly. "Would you mind filling this out for us so we can put you on our mailing list and let you know about upcoming activities?"

She smelled fresh, like baby powder.

Christy quickly filled out the small card with her name and address. The last line said, "Hobbies."

"What should I put?" Christy asked Janelle. "I don't have any hobbies."

"I know," said Janelle. "That's so dumb. Do you like to ski or swim or sew or anything like that?"

"Not really."

"I know!" said Katie with a mischievous twinkle in her eye. "Put down 'toilet papering.'"

"Yeah, right!" Christy said.

"No, do it! It'll be funny," Janelle urged.

Oh, well. The girl said they just needed it for their mailing list. So she wrote it down.

"Thanks," said the girl, who had patiently waited for Christy to fill out the card. "We're really glad to have you here visiting us. Hope you'll come again!"

"She's nice," Christy said.

"Who, Wendy?"

Christy nodded and looked toward Wendy. Her blond hair, pulled back in a French braid, looked as if gold threads had been carefully woven into it by the sun.

"Wendy's our model," Katie said. "She's so perfect. We all wish we could be like her by the time we're seniors."

"She's also Rick's girlfriend."

Christy's heart froze. The mention of Rick made her feel squeamish.

"They're not going together," Katie said bluntly.

"I heard they went out twice already, and she was at the game Friday night. They probably went out after the game, too."

"So they've gone out two, maybe three times, huh? I suppose in your opinion, Janelle, they're practically engaged."

"I didn't say that."

"But that's what you insinuated."

"Katie, I hate it when you use all your big words," Janelle said.

Christy ventured to disrupt their play-fight. "What's 'insinuate'?"

Katie looked at Janelle and then turned toward Christy, her shiny hair doing its little swishing fan motion. "It means, maybe that's not what Janelle said, but that's what she meant. It's the same as 'intimated.'"

"Intimated?" Christy questioned, scrunching up her nose.

Janelle and Katie looked at each other, and then they both burst into laughter. Christy couldn't tell if they were laughing at her or at each other or what. All her self-conscious feelings began to rise. She considered ducking out, finding the rest room, and hiding there for a while.

A guy in his late twenties with brown hair stepped to the microphone in the front of the room: "Good morning, everyone!" People started quieting down and finding their seats. The guy at the microphone ran through some quick announcements and then said, "We'd like to take a minute now to introduce our visitors."

Suddenly, Rick Doyle stepped up to the microphone. Tall and smiling, dressed in dark slacks and a white shirt, he held a few cards in his hand. He scanned the room for a second, and then, as if he found what he was looking for, his gaze stopped at Christy and stayed there as he spoke to the group.

"Okay, listen up everybody. We have four visitors this morning, and I want you guys to make them feel welcome. First one here is Christina Miller. Would you stand up, Christina?"

Christy froze in her seat. Her heart pounded. She couldn't move.

"Stand up," Katie urged, pulling her up by the arm.

"Come on," Janelle nudged. "Stand up!"

"She's kind of shy," Katie said loud enough for the whole room to hear.

Everyone turned and looked at her. With every ounce of nerve, Christy fought the panic that paralyzed her and stood, trembling. *Why didn't they tell me I was going to have to stand up and be introduced? I never would've filled out that card! And why is Rick the one doing the introductions?*

"Christina is a sophomore at Kelley High," Rick read from the card, "and it says here that her hobby is 'toilet papering.'"

The whole room burst into laughter.

"At least she admits it!" Rick said loudly into the microphone. He was looking right at her and smiling broadly. "We're real glad to have you here, Christina."

Christy dropped to her seat and kept looking straight ahead, her teeth clenched, her face burning with embarrassment. Janelle and Katie giggled beside her as if they'd planned this little prank all along. Rick introduced the other three visitors.

Christy wanted to melt into her seat or somehow evaporate into the air. This had to be the most embarrassing moment of her entire life.

In a few minutes the group was dismissed to go into separate classrooms. Christy kept her head down, staring at her feet, reluctantly following Janelle and Katie to their elective class on First Corinthians.

Suddenly someone stood before her, blocking her exit. She looked up hesitantly, holding her breath. It was Rick!

"So," he said, smiling broadly, "your name is Christina." He stood there, tall and confident, completely overwhelming Christy. She could barely make her head nod and her mouth form a light smile.

"I'm Rick." He stuck out his hand to shake hers.

Christy forced her sweating palm into his strong grip. She tried to push the word *Hi* from her throat, but it wouldn't come.

Rick let go of her hand. "I've been telling everybody about the night you popped out of the bushes at my house. That was incredible. And then didn't I see you in the hall at school last week?"

Christy forced out a breathy laugh and nodded her head ever so slightly.

"Well, we'd better go to class," Rick suggested. "I think your friends went in here." Rick opened the door to a small classroom where about thirty-five chairs formed a half circle.

Janelle and Katie were both sitting in the back row, chatting briskly about something. They immediately stopped and

254 ● ● ● ● ●   Robin Jones Gunn

stared wide-eyed when Rick held the door open for Christy
and pointed to two empty seats for them in the front row.
Christy noticed that Janelle and Katie weren't motioning for
her to sit by them, and when someone took the seat next to
Janelle she didn't act as though she were trying to save it for
Christy. Pulling together her courage and composure, she
gracefully slipped into the seat in the front row where Rick
was offering for her to sit beside him.

As the class began, Christy found it nearly impossible to
pay attention to what the teacher was saying. She did manage to find the verses that he referred to in her Bible, but
the letters looked blurred as Rick, who didn't have a Bible,
looked on with her.

*This is so stupid! What good is it to have my dreams come true if I'm too
jittery to just relax and enjoy it?*

She had done the same thing on a bike ride to Balboa
Island with Todd last summer, and she had vowed that she
would never again space out when she was with a guy.
Thinking of Todd brought a calm sensation over her.

*Why am I even worried about what this guy thinks of me? What does
that say about my feelings for Todd? Was that just a summer thing? Is Brittany
right about moving on, since Todd is never going to write to me? Why am I
thinking all these things right now? We're supposed to be studying the Bible!*

Christy forced herself to listen and try to comprehend
what the teacher was saying about the verse before her. She
focused on the passage until she could read it: "Do not be misled: 'Bad company corrupts good character'" (1 Corinthians
15:33).

Someone raised a hand and asked, "I still think you
should try to have friends that aren't Christians, because
how else can you lead them to the Lord?"

"True, true," the teacher, an older man with thick glasses and black hair, answered. "But the key question is, are they bringing you down? In other words, are you having an influence on them, or are they having the greater influence on you?"

"Most of my friends aren't Christians," one of the guys said. "There are hardly any Christians at my school. And if you really want to know the truth, some of the girls I've gone out with from my school are, like, way more moral than some of the Christian girls I've dated."

"Okay, that's a valid point," the teacher said, standing up. He looked as if he were really getting into the discussion. "Let me give you something to think about: Is it okay for a committed Christian to get involved in an ongoing dating relationship with someone who's not a Christian?"

"How else are they going to come to the church and learn about God and everything?" one girl asked.

"I didn't say a one-time date, like bringing them to a church activity or group dating with a bunch of your church friends. I said an ongoing dating relationship. Going steady, or whatever you call it now. What do you think?"

Everyone hesitated to answer aloud, but Christy could hear them murmuring among themselves. She thought it was okay. As long as the Christian stayed strong. But she didn't say anything.

"Let me show you something," the teacher said. "Here are my feelings on 'missionary dating.'"

"Missionary dating?" one of the girls behind Christy echoed.

"Yes. You know, when you feel like you're a missionary called to go steady with all the cute unbelievers in Escondido."

Everyone chuckled.

"Rick, come up here. Stand beside my chair, will you? Go ahead. Just stand up here. Now, let's see...Katie! You come up here too. Katie, you stand on top of my chair. That's right, right here. Okay now, Rick, you are 'Peter Pagan.'"

Everyone laughed. Christy smiled. Rick looked so self-confident and bold standing beside the chair with his arms folded across his chest.

"And Katie, you are 'Katie Christian.'"

Katie made a cute little curtsy, balancing gingerly on the chair, her bright green eyes flashing. Christy felt a tiny twinge of jealousy. But she knew she would have died if the teacher had called her up to stand next to Rick in front of the class.

"Now, Katie, you are a sold-out Christian. You have surrendered your life to Christ, and you are committed to living for Him and following Him obediently.

"Rick, I mean, Peter Pagan, you are clueless when it comes to things of the Lord. Not that you haven't heard the gospel. After all, you're a red-blooded American, right? But you haven't given your life to Christ, and so all you know is the way of the world and following after your own desires."

Rick posed with a toothy smile, raising his eyebrows and twirling an imaginary mustache like a villain in an old-time play.

"Katie, you are convinced that missionary dating is the only way to reach this guy, so you begin going out with him regularly."

"Oooo, Katie!" Janelle hooted as others laughed.

"So, Katie, you and Peter Pagan hold hands." Katie obeyed; her cheeks instantly turned a shade of red that almost clashed with her orangish-red hair.

"Katie, you are such a strong Christian," the teacher said, "that you are going to influence Peter Pagan for good. You're going to bring him to God. Go ahead. You pull Peter up to the chair where you stand. Go ahead, pull harder."

Katie yanked and tugged, but Rick barely moved.

"Not so easy, is it? Now, Peter Pagan, try your influence on Katie. You bring her down to your level."

With one quick tug, Katie toppled off the chair and literally fell into Rick's arms. His quick reflexes allowed him to catch her with a solid thud before both of them crashed to the floor.

The classroom filled with laughter as Katie pulled away from Rick's chest.

With a crimson face, she asked the teacher, "May I sit down now, or do you want me to go lie down in front of a train or something?"

"Thanks, Katie. I knew you'd be a good sport. You can sit down now."

Rick and Katie both returned to their chairs as the teacher drove home his point. "What do you think? Was it easier for Katie Christian to pull her boyfriend up to her level, or was it easier for Peter Pagan to pull her down to his level?"

There was a pause. No one needed to answer aloud. It was obvious that everyone got the point.

"This verse makes it very clear. Let's read it again, 'Do not be deceived: "Bad company corrupts good morals."' If you don't remember anything else from this chapter, remember this verse. Bad friends could ruin your whole life. Be wise when it comes to choosing your friends. You set the standard. You be the one who stands strong. Don't be a follower."

The teacher paced the floor in front of the class for a brief moment, pulling up his next thoughts. "And for all of you who think God has called you to a life of missionary dating, well, don't be misled. I should bring my sister in here next week. She could tell you all about her results with missionary dating. She ended up marrying the guy, and he still isn't saved. They've been married for twelve years and have three kids, and my sister is the loneliest person I know." He looked at his watch and then looked up, showing his feelings of pain for his sister by the pinched look on his face.

"That's all for this week. We'll finish chapter fifteen of First Corinthians next week. Any of you who wants a jump start on this, read from verse thirty-five to the end of the chapter. Next week we're going to talk about the Resurrection."

Rick stood and began talking to some of the guys beside him, who were teasing him, calling him Peter Pagan. He wasn't exactly ignoring Christy, but he wasn't including her in the conversation either. She hung around for a few minutes until Janelle and Katie walked by close enough for her to slip into the herd that moved with them. All the other girls were teasing Katie and talking about the chair demonstration.

The group of seven girls all sat together in the sanctuary. Right before the service began, Rick walked past the row where Christy sat. The girls watched him go up two rows and slide past four people to an empty seat by Wendy. Wendy, the perfect girl. It appeared that she had saved the seat for him.

"See," Janelle whispered around Christy to Katie, who was sitting on her other side. "I told you they were going together."

"So what?" Katie answered in a singsong voice. "He held hands with me in public!"

The two girls laughed quietly at Katie's comment, and Christy sat perfectly still between them, something bothering her. *Why did Janelle tell Brittany that Rick was interested in me if Janelle was so sure that Wendy and Rick were going together?*

She was finding it hard to understand her new friends. It still bothered Christy that they hadn't saved a seat for her in the classroom, but she didn't know how to tell them it had bothered her. What bothered her more was that Brittany had fed her all this information about Rick asking about her, and now it didn't seem to be making sense.

Christy tried hard to remember all the things Brittany had said about Rick being intrigued with her. Every time Brittany had said her source of information had been Janelle. So, why wasn't Janelle telling Christy these things? All Janelle seemed convinced of was that Wendy and Rick were dating.

Christy stood at the appropriate times in the service and sang the words to the songs, but her mind played laser tag with all the unanswered questions about Rick and what Brittany had said.

When the sermon began, Christy jotted a note to Janelle on the back of her bulletin: *Janelle, did you tell Brittany that Rick wanted to meet me?*

Janelle read it and gave Christy a look that said, "Oh, come on! You've got to be kidding!" She wrote, *No. Why?*

Brit said you'd talked to him a couple of times and that he knew you had the slumber party. He wanted to know who I was. Is that true?

Janelle discreetly read the note and then gave Christy a look that said, "I'm sorry, but no," and gently shook her dark, curly hair.

Christy bit her lower lip and blinked quickly before any tears could form. Why did Brittany lie to her? Why would she make up all that stuff? Was it just so Christy would be convinced she needed to lose weight, like Brittany was?

Janelle, noticing the look on Christy's face, quickly scribbled another note on the front side of the bulletin: *Don't worry about it. It looks as though you managed to meet Rick fine all by yourself. You didn't need Brit to arrange it for you.*

Christy smiled a "thank you" to Janelle, but her heart still felt squashed. She tried to pay attention to the sermon, but her eyes kept darting over to the back of Rick's head. His curly, brown hair was tilted only a few inches from Wendy's gold-spun French braid. They even looked good together from the back.

Soon the congregation stood to sing the last song and then be dismissed. Katie, Janelle, and Christy stood around talking with some other girls. Rick huddled with some guys only a few feet away.

"Come on," Rick said to the other guys, "let's ask them." He and the guys moved toward the group where Christy stood.

"You girls want to go out for pizza with us?" Rick asked.

"Sure," said Katie. "Who else is going?"

Rick recited a list of names, with Wendy's name appearing at the top of the list.

"I can't," Janelle said. "We're going to see my grandma."

"How about you?" Rick said, looking at Christy.

"I guess not. I came with Janelle."

"I'll give you a ride home afterward," Rick offered.

Christy wasn't sure. Then she remembered her mother telling her to take her key because they might run errands. *They're probably not even home,* Christy thought. She looked up at Rick. "Sure, that would be okay."

"It would be more than okay," Janelle said in a muffled tone behind Christy's back. Aloud she said, "Have fun."

8

Slow Down, Honey

Christy and Katie followed the guys to the parking lot as the group headed out for pizza. Squished into the backseat of Rick's cherry red Mustang, Christy and Katie kept bumping knees. A guy Christy hadn't met sat in the front seat.

"Your car is in great shape," Katie said as Rick pulled out of the driveway. "What year is it?"

"'68. Used to be my mom's. My parents had it up on blocks in the garage for a long time. That's why it's still in good shape. You drive yet, Katie?"

"No."

"How about you, Christina?"

"No."

"Then you must be under sixteen," he said, looking at them in the rearview mirror.

"We're both fifteen and proud of it," Katie said.

"Just babies," the guy next to Rick said.

Katie slugged the guy in the arm. "Hey! Fifteen is a very nice age, thank you very much."

Katie and the guy exchanged quick, rude little comments all the way to the pizza place. Christy sat back and watched, feeling excited and nervous. Twice she caught Rick looking at her in the rearview mirror. *I wonder what he's thinking?*

Rick parked the Mustang next to Wendy's car and held the seat forward as Christy tried to step out gracefully. She feared she might do something klutzy, like trip or tear her dress. But nothing happened. Maybe her awkward days were over. Maybe she was becoming as mature as she felt in this blue dress.

Rick walked beside her and held open one of the double doors of the restaurant. "After you, miss," he said, bowing playfully. "Nice dress," he added.

"Thanks," Christy said, looking up at him bravely, wondering if he would sit by her. He was so tall that he actually made her feel petite. No guy had ever made her feel petite before. Just as she slid beneath his arm, which was propping the door open, he leaned forward and said softly into the back of her head, "You're not going to run away this time, are you?"

Christy blushed and turned to look at him, smiling. He was so good-looking.

"No, not this time," she said softly.

"Good." Rick's smile melted Christy's heart. He slid past her, leading the way to the counter where a group of eight of them stood deciding on what kinds of toppings to order on their pizzas.

"I've got only five dollars," Christy said quietly to Katie. "Who should I give it to?"

"You've got more than I do. Here, I'll take it." Katie

moved up beside Rick and flashed a bright smile. "Oh, Peter Pagan!" she said loudly. "Here's nine dollars for Christy and me. And we want Coke if you're going to order by the pitcher." Katie turned to get Christy's attention. "You like Coke, don't you?"

Christy nodded as her mind flashed back to a searing memory of the party she had gone to in Newport Beach last summer. She had been left all alone to try to fit in. She had asked for something to drink, "some Coke." To her horror, one of the surfers thought she was asking for cocaine and sent her upstairs to the bedroom where a small group sat around smoking dope. She had run from the house, feeling like a baby. But that's when Todd had caught up with her, and they had sat together on the jetty, watching the sunset and talking.

I'm glad I ran out the door that time. But I'm not running away any-more, Christy thought. *Not from Rick, not from anything.*

After ordering the pizzas the group moved to the back room. Christy sat at the same booth as Katie, and to her delight, Rick moved briskly past another guy and slid onto the red vinyl seat next to Christy.

Wendy and her friends sat in their own separate booth across the way. It looked as though two of the guys were competing for Wendy's attention.

She must not be Rick's girlfriend! Christy thought triumphantly. *And he's sitting next to me!* Feeling flirty and fun-loving, Christy laughed at everything Rick said.

But it was Katie who kept the conversation rolling, and the guys loved her. She had a fresh, tomboyish way about her that made everyone feel comfortable around her.

Christy didn't say much. All the others were talking so

quickly that she couldn't squeeze much in. Plus, it seemed that whenever she thought of something clever, the group had already passed that particular subject.

Katie was quick. She had unbelievably fast comebacks. Christy wished Katie could go to Palm Springs with them next weekend.

Once the hot pizza, covered with simmering pepperoni, arrived, Christy ate only one piece. Katie had several, and the guys devoured the rest. Rick must have eaten at least ten pieces.

"I think Christy and I should get a refund," Katie said, eyeing the emptied pans before them. "We didn't get our nine dollars' worth. We merely made a contribution to support you guys' pizza habit."

"Let me be the first to thank you," one of the guys said. "I was beginning to have pepperoni withdrawal. You saved me, Katie Christian!"

"Oh, great! Just when I was getting used to Katie Cougar!"

"Here," Rick offered, pitching her a quarter, "here's your refund."

Another guy tossed a quarter in the center of the table. "Hey, remember Hume Lake?" he asked. "Time to defend your title, Katie. Come on, guys! The quarter game!"

"Do you know how to play this?" Rick asked Christy.

"No."

"We have two quarters that we pass under the table. Katie's going to stand at the end of the booth watching, and when she says stop, we put our fists on the top of the table."

"Like this," the other guys said, putting the thumb side of their fists up and pounding on the table like a drum.

"Then Katie says stop again, and we have to put our hands flat on the table. See, if you have one of the quarters, you try to keep it from being seen or heard. Then Katie has to guess which two hands have the quarters."

"Got it?" Katie asked.

"I think so," Christy said, scooting up to the edge of the table. "Let's practice."

Katie stood at the front of the booth. "Ready? Go!"

Christy placed her hands on top of her knees under the table, waiting for the quarter to be passed to her. All the guys were moving their arms, and she couldn't tell who was passing the quarters.

Suddenly the guy on her right pressed a quarter into her open palm. Christy quickly passed it to her left hand, then moved her hand toward Rick to pass it on to him. At the same moment that she touched Rick's hand, ready to give him the quarter, he pushed the other quarter into her hand.

"Stop," Katie yelled, and ten fists went up on the table. Christy squeezed her hand tightly as she pounded the table with the others.

"Stop."

All the guys laid their hands flat. Christy fumbled a bit, trying to get her fingers out and the quarters to lie flat. It didn't work. One quarter stuck out through her middle fingers, and the other one slid off the table and onto the floor.

Christy burst into laughter, and Katie said, "Now, let me guess. Could it be Christy?"

"That was a trial run," Rick said quickly. "Practice only. It doesn't count."

"Okay," Katie said, retrieving the quarter and placing it on the table. "This one counts for real. Okay, guys?" Her bright jade eyes scanned each player as the quarters made their rounds.

"Stop."

They pounded the table.

"Stop."

All fists lay flat. Katie picked two hands, but neither had the quarters. Rick had one of them, and he laughed when Christy said, "That's no fair! Your hand is twice the size of mine."

"Here," Rick said, poking his hand into his pocket. He pulled out a dime and handed it to Christy. "Is this more your size?"

They all laughed.

"Come on," Katie said. "Quarters only. Let's get going."

They played round after round, and Christy spent most of the time as the "spotter" since she got caught nearly every time she had the quarter. She didn't mind. She was having a great time.

"I've got to get going," one of the guys said.

Christy didn't want to leave. This was too much fun. She wanted to sit next to Rick and laugh and have a good time all afternoon. But everyone else got up and walked out to the parking lot.

Christy slipped into the backseat with Katie again, and Rick asked, "You guys going to church tonight?"

"I don't know," Christy answered. She wasn't sure her parents would let her, and she had some homework she hadn't done yet.

"I probably am," Katie answered, "but I don't think you were asking me, were you?"

Rick didn't answer. He had turned on the radio, and the guy in the front seat began drumming the dashboard in time with the music.

When Rick pulled into Christy's driveway she was surprised to see the car there. She thought her family would still be out shopping. Their car looked so old and junky compared with Rick's polished red Mustang.

"Thanks for the ride, Rick," Christy said when she slipped out.

"Anytime," he returned.

"I'll see you guys later." Christy waved good-bye and swung open the front door, her heart singing.

"Where have you been?" Christy's mom jumped up from the couch.

"At church. I told you I was going to church."

"Church? From eight-thirty in the morning until two-thirty in the afternoon? You've been at church this whole time?"

"No, I mean yes, I mean..." Her dad walked in from the back of the house, and Christy caught her breath. "I was at church until noon, and then I went out to lunch."

"You didn't ask us if you could go out to lunch."

"I didn't know until after church."

"You should have called, Christy," her dad said firmly. "We've been worried sick. We had absolutely no idea where you were. We didn't even remember what church you were going to."

"I thought you were going to run errands. I didn't call because I didn't think you'd be home," Christy said.

"We did run errands," Mom said. "But we got back before noon. We had no idea where you were."

David burst through the front door. "Who was that guy in the red car, Christy? Did you see his car, Dad? I tried to race him to the corner on my bike, but he beat me."

Dad's eyebrows rose as he looked his daughter in the eye. "You went out to lunch with a young man?"

"Yes, well, sort of. A bunch of us went, guys and girls, all from church. Rick just gave me a ride home. Two other people were in the car. Katie was in the car." Christy talked fast, afraid that she was in big trouble.

"What happened to Janelle?" Mom asked, crossing her arms in front of her.

"Janelle had to go home after church, but Katie and I went to lunch with everybody because Rick offered to give us a ride."

"Why didn't you come home when Janelle did?" Mom asked.

"I-I don't know. I guess I wanted to go out to lunch with everybody."

Christy's dad looked at her mom; then they both looked at Christy.

"Listen carefully, young lady," Dad said in his sternest voice. "I'm sure you didn't mean to worry us like this, but you should have used better judgment. You should have come home with Janelle or at least called and asked about going out to lunch. You're not allowed to date yet, and that includes accepting rides with people we've never met—especially teenage guys. Actually, I don't want you riding in a car with a bunch of teenagers at all. Is that understood?"

"Yes. I'm sorry," Christy said. It was the first time she'd

ever heard him actually say she wasn't allowed to date. The question had never come up when they lived in Wisconsin. "I didn't think it would be a problem since it was with a bunch of people from church."

His expression softened. "Well, too many kids don't think, and that's the problem."

"You've got to be more responsible, Christy," her mom said, sitting back down on the couch. "You can't take off for hours without us knowing where you are. Don't you see?"

"Yes, I see," Christy said. She didn't like this thick, heavy, sick feeling she always got in the pit of her stomach whenever her parents "counseled" her like this. She always ended up feeling miserable and foolish for not thinking things through ahead of time. She turned to go to her room.

"One more thing," her dad added. "Where in the world did you get that dress?"

"From Aunt Marti. She bought it for me in San Francisco."

Her dad shook his head. "You kids always want to jump ahead and try to look older than you are—try to use up your youth. Don't you realize that once it's gone you can never get it back?"

He stepped closer to Christy; his eyes looked misty. "Slow down, honey," he said in a tender, hoarse voice. "Just slow down, will you?"

Her father's words plagued her all week long. At home, walking down the hall at school, playing volleyball in P.E. class—everywhere she went she could hear him saying, "Slow down, honey."

After about three days of sloshing that phrase around in her brain, she wrote in her diary:

The thing is, I'm not really trying to grow up too fast. All these things are happening to me, and I'm just trying to keep up with them. I think it would be different if I were rebelling or something. But I'm trying to do the right thing. Well, at least most of the time.

I'm sure Dad's right, that I don't always think things through. But he doesn't know all the good choices I've made or all the stuff I've already said no to.

I've been trying to figure out what God wants me to do. I think He wants me to try really hard to do the right thing and say no to everything that looks like it wouldn't be good for me.

No, no, no, no. There, my daily practice in saying no.

9

Fun, Fun, Fun

The week zoomed by. Christy's mom got the job at Mr. Taylor's real estate office. David fell off his bike and had to get four stitches in his chin. Christy's dad planted some bushes and fixed the screen door.

Although Christy scanned the halls every day for Rick, she never saw him. By Thursday afternoon she hardly gave him a thought. She was going to Palm Springs with her friends, and the three of them were brimming with excitement.

"You girls all ready to go?" Uncle Bob asked as he tightened down a suitcase on the trunk rack of his Mercedes convertible. The luggage for the five of them had been more than the trunk of his car could handle.

He checked his pockets for his keys and said, "Oh, here, Christy. A couple of letters for you. The one I told you about over the phone last week," he said, handing her an envelope addressed in Paula's handwriting. "And here's another one that came yesterday."

For one hopeful moment, Christy thought, *Todd! He finally wrote to me!*

She reached for the envelope and looked at the return address. It was from Tracy. Tracy, the girl from the beach whom Christy had tried so hard to not like. But sweet Tracy had always been kind to Christy. *Why would Tracy be writing to me? She and Todd are close friends. Maybe there's some news about Todd.*

The three girls settled snugly in the backseat of the comfortable car. Aunt Marti's perfume filled the air around them since Bob had left the top up on the car. With one last wave to Christy's mom and a dejected-looking David, they were on their way.

While Janelle and Brittany discussed different kinds of perms with Aunt Marti, Christy quietly read her letter from Paula. Paula wrote with strong emotion, saying how much she missed Christy and that she couldn't wait until June, when she would come out to California. She said she would never find another friend like Christy. Her birthday party this Saturday night would be the first time since kindergarten that Christy had missed celebrating with Paula.

Christy faced the window. The dry scenery rolled past as she blinked back the tears. *I wish you were here now, Paula. I wish you were going to Palm Springs with us. I miss you too.*

Christy realized that her relationship with Paula had become something different. Still friends, still close, even though apart. Still a part of each other's lives. Yet they had definitely stepped into a different season of their friendship. What really hurt was that Paula didn't understand Christy's summer promise. She didn't see that to have a relationship with Jesus you must first make a commitment to Him. *It took me awhile to understand it, Paula. I'll keep praying for you the way Todd and Tracy prayed for me.*

She tucked Paula's letter into the side pocket of her

purse and then quickly scanned Tracy's note card. It was short and sweet, just like Tracy.

> *Dear Christy,*
>
> *I read this verse today, and I thought about you, so I decided to send it your way:*
>
> *"The Lord himself goes before you and will be with you; he will never leave you nor forsake you. Do not be afraid; do not be discouraged" (Deuteronomy 31:8).*
>
> *I hope everything is going well for you and that you're making lots of friends at your new school. Let us know whenever you're up here at the beach again. We all miss you.*
>
> *Love,*
>
> *Tracy*

Of all the girls Christy had met at the beach last summer, Tracy was the friendliest. She had gone out of her way more than once to be kind to Christy.

I'd like to be more like Tracy, Christy thought. *She thinks about her friends and their needs more than she thinks of herself.*

"Do you girls mind listening to one of my oldie-moldy favorites?" Bob asked. Before they answered, he popped a CD into the stereo and cranked it up.

"Really, Robert!" Marti scolded. "Must you turn it up so loud?"

Janelle and Brittany were already singing along. Bob respectfully turned it down a bit and slipped his sunglasses up on top of his head, looking his wife in the eye. "Come on, babe! Tell me this doesn't bring back memories!"

She smiled and reached across the seat, giving his arm a

squeeze. "You haven't changed a bit, Bobby. Always Mr. Fun, Fun, Fun..."

Janelle knew the words to every song. "My brothers have this CD. I love it!"

Bob really got into it, drumming on the steering wheel, bopping his head back and forth. "Think your hair can take the breeze if I put the top down?" he asked Marti.

"Yes! Let's put the top down!" Janelle said enthusiastically.

"Oh, no, dear. I don't have a scarf with me. I'd prefer you left it up. Besides, the air conditioning feels so refreshing."

"What are we going to do tonight?" Christy asked sometime later, after the song fest died down.

"We'll go straight to the hotel and check in; then we'll change and go out for dinner," Marti announced.

Aunt Marti, you would have made a great cruise director on a luxury liner, Christy thought with a smile.

"You girls like Italian or Chinese?" Bob asked, turning off the stereo.

"What?" Janelle asked. "Guys or food?"

Bob laughed. "Either."

"Both!" Janelle giggled.

"I see I've met my match in your friend, Christy," Bob said, pulling off the freeway onto a long road that appeared to be heading straight for a high range of mountains. The car traveled in the shade now; everything looked different—purple-tinted.

"How much farther?" Christy asked.

"A few miles. You can almost see the aerial tramway from here."

"What's that?"

"The Palm Springs tram runs from the desert floor to the top of Mount San Jacinto there. It's about eight thousand feet up, and in the winter it's covered with snow."

Bob bent his head forward, looking out the windshield. "I've got a great story about that mountain. A few years ago I went up in November with some of my golf buddies to go hiking. When we got on the tram it was cloudy, but by the time we got to the top it was freezing. After we ate lunch at the restaurant up there, we were all set to go on our hike when it started snowing. The crazy part was I got sunburned golfing the day before!"

"You girls would enjoy going up on the tram, wouldn't you? You could take them on Saturday, couldn't you, Bob?" Marti said.

"Sounds like a plan. Or we could take a ride in a hot air balloon."

"Really?" Christy squealed.

"That's something I've always wanted to do!" Brittany said.

"That'd be hot!" chimed in Janelle. "Get it? Hot? Hot air balloon?"

"We get it, Janelle," Christy said. "That's why we're not laughing."

How fun! Christy thought. *I always wanted to ride in a hot air balloon.* She hummed to herself the rest of the way while the others kept discussing their plans. "And we'll have fun, fun, fun..."

"Here we are," Bob said as they drove down a street lined with shops, restaurants, and office buildings. "Palm Canyon Drive."

Christy wasn't impressed. After all she had heard about Palm Springs, she expected some wonderfully glamorous, fancy town. The shops and everything looked nice but not spectacular.

Bob pulled into a hotel parking lot and stopped under a huge portico supported by white pillars. A valet opened the door, and a rush of hot desert wind engulfed them. The valet offered his hand to each of the girls as he helped them out of the car. Christy loved being pampered like this.

Another uniformed man piled all their luggage onto a cart and followed them to the reservations desk.

"Look at that fountain!" Janelle gasped when they entered the spacious lobby.

Christy thought the lobby, with its adobe-style décor, looked like a movie set. It was so grand and different from anything she'd ever seen before. The floor was a pinkish-clay color, and the walls were a white tile with a lot of Native American rugs hanging on them. There was a lot of open space and light. The hallways were decorated with big clay pots holding tall cacti.

"Look," Janelle said, pressing one of the stickers on a cactus. "They're fake." The pointed needle sticker that appeared so dangerous bent beneath Janelle's touch like an overcooked spaghetti noodle.

They were led down the wide hallway, and Christy thought, *This is like a movie. It's not real, but it's so fun! I love playing the part of the spoiled little rich girl.*

"I trust you'll be pleased with your rooms," the bellhop said, opening the door to the girls' suite.

Their eyes swept the spacious room. It had a sliding glass door opening onto the pool and deck. The bedspreads and curtains had the mosaic look of Native American rugs, only done in softer colors. On the walls hung several pictures of blooming cacti and desert wildflowers. Christy decided she liked the old-fashioned, Victorian look of the St. Francis in San Francisco better.

"This is totally hot!" Janelle said.

"Then you may wish to adjust the thermostat over there," the bellhop said with a straight face, pointing to the wall by the bathroom.

The three girls looked at each other and burst into laughter. Bob handed the attendant some money and said, "They're my fan club. I take them with me wherever I go. Keeps me young."

"Now you girls get yourselves situated," Aunt Marti directed. "Our room is right next door. Shall we leave for dinner in, say, half an hour?"

"Sure."

"Sounds good to me."

The three of them quickly unpacked, chattering and laughing as Janelle explored the room, trying out every light switch and faucet and examining the complimentary basket filled with soap, shampoo, conditioner, lotion, and a shower cap.

"How does it look?" Janelle asked, stepping out of the bathroom with the shower cap over her head. "Should I wear it to dinner tonight in case it rains?"

"Quite stunning!" Christy said. "It goes so well with your tennis shoes."

They all laughed, and Brittany asked what they were going to wear to dinner.

"I didn't even bring a dress," Christy moaned. "I just

didn't think of it when I packed last night."

"I brought a couple," Brittany said. "You can wear one of mine."

Christy chose a turquoise knit dress of Brittany's and slipped into the bathroom to put it on. She couldn't get it over her hips. Jerking open the bathroom door, she hollered out, "What size is this thing?"

"A three. Why?" Brittany said. "What size do you wear?"

"Not a three, that's for sure." Christy tossed it back at Brittany.

"Here," Janelle said. "I brought a dress and a skirt. Do you want to wear one of mine?"

"Throw me the skirt. I've got a couple of T-shirts. I'm sure I can find one to wear with it." Christy zipped the skirt up with no problem.

"A three," she muttered to herself. "Nobody wears a three. A size five, maybe, but not a three."

The girls quickly put on their makeup and did their hair.

"You should use more eyeliner," Brittany told Christy. "Try this one," she said, handing Christy a container. "It's Plum Passion. It would look good on you."

"Purple?" Christy exclaimed. "I don't know…"

"Here, I'll do it," Janelle said, and she and Brittany both went to work on Christy.

When they stepped away and Christy saw her image in the mirror, her first reaction was, "Yuck!" But she didn't want to hurt her friends' feelings as they admired their handiwork. Her eyes looked squinty with the thick mascara and heavy liner. She felt ridiculous. Like a toddler with Mommy's makeup on.

Then someone knocked on the door, and it was too late to change anything. Uncle Bob, dressed in a tan sports coat and navy blue slacks, whistled through his front teeth. "Wowie kazowie! You gals look great. We'd better get out of here, though. It smells like a perfume bomb just exploded in your room!"

They laughed and met Marti in the hallway. Christy had to admit her aunt was a classy woman. She always looked just right for the occasion. Tonight her soft, cream-colored silk dress shimmered in the light, and her diamond necklace and earrings sparkled brightly.

"Christy," Marti said, eyeing her makeup, short skirt, and sandaled feet, "I don't suppose you brought your blue dress with you, dear. You know, the one I bought you this summer at Macy's."

"I didn't think to bring it." Actually, after her dad's comments over the dress last Sunday, she had stuck it in the back of her closet and decide to leave it there until she was at least eighteen.

"Is that the only skirt you brought?" Marti prodded.

"Actually, it's Janelle's. I packed in such a hurry, I didn't think to bring anything really nice."

"Well, we plan to do some shopping tomorrow, anyway. Now we'll know what to look for first."

Christy shrank into the backseat of the car as the other two girls, in their crisp, perfect-for-the-occasion dresses, chatted away. Christy hated it when her aunt made her feel this way: scruffy, like a well-used rag doll. It was bad enough last summer, but now, in front of her friends, it was even worse.

When no one was looking Christy licked the waxy-tasting lipstick off her lips and ran a finger across each eyelid, wiping off the Plum Passion as best she could.

At the dimly lit Italian restaurant they went over the extensive menu, asking Bob what everything was. On her uncle's recommendation, Christy ordered the fettuccine. It sounded so exotic, but when the waiter set it in front of her she thought, *This looks like squished, milky spaghetti.* That's kind of how it tasted to Christy's unsophisticated tastebuds too.

A man in a tuxedo playing a violin stepped up to their table. Uncle Bob asked him to play some song with an Italian title that Christy had never heard of.

The musician smiled and nodded. Then, tucking the violin under his chin, he began to play. Slowly at first, then vigorously, he pulled the bow back and forth, putting his whole heart into it. Christy found herself holding her breath on the last few high notes as if she were squeezing them out of her lungs along with the musician. He ended as dramatically as he had begun and then drew his violin under his arm and bowed low.

"Bravo!" said Marti.

"*Molto bello!*" exclaimed Bob and slipped the artist what Christy thought looked like a twenty-dollar bill.

The man smiled and nodded; then, taking Marti's hand, he kissed it. He moved to Janelle and did the same thing. She giggled and looked at Christy, who was next in line.

Christy thought it was a little embarrassing but very exciting at the same time. The musician barely brushed his lips across the top of her hand. She turned to see how Brittany would react to the gracious gesture, but Brittany was gone.

"She probably went to the bathroom," Janelle suggested.

In the ten minutes that followed, Christy sloshed the fettuccine around on her plate and ended up eating another piece of garlic bread before deciding she was full.

"Do you suppose your friend is all right?" Marti asked.

"I'll go check on her," Christy offered.

"I'll go with you," Janelle said. As they walked away from the table, Janelle said softly, "She's probably throwing up. She's on this weird diet. I think she's too skinny."

"I know," Christy agreed. "She told me she takes her mom's diet pills."

Suddenly Christy remembered the prescription bottle of diet pills Brittany had given her. She still had them in her purse, which was back at the table. *I've got to throw those things away,* she thought.

They found Brittany standing by the sink, combing her hair.

"I think I'm going to try another brand of hair spray," Brittany said. "The one I use now is drying my hair out too much."

Christy noticed a clump of hair in the sink. Brittany squirted her wrists with perfume and asked, "Is everyone else finished?"

"Almost," Christy said. "We came to check on you. You okay?"

"Of course." Brittany laughed nervously. "I'm ready for dessert!"

"Brittany," Janelle sounded like a parent, "you didn't just throw up, did you?"

Brittany lowered her voice and raised her eyebrows,

looking innocent. "Of course not! Why do you ask?"

"Brittany! Tell me the truth. Are you done with your diet or are you still taking laxatives and stuff?"

"No, I'm not on a diet anymore, honest. I was only saying that dessert sounds good to me tonight."

Christy couldn't tell if she was lying or not.

Janelle seemed convinced. "I think we'd better get back. They're probably ready to go."

Marti suggested that, instead of returning to the hotel, they park the car and do some window-shopping. A wonderfully warm desert breeze twirled around them as they strolled past brightly lit window displays. Janelle came up with all kinds of jokes about the things they spotted in the windows, practical necessities like black leather miniskirts and stainless-steel pasta makers.

She still had them laughing when they got back to the hotel. Christy pulled the key to their room out of her purse and thanked Uncle Bob for the fun evening and good dinner.

"My pleasure, ladies," he said. "I've got an eight o'clock tee-off, so I'll probably grab a donut in the coffee shop. Maybe you girls would like to sleep in and have your breakfast out by the pool. They have a buffet brunch, don't they, Marti?"

"I think it's only on Saturday and Sunday."

"Well, if you girls get hungry at anytime, give room service a call," Bob said. "We'll see you sometime tomorrow, then. Good night."

"Sweet dreams!" Marti said.

The three of them changed into their nightshirts, and Janelle said, "I'm too hyper to just watch TV. Let's put our bathing suits on and go swimming!"

"I don't think we can," Christy said. "Doesn't the pool close at ten?"

"Maybe if we're real quiet they won't know we're in there," Janelle said with a giggle.

"Oh, right!" Christy said. "Three girls jumping in the pool. That's going to be real quiet."

"Then let's go walk around the lobby," Janelle said.

"In our pajamas?" Christy asked.

Janelle kept trying to convince them to think of something fun to do, and Christy kept coming up with excuses for why they couldn't do any of Janelle's crazy ideas. To Christy's relief something Brittany said prompted Janelle to start asking Brittany questions about Kurt.

Propping pillows against the headboard, Janelle quizzed Brittany. "I saw you talking with Kurt last week after school. Are you going to start going out with him again?"

"Are you kidding? I was telling him to get lost. He turns my stomach. What about you and Greg?" Brittany asked Janelle. "What's happening with him?"

"Not much. He did talk to me a couple of times last week. But he only flirts with me when there aren't any junior or senior girls around. I like him, but he almost scares me, you know what I mean?"

"He scares you?" Christy asked.

"It's like he's always a step ahead of me. I look at him, and I can't figure out what he's thinking. He's very mysterious and untouchable. I like that, but it also scares me. And speaking of untouchable guys, Christy, do you have any updates on Rick?"

Christy didn't say anything. She looked at Brittany for her reaction. Brittany looked her usual cool self. Christy decided now was the time to get everything out in the open about what Brittany had been telling her about Rick.

"Brittany, why did you say that Rick was interested in meeting me and that Janelle was giving you all the inside information?"

"That's right," Janelle joined in. "I heard you were saying some stuff about Rick that I never said. I want to know where I got all this detailed information that I supposedly passed on to you. Rick never asked about my slumber party or who Christy was."

Brittany sat perfectly still on the bed, her legs crossed under her. Her facial expression didn't change, but it seemed to Christy that Brittany's mind was spinning behind those steady eyes, trying to come up with the right answer.

Brittany jumped up from the bed. "Oh no! I think I left my curling iron on!" Sprinting into the bathroom, she closed the door.

"Oh, now that was convenient," Janelle said. "Why can't she just admit she's wrong and move on from there?"

"Should we go check on her?" Christy asked.

"No. She has to come out eventually. Sometimes she's a real case," Janelle said.

"She has some problems," Christy said, keeping her voice low. "We have to try to be fair. You know about her parents splitting up. Her dad is never home. I feel sorry for her. I think we should try to help her."

"I guess you're right. I should be more understanding. But why did she make up all that stuff about Rick?"

"I don't know." Christy shrugged and glanced over at the closed bathroom door. "There's no point in even talking about Rick. You were the one who said you thought Rick was going out with Wendy."

"I don't know. I thought they were, but I guess he's the kind of guy who likes to play the field. He's a sweet talker, if you know what I mean. He can get any girl he wants, and he knows it. I guess nobody really knows what's going on inside the head of Rick Doyle." Janelle stretched out and made herself more comfortable with a pillow stuffed under her arm. "What about that guy you met last summer?"

"Todd?"

"Whatever happened to him?"

Christy took a deep breath. "I have no idea. The little sweetheart hasn't written me at all. I've sent him at least five letters. Somehow, I don't feel like it's over, though. I keep hoping I'll see him again someday."

"He sounded like the perfect dream guy."

Christy glanced up at the painting on the wall behind the bed and smiled. "He is. Todd is one of a kind. I'll never forget him." Her eyes misted over with tears, and as she blinked all the wildflowers in the painting began to run together in a swirl of smeared pastels.

"There's nothing wrong with liking two guys at the same time, Christy. Or a whole bunch of guys, for that matter," Janelle said. "My mom says this is the time of our lives when we should go for as much attention as we can get. We should be the ones who decide who we go out with and not wait around for the guys to decide if they're interested in us."

Christy blinked back the tears. "That could be, but it sure helps if at least one of those guys likes you back."

Janelle laughed. "Well said, Christy, well said. Now, if

only Greg would ask me out and Rick would ask you out, then we could go on a double date!"

"Oh, right. Like that would ever happen."

"It could happen. Like for homecoming next weekend." Janelle's eyes took on their exotic glimmer. "Wouldn't that be fun?"

Christy was noticing that *fun* seemed to be Janelle's favorite word—or at least the motivation for most of her decisions.

The bathroom door opened, and Brittany walked out, cool and composed. "Is anybody hungry besides me?" She opened the room service menu on the dresser and began reading the list.

Christy and Janelle exchanged wary looks, and Christy wondered if they should say anything to Brittany.

"A hot fudge sundae—$9.50!" Brittany squawked. "And look at this: soft drinks—$4.50! What a rip off!"

"I don't think I could order anything with a clear conscience, knowing your uncle had to pay for it," Janelle said.

"He doesn't mind," Christy said. "Money doesn't mean the same thing to him that it does to my family."

"Hey, you guys, we still haven't done anything fun tonight. Don't you just feel like doing something wild?" Janelle asked.

"Like what?" Christy asked cautiously.

"I don't know. Like running up and down the hallway."

"I think I saw some vending machines at the end of the hallway," Brittany said. "Let's go and get a candy bar and a soda. It'll be cheaper than ordering from room service."

"I don't know if we should," Christy hesitated.

"Oh, come on! It'll be fun." Janelle was already standing up, ready to go.

"Should we go like this? In our nightshirts?" Brittany asked.

"Not me!" Christy said. "I'm putting on my jeans."

The others did the same, quickly dressing in a haphazard fashion.

"Let me get the key and some quarters," Christy said.

"Wait a minute!" Janelle ran into the bathroom. She emerged with the shower cap on her head and a bath towel wrapped around the outside of her clothes. "Now I'm ready!"

Brittany and Christy burst into laughter. It felt good to have the earlier tension with Brittany gone. Janelle opened the door and held her hand over her eyebrows, like a trail scout looking up and down the hallway.

"Okay, fellow adventurers," she said in a deep voice. "The coast is clear."

Repressing their giggles, the three girls clumped together and toddled down the hallway. They made it to the vending machines before anyone saw them and quickly pooled their quarters. They had enough for a candy bar each and one soft drink, which they decided they would split back in the room.

The vending machine made a loud rumbling noise as it dropped out the can of soda. Janelle pressed her index finger to her lips, saying, "Shhhhh!" to the machine.

The other two giggled as they huddled together, and in unison all three looked down the hallway.

"What are we hiding from?" Christy asked.

"Shhhh!" Janelle motioned again. Then with exaggerated tiptoeing, Janelle led the way back to their room. Suddenly they heard voices behind them and turned to see a young couple who had just gotten off the elevator and were heading in their direction.

"Hurry!" Janelle ordered, breaking into a dash for their room.

They were almost to Bob and Marti's door when Janelle let out a "Yikes!"

Christy ran to their door. She jammed in the key, turned the handle, and ducked inside as the other two pushed their way in behind her. She quickly slammed the door, and they all started laughing.

Christy pointed to Janelle. "What happened to your towel?"

"I lost it in front of your aunt and uncle's door! That's why I panicked."

"We've got to go get it," Christy said. "We can't leave it there!"

For almost a full minute they squabbled over who would retrieve the towel. Finally Brittany settled the argument by stating, "All right, you cream puffs. I'll go get the towel."

Slowly they opened the door and looked to the right, to the left, and then they looked down at their feet. Someone had already picked up the towel, folded it neatly, and placed it in front of their door.

"One thing I can say about this hotel," Janelle said, snatching up the towel and quickly closing the door. "The maid service here is incredible!"

10

Making Choices

The next morning Brittany was the first one up, and she was brimming with energy.

"Wake up, you sleepyheads," she called. "Anyone interested in a morning jog?"

Janelle threw her pillow at Brittany. "Go away! It can't be morning yet."

"It's almost eight-thirty," Brittany sang out. "The day is slipping away while you two sleep."

"Wake me when it's noon," Christy said, pulling the covers over her head.

"I'll wake you deadheads when I get back."

Christy grunted and drifted back to sleep. She woke up with a start when the phone rang a short time later. It was Aunt Marti telling them to meet her for breakfast in half an hour at the Sundance Coffee Shop in the lobby.

Brittany returned from her morning jog, perspiring and breathless, and the three of them scrambled to get ready in time.

"I didn't know you were really going jogging," Christy

said. "I don't think you should've gone out like that."

"Oh, I just went around the hotel. I was perfectly safe," Brittany said, applying her mascara with a shaky hand.

"Come on, you guys," Janelle hollered from the door. "Your aunt is probably waiting."

"What? No shower cap this morning?" Christy teased as she slipped past Janelle. The three of them hurried to catch the elevator.

Aunt Marti stood waiting in the entrance of the coffee shop. Right next to her stood the young couple from the night before. The three girls suppressed their giggles and kept their heads down.

As soon as they were seated, Aunt Marti laid out their plans for the day. They would spend some time by the pool relaxing and then go shopping; dinner would be at six-thirty at Bob's favorite Mexican restaurant.

"This is the way to live!" Janelle exclaimed to Christy a short time later. The poolside waitress was serving them iced teas they had ordered from their lounge chairs. "I've never been to a resort like this in my life. I just decided I could very easily be a rich person. It suits me, don't you think?"

Brittany was in the pool with her arms propped up on the side. She playfully flung a handful of water on them. "Hey, you rich and famous wannabes, are you coming in or not?" she yelled.

"I'm ready," Christy said. "Coming, Janelle?"

Janelle stretched like a spoiled cat and in her best movie-star voice said, "Oh, I suppose, darling. If I must."

The two girls slowly lowered themselves into the pool at the shallow end. Christy hated that shivering sensation that sliced through her every time she got her stomach wet. She quickly ducked the rest of her body underwater and swam leisurely, with Janelle dog-paddling beside her. Brittany kept challenging them to swim laps with her, as if it would be fun to start some kind of competitive race. Christy turned down all the offers, saying she was happy going at her own slow pace.

Marti came out to the pool and settled in a lounge chair shaded by an umbrella. She waved at the girls and then motioned for the poolside attendant to come take her order for something to drink. Christy thought her aunt looked as if she were enjoying this as much as they were. She knew Marti would also enjoy the planned shopping trip that afternoon. What Christy was really looking forward to was the promised hot air balloon ride. Maybe tomorrow.

Brittany pulled herself out of the pool at the deep end after swimming several laps by herself. "I think your aunt's trying to tell us she's ready to go shopping," Brittany said. "Mind if I go in first and take a quick shower?"

"Go ahead. We'll be there in a few minutes," Christy said. "The key is in my bag under my chair."

Christy and Janelle got out of the pool and patted themselves dry with the thick hotel beach towels.

"Were you trying to tell us it's time to go shopping?" Christy asked Aunt Marti.

Aunt Marti, who sat only a few feet away, ignored Christy's question and seemed to be studying Brittany's skeleton-like frame as she walked away from them.

"I think your friend is far too thin," Marti said. "I've never seen hip bones stick out like that on a teenager. It doesn't look right. And where's her rear end? She hardly has enough bottom to hold her bathing suit on."

Christy didn't know how much she wanted to confide in her aunt, but Janelle jumped right in. "We know. She's got some strange problems with food. She's always on a diet, and then she overeats and makes herself throw up."

"I've read about girls like her," Marti said in her direct manner. "She needs professional help to overcome this problem. Eating disorders are very common and also very dangerous. Thank goodness that's something Christy hasn't struggled with! You've always had a healthy appetite, dear."

Christy couldn't tell if her comment was a put-down or a compliment.

"Well," Janelle said, "I'd feel awful if anything bad happened to her. Like if she got really sick or something. What should we do?"

"Leave it to me. I'll handle this," Marti stated.

For some reason, Christy felt a knot forming in her stomach at her aunt's words. Marti was a well-meaning woman, but she had messed up things for Christy more than once. How would she handle Brittany?

About an hour later, after quick showers and an even quicker scramble to dress, Marti steered them through the streets of Palm Springs as if she were in her hometown. She took the girls to several small boutiques, where they received plenty of personal attention.

Marti talked Christy into getting a short, black dress that Brittany said she had seen in one of her fashion magazines that month. Janelle said it made Christy look at least seventeen.

Oh, great! Christy thought as she surveyed herself in the mirror. *The last thing I need is another dress that makes me look older! What will Dad say?*

But Marti insisted, and in the end they left the boutique with the dress, some fun, strappy black shoes to match, and a pair of dangly earrings that Christy thought were way too expensive, even if they were a custom design.

Christy and Janelle slid into the backseat of the car, and Janelle said softly, "Now you have something to wear to homecoming when we go on our double date with Rick and Greg. I figured out a way to get the guys to go with us. I'll tell you about it later."

Christy forced a weak smile. *Homecoming? Double dates? Who said I even wanted to go out with Rick? When am I going to start standing up for what I truly think and feel and stop letting everybody else make decisions for me? Like this dress. I don't even like it. Why did I let my aunt buy it?*

The next place they went was the Desert Fashion Plaza. The minute they entered Saks, Christy knew they were about to see some serious money being spent. Marti reminded her of a tropical bird that had suddenly been transported to its native banana tree. Watching Marti coo and strut between the racks of clothes, Christy could just picture her aunt pulling out her credit cards and fanning them like a peacock's tail.

This time I'm going to decide for myself, Christy vowed.

All three of the girls entered the large, elegant dressing area. The saleswoman had already hung their choices on the outside of three individual rooms, and now she stood ready to serve them in any way she could.

Christy was the first to call out from her dressing room. "I think this shirt is a little too big on me."

"What size is it?" the saleswoman asked. "I'll bring you another one."

"Step out, dear. Let's see the whole outfit." Aunt Marti

smiled when she saw Christy. "Oh, yes, I like those bright colors on you very much. Very striking."

Christy looked in the full-length mirror. Several months earlier she would have eaten up every word her aunt said, along with all the glamour and excitement that accompanied such a trip as this. But this time she forced herself to see the outfit clearly, from her own point of view. She didn't like it. Time to practice standing up for herself. *No, no, no, no.*

"I don't know," she said cautiously to her aunt. "I'm not a bold, striking type of person. I think I like the peach better."

"Let's see," Janelle said, stepping out in a long rayon dress. She made a face at Christy that only confirmed Christy's opinion of how she looked in this outfit. "I think I need a bigger size on this dress," Janelle said to the saleswoman. "It's too tight under the arms."

The saleswoman checked the tag and then left. Marti paused for a minute, tapping her index finger along the side of her mouth. "I suppose you're right, Christy. You wear peach very nicely, especially that deep salmon shade."

Christy held up a light peach shirt. "This is the peach I mean. Light peach. Pastel. What do you think?"

Marti blinked her eyes as if her feelings were hurt, but then her expression softened, and with a chuckle, she said, "I think it obviously doesn't matter what I think. You've made up your own mind. And that's very commendable, Christina. Did you match it with your color swatches?"

Christy ducked back into the dressing room and rummaged through all the junk in her purse, trying to find her color packet. The packet came from a color consultant

Marti had taken Christy to last summer. The consultant had evaluated Christy's natural coloring and provided her with a collection of color swatches. The consultant had instructed Christy to never wear a color that wasn't in her packet. Now if only she could find the packet in her messy purse!

Her hand circled around a small plastic prescription bottle, and she suddenly froze. *Brittany's diet pills! I have to get rid of these! But not here. Not in front of Marti, especially now that she's noticed that Brittany has a problem. She'll think I'm trying out Brittany's crazy diet techniques. As soon as we get back to the hotel, I'm getting rid of these. And I'm not giving them back to Brittany. I'm going to throw them away.*

"Absolutely adorable," Christy overheard her aunt say to her friends outside the dressing room. The color swatches forgotten, Christy hurried to take off the outfit. She was eager to get back to the hotel.

"Now, listen," Marti said to Janelle and Brittany. "I'd like to buy each of you one new outfit, so choose whatever you like. It'll be my treat."

"Really?" Janelle squeaked. "That's so nice of you! I can't believe it."

"You don't have to," Brittany said. "My dad gave me his Visa card in case I wanted to buy anything."

"Well, let me buy it for you, dear. I'd like to do that. Do you like the outfit you have on?"

"Pretty much," Brittany answered. "I was thinking of getting it."

"That settles it; I'll get it for you," Marti offered. "It looks nice on you, although the shorts are a bit baggy in the back, don't you think?"

Oh no! Christy squeezed her eyes shut in the privacy of

her dressing room. *Here comes my aunt's subtle way of dealing with Brittany's weight problem.*

"It's the smallest size they have," Brittany answered. "I like them baggy. They make me look thinner."

"Honey, you are about as thin as a person can possibly get. How much do you weigh, dear?"

Brittany didn't answer right away. "I don't know. I haven't weighed myself lately."

"In my opinion, dear, you could stand to put on a few pounds. Start eating some good, healthy pasta and bread at every meal."

Christy slowly opened the door to see Brittany's reaction to Marti's words. Marti had turned abruptly away from Brittany and was evaluating Janelle's outfit. "Now with your dark hair, dear, you shouldn't wear such a deep shade right next to your face. What about that mint green sweater I suggested? Ah, here it is. Janelle, this would be a gorgeous shade on you, don't you think?"

The rest of the afternoon and the evening continued the same way, with Marti in control. When they got back to the hotel, Marti stayed in their room, directing each of them on what to wear to dinner. Marti insisted that Christy wear her new black dress. Even though the other girls and Bob made all kinds of flattering comments during the night, Christy still didn't feel like herself. She felt like Marti was trying to make her into someone else, and she didn't know how that "someone else" should sit or speak or smile.

Bob was acquainted with the owners of the Mexican restaurant they went to and asked the waiter if "Joaquin" was running the show that night.

Soon a tall, handsome, dark-haired man appeared at

the table, and Bob rose to greet him with a hearty hand-shake. "How've you been, Roberto?" the man asked. "And Marti, you become more beautiful every time I see you!"

Marti held out her hand, and Joaquin kissed it, then raised his head to view the three girls. "And who do we have here? You have been holding out on me, Roberto!"

"Joaquin, I'd like you to meet my one and only niece, Christina, and her friends, Janelle and Brittany."

Joaquin shook Brittany's hand. "Beautiful hair," he said. "Like the golden sunshine on the desert sand."

As he shook Janelle's hand he said, "Your smile could light the darkest night."

Then, turning to Christy, he smiled and said, "Christina, Christina." The *R*s rolled off his tongue with great flair. "You have eyes like rare gems. Never have I seen eyes like yours. One look into those eyes, and a man is taken captive forever."

Christy turned away, feeling herself blush from her neck up.

"Such innocence," Joaquin said to Bob. "It is beautiful on a woman."

Changing his tone and addressing everyone at the table, he said, "Listen, my friends, tonight you must try the crab enchiladas. They are the best."

"That sound good to everybody?" Bob asked.

"I'll just have half of a chicken tostada with the guacamole on the side," Marti said. Then she added, "Brittany, you be sure to order enough, dear. Order anything you like."

All three girls and Bob ordered the crab enchiladas. Christy thought they were delicious. They were mild, for Mexican food, and covered with cheese. She knew it must be the influence of growing up on a Wisconsin dairy farm, but that was just the way she liked her Mexican food. After eating her entire dinner, Christy felt so full she didn't think she could stand up.

The waiter came to clear their plates and said, "Your dinner is on the house tonight, sir. Would you care for anything else?"

"Girls?" Bob asked.

"I couldn't eat another bite!" Janelle said.

The others agreed.

"I guess that's it," Bob said. "Tell Joaquin thanks for us. The crab enchiladas were terrific. And here, this is for you." Bob handed the waiter a fifty-dollar bill.

"Thank you, sir!" the waiter said, his eyes wide with surprise. "Thank you very much!"

"Robert," Marti scolded in a low voice, "don't you think you overtipped him a bit?"

"That's the smallest I had. Besides, the dinner was free." He turned to Christy and her wide-eyed friends. "So how about it, girls? You ready for a movie?"

"As long as you don't buy us any popcorn," Janelle said. "I'm so full."

"How about you, Brittany?" Marti asked pointedly. "Did you get enough to eat?"

"Yes, I did. Thank you." Christy thought Brittany sounded like a robot answering Marti's obvious questions. She wondered if she sounded that cold and rude when she answered her aunt during the times when Marti bugged her.

"Then let's go, shall we, Robert?"

When they arrived at the theater they found the film was sold out, and the next showing was at 10:10. After much debate they finally agreed to go back to the hotel and go to bed. They would all meet in the lobby for brunch in the morning, if any of them felt like eating by then.

The girls lounged in their room, watching TV and feeling bloated and lazy.

Brittany went into the bathroom, and Janelle jumped up to turn down the TV.

"Listen," she whispered to Christy. "She's doing it again. She's throwing up."

"I can't say at this moment that I don't feel like throwing up myself," Christy said.

"I know, but she did it this afternoon too. When we came back from the pool. She didn't think I heard her, but I did."

"She told me she wasn't doing that anymore," Christy said.

"She told you a lot of other things, too," Janelle said, looking very serious. "This isn't good. I think we should try to help her. After all the things your aunt said at the pool, I'm really worried."

"I know, but what can we do?" Christy said softly.

"We could try talking to her about it," Janelle suggested.

Right then the bathroom door opened, and Brittany came back into the room. She realized the two girls had taken their eyes off the TV and were focusing on her. Janelle turned off the TV and looked over at Christy and then back at Brittany.

"What?" Brittany asked. "What's wrong?"

Christy didn't know what to say. Janelle was the gutsy one. Christy hoped Janelle would start this difficult conversation.

"Brit, well, it's like this," Janelle said. "We know you've been trying to lose weight and everything, and you've lost a lot of weight already. Really fast, too."

Brittany stood perfectly still. Her face was expressionless.

"And, well, we're worried because it's not good for you to throw up a lot, and we know that you have been."

Brittany's face softened. "I know. I don't want to throw up. I'm not trying to. It's just that I've had this terrible stomachache all day. I didn't want to tell anyone because I didn't want to ruin the shopping trip and everything for the rest of you. I think my stomach just couldn't handle those heavy enchiladas tonight."

"Why didn't you say something?" Christy asked. "Are you feeling better now?"

"Not really. My stomach is still upset."

"Can we do anything to help you?" Janelle asked, her face showing her sincere concern. "Do you want Christy to check with her uncle and see if he has anything you could take for your upset stomach?"

"No," Brittany said, sitting on the edge of the bed. She folded her arms across her middle and let out a little groan. "I think I'll just go to the drugstore and get some antacid tablets. I know that would help. When I was out jogging this morning I went past a drugstore about a block from here."

"I'll get my uncle to take you," Christy said, reaching for the phone. "What's their room number?"

"No! Please!" Brittany insisted. "I don't want to bother them. They're probably already asleep, and after all the things your aunt was saying to me today, the last thing I want to do is get on her bad side. I'll run to the drugstore by myself."

"You can't go by yourself," Janelle protested.

"I did this morning."

"That was different. It was daylight then. Muggers and weirdos don't work when the sun's up," Janelle said. "We'll go with you."

"I don't think we should," Christy said.

"It's only a block away," Brittany said. "Maybe less."

"We left our room last night, and nobody knew it," Janelle reasoned. "I think Brittany's right. We shouldn't bother your aunt and uncle for something minor like a little roll of antacids."

"I don't know, you guys," Christy said. "I don't feel right about it."

"Look, Christy," Janelle said, pulling her thick, wavy, black hair back in a scrunchie. "The weekend is only half over. The last thing we want to do is get your aunt upset at us for waking her up and disrupting her beauty sleep. Besides, if you were the one with the upset stomach, Brittany would go to the drugstore with you. Wouldn't you, Brit?"

"Oh, definitely. We'll only be gone for five minutes. They'll never know. You don't have to come with us, Christy."

Christy absolutely hated moments like this! She had never been good at making split-second decisions. She hated the feeling of being an outcast, yet she knew they shouldn't leave the hotel by themselves at night.

"Listen," Janelle said quietly to Christy while Brittany looked in the closet for some shoes. "This is a way we could really help Brittany. You're the one who said we should try to be her friend and help her."

"I know, but..."

"Come on. It'll be fun. The drugstore is right next door. Isn't that what she said? It might even be part of the hotel."

"She said it was a block away."

"Okay, a block. Christy, we should think of Brittany now, not ourselves." Janelle slipped on her sandals and went over to the door next to Brittany.

"We're going," Janelle said. "Now are you coming with us or not?"

"Oh, all right." Christy spit the words out and jumped up from the bed. "Where's my purse? I don't want to get locked out. You sure it's only a block away?"

"Maybe a block and a half. It's not far. Trust me," Brittany said, opening the door.

Janelle imitated their antics of the night before, looking up and down the hallway before exiting. "Come on," Janelle whispered to Christy. "The coast is clear!"

Christy reluctantly stepped into the hallway. The door automatically locked behind them.

11

Midnight Run

"How much farther is it, Brittany? We've already gone over two blocks!" Christy felt as panicked as she sounded.

"It's down this street here," Brittany said calmly. "You surprise me, Christy. After we papered Rick's house, I thought you were a professional at late-night adventures on dark streets."

Christy clenched her teeth. *Am I being a baby?* She shot a glance at Janelle.

Janelle's usual carefree look had disappeared. Anger now spread across her face. "I think it's too far," Janelle said. "Let's go back and ask Christy's uncle to drive us."

"Hey, if you guys want to go back, that's fine with me," Brittany said. "But I'm going to the drugstore. Look. There it is." Brittany stepped up her pace, and the other two trotted along beside her.

Inside the brightly lit store, Christy felt a little more secure. The trip actually seemed rational once they could see other people, normal people, standing in the checkout lines, buying normal things. Still, her heart pounded with the fear that if her parents ever knew she had done this she would be in big trouble.

Why didn't I chicken out? she thought. *I wish I'd stayed back at the hotel. Why am I doing this?*

"Over here," Janelle called from one of the well-stocked aisles. "What kind of antacid do you want? Hurry, so we can go back."

"I don't know. You look at what they have. I'll be right back." Brittany shot like an arrow to the back of the store.

"Where's she going?" Christy asked.

"I don't know, but we'd better find out."

Janelle and Christy found Brittany at the pharmacy window, reaching for a small bag the clerk held out to her.

"What's she doing?" Janelle asked.

"Oh, no!" Christy felt a rush of horror through her veins. "I hope that's not what I think it is."

"What?"

Christy stepped up to Brittany as she turned to walk away from the counter and boldly confronted her. "Are those your mom's diet pills?"

"What do you mean?" Brittany returned a blank stare.

"Brittany!" Janelle reprimanded. "You don't even have a mother! What are you trying to do?"

The window to the pharmacy area was still open, and the clerk stood there, casually observing the girls.

"Janelle, it's not funny when you act like this. I don't appreciate it at all. You know my mom asked me to pick up her medicine for her." Brittany's eyes opened wide as she coaxed Janelle to go along with the story. "Come on. We're going to be late, and she'll be really mad."

Janelle looked as if she might explode with anger at any moment. "Come on, Christy," she said, turning and pulling Christy by the arm. "You and I are leaving. I can't believe she did this to us!"

"I just figured it out," Christy said as they marched down the hair-care aisle. "Brittany must have left the empty prescription bottle here this morning when she said she went jogging. This whole scene tonight with the stomachache was to get us to go with her to pick up her diet pills."

"Right. And we were dumb enough to fall for it. We're going back to the hotel—now."

"I can't believe she lied to us. I can't believe I didn't just tell her no!" Christy moaned.

"We don't have to tell anybody," Janelle said over her shoulder as they neared the front of the store. "Let's hurry back to our room and wait for Brittany. If she gets caught, we'll say she snuck out without us."

"Janelle, we can't lie!"

"Why not? She lied to us! Do you think we should wait here and help her pay for her pills or something?"

Just then Brittany rounded the end of the next aisle and met them at the front of the store. She looked as if she'd run to get ahead of them but other than that seemed unaffected by the whole scene. "You guys ready to go?"

Christy and Janelle exchanged looks of confusion. "Aren't you going to buy something?" Christy asked.

"No," Brittany answered calmly. She stepped toward the exit, and the glass doors opened automatically for her.

Christy felt completely flustered and confused. All she wanted to do was get back to the hotel so this whole night could be over.

Suddenly a voice boomed behind them. "Ladies, hold up a minute there."

A large man dressed in a security guard uniform towered over them. "Would you young ladies come with me?" his voice demanded.

Numbed and silent, they followed him back into the store to a small office. Brittany hung behind at first; then all of a sudden she tugged at Christy's purse and hung onto the strap. Christy could feel the purse strap dig into her shoulder as Brittany whispered, "We don't have to take this, you know. We have rights. Remember what Ms. Archer is always telling us?"

"Forget it, Brittany. This is the last time I let you talk me into anything, and I mean it!"

The guard pushed open the door to a small office. It felt unbearably hot inside the small room.

"Have a seat," he commanded, pointing to a narrow couch in the corner. They squished next to each other while the guard swung open the back door to let in the evening air.

"Stupid air conditioner," he mumbled. "I need to ask you girls a few questions." Turning his back on them, he adjusted the thermostat on the air conditioner.

"Come on!" Brittany hissed. She grabbed Janelle's arm, and the two of them vanished out the open door.

Christy jumped up, then sat down, then jumped up again.

"Sit down," the guard bellowed.

Instantly she obeyed.

"Stay where you are!" the guard ordered and dashed out into the darkness.

Christy trembled. Everything within her fought the urge to run. *It's just like the night we papered Rick's house! They ran off and left me again. What am I going to do? What's going to happen?* Christy drew in a deep breath, her chest pounding. *I can't believe this is happening! What am I going to do?*

In the stillness a sudden thought pierced her. Something she had read: "Do not be afraid."

It was part of the verse in Tracy's letter! Christy grabbed the envelope from the side pocket of her purse and pulled out the card.

She read it slowly: "'The Lord himself goes before you and will be with you; he will never leave you nor forsake you. Do not be afraid; do not be discouraged.'"

Christy felt a quietness trickling over her like a warm shower. She read the verse again and again. The comforting sensation continued to calm her. It was as if Jesus were sitting right beside her, putting His arm around her, talking softly to her. She never heard a voice or anything, but it was the closest she had felt to the Lord since last summer.

Suddenly the guard appeared in the doorway, perspiring and heaving deep breaths. "Your friends must be experienced at running away." He pulled out a handkerchief, wiped his forehead, and then positioned himself on the edge of the desk.

"Don't make this any harder on yourself. First of all," he began, "how old are you?"

"Fifteen." Then she added, "Sir."

He pulled out a notebook and began writing. "Okay, that's one. Violation of curfew. Not something you want to mess with in Palm Springs. What's your name?"

"Christy Miller, or, well, Christina Miller, sir."

"Your parents' name and address?"

She rattled off her address and then went into a jumbled explanation of how she was in Palm Springs with her aunt and uncle.

"Where are you staying? What hotel?"

"Um, I think it's the West something....I don't remember. Oh, maybe it's on my room key." With sweaty hands, Christy pulled her purse up to her lap and reached for the key.

Suddenly she froze. The first thing her hand touched was a crackly paper bag—a slick, white pharmacy bag.

"May I see that?" the guard asked, reaching for the bag that Brittany had so slyly slipped into Christy's purse.

"It's not mine," Christy said defensively. "I didn't take it."

"Where's the receipt for these?" he asked, pulling out three boxes of laxatives.

Christy gasped. "I-I don't know. They're not mine!"

"You're saying these aren't yours either?" He held up the prescription diet pills.

"No! No! They're not mine! Really!"

"We'll let the police decide about that." He continued to go through her purse, dumping the contents on the table. He flipped through her wallet, fanned through her color swatches, and then lifted up a prescription bottle, held it to his ear, and shook it. Two pills rattled inside.

Oh no! No! Christy screamed under her breath. *No! No! Why didn't I throw those stupid pills out the day Brittany gave them to me? I can't believe they're still in there!*

The guard read the prescription, then opened the bottle and examined the tiny pills in the palm of his hand. Christy's eyes burned with tears as he opened the new prescription bottle of the same diet pills and compared them.

"I suppose these aren't yours either?"

"No, sir. They were given to me. They've been there for weeks." The words jerked their way out of her throat in spasms.

"I see," he said, writing furiously in his notebook. Then he picked up the phone and talked to somebody named Pat.

"Yeah, Pat," he said. "I've got a curfew violation with a possible illegal possession. Tourist. Sure. I'll have the report finished by the time you get here." He hung up the phone and continued writing.

"Can I go now?" Christy asked meekly.

"Can you go? I don't think so, missy. You're caught, young lady. The jig is up, as they say. Your whole life is about to change. You sit tight. The police are on their way."

Police! Why? I told the truth. They're not my pills. Christy couldn't sit still. Her body throbbed with the drumming of her heart. She felt the perspiration rolling down the front of her, soaking her shirt, forming a river around her waist. Her mind pulsated as each terrifying thought rode on a different vein, shooting wildly through her head. *Why is this happening to me? Where did Brittany and Janelle go? Why did they leave me?*

The door of the office opened, and in stepped a short, thickset police officer with a wide, bushy mustache. "Yeesh! Sure is hot in here. Air conditioner broken again?"

"Yeah, Pat. How you doing?"

"All right. Is this the suspect?"

"Right. Her name is Miller, Cathy."

"Christy," she corrected him. Her voice came out squeaky like a screen door closing.

They both ignored her. The security guard handed the police officer the report forms he had been filling out. "There are two others. Females, same age roughly. They bolted. This one had enough sense to face the music."

"I see. Cathy, what are your friends' names?"

"Christy." She still sounded squeaky.

"One of them is Christy? And the other?" The officer pulled out a pen and began writing on the report forms.

"No, see, my name is Christy. Christy Miller. Or, well, Christina Miller. You called me Cathy."

"I see. Okay, Christy. What are the names of the other two girls?"

"Janelle Layne and Brittany Taylor. They live in Escondido."

"And who is Merriah Jasmine Taylor?"

"I don't know."

"Are you sure?" The officer held up the diet pill bottle to read the name on the label again.

"Oh, that must be Brittany's mom. I've never met her. They're divorced. Her parents, I mean. Brittany's parents. She lives with her dad. His name is Hank Taylor."

"Okay, okay." The officer stopped her. "That's fine. Let's go down to the station and finish this. These charges are rather serious. Did you know that?"

Christy shook her head and looked at him blankly.

"Miss Miller, you have the right to remain silent. Should you give up that right, anything you say can and will be used against you in a court of law...." The officer continued reciting her rights as if she were a crook or something. It all seemed like a bad scene from some TV rerun.

"Come with me," the officer said. He took her arm and held it all the way to the police car. People in the parking lot were looking at her. She bent down and slid into the backseat. Straight ahead of her the grille between the front seat and the back made her feel caged in and helpless. They drove the mile or so to the Palm Springs Police Station with only the crackling messages on the police radio breaking the dead silence of the night.

Christy trembled all over. Her lower jaw shivered until her teeth chattered. She kept trying to repeat the verse over and over again: "'The Lord himself goes before you and will be with you; he will never leave you nor forsake you. Do not be afraid; do not be discouraged.'" Every time she said it she felt a little stronger, a little more clear-headed.

They entered the police station lobby. The officer went up to the front desk, and Christy tried to ignore the other people around her and keep her knees from shaking so much. She focused her attention on a picture on the wall. It was a print she had seen before of a small boy and a large police officer sitting beside each other on counter stools at a diner. The boy looked as though he had tried to run away from home, but the officer had found him and was treating him to a little snack. Christy never thought she would be living out the part of the runaway. And her officer didn't look as if he were about to treat her to anything.

"Follow me," he said, leading her down a hall to a small room with a table and three chairs. "Have a seat. Now tell me about the laxatives and pills found in your possession. Where did you get them?"

"My friend Brittany stuck them in my purse. They were hers."

"But the prescription was made out to Merriah Taylor, not Brittany Taylor."

"I guess, I mean, they were originally her mom's, or at least the prescription was her mom's, but Brittany got them refilled today and picked them up tonight. That's why we were out after curfew. But we really thought she was sick. Janelle and I. Brittany was sick, I mean. We didn't know she was just using us."

"Let's start over," the officer said.

Christy slowed down and carefully told him the whole situation, starting back with how they came to Palm Springs with her aunt and uncle. She explained how Brittany had given her the diet pills weeks ago and how she had only carried them around but never took them.

"Do you realize that you were in possession of illegal drugs that whole time?"

Christy shook her head. "No, sir. She told me they were just diet pills."

"Prescription diet pills. Prescribed for someone else, not for you. That's nothing to mess with. It's a health and safety code violation. Drug-related violation. This will go on your record."

"But, but, I—"

"I want you to know I believe you're telling the truth about holding the drugs for your friend and that you never took any. However, you were in possession of the shoplifted items and prescription drugs, obtained through falsification. We'll have to hold you until we can contact your aunt and uncle."

Christy sat perfectly still, yet her mind jumped and twisted and hopped at a frenzied pace. She thought of the illustration in Sunday school when Peter Pagan so easily yanked Katie Christian down to his level.

It can happen so fast! What if I'd taken the laxatives and diet pills like Brittany wanted me to? If only I'd said no tonight. If only I'd stayed at the hotel room—none of this would have happened.

Then Christy remembered Leslie saying that you could go crazy trying to live in the Land of If Only. *I've got to believe God is in control, even now.*

An officer took Christy to be "printed." Each finger was rolled in black ink. As she stood there looking at her ten blackened fingertips, she felt dirty.

What was that verse from Sunday school? Something about bad company corrupting good character? Christy felt corrupted as she tried to wipe the black ink off her fingers with a rough paper towel.

A woman officer, the keys jingling on her belt, led Christy down a hall past a row of cells. They stopped in a small room with a camera. Christy was directed to stand on a mark on the floor while a mechanical arm moved in front of her. She trembled all over when she realized that the mechanical arm displayed a number—a jailbird number, black and white.

She looked forward, and the camera snapped with a blinding flash. She turned to face the wall, and a second picture was taken. Never, ever in her life had Christy felt like this—so utterly humiliated and completely misunderstood. She felt dirty and ugly and bad. And to make it worse, this whole painful experience was being recorded, kept on file, captured with a picture.

"The suspect's guardians have arrived," an officer said, poking his head in the room a short time later. "I'll take her."

Christy was led back to the lobby, where Bob, Marti, and Janelle sat on a bench. She approached them cautiously, her head down. Then she spotted Brittany standing to the side, holding her head high, looking cool, calm, and confident.

"Christina Juliet Miller!" Aunt Marti sprang from her seat. "I hope you realize what kind of trouble you're in! Running out in the middle of the—"

"I'll handle this, Martha." Bob reached over and squeezed Christy's shoulder. "You all right?"

She nodded, her eyes filling with tears. "I'm sorry, Uncle Bob. We shouldn't have left our room. I'm so, so sorry."

"Okay." The police officer named Pat stood before them with a bunch of papers in his hand. "I'm sure you folks are anxious to get this cleared up. Let me take the girls one at a time. Janelle, I'd like to talk to you first."

Janelle's usual carefree, just-flew-in-from-Tahiti look had disappeared. She looked as shaken up as Christy felt. With cautious steps, Janelle followed the officer down the hall.

Brittany appeared completely unaffected. She stood rather than sat and looked out the front door into the darkness, as if she were involved in something going on outside.

How can you be so detached from this, Brittany? Christy thought. *I feel sorry for you.*

Christy realized that as much as she'd wanted to be Brittany's friend and help her, there was something much more complicated going on here. Maybe Brittany needed more than a friend right now. Maybe she needed to get "caught."

316 ● ● ● ● ●   Robin Jones Gunn

"Did you tell the officer the truth, Christina?" Aunt Marti asked, grabbing Christy's arm and digging her fingernails into the flesh.

"Ouch!"

Marti released her grip. "Tell me, dear. What happened?"

"I told him everything I knew. I told the truth."

Brittany snapped her focus onto Christy and pierced her with the most spiteful look Christy had ever received.

"Of course she told the truth!" Bob defended. "I'd never expect anything but the truth from this young woman. She's a woman of honor." His look, his words, his warm arm around her shoulder, drenched Christy with a healing she desperately needed. It left her weak. It brought release.

As if all the plugs had been suddenly pulled from her pent-up emotions, Christy doubled over, dropped her head in her hands, and wept a thousand salty tears.

"Whatever is the matter with her, Robert?" Marti snipped. "What did you say to the poor child?"

"Let her cry, Martha. Just let her cry."

As Christy tried to curtail her tears, her aunt rose and walked calmly over to Brittany.

"Brittany," Marti began sweetly, "is there anything you'd like to talk about before the officer questions you?"

Christy pulled up her head and dried her eyes, listening intently for Brittany's response.

"No."

"Now, dear, I'm sure you realize this is all very important, and we are here to help you in any way we can."

Brittany pulled away. Aunt Marti didn't. She was used

to having her way. Her voice raised, her head tall, her face directly pointed toward Brittany, she said, "Do you realize we have a serious problem here? You need professional help, child."

Brittany slowly coiled back like a snake about to strike. Then she thrust her head and her voice forward with a loud burst of laughter.

Stunned, Marti turned to Bob for support. None of them knew what to do or what to expect next. Brittany kept laughing until the tears rolled down her cheeks, and Marti stood in utter silence. Then the officer returned with Janelle and asked to see Brittany.

Wiping the tears and still chuckling to herself, Brittany followed Officer Pat.

"What's with her?" Janelle asked.

"I don't know," Christy answered, wiping her eyes with a tissue Marti handed her. "What happened with you?"

"He asked me a bunch of stuff, and I told him what I knew. He said he believed me, and that was all."

"What happened after you guys ran out of the drug-store?"

Janelle positioned herself sideways next to Christy on the wooden bench and looked up at the picture of the little boy and the policeman above them. "I always liked that picture. My dad has a big book of pictures by that artist."

Bob twisted his neck to see. "Norman Rockwell," he said. "My all-time favorite."

"Janelle!" Christy squawked. "Forget about the picture and tell me what happened!"

"First Brittany grabbed my arm and pulled me out of that little office. I guess I could have broken away from her, but I didn't know what to do. We hid behind a big Dumpster at the back of the store and waited until the security guard went back inside."

"Why did you do that?"

"I don't know. Why did we do any of it? It all happened so fast. I wanted to go back to the hotel, but I said we didn't have the key, and then Brittany said, 'Oh, don't we?' She held up the room key and said you gave it to her."

"I did not! She took it out of my purse and left me with the bag from the pharmacy."

"You're kidding!"

"No, I'm not kidding! That's why I got in so much trouble. They thought I was the one getting the prescription drugs. Plus, there were three packages of laxatives in the bag, which she apparently didn't intend to pay for."

"You mean she was going to steal them?"

"I guess so. At least that's what the guard accused me of doing when he called the police."

Janelle leaned her head against the wall. "What a mess! Brittany said they'd let you go. You're a minor. I never thought they'd call the police."

"So, what did you guys do? Jog back to the hotel and think you'd wait around for me to come waltzing back? Thanks a lot."

"No, wait!" Janelle said. "Let me finish. We practically ran back to the hotel. Brittany didn't want me to, but I went right over to your aunt and uncle's room and woke them and told them everything."

"Then Janelle and I drove straight to the drugstore, but they said you'd been brought here," Bob said. "So we went back to the hotel, picked up Brittany and Marti, and came down here. Janelle told me everything, Christy. Don't accuse yourself too harshly. It's clear that the fault lies with Brittany. You made the mistake of not saying no when it really mattered."

"I wonder what's going to happen to her," Christy said.

"Perhaps you should wonder what's going to happen to you, Christina. This is no laughing matter," Marti scolded.

The officer stepped into the lobby without Brittany and addressed them. "Okay, the story checks out. The charges against your niece will be minimal. She'll have this on her record—possession, shoplifting suspect—but she can have her record sealed once she turns eighteen. Something like this shouldn't ruin a kid's whole life." He sounded softer, more human now and less like the bulldog he had seemed to be earlier.

"What about Brittany?" Christy asked.

"What about me?" Janelle asked.

"Okay, Janelle, you did the right thing in contacting the adults. Your only charge is curfew violation. Under the circumstances, we'll let that go."

"Are you going to have to call my parents tonight?" Janelle asked.

"We already have. They agreed that we could release you to your friend's aunt and uncle here. We're holding Brittany until we can reach her father. He doesn't seem to be home."

The thought of the police officer calling her parents made Christy feel sick. Bravely she ventured the question, "Did you call my parents?"

"Yes, we did. I might add they weren't too happy about the situation, miss. Actually"—the officer glanced at his watch—"it's almost midnight. Let me talk to the sergeant and see if we can't release Brittany to you tonight. She'll have to appear before a judge for sentencing in about a month."

"Will she come back here?" Bob asked.

"No. The Indio County Courthouse. She'll probably appear before a juvenile referee. My guess is that they'll require her to enroll in a treatment program for her eating disorder. They might place her on probation, require her to do some kind of community service work."

"Will the program help her eating problems?" Christy asked. "I'm really worried about her."

The officer paused for a moment and then answered in the most human-sounding voice he had used yet. "Let me tell you about kids with eating disorders. My brother's kid was sixteen when they finally put her in a hospital program. She weighed only eighty-two pounds the day they admitted her. She was in there for months.

"Seemed to like it, being with a whole ward full of 'her kind' and having a shrink to talk to whenever she felt like it. My brother shelled out thousands of bucks to get her straightened out. She died. They found her on the bathroom floor in the hospital with a box of laxatives in her hand. Some friend had smuggled them in to her. She was a beautiful girl. Could have had a great future...." His voice trailed off.

Christy and Janelle looked at each other in stunned silence.

"I knew it was serious," Marti spoke up. "I tried to tell that girl, but she simply wouldn't listen. Let this be a lesson to the two of you!" She eyed Janelle and Christy.

"Girls like that need help," the officer said. "It's as though there's a voice in their heads telling them they're fat and they need to be thin, because once they're thin they can do anything, have anything, be anything."

He turned to Janelle and Christy and said, "I'm sure you two meant well, trying to help your friend tonight. Fact is, she needs more help than the two of you could give her. If you don't mind me giving you a bit of advice, I'd encourage you to think twice before you let somebody else lead you into foolish mischief. It could change your whole future."

12

One Quiet Word

The car stereo in the Mercedes played elevator music while Bob hummed along. Marti silently flipped through her magazine. The three girls sat perfectly still in the backseat. No one said a word.

Christy stared out the window at the dry desert scenery as they sped away from Palm Springs and headed home. The midmorning light brushed the landscape with its amber hues. Already the heat rose from the pavement like iridescent snakes charmed by the sun.

Right now we should be riding in a hot air balloon or going up the aerial tramway or at least swimming in the hotel's pool. But now all the fun is over, and I have to face my parents. They are never going to understand. Christy felt miserable.

That morning they had packed in a rush and checked out of their hotel early. The night before, the police sergeant had agreed to release Brittany to Uncle Bob as long as she would be returned home to her father the next day.

Christy's mind played with nightmarish scenes of what her parents would say when she got home. She closed her eyes and prayed. She tried to remember the verse Tracy sent her and say it over and over. *The Lord Himself goes before you....*

Around eleven o'clock Bob pulled up in front of Christy's house. She bravely got out of the car, walked up the front steps, and opened the door. Her parents, Janelle's mom, and Mr. Taylor were all sitting at the kitchen table.

"Where's Brittany?" Mr. Taylor said, jumping up.

"In the car," Christy answered, checking her parents' faces for an indication of how they would deal with her. She felt weak and empty and wanted to run to them and feel their reassuring hugs. At the same time she wanted to stand her ground and tell them that she wasn't a baby anymore. She'd grown up, and they could trust her now more than ever because she was determined not to meekly follow others.

Mr. Taylor hurried out the front door. Christy watched as he greeted Bob and spoke with him briefly. Brittany emerged from the car with Janelle right behind her. Mr. Taylor hustled his daughter into his BMW. He seemed nervous and embarrassed when he called out, "Thanks again, Bob. See you folks later."

Bob pulled the suitcases from the car. It was uncomfortably quiet. Christy, her parents, and Janelle's mom had all joined the group outside. Janelle's mom reached for Janelle's luggage, but Christy's dad offered to carry it to the car for her.

"I guess we kind of messed up the weekend," Janelle said, giving Bob an apologetic look.

Janelle's mom sliced through the tension with a laugh. "Good heavens! I did worse things than sneaking out of a hotel room when I was a teenager. What matters most is that no one was hurt. I'm thankful for that."

Janelle and Christy exchanged serious glances.

"So are we," Janelle answered for both of them.

Christy was thinking about how there are different kinds of hurts and not just the ones that are obvious to everyone else. She knew something about such hidden hurts and the kind of scars friends can leave on your heart.

After thanking Bob, Marti, and Christy, Janelle followed her mom to their car, a lighthearted bounce returning to her steps. If Janelle was about to get in trouble for what happened, she sure didn't appear worried about it.

Once Janelle and her mom were down the street, Mom invited Bob and Marti to come in. The five of them fit comfortably around the kitchen table as Mom offered everyone coffee.

I can't stand this suspense! Christy thought. *Why doesn't somebody say something?* Her lower lip felt numb, and she realized that for the last two hours she had been chewing on it.

At last Dad said, "Christy, what do you have to say for yourself?"

She wanted to cry but fought back the tears. "I'm really sorry. I know we should never have left the hotel room. It was really dumb, and I should've talked my friends out of it."

All four of them were looking at her. She wished she could jump into a time machine and go back twenty-four hours. She would do everything differently.

"Personally, I think Brittany was the one at fault here," Marti interjected. "She's wrapped up in a whole world of problems, and she pulled the other two right down with her. I'm so relieved that she'll be getting the help she needs."

"This was a raw deal any way you look at it," Bob said. "I

was proud of Christy. The police really shook her up, but she showed me that her heart was in the right place."

"Yeah, but her brain wasn't in the right place," David announced from the hallway.

"David! Go outside. Right now," Dad said.

David hurried out the door, and Christy avoided looking at him. For the next fifteen minutes the adults discussed the series of events. Christy felt like a spectator as they evaluated her life.

Once all the facts were clearly laid out, Christy's mom turned to her and said, "Tell us what you learned."

"I learned I have to say no," Christy answered quickly. "And I have to choose my friends more carefully." It felt strange to have all of them looking at her so intently.

A comforting smile pressed across Bob's tanned face. "I know a few forty-year-olds who haven't learned that yet. I'd say the weekend wasn't a total loss."

"I also learned," Christy added, "that no matter what happens to me, the Lord always goes before me and He's always with me." She felt a little bolder than usual, a little surer that her summer promise to Jesus was real and lasting.

No one said anything.

Didn't they agree with her? Did her parents and aunt and uncle understand? It seemed so clear to her.

"Nevertheless," her dad began, sitting up straight in his chair, "there are consequences. You will not be allowed to go anywhere except school for the next two weeks. No social activities of any sort. Do you understand?"

Christy nodded, swallowing hard. She had expected it to be much worse. In an unspoken way she knew her parents were on her side in this whole thing.

When she wrote about the weekend in her diary that night, she penned:

> *The only thing that's going to be hard is not going to church and see-ing Rick. I never see him at school. That afternoon at the pizza place was the best time I've had since we moved here. Rick's probably already forgotten about it. He'll probably have another girlfriend by the time I get off restriction.*
>
> *Why do guys do that? They act all interested in you, and then they forget about you as soon as you're out of their sight.*
>
> *Like Todd. I'll never forget Todd. Ever. But I bet if he saw me right now, he wouldn't even remember my name. If only guys weren't so strange. If only they...*

Christy stopped writing. She had written herself right into the middle of the Land of If Only. She knew if she stayed there tonight she would only get depressed.

Putting away her diary, Christy wrote a short note to Tracy.

> *I can't tell you how much that verse helped me. It came at a time when I needed it more than I even knew. Thanks so much for think-ing of me and for taking the time to write.*

She licked the envelope, sealed it, and then pulled out a belated birthday card for Paula. She had bought it in the hotel gift shop that morning while Uncle Bob was checking them out of the hotel. It seemed perfect for Paula. The card said on the front, "Something has come between us," and inside, "A few thousand miles! Hope you had a nice birth-day at your end of the world."

Christy wrote Paula a little bit about what had been going on but not many of the details. She wasn't sure Paula would understand, since Christy had been the one who accused Paula of hanging out with the wrong kinds of friends when they were in Paula's bedroom. If Christy told Paula everything that happened this weekend, Paula would have every right to give Christy's own lecture back to her. Her closing paragraph to Paula said:

> I can't wait for you to come see me next summer. We are going to have the best time ever. I really miss you. You do know that you're the best friend I've ever had, don't you? Please always remember that. Even though things have changed since I moved, I want you to always know how glad I am that God gave me a best friend like you.
>
> Love,
> Christy

The last person she wrote was Alissa. For some reason she felt freer to tell Alissa about all the trouble she had gotten into in Palm Springs. She also told Alissa about the Bible verse that Tracy had written in the card to her and how reading that little bit of God's Word had comforted her when she needed it most. Then she wrote:

> You asked why I would make such a big deal about promising my life to Jesus if He were dead like Buddha or Mohammed. The thing is, Jesus isn't dead! Yes, He died on the cross, but then He came back to life, and He's still alive today. I can't explain it, but He's living inside me. He's as real as any person I know. I don't know Him as well as I want to, but we're getting better acquainted. I've always

prayed—you know, talked to God. But now I'm starting to read my Bible, which is like listening to Him.

Maybe you could find a Bible and start reading it or find a good church you could go to there in Boston. I'll start praying that you'll meet some other Christians who are strong like Todd was and that they'll be able to explain all this to you.

Love,

Christy

Setting all her letters on the floor beside her bed, Christy slipped under the cool, crisp sheets. She propped her knees up and balanced Pooh Bear. She felt clean and fresh and invigorated, as though everything were in order. She was ready for a fresh start at school tomorrow.

"Okay, Pooh. Repeat after me. No, no, no, no! When in doubt, chicken out. No, no, no, no..."

The next morning Janelle caught up with Christy in the hall. Janelle's dark, tousled hair looked like a garland of wild black orchids around her head.

"Guess what!" she squealed breathlessly. "Greg asked me to homecoming Friday night! Can you believe it? And I didn't even get to try out my plan to get him to go with me."

"That's great! But what was your big plan, anyhow?" Christy remembered how Janelle's plan had included Rick, and for some reason that still captured her curiosity.

Janelle didn't answer. Her dark eyes had taken on an exotic glaze, indicating that her mind had flown to parts unknown. Christy knew she wouldn't be back for days.

After school Christy flipped through her locker combination and began yanking her books out when someone tapped her on the shoulder. She spun around and accidentally knocked into the person, spilling her books all over the floor.

"Oops! Sorry!" Christy said before she saw who it was. She stood at eye level with the shoulder of a blue and gold letterman's jacket. Her gaze shot up to the guy's face and looked into the chocolate brown eyes that could only belong to Rick.

"Hi!" she said with a giggle. "Did I hit you? I didn't mean to...I mean, I didn't see you...."

"You ever consider going out for track?" Rick teased. "You could throw a mean discus."

Christy blushed.

"Here," Rick said, scooping up her books and handing them to her with a smile. "Looks as though you've got a busy week ahead of you."

"Not exactly," Christy said.

"You just like to look smart, right?"

Christy felt as though she were blushing on top of the first blush. Her cheeks must have looked candy apple red.

"Are you going to take time out from all your studies to go to homecoming on Friday?" Rick asked, leaning his arm casually against her locker.

Christy lowered her eyes. "No, I'm not going." She hoped he wouldn't ask why. It would be so embarrassing to admit that she was on restriction.

"Not even going to the game to see us trample Vista High?"

Christy looked up hesitantly and shook her head.

"How about this?" Rick suggested in his deep, strong voice. "How about if I pick you up after the game and take you to the homecoming dance?"

Christy's clear, blue-green eyes opened wide in disbelief. *He's actually asking me out! What should I say?*

"Rick..." Christy tried to find the words. "I would really, really like to go out with you. But you see..." She took a quick breath. "Well, I'm not allowed to date until I'm sixteen."

Immediately panic seized her. *Will he think I'm a baby? Did I ruin everything by telling him that?* She looked down at the books in her hands and then slowly back up at him.

Rick didn't move. The corners of his mouth were pressed into a warm grin. "Maybe that's one of the things that intrigue me about you so much."

Christy's eyes opened wider as she gazed at him more intently.

"It's your honesty. I think the most beautiful girls are the most innocent ones."

Christy couldn't believe her ears. Her heart raced. *This is the kind of thing a girl dreams of having a guy say to her! Did he really mean it?*

"So," Rick said, pulling his arm back and shifting his books to his other hand, "when's your birthday?"

Christy laughed. "Not until July. July 27th."

"That's only—what?—eight, nine months away? For a girl like you, I could wait that long."

Christy didn't know what to say. She wanted to throw her arms around him and hug him. She wanted to tell him that was the most wonderful thing anyone had ever said to her, that she thought he was the most fantastic guy on the face of the earth. But absolutely no words came out of her mouth. She wished something bright and clever would pop into her mind, but all she could do was smile and swallow hard and smile some more.

"You going to church Sunday?" Rick asked.

"Yes," Christy said, finding her voice. "My whole family is. My dad said this morning that he thought it was time we found a good church, and I told him how much I liked yours."

"Good. Well, I have to go. I'll see you Sunday, if not before."

"Okay. Bye!"

Rick smiled over his shoulder as he started to leave. Suddenly he turned and said, "By the way, can I call you sometime?"

"Sure!"

"You're not too young to accept phone calls?" he teased.

Christy felt the blush returning to her face. No guy had ever made her blush so much.

"No." She laughed along with him.

"Good," he said, taking long-legged strides backward. "I got your number off the card from church. I'll call you sometime."

Christy floated home. For the next hour and a half she relived the conversation over and over in her mind—everything Rick had said, the way he'd said it, how she had reacted.

Janelle had said he was a smooth talker, and boy, was he! Christy thought it was wonderful. Todd would never say those kinds of things to her. Rick had actually asked her out. It was like a dream. Why did she always have to turn red, though? The next time she talked to Rick she would be more confident—definitely. More outgoing, too.

David came in from riding his bike and looked at

Christy as she lounged on the couch, gazing out the front window. "What are you looking at?"

"Nothing."

"What are you doing?"

"Just making a few wishes."

David walked away, shaking his head. The phone rang, and Christy sprang from the couch, but David had already grabbed it.

"Hello?" he said. Then, "Yeah, she's here."

Christy grabbed the phone from him and, covering the mouthpiece, said, "Who is it, David?"

"I don't know. Some guy."

Christy's heart bounced into her throat as she put the phone to her ear. Very confidently she said, "Hi, Rick?"

"Rick?" The male voice on the other end responded.

Christy fumbled through her memory to identify the vaguely familiar voice. "Hello?" she said quickly.

"Is Christy there?"

"This is Christy."

"Hey, Christy, how's it going?"

"Todd?" she asked in disbelief.

"Yeah, how's it going?"

"Todd! I can't believe it's you! How are you?" *Oh no! I hope he didn't notice that I called him Rick!*

"Pretty good."

"How did you get this number?"

"I called your uncle."

"Oh. Where are you?"

"Florida. At my mom's."

"What...I mean how...I mean...well, it's just that I'm surprised to hear from you because you never wrote or anything." The instant she said it she regretted it.

"Yeah, well, I'm not much of a writer. Not like you. Your letters are incredible. I feel like I'm right there talking with you. So, what's been happening? I haven't heard from you in a while."

Christy felt herself relaxing and visiting comfortably with Todd the way they'd talked long hours on the beach last summer. She gave him a quick summary of the disastrous weekend.

He listened intently and said, "Friends can either lift you up or really drag you down."

"I sure learned that," she said. "I've made some big decisions about taking a stand and saying no to people and things that are bad influences on me." She thought Todd would be proud of her decision.

"Sounds cool."

There was a tiny pause, and then Todd said, "Have you started saying yes yet?"

"Yes? Yes to what?"

"Yes to the Lord."

Sometimes Todd's way of thinking was not exactly Christy's way of thinking. "I'm not sure I know what you mean," she said cautiously. She hated to sound dense around him, but she loved hearing his thoughts.

"When I first became a Christian, I was saying no to everything: No to drugs, parties, my old friends, everything. Pretty soon I was a total loner. I felt as though I were the strangest creature on the face of the earth."

"You? I can't believe that," Christy said.

"Well, then I figured out I needed to start saying yes to something. I mean, no is a good place to start, but being empty is no way to live. So, I started saying yes to God's way of doing things. That's when I found out that His way of doing things is usually the opposite of my way of doing things.

"Anyway, I made a bunch of good friends who were full-on Christians, and before I knew it, instead of all the empty holes from what I'd said no to, my life became really full of all the stuff Jesus was teaching me to say yes to."

"I see," Christy said, trying to understand what he was saying.

Todd probably read her confusion, because he added one of his famous stories. "It's like that boat ride to Hawaii I told you about, remember?"

"Of course I do. I'll never forget that!"

"Okay, let's say you're on the boat. It's this awesome cruise ship with everything you need already on board. I didn't say everything you want, but everything you need. So, you get on board with all these heavy suitcases and bags of junk that you lived off of back on shore. You with me?"

"Go on."

"You try to get into your assigned room, but you can't get through the door because your arms are too full. So you go on deck and watch everybody else swim and eat and have fun, but you're hating life because you've got your arms full of all the old junk and you can't do a thing.

"That's when you say no. No to the old stuff you're still carrying around. You dump all that garbage overboard. You see what I'm saying?"

"Yes, I do."

"But then you can't just stand there and keep saying no when the good stuff comes. Like if they ask if you want to eat at the captain's table or play volleyball, you don't keep saying no to everything just to be safe. You've got to learn to make good choices and say yes to the new stuff that God brings to you.

"You see what I mean? There's stuff you have to say no to, but that's only a tiny part of it—the first step, really. If you want to enjoy the cruise, you have to start saying yes. Yes to reading your Bible and going to church and getting close to some strong Christian friends."

Christy took his words to heart. "Todd, I don't know how you come up with these great illustrations, but I love them. You've helped me understand Christianity and what it really means more than anyone else. I really like your stories."

"Yeah, well, I figure Jesus liked stories too. He told a lot of stories. Have you read the book of John yet?"

"No." The awful truth was she hadn't read much from the Bible he had given her at all. But she planned to start reading a little bit every day, and she'd decided that even before he called.

"I like John. It's one of the Gospels, you know. And it's full of great stories that Jesus told."

"I'll start reading it tonight," Christy promised.

There was an awkward pause. Christy scrambled for another topic. She loved listening to Todd, and she didn't want him to hang up. Not yet!

"You haven't told me what's new with you," she said. "How's everything in Florida?"

"Oh yeah," Todd said. "The reason I called was to tell you my mom's getting married again."

Christy didn't know how to respond. "Really?"

"Their wedding is in December, and they're moving to New York."

"You're moving to New York?"

"Not me. My mom and her boyfriend. I'm moving back with my dad. To Newport Beach."

"You're kidding!" Christy practically screamed into the phone. "When?"

"Christmas vacation."

"Todd, that is so great! I wondered if I'd ever see you again, and here you're moving back to California!"

"Yeah, it's pretty cool. The thing I'm looking forward to the most is going to the beach some winter morning and cooking breakfast. Shawn and I did that a couple of years ago. We burned the eggs, but the bacon turned out pretty good."

"That sounds like fun," Christy said.

"There's nothing like the beach in the winter. I almost like it more than in the summer. In the morning it's totally deserted except for a few hard-core surfers and about a million seagulls."

"Todd, I'm so excited that you're moving back here! I can't wait to see you again."

"Yeah. It'll be good to see you, too. Hey, I have to go. Do me a favor and practice making scrambled eggs, will you?"

"Okay. Why?"

"So that when we have breakfast on the beach, we can have some decent food."

Christy laughed. "Okay. I'll practice every chance I get."

"Good. Oh, and hey, start saying yes to Jesus too. He's the best friend you'll ever have."

"I know He is. I will. Thanks. Bye, Todd."

"Later, Christy."

She waited until she heard his end of the line click and the dial tone hum in her ear. Then she hung up and headed straight for her bedroom.

Her pesky little brother stood by the kitchen doorway. "Who was that?"

"That was a wish come true," Christy said. She impulsively grabbed David and planted a big kiss on his cheek.

"Yuck!" David quickly wiped off his cheek and called to their mom, who was cleaning out the refrigerator. "Mom, Christy's kissing me! Tell her to stop it."

Christy laughed and said, "Sorry, David. I couldn't help myself. I'm just so happy."

Mom appeared behind David with a droopy stalk of celery in her hand. "What's the problem here?"

"Nothing," Christy said before dancing off to her room.

"She kissed me!" David said.

"She kissed you?"

"Don't worry," Christy called over her shoulder. "I can almost guarantee you it will never happen again in your lifetime."

As Christy closed her bedroom door she heard her brother say, "Why is she acting like that?"

Christy didn't wait to hear her mom's explanation. She twirled around twice before flopping onto her bed, still grinning from ear to ear. Then, scooping up Pooh Bear, Christy hugged him tight and laughed out loud.

Todd is moving to California! Rick actually asked me out! This is one of the most amazing days of my life. After this weekend I thought my whole life was falling apart, and now look.

She thought of Todd's story about the cruise and about saying no to all the old stuff so you can start saying yes to all the new adventures God has ahead.

Christy tilted her smiling face upward. *You really do go ahead of me, don't You, God? You're working everything out. You promised You would never leave me, and I believe You because You're right here with me, this very minute, aren't You? I know You are. And You will be with me— forever.*

Christy squeezed her eyes shut, and into the sacred silence that filled her room she whispered one quiet word: "Yes!"

BOOK THREE

Yours Forever

To my favorite man of God, my husband,
Ross Gunn III.
We are His forever.

I

The Gift

"See, Katie! I told you he wouldn't be here," fifteen-year-old Christy Miller whispered, standing stiffly in the corner of the gym.

"Trust me, Christy. Rick told me he was coming to church tonight to play basketball. He'll be here." Katie's copper-colored hair swished as she quickly glanced over her shoulder, checking the entrance.

"Well, even if he does come I'm not going to give him this Christmas present. It was a bad idea." Christy slipped the small gift into the purse slung over her shoulder.

"No, it wasn't!"

"Yes, it was, Katie. I hardly know Rick, so why am I chasing after him to give him a present?" Christy felt her face getting hot. She felt hot all over. Quickly running a finger over each eyelid, she asked, "Is my eye makeup all smeared?"

Katie looked into Christy's distinctive blue-green eyes. "No, not at all. I can't even tell you have any on."

"Maybe I should go in the bathroom and put on some more."

"Christy, stop with the Barbie Beauty Shop, will you? You're a natural beauty—and Rick knows it." Katie put her hand on her hip. "As long as you've known Rick Doyle, you've been running away from him. Now that he's finally showing some interest in you, why don't you stand still long enough for him to catch you?"

Christy looked around, avoiding the question. The truth was Rick could melt her with a single look. She was fine around him as long as they were teasing each other. But standing here, waiting for him like this, pushed her out of her comfort zone.

The church gym began to echo with the *thump, thump* of basketballs and the loud hoots and calls of the athletes warming up for the usual Friday rec night. The only other girls Christy noticed were sitting in a clump on the bleachers.

"Katie, I wish we hadn't come." Christy fingered her shoulder-length, nutmeg-brown hair. "I'm not into sports like you. I feel totally out of place here."

Katie's face suddenly lit up. "Don't turn around," she muttered under her breath, "but there he is!"

Christy's heart felt as though it was *thump-thump*ing as loudly as the basketballs that pounded the gym floor. "Did he see us? Is he coming over here?"

Katie looked pleased. "The answer is yes and yes, and you're on your own now. I'll see you later."

"Katie!" Christy called out as her friend jogged across the court, scooped up a basketball, and filed into line with a bunch of free-throwers.

"Hi," came a deep voice from behind Christy.

She turned slowly, letting her gaze melt into Rick's chocolate brown eyes. His dark hair looked especially good tonight, all wavy on the sides.

"Hi," she answered, feeling petite at five-foot-seven in the shadow of his six-foot-four-inch frame.

"Katie said you were coming tonight."

"And you came just to see me, right?" Christy switched from her nervousness to the lighthearted, flirty way she had been talking with Rick lately.

He played right along. "I've been counting the seconds."

"Oh yeah? How many did you count?"

"Billions."

"I didn't know you could count that high," Christy teased.

Rick playfully grabbed her by the elbow. "Is that any way to talk to the only guy here who brought you a Christmas present?"

"You did?" Christy felt her cheeks flush with surprise. Maybe what everyone had been telling her was true. Maybe Rick really did like her.

"Maybe I brought you a present and maybe I didn't." Rick grinned. "All depends. Have you been a good girl this year?"

"Oh, yes, Santa. I've been very good."

"In that case, you'd better come out to my sleigh and get your present. Especially since my elves tell me you're leaving town tomorrow."

"My whole family is going to my aunt and uncle's in Newport Beach. But we'll be gone only a week."

"A week!" Rick clutched his chest as if he were having a

heart attack. "Do you know how many billions of seconds are in a week?"

Christy laughed. "No, how many?"

"I don't know. That's why I asked you. I can't count that high, remember?"

Christy playfully swatted Rick on the shoulder, then followed him out of the gym and into the parking lot. It was a mild southern California evening. Rick had on shorts and a gray sweatshirt. Christy felt overdressed in her best jeans and nice shoes. Christy thought her outfit looked good. She thought it might help her capture Rick's attention. Apparently she didn't need a particular outfit to do that.

They batted jokes back and forth on their way to Rick's cherry red Mustang. Ever since he had given her a ride home from church over two months ago, she had watched for his car everywhere—at school, at church. It was usually full of guys and girls, and Rick was so busy with his fan club that he never noticed Christy watching from afar.

Then two weeks ago he talked to her at church, and for some reason they started this game of who could tease the other one the most. They had talked to each other every day since then, and people had started to ask Christy if they were going out.

Now, standing at the far end of the parking lot in front of Rick's car, it seemed unusually quiet after all the hubbub in the gym. Rick unlocked the front door, bent over, and grabbed a box wrapped with a huge red ribbon.

"For you," he said.

"You shouldn't have, Rick."

"I know. I know."

"Should I open it now?" She felt excited and full of

anticipation—and relieved she had a present for him too.

"Sure. Go ahead. Live dangerously," Rick said, folding his arms across his chest. "To be honest, I didn't know what to get you. My sister suggested a book. She said most girls like to read."

Christy opened the box, and, sure enough, it was a book. She held it up to read the title in the faint light: *One Hundred-Twelve Uses for a Dead Hamster*. Her emotions did a nosedive.

What kind of present is this? Does Rick actually think I'd like a joke book for a Christmas present?

Rick grinned. "I got one of the few copies left. It's bound to be a best-seller this Christmas."

"Rick, you're a sick person!" Christy felt like throwing his morbid book at him.

"Check out number fifteen," Rick said, turning the pages for her. "This is my favorite. See, you bend a coat hanger between two of them, and you've got ear muffs."

Christy didn't look at the illustration. She glared up at Rick.

Rick caught her look and held it a moment; then he thumped his forehead with the palm of his hand and said, "Oh, man! How could I have been so stupid? You already have this book, right?"

Christy burst out laughing. "You are so strange, Rick Doyle! You have to be the strangest person on the face of this earth."

"That's why I need someone like you. Someone who's pretty and charming and whose manners might rub off on me."

Christy stopped laughing. She stood perfectly still,

looking up at him, her blue-green eyes searching his in the dim light. How did he do that? Tease her mercilessly and then compliment her in the same breath.

"You really are," Rick said. "Charming, I mean." He moved a little closer to Christy and in a hushed voice said, "Actually, what I really wanted to give you I couldn't put in a box."

"Oh yeah?" Christy felt her stomach tighten. She wasn't used to being serious with Rick. "What was that?"

"This." Rick grasped her by the shoulders, bent down, and kissed her. Then he stood up straight and looked around, as if to make sure no one had seen them.

Christy swallowed and tried not to look as though the most shocking thing in the world had just happened to her. *Why did he do that? Now what? What should I say? What should I do?*

Rick stood firm, waiting for Christy's response.

"I, um, I have a present for you too," she said.

"Oh yeah?" He smiled one of his half-face grins in which only the left side of his mouth curved upward.

"Here." Christy pulled the wrapped CD from her purse and handed it to him. "I hope you don't already have this one."

The grin disappeared.

Is he disappointed that I ignored his kiss? Should I have waited longer before giving him the gift? Christy felt awkward and not at all charming.

Rick pulled the wrapping off and said with mild enthusiasm, "Oh, thanks. I don't have this one."

The weird, confusing feelings that had overwhelmed her when Rick kissed her began to evaporate. She imagined they would walk back to the gym now, both acting as though nothing out of the ordinary had happened. They would be just friends again and would go back to their flirty little games. It would be fun again instead of puzzling.

"Thanks a lot, Christy. That was really nice of you," Rick said, tossing the CD onto his front seat and locking the car door. He stuck the keys in his pocket and said in a low voice, "I was kind of hoping your present didn't come in a box either."

Her heart began to pound. *He wants me to kiss him! But do I want to kiss him? Did I even want him to kiss me the first time? Or is this part of our game, and now it's my turn to make a move if I want to keep the game going?* Before Christy could tie all her thoughts together, Rick leaned over and kissed her. This time it was longer than the first kiss.

Christy pulled away quickly. He was coming at her too fast. This was too confusing. What was he thinking? She lowered her head, and Rick let go. They stood there, silent, while Christy's heart and mind raced with mixed messages.

"Well," Rick said, clearing his throat, "I guess we'd better get back in." He nodded his head toward the gym. His expression showed that he was hurt. Or angry. Or both. Christy didn't know what to say. They walked quickly, with a tight strain between them.

The rest of the evening seemed to go on around Christy in slow motion as she kept replaying the scene in the parking lot. What had gone wrong? She liked Rick. All the girls liked him. She loved being around him and having people see them together. She loved teasing him and the way he joked with her. He had a personality like no other guy she had ever known. And he was so good-looking. He made her feel pretty when he looked at her.

And, yes, she had dreamed about what it would be like to kiss him. But in her dreams it was nothing like the way it turned out tonight. In her dreams the kiss was sweet and innocent and romantic—like it had been last summer when Todd kissed her the day she left Newport Beach. She and Todd had stood in the middle of the street with the whole world watching, and she had felt all warm and glowy inside.

With Rick she felt surprised and confused and as if they were hiding from the whole world in the dark parking lot. She wasn't ready for what had just happened.

Christy didn't take her eyes off Rick all night as he played basketball. But he never once looked her way. Was he confused too? Or was he mad at her? Had she ruined everything by not responding in a way that would let him know she liked him?

Determined to say something before she left, Christy positioned herself only a few feet from the exit and waited. Rick brushed past her, arguing with the guy next to him over who was supposed to be covering whom on the last play. Rick didn't even look at her.

The worst part was Katie's prodding on the way home. "So, he gave you a stupid book and then what?"

"I gave him the CD." Christy wasn't about to say any more, especially with Katie's mom listening as she drove the car.

"Well, did he like it?"

"He said he did."

"Then what was the problem with you two tonight? He didn't even say good-bye or anything when he left. And you were only standing a few feet away from him."

"It's no big deal. We're just friends," Christy said defensively.

"So…" Katie paused before switching subjects. "When do you leave for your aunt and uncle's?"

"Tomorrow. We'll be back on New Year's or the day after."

"Did Todd ever call? Are you going to see him next week?"

"I don't know, Katie. He hasn't called yet." The words stung as Christy said them, and Katie backed off again.

The two girls had gotten into an argument just last week over Todd. Katie told Christy to forget him, since he hadn't called or written in months, and she told Christy to go after Rick, since he was suddenly interested in her.

Christy argued that her relationship with Todd was so solid that even if she didn't see him for months, they could still pick up where they had left off last summer. Nothing would have changed between them.

Now reality was about to hit. Tomorrow she had to get in the car with her mom, dad, and eight-year-old brother, David, and drive the hour and a half from Escondido to Uncle Bob and Aunt Marti's house in Newport Beach. Todd would be there, living at his dad's house.

Then what would happen? Would Todd remember that he had called her in October and promised they would have breakfast together on the beach? Would everything still be the same between them? And what would happen with Rick while she was gone?

When she got home, Christy retreated to her bedroom. There she lifted an old Folgers coffee can from her dresser and poured out a mound of dried carnations onto her yellow patchwork comforter. The faint scent of coffee came tumbling out with what was left of the bouquet of white carnations Todd had given her the day he kissed her.

Twirling one of the withered petals between her thumb and forefinger, Christy whispered, "Lord, what's going to happen with Todd? What should I do about Rick? Everything seemed fine until tonight. Does stuff like this even matter to You? Of course it does. What am I saying? It's just that You don't speak to me and tell me what I'm supposed to do. That would make it a whole lot easier, You know."

Christy paused and pressed the flower against her cheek. "I want a second chance with Rick. I want to start over and not let everything get all weird. And I want everything with Todd to be just like it was last summer. That's all I want for Christmas, Lord. Oh, and one more thing. I want to make You happy. I mean, I don't want to mess up and make You or anybody else disappointed with me."

Christy got ready for bed, wondering if she should have prayed the way she just did, giving God a wish list as if He were Santa Claus. *At least I was honest,* she thought. *I don't want to hide anything from God. Doesn't He already know everything?*

Christy slipped between the cool sheets and curled up with the comforter tucked under her chin, clutching in her right hand a withered carnation.

2

A Promise Kept

"You about ready, Christy?" Christy's dad rapped on her bedroom door.

"I'll be right there." Christy grabbed her purse and a bag with cosmetics and hurried out to the car.

Christy's mom, a short, round woman, stood by the front door, brushing back a strand of graying hair. "Norman," she called to Christy's dad, "you'd better take your Bible. I don't know if Bob and Marti have one in their house."

"Maybe that's what we should have gotten them instead of that box of international cheeses," Dad called back in his deep voice.

Christy could tell he was teasing. Her mom had tried so hard to come up with a nice gift for Bob and Marti, the couple who had everything. When Mom came home from the mall with a big gift-wrapped box of international cheeses, for some reason Dad thought it was hilarious and had teased her for days.

"Christy," Mom said, ignoring Dad's joke, "will you put

the rest of these things in the car and tell your brother to get ready to go?"

Christy found David climbing a tree in the backyard and coaxed him down. A big kid with reddish-brown hair, he resembled their father. David had begun wearing glasses a few weeks earlier and had developed an annoying habit of scrunching up his nose to keep them from sliding off.

Christy thought it looked disgusting and kept saying, "David, don't do that!"

He would only scrunch and squint more and say, "Don't do what?" He did it about twenty times in the car during the drive up the coast to Bob and Marti's.

Finally Christy said, "You look like a hamster, David."

"I do not!" he spouted. "Mom, Christy called me a hamster!"

"Please don't start, you two. We'll be there soon. Just look at the ocean. Isn't it beautiful? Such a unique color today—almost like gray glass," Mom said.

"I miss the snow." David stuck out his lower lip in a pout. "Doesn't seem like Christmas without the snow."

"That's because you never spent Christmas day shoveling the driveway for four hours," his dad said. "I don't miss it a bit."

Mom smiled. She reached over and squeezed her husband's shoulder. Christy felt warm inside. She hadn't seen her parents this content in years. Things had been awfully hard for them back on the farm in Wisconsin. Since they had moved to Escondido in September their family had gotten much closer. Christy noticed the biggest changes in her parents after they started going to church and joined a home Bible study group. They were settled and happy.

"Can I go out on the beach as soon as we get there?" David asked.

"We'll see," Mom said.

Uncle Bob greeted them at the door of his beautiful house in Newport Beach. "Welcome, welcome! Merry Christmas! Come on in!" He had on a red vest and a matching bow tie with white lights that blinked off and on.

"Hey, cool!" David said, reaching up to touch the bow tie. "How does it do that?"

Bob patted his right pants pocket, where he had a small box with batteries. Then he lifted his vest to reveal the wire leading up to the tie.

"We special-effects guys never give away our secrets," he said with a wink to David. "But we just might have another one of these gizmos lying around. You never know."

Marti rushed up behind Bob. "Why didn't you tell me they were here, darling? Come in, come in." She wore a festive sweater that was black with a Christmas tree woven into the front and trimmed in silver with a star on top. Her earrings were little presents that matched the ones under the tree on her sweater.

Christy glanced at her family, all dressed in jeans and crumpled sweatshirts. Familiar feelings of inferiority and embarrassment spread over her. But her mom didn't seem to be ruffled, so Christy decided to not let it bother her either.

They all stepped into the living room and admired the elegant decorations. Everything was white, including a new leather couch and love seat. White and silver garlands hung across the huge window and fireplace mantle. And in front of the window stood a magnificent white-flocked tree, loaded with tiny silver balls and lamb ornaments. Dozens of gifts poured out from its base.

"Christy, remember when we picked out all these lamb ornaments in San Francisco last summer? Didn't it turn out adorable?"

"It's really pretty, Aunt Marti," Christy said sweetly. Inwardly, she missed the smell of evergreen and the homemade strings of popcorn and cranberries that laced their small tree at home.

"We brought our nativity scene," Christy said. "Could we put it up on the coffee table?"

"I suppose so," Marti said slowly. "As long as it doesn't scratch the glass, dear."

"I'll be careful."

While Dad carried in the luggage and Mom busied herself in the kitchen, Christy set up the nativity scene. She kept glancing out the huge windows at the view of the beach. Her mind flooded with thoughts of Todd. Where was he now? When would he call? Would he stop by? Would they have breakfast on the beach as he promised? Escondido and Rick and Katie all seemed far, far away. Todd and all her summer beach friends were all that mattered right now.

The family gathered around the kitchen table for soup and salad.

"I planned a light dinner," Marti explained as they sipped their French onion soup. "We have so much snack food around here, I knew we'd be nibbling all night. So many of our friends gave us food this year. And some store must have had a sale on cheese because we've been given three boxes of international cheeses!"

Dad tried to suppress a choking laugh, but he couldn't

do it. He sprayed his spoonful of soup into his napkin and then tilted his head back and roared a contagious laugh. David laughed wildly and fell off his chair for added attention. Christy giggled uncontrollably. Poor Mom looked as though she were about to cry. Then, slowly, she began to chuckle along with the rest of them.

"Was it something I said?" Marti looked bewildered, not sure if they were laughing at her or at something she had accidentally said. She looked to Bob for support.

Gentle, wise Bob calmly sipped his soup and said, "Perhaps we'll understand when we open their gift tonight." He winked at Christy's mom. "I like the Brie, myself."

Marti still looked confused, but as soon as everyone stopped laughing, she carried on as if she were still completely in control of the situation. "I thought we'd open all the gifts tonight. That way we can sleep in tomorrow morning, and we'll have a lovely Christmas dinner at one o'clock. What time do you need to get back to Escondido?"

"We both have to work the next day, so we should try to leave by five or six," Mom said.

"Which reminds me," Dad said, leaning across the table and wagging his soup spoon at Christy and David. "You two keep in mind that you're guests of your aunt and uncle this next week. They didn't have to invite you, you know. You need to make sure you do your best to fit into their plans, all right?"

They both nodded.

"Good," Dad said, and he stuck his spoon back into his soup.

Christy's mind left the family conversation and constructed elaborate dreams of when she would see Todd and what it would be like.

That evening the family gathered by the fire in the living room. Before they dove into the mound of presents, Christy's dad offered to read the Christmas story from the Gospel of Luke. He had done this every year since Christy could remember, and she nearly had the passage memorized. This year it was different. Not just because they were at Bob and Marti's, but because this year she really knew Jesus. To her, He wasn't just a little baby in a manger anymore. Last summer she had surrendered her life to Him and promised Him her whole heart. Jesus was real to Christy. His Spirit lived inside her.

"That was lovely," Marti said when Dad finished reading. "It's good for us to remember the true meaning of Christmas." Instantly, she sat upright and pointed to a small package in the front. "David, you open that one first, all right, dear? We looked all over town for this one," she confided to Christy's mom. "I couldn't believe how the price had gone up since three years ago when I got Bob's, but I knew David would want one."

David tore open the box and pulled out his own flashing bow tie. "All right!" he cheered. "How do you hook it up, Uncle Bob?"

And that's how it began: over two hours of wrapping paper flying and expensive gifts emerging, one right after the other. Next to Christy on the couch sat a pile of wonderful gifts—clothes, perfume, makeup, a CD player, and an iPod. Although she thought it was all very nice, something felt hollow. She had been through all this money-and-clothes thing with her aunt and uncle in the past, and she never felt really good about it. Right now she wished her dad would read the part about the angels and shepherds again.

She felt kind of bad too, because nobody seemed overly excited about the T-shirts she gave them. She and another friend from Escondido, Janelle, had gone to a craft store and bought the paint, stencils, and T-shirts. It cost every penny she had just for the supplies. For three days she and Janelle had worked on designing and painting the shirts. They had a great time working on them, and Christy had felt pleased at how they had turned out.

But now, watching Marti hold up the T-shirt with the large yellow sunflower carefully painted on the front, Christy knew it was a waste. Her aunt would never wear it. David liked his shirt, though, with the neon-colored surfer splashed across the front.

Then Bob lifted an envelope off one of the flocked branches of the tree and handed it to Christy. "Merry Christmas to our favorite niece," he said.

It was a bankbook for a savings account in her name, and printed in the ledger was the amount: "$10,000.00." Christy swallowed hard and showed the bankbook to her parents.

"Bob," Dad said in gruff voice, "this is going too far. We can't accept this." He looked hurt and angry at the same time.

"Let me explain," Bob said smoothly. "One of my real estate investments out in Rancho California paid off exceptionally well this year. I thought it would be profitable for me to reinvest the money into a very promising, worthwhile cause, namely, Christy's future. I set this up as a college fund. She can't touch the money until she's eighteen. I don't see how any kid can get into a decent college these days without some little nest egg stored away."

Mom looked as though she might cry.

Dad still looked angry.

"Believe me," Bob said, "you're doing me a favor. It's either a scholarship account or else I have to pay exorbitant taxes on it."

Mom smiled at her husband.

He said in a hoarse voice, "Thanks, Bob."

Christy rose and kissed Uncle Bob on the cheek. "Thank you," she said with a smile.

"What a rip!" David said. "All that money, and she can't even touch it until she's eighteen!"

"David!" Mom scolded.

Bob laughed and pulled another envelope from the tree. "This 'rip' is for you, David. You can't touch yours until you're eighteen either! I figure during the next decade this will pull in some favorable interest for you."

"Wow! Five thousand bucks!" David said, looking at the total. "Couldn't I just take a little bit of it out to buy a new bike?"

"No!" his parents said in unison.

"Bob," Marti said brightly, "why don't you give David his last gift?"

Bob pulled a small wrapped box off a top branch and handed it to David. David tore it open and pulled out a piece of paper, then read the note aloud. "Go to the closet in the hallway and see what Santa left for you."

They all followed David to the hall closet. He opened it up, and on the floor was a big bow with a long ribbon attached. The ribbon ran up and over the doorway and across the kitchen floor.

"This is cool!" David shouted. They all followed him

through the kitchen, in and out of the dining room, back through the kitchen, through the laundry room, and into the garage. There, in the center of the garage, stood a new bike with a big, white bow on it. David whooped and hollered, and there was so much commotion that when Bob turned to Christy and said, "Would you get the phone for me? It's probably your grandmother," Christy strained to hear if it was really ringing. She grabbed it in the kitchen and answered full of cheer: "Merry Christmas!"

"Hey, how's it going?"

"Todd?"

"Yeah, hi. How's it going?"

"Hi! Are you at your dad's house?"

"Yeah."

"Are you having a merry Christmas?" *That sounded so dumb!*

"Pretty good. Hey, you want to have breakfast on the beach tomorrow morning?"

"On Christmas morning?"

"Sure. Unless you have family plans in the morning. I thought I'd give it a shot."

"Yeah, I mean, no. Everyone was going to sleep in. Let me ask my parents real quick, okay? Hold on."

Christy scurried to the garage, breathless. How was she going to ask this? Would her parents understand how much this meant to her?

"Mom?" Christy broke into the group of adults as they watched David ride around in circles in the cleared garage. "Mom, one of my friends from the summer is on the phone, and they want to know if I could have breakfast with them tomorrow morning."

"On Christmas morning?"

"Well, I thought you guys were going to sleep in tomorrow."

Marti nudged her way into the conversation. "That's right. That's what we planned. I don't see why you couldn't go."

"Where are you going to eat breakfast?" Mom asked.

"On the beach. We were going to cook it out on the beach."

"I don't know, Christy." Mom hesitated.

Bob stuck his head over and said in a calm voice, "It's perfectly safe. You can see the fire pits from our living room window."

"I suppose it's all right; I'll have to ask your father. Norm?" Mom turned to get her husband's attention. "Christy wants to go out on the beach in the morning with some of her friends—for breakfast. Is that all right with you?"

"Why in the world do you want to do that?" Dad turned to look at Christy.

She glanced at her mom and Bob and Marti. They all were looking at her dad with favorable expressions on their faces. Bob was nodding his okay.

"Oh, I don't care," Dad said. "Whatever your mother says."

Christy dashed back to the phone. "Todd? Are you still there?"

"Yes."

"It's okay. I can do it. What time, and what do you want me to bring?"

"Is seven o'clock too early?"

"No. That's fine. What should I bring?"

"I went to the store already and got bacon and eggs and

orange juice, and we've got plenty of firewood here. I guess all you need to bring is yourself."

Christy smiled. "Okay. I'm really looking forward to seeing you, Todd."

"It'll be good to see you too. I'd better let you get back to your family. I didn't mean to interrupt anything."

"You didn't. That's okay. I'll see you tomorrow morning."

"Later," Todd said and hung up.

Christy held the receiver to her ear, listening to the dial tone. She whispered into the mouthpiece, "Good-bye, Todd. I'll see you tomorrow."

3

December Dawn

"What do you mean I have to take David with me?" Christy squawked.

"Your father and I thought it would be good for David to meet some of your friends. He doesn't know anyone here, and since you're both spending the week with Bob and Marti, we thought he should have a chance to make some friends."

"But, Mom," Christy said cautiously, "there won't be anybody there his age. I don't think he would have a good time. Really!"

"Then it's up to you to see to it that he does have a good time. Our decision is final. Either you both go to this crazy breakfast on the beach, or neither of you goes! What's your choice, Christina?"

"I guess David will go with me," Christy said slowly.

"Fine," her mom said, squeezing her arm and heading for the bedroom door. "Sweet dreams. And have fun in the morning."

Mom closed the door, leaving Christy alone in the bedroom that had been hers during her summer stay with Bob and Marti. She slipped under the flannel sheets and gave her pillow a few well-aimed karate chops.

"This is so unfair!" she muttered. "David is going to ruin everything! This was supposed to be just for Todd and me. I've waited weeks and weeks for this breakfast, and now David is going to ruin everything!"

Deep down she knew it was her fault. She had stretched the truth with her parents by making it sound as though the breakfast was with a bunch of friends, not with just Todd. If they knew it was only Todd they wouldn't let her go. Or would they? Rather than coming right out and asking, she had covered up the real plan, and now she was facing the consequences.

Nevertheless, she was going to see Todd in only a few hours. She couldn't let anything ruin that. Not even David. Why did Todd wait until the last minute to call her? Why was he always so easygoing and noncommittal?

Todd, you are so unpredictable! You frustrate me to pieces. Why do I feel so many deep, strong emotions toward you? What is it going to be like to see you tomorrow? Are you going to hug me? Are we going to be able to have good, long talks like we did last summer? Do you even care about me at all?

"Of course he does," Christy answered aloud. "He called, didn't he? He kept his promise about the breakfast. He even bought the food already. See, he likes you. He's been looking forward to seeing you. Don't be so insecure!"

She coaxed herself to sleep, concentrating on Todd—what he would look like after almost five months, how she would greet him, what she would wear, what they would talk about.

She smiled. As a child she had dozed off to sleep on

Christmas Eve with dreams of a new toy. Tonight she was dreaming bigger dreams—more complicated, but much more exciting. She would awaken not to Santa Claus and his gifts, but to Todd and breakfast on the beach.

At five-thirty the alarm's shrill buzz rousted her from her sweet dreams. She wanted to sleep for ten more minutes, but she didn't dare. It took more than an hour to shower and get ready. Then Christy put on some of the new eye shadow Marti had given her for Christmas. She tried the lavenders and browns but decided they made her look dull and groggy. Quickly washing the colors off, she went for three shades of very light green and a dark eyeliner. It was more than she usually wore, but she wanted to look her best. Older. *Will Todd notice?* she wondered.

Choosing what to wear was easy. Aunt Marti had given her a sweater she fell in love with the minute she pulled it out of the box. It was ivory and soft and very Christmas-y feeling. Christy slipped on her favorite pair of jeans and the new sweater. She felt snuggly and romantic—ready to see Todd.

"David, wake up!" Christy said, standing beside the hide-a-bed in the den, where her brother lay, sound asleep.

"Go away."

"Fine." Christy began to tiptoe away, her mind spinning with a plan. If she tried to wake David, but he wouldn't get up, then it wouldn't be her fault that he didn't go out on the beach with her, would it?

Suddenly, David popped his head up. "Wait a minute! We're supposed to go to the beach, huh?"

Rats! "Yes, David. Are you coming or not?"

"What's that smell?"

"What smell?"

"It smells like stinky flowers."

Christy sniffed and realized he had caught a whiff of her new Midnight Gardenia perfume. She had sprayed it in her hair and on her clothes so it would last. Maybe she had overdone it a bit.

"Just get going, David. I'm leaving in five minutes. You'd better be ready."

He sprang from the bed and hollered, "I will, I will. Close the door."

Christy popped her head into the kitchen. Uncle Bob was already up and was putting together a picnic basket.

"What are you doing?" Christy asked, surprised to see him up.

"Good morning, Bright Eyes. Don't you look terrific." He sniffed the air. "You smell pretty...ah...pretty"—he gave an impromptu cough—"pretty. That's it. You smell pretty."

Christy laughed. "I think most of it will blow away in the morning air, once I get outside."

"Let's hope so—I mean, I imagine so." Bob winked. "I tossed a few goodies into this basket for you and your friends. Hope it's enough. I didn't know how many of your friends were going this morning."

Christy felt horribly guilty. "Uncle Bob? Can I tell you something?"

Bob stopped filling the basket to give Christy his full attention. "Of course you can."

"Well, a couple of months ago Todd called me. He was still in Florida then. He said he was moving back here to live with his dad. See, his mom was getting remarried and moving to New York. Anyway, he asked me if I wanted to have breakfast on the beach with him. Then he never called again, until last night."

Uncle Bob smiled. "And you were afraid your parents wouldn't let you go alone, so you made it sound as if the whole group would be there. Am I right?"

Christy nodded.

"Somehow I thought that might be the situation." Bob reached over and squeezed Christy's hand. "Listen, I talked with your folks about it last night after they told you David was going with you. I put in a good word for Todd. They figured it would be okay, since David would be with you. But, Christy, you need to know that it hurt your parents. You're making it difficult for them to trust you. I expect more from you. Your parents deserve more than you're giving them."

By now Christy had shed big tears that dripped down her cheeks, leaving streaks from the eyeliner. She felt awful. In barely a whisper she asked, "What should I do?"

Bob straightened up, his expression tender. "Go for it, Christy. Go have a wonderful breakfast. When you get a chance this afternoon, tell your parents the whole story. They'll understand. They were teenagers once."

David pushed open the kitchen door and headed for a box of candy on the counter. "When are we going?" he asked, stuffing two chocolates into his mouth.

Christy grabbed a paper towel and dried her eyes. "I'm almost ready."

"One more spot on the side of your cheek," Bob said as Christy dabbed the last streak of runaway eye makeup.

"There, you got it. You look great."

Christy gave him an "Are you totally sure?" look.

He winked. "I like you better as a natural beauty anyway. The blue in your eyes needs no competition."

She felt a little better.

"Here's a blanket for you to sit on, and this Thermos is full of steaming cocoa. My own recipe," Bob said. "The mugs are in the basket with the croissants and fruit."

Christy scooped up the gear in her arms.

"Come on, David," she called, "let's go!"

David stuffed two more pieces of candy into his mouth and mumbled, "Okay, okay!" Then he grabbed four more chocolates and waved his full fist at Uncle Bob.

"Thank you, Uncle Bob," Christy said, tossing the blanket at David. "Here. Carry this."

"Aw, do I have to?" David complained, his paws full of candy.

"Would you rather carry this basket and Thermos?"

"No," he mumbled, stuffing the blanket under his arm and stepping into the early morning mist with his sister.

The Christmas morning sky matched the creamy blue-gray of the foaming ocean. The air, the sand, even the quick breaths Christy took felt damp and chilly.

"Lord," she whispered, "I'm sorry I messed things up. I don't want to hide stuff from my parents, and I especially don't want to hide stuff from You. I'm sorry."

She took a deep breath, filling her lungs with moist morning air and her heart with anticipation. Then she stopped.

There he was!

Tall, broad-shouldered, blond, wearing shorts and a navy blue hooded sweatshirt, Todd bent over the fire pit, poking the logs.

Christy started meshing her feet faster through the sand, David following right behind her. There Todd stood, only a few yards away, yet she couldn't get a single word out of her heart, through her mouth, and into the space that hung between them.

Suddenly David called out, "Hey, dude!"

Todd spun around.

"David! Why did you say that?" Christy scolded.

"That's what surfers say. I saw it on TV."

Christy looked up. Only a few feet away stood a confident, grinning Todd. Christy halted. Everything she had ever felt for him rolled itself into a big wad and landed in the pit of her stomach. She couldn't say a word.

Todd only grinned. Then he looked at David. "Hey, how's it going, dude?"

"See, Christy?" David said proudly. "I told you all surfers say 'dude.'"

Todd laughed. "So, what's your name, dude?"

"David."

"You ever gone out on a skim board, dude?" Todd said playfully.

"You mean in the water?"

"C'mere, dude. I'll teach ya."

Todd flashed a wide smile at Christy. His screaming silver-blue eyes pierced hers. Then he turned, slid the oval fiberglass board under his arm, and threw his other arm around David's shoulders. The two of them trotted down to the water.

Christy stood perfectly still. *Wait a minute! What's happening here? Todd! What are you doing taking off with my pesky little brother and leaving me here like this?* Christy still held the basket and blanket in her arms. *I should have dropped these the moment I saw you! I should have dropped this junk and run into your arms and hugged you the way I planned it in my dream last night.*

Now here she stood, alone, hugging her stupid blanket. *Come on, Christy. Get a grip. Act busy, like you're having fun. They'll be back up in a minute.*

She set to work, spreading out the blanket and surveying the food situation. Her mind scrambled to construct a Plan B in which she, not David, would be the center of attention. Within a few minutes, she had found everything she needed, stretched out the bacon strips in the frying pan, and placed it on the grill.

She kept glancing down the shore to where Todd was demonstrating the skim-board technique. He would wait until a wave receded, and then he would toss the board on the wet sand, run, jump on it, and skid a few feet down the shoreline before the next wave came. As it receded he would go through the same steps all over again.

Todd looked taller and more athletic than she had remembered. His hair was a darker shade of blond than in the summer, but he still wore it short. Watching him at this distance made it seem as though she were watching a home video, not actually preparing their dream breakfast on the beach.

The popping bacon called her attention back to the fire. It smelled great. Christy carefully turned each strip, making sure none of it got too well done. It looked as though Todd had remembered everything: plates, silverware, even paper towels to drain the bacon. The eggs were hard to crack, maybe because her fingers were slick from the bacon grease. But once in the frying pan, scrambled around, the eggs cooked extremely fast. Christy felt like a little pioneer woman and couldn't wait for Todd to see.

"Hey, dudes!" Christy yelled down the beach. They didn't respond. She walked closer to them and hollered again. They still didn't hear her. She glanced up and down the beach. Not another soul was out this morning. "Come on, you guys!"

They heard her and waved but kept on skim-boarding.

"Come on!" she yelled, waving for them to come. Then she whistled loudly and stood there, emphasizing the point with her hands on her hips.

They finally obliged, and Todd, red-cheeked and out of breath, jogged up to her, the wet board under his arm. He slipped his free arm around her shoulder and gave her a quick hug. Everything inside her shivered. Without saying anything, Christy slipped her arm around his waist, and they headed toward the fire pit, lost in a dream.

Suddenly Todd let go and took off running and shouting, waving his arm over his head.

"What's wrong?" Christy called out after him. David came running up beside her, and together she and David ran to the fire pit. "What happened?"

"Seagulls," Todd said, holding up a paper plate with only one strip of bacon left. "Guess they thought it was their Christmas present."

"Oh, no!" Christy cried. "Look at the eggs! They ruined everything!"

Overhead the gulls circled, their shrill appeals for more, more, more piercing the air.

"Hey, it's cool," Todd said. "We've still got some orange juice."

"But, Todd," Christy said, trying hard not to cry, "everything was perfect!"

"I already ate," David said, the telltale chocolate marks lining his lower lip. "Can I go use your skim board some more?"

"Sure, dude," Todd said, chomping into the slice of bacon. He turned to Christy. "Not bad. No wonder the birds liked it."

He looked so content—so unruffled by the catastrophe. It frustrated Christy yet set her at ease at the same time.

"I just remembered!" she said. "My uncle packed some stuff." She lifted the lid to the basket. "There's plenty in here, look! Do you like croissants?"

"Sure. What's this?" Todd held up a foil wedge of Dutch Gouda. Christy laughed and told Todd the story of the abundance of international cheese at Bob and Marti's.

He smiled, and she could see his dimples. Stretching out on the blanket, he broke open a croissant and smeared it with strawberry jam. He propped his wet feet up by the fire and said, "Good morning, Lord Jesus! Are You having a good birthday?"

Christy didn't know if she should close her eyes and bow her head or look up into the sky the way Todd was. She had never heard anyone pray like this before, but then Todd wasn't like anybody else. And the way he talked to God wasn't like anybody else either.

Todd finished with, "Amen," and then chomped into the flaky croissant. He looked at Christy and smiled. "Hey, tell your uncle thanks for me. These are good."

Christy reached for a paper towel and gently wiped the side of Todd's mouth. "You had some jelly right there," she explained. Then she immediately felt self-conscious. *Why am I wiping his mouth like he's my baby brother? Did that bother him?*

"Thanks," Todd said. Then he looked at her as she never remembered him looking at her before. It was a strong, deep, intense look that shot through her and ignited every memory she had of Todd. Every emotion. In that instant, she realized this was really Todd. They were really back together on the beach. This was the morning she had dreamed about for weeks, and her dream was coming true.

4

The Way to a Man's Heart

It seems that when dreams come true they never turn out the same way you dreamed them. They twist and turn and disappoint, leaving you wanting so much more. I don't know which to blame: the dream itself or the reality that dissolves the dream.

That's how Christy began her journal entry on Christmas night, snuggled under her warm covers in the privacy of "her" room.

The morning on the beach hadn't exactly turned out the way she thought it would. It had gone too fast. They ate, and Todd talked some about his mom's wedding. But right when Christy was finally beginning to feel at ease and enjoy their time together, Todd had jumped up, announced he had promised Shawn's parents he would be at their house at nine, and left. No big good-bye. No hug. Absolutely no hint of when he would call her or see her again.

Christy knew Todd and Shawn had been close friends for years, but Shawn had died last summer. Why was Todd leaving her to go spend the day with Shawn's parents? It didn't make sense.

She wrote in her diary how she had felt sitting alone by the dwindling fire and watching Todd walk away, his arms full of gear. He didn't even look back. Their dream breakfast was over, and she felt abandoned. Forsaken.

She probably would have stayed there, shivering in the morning chill, feeling sorry for herself, if it hadn't been for her soaked brother's whines to go back to the house. Gathering her things, she had trudged through the sand, miserable and cranky. Behind her only the fire remained, burning into ashes.

Back at the house her parents asked about "the crazy breakfast." Christy joined them at the kitchen table and began by apologizing for not being up-front about the situation. Marti kept interjecting her approving comments about Todd, and David joined her, giving full details of how Todd had taught him to skim-board.

"Sounds like a boy we'd like to meet someday," Mom said.

"But remember, Christy, you're not allowed to date until you're sixteen," Dad said. "We don't mind if you spend time with Todd and your other friends this week, as long as you're not going on a date." His tone was gruff; then he added, "Don't ever lie to your mother and me. If you want more freedom and privileges, then you show us you're trustworthy."

"She is," Bob interjected quickly.

"We want to trust you, Christy," Dad said a bit more gently, "but trust is something you earn by making wise choices and by being honest."

Christy felt humiliated, having everyone looking on as her dad lectured her.

"If we didn't trust you, Christy, we wouldn't let you stay here this week," her mom added. "Just don't take advantage of the privilege, all right?"

Christy nodded. Her stomach felt awful. She had so many things she wanted to say, like, "You can trust me. I've made a lot of wise choices you don't even know about. I'm really trying hard, even though I slip up every now and then." But all she did was force a smile and nod.

Mom smiled. Marti smiled. Bob smiled. Nobody said anything. They just smiled tight, forced smiles.

"Well," Christy said, excusing herself, "thanks for letting David and me stay this week. You can trust me. I'll do my best."

"We know you will, honey," her dad said.

Christy slipped out of the room and changed into sweats. She knew her dad was right about needing to be honest and trustworthy, and she knew she deserved the lecture. Still, it made her feel small and shaken, stripped of what little magic the morning had held.

Now, at day's end, trying to write all these feelings out, she felt even more dismal. She knew she couldn't mess things up this week. But somehow, without getting around her parents' directive, she had to spend as much time as she could with Todd. They said she could see him, just not go out with him. She would have to plan a bunch of group things, then. Get all the gang from the summer back together so she could be with Todd.

Her final entry in her diary read:

This week I've got to find out where I stand with Todd. I need to know where our relationship is and where it's going.

She had his phone number. Turning out the light, Christy determined that if he didn't call by noon tomorrow, she would call him, and she would have something planned for them to do.

The phone rang at exactly 11:45 the next day. But it was Tracy, not Todd. At first Christy acted frustrated that Tracy had called right then, but then she caught herself.

This was Tracy, her friend! And she really wanted to spend time with Tracy, too. Tracy was close friends with Todd. They could all do something together. She quickly changed her tone of voice and invited Tracy over to make cookies.

Right when she hung up, Marti came swishing down the stairs, dressed in navy blue pants, a white blouse, and a navy blue, V-neck sweater with some kind of emblem on the pocket. She looked cute—like a schoolgirl in a new uniform.

"Ready, Christy?"

"Ready for what?"

"Why, shopping, dear. I thought we'd go shopping. We're getting an awfully late start. If you want to wear what you have on, it's all right." Marti reached for her purse on the front hall tree and turned to look at Christy over her shoulder. "Well, come along, Christy. Don't just stand there."

Christy took a deep breath and two steps forward. She was taller than her aunt, and at that moment even that tiny bit of leverage helped give her courage.

"You know what, Aunt Marti? I didn't know we were supposed to go shopping. Did you mention it to me earlier?"

"I suppose not. But everyone goes shopping right after—"

Christy gently interrupted. "Since I didn't know your plans, I made my own plans. I invited Tracy over to bake cookies. Uncle Bob said it was okay."

Marti looked stunned. She stammered, "Well, then, I..."

"I didn't mean to mess up your plans. It's just that you didn't tell me."

"I see. Yes, I understand," Marti stated, pursing her lips. With a brisk turn of her head she called into the den, where the TV blared. "David! David, come here, dear."

"What is it?" David called back without moving.

"David, I want you to turn off that television and come here, darling."

"David," Christy yelled above her aunt's controlled voice. "Do what Aunt Marti says—now!"

"Okay, okay!" David, wearing cargo pants and a skateboard T-shirt, appeared in the entryway. He scrunched up his nose and squinted through his glasses. "What?"

"David, we're going shopping. Now. You need to comb your hair and get your shoes on." Marti looked awfully smug.

"Aw, do I have to go?"

"Yes!" Christy stated sternly, yet inwardly suppressing a laugh. She didn't know who would drive whom nuts first, Marti or David. This would be a shopping trip to remember.

Within five minutes they were out the door, David already begging Marti to take him to McDonald's for lunch.

Bob helped Christy find what she needed in the kitchen. It really amazed her. At home they never had this much food in the refrigerator at one time. Their cupboards never held so much nor such a variety. Bob even had different kinds of chocolate chips, including white chocolate. These cookies were going to be gourmet!

Tracy arrived and handed Christy a plate of fudge. "This is for you. My mom and I make fudge every year. I hope you like it."

"Are you kidding? I love anything chocolate. Thanks, Tracy. But now I feel bad that I don't have something for you."

Bob's voice came from the den. "Do you like cheese, Tracy?"

"Pardon me?" Tracy called back.

"Never mind," Christy said, laughing and steering Tracy away from her crazy uncle and into the kitchen. "Come on. Let's make some cookies. We have enough ingredients to make a couple of batches. I thought maybe we could take some to some people this afternoon, if they turn out well."

Petite Tracy, her shoulder-length brown hair pulled back in a ponytail, smiled a knowing smile. "You mean, maybe we could take some to Todd?"

Christy blushed. "Yes. And everybody else, too. Heather and Doug, and you know, all the guys from this summer."

Tracy placed her hand on Christy's arm and, with a teasing look on her face, said, "You don't have to explain, Christy. I know who you mean. And yes, I think Todd would really appreciate it."

They both giggled.

"Is there anybody in particular you'd like to deliver a box of cookies to?" Christy probed, curious if Tracy had her heart set on any certain guy.

"Well, actually..." Tracy didn't look up as she hesitated;

then she said, "I'm sort of interested in somebody, but I don't think he's interested in me."

"Who?"

"I don't want to say. I'd feel horrible if everybody knew that I liked him, especially if he's not interested in me."

"Oh, come on! Tell me!"

"I'll tell you this week if he acts at all interested in me. Otherwise, I'm going to give up on him."

"You'd better tell me."

"I will. I promise. Only if it looks like there's any hope, okay?"

"Okay."

The girls shook hands on it and set to work.

Bob had a great kitchen for cooking: plenty of counter space and every possible size of measuring cup and mixing bowl. They started with a huge mixing bowl and doubled Bob's own recipe for gourmet chocolate chip cookies, using real butter and mixing it with brown and white sugar until it looked like caramel pudding. Next came eggs, flour, baking soda, and then the chocolate chips.

"Which kind should we put in?" Christy asked, snitching some white chocolate chips and popping them into her mouth.

"How about both?" Tracy said, pouring both bags of chips into the bowl.

Christy laughed and grabbed a scoop of dough. "These are going to be so good!"

They worked together, nibbling on the dough, then placing rounded balls on the cookie sheets.

"Do you want anything to drink?" Christy asked, looking in the refrigerator.

"Do they have any diet drinks?"

Christy turned around and burst into laughter.

"What's so funny?" Tracy asked, popping another ball of cookie dough into her mouth.

"I just think it's funny that we've eaten about ten thousand calories in cookie dough, and you ask for a diet drink."

Tracy laughed and washed the dough off her hands. "Never mind. I'll just have some water. I feel kind of sick to my stomach from all this dough."

"Me too. Let's get these two cookie trays going so we can take them to Todd's. You put them in the oven, and I'll find a couple of boxes to put them in," Christy said.

She set to work lining two nice boxes with tissue paper. Within half an hour the boxes were filled with warm, soft, delicious cookies.

"Should we take these over now?" Christy hoped Tracy wouldn't think she was being pushy or acting as if she didn't want to be with Tracy but only wanted to be with Todd.

"Sure," Tracy agreed without hesitation. "We can freeze the rest of this dough. That's what my mom always does. We'd better clean the kitchen up, though."

"I'll do the dishes," Christy volunteered. "Do you want to get your box of cookies ready for your mystery boyfriend? Now, what was his name...?"

"Christy, Christy!" Tracy said in a mock scolding voice. "I told you, I'd only tell if he showed interest in me on his own. I don't like it when it turns into a game and everybody except the guy knows you like him. Then all your friends go up to him and say, 'Guess what? Tracy likes you!' And then the poor guy has to decide if he's going to break your heart or play along with the game. I don't want to play that game with—" She caught herself.

"With…?" Christy prodded.

Tracy covered her mouth with her hand. "I can't believe it! I almost said his name, didn't I?"

"Your secret would have been safe with me."

"I know it would, Christy. But haven't you ever been caught in the middle of a relationship, and you suddenly look at it for what it really is, and you say, 'Wait a minute! This is everyone else's idea, not mine'? And you wish you could start all over and just be friends for a while without all the pressure everyone else puts on you to be boyfriend and girlfriend?"

Christy pulled up a stool and sat down. "Tracy, I know exactly what you mean. There's this guy at school, Rick, and I don't know if I really like him or if I just like him because everyone keeps saying, 'Oh, Rick asked about you today. He likes you—we can tell.' So, yes, I know exactly what you mean, and I won't bug you anymore."

"Do you like Rick?"

"Yes and no. It's not the same as it is with Todd. Like yesterday. Nothing turned out the way I thought it would when we made breakfast on the beach. Todd left without saying if he'd call or anything. I felt depressed about it, but I didn't worry about whether or not Todd liked me anymore. I feel that the next time I see him, we'll just pick up where we left off."

"Todd has that way about him, doesn't he? He has to be the most loyal guy in the world," Tracy agreed. "Once you're his friend, you're always his friend."

"Exactly! But it's not that way with Rick at all. When I

came up here a couple of days ago, he wasn't speaking to me. I can't even guess what things will be like when I see him again."

"Don't you hate that?"

"Yes!"

Tracy pulled the last cookie sheet from the oven and turned it off. "And that's why, even though I like this one guy a lot, I'm going to wait for him to show some interest in me, unprompted by all my well-meaning friends."

"You're a good influence on me, Tracy," Christy said as she returned to the sink and finished loading the dishwasher. "I don't know if I ever thanked you for the Bible you and Todd gave me."

"You did. And speaking of Todd, I'm going to call him and make sure he's home," Tracy said.

"Good idea!" Christy couldn't wait to get going. "I'll be ready as soon as I brush my hair and tell my uncle where we're going."

Christy loved this feeling of independence, being able to bake cookies, talk so openly with Tracy as if they'd been best friends all their lives, and now go over to Todd's house.

That last part seemed too good to be true. After five months of being thousands of miles apart and carrying on a one-sided correspondence with Todd, he was so nearby that she could simply walk over to his house and see him and talk to him and be close to him.

The painful part was that they had only a few days to be this close. Christy knew that every moment with Todd had to count.

5

All-Time Friends

"Hold on a minute, girls," Uncle Bob called as they headed out the door. "Almost forgot. I've got something for Todd too." Uncle Bob appeared at the door with a gift bag all tied up. "Have fun, ladies!"

"What is it?" Christy asked, shaking the bag.

Uncle Bob gave her one of his "twinkle-grins" and said, "A little something a guy like Todd might appreciate."

The afternoon was clear and warm, yet the brisk wind made Christy glad she had put on a sweatshirt. She wondered if Todd still wore the sweatshirt she got for him in San Francisco last summer. A bigger question was whether he would like the T-shirt she painted for him.

"Did you get anything for Todd?" Christy asked Tracy.

"Yes, I usually buy him a present. This year I got him a CD. The new Debbie Stevens one. Do you have it?"

"No. I bought one, but I ended up giving it to Rick. I kind of wish I hadn't because I don't think he liked it."

"What did Rick give you?"

"A stupid book. It was a joke. Some guys have such a strange sense of humor."

Tracy laughed. "Don't I know it!"

"I have a T-shirt for Todd," Christy explained. "But I don't know if I should give it to him. I painted a surfer on it. I was going to give it to him yesterday, but I completely forgot about it. It was probably a good thing, because he didn't give me anything."

"Except the breakfast," Tracy reminded her. "I was pretty impressed when I heard he bought the food and set the whole thing up. That's a nice gift, if you ask me."

"You're right. I should be more grateful. It's just that the birds ate everything, and my little brother ended up spending more time with Todd than I did."

"Still, Christy. What girl wouldn't love for her boyfriend to go to all that trouble for her?"

"My boyfriend?"

"Well, you know, Todd's your friend, and he's a boy. I don't know what else to call him." Tracy led Christy around a corner and down the street to where Todd lived.

"You know what? I wish there was a word for something between 'just friends' and 'boyfriend.'"

"I know what you mean," Tracy said. "And there needs to be a word between 'like' and 'love' too. Either you 'like' a guy or you're supposedly 'in love.' There's definitely a middle area, but there's no word for it."

"Then let's make up a word!"

Tracy laughed. "Should we ask Todd to help us? This is his house." She stopped in front of a narrow two-story house that faced the street, not the beach. From the outside it looked smaller than Bob and Marti's, but newer.

"Merry day after Christmas!" Christy said brightly when Todd answered the door.

"Hey, how's it going?" Todd said, welcoming them into the messiest living room Christy had ever seen. Newspapers, dirty dishes, and clothes were all over the place. The most obvious thing to her, though, was the absence of any Christmas decorations. No tree, no wreaths. No evidence that a family lived here or had celebrated Christmas.

"Sorry it's such a mess," Todd apologized, clearing a place for them to sit on the couch. "The housekeeper hasn't come yet this week. My dad's in Switzerland."

"Switzerland?" Christy said in surprise.

"How long has he been gone?" Tracy asked.

"Four or five days. I think he gets back on Saturday."

"Todd!" Tracy looked as distressed as Christy felt. "What did you do for Christmas?"

He turned to Christy and smiled. "Had breakfast on the beach and then hung out at Shawn's."

Tracy hesitated and then said, "I bet they appreciated your being there." She held out her bag full of gifts.

Christy followed, handing him her bag and saying, "Merry Christmas from us a day late, or a year early, whichever you prefer. Go ahead! Open your presents!"

Todd sat down and gathered the boxes on his lap. He opened Bob's gift bag first. Christy groaned when Todd pulled out a handful of international cheese triangles.

"Cool!" Todd said. "Is this the same kind we had for breakfast?"

"Who knows," Christy said, shaking her head. "We have such a variety of cheeses to choose from! My uncle sent them over. I didn't know what he put in the bag. Open the box. I know you'll like what's in there."

"Oh, man!" Todd exclaimed, pulling off the lid and grabbing a soft cookie. "Did you make these?"

"Tracy and I did. Just this afternoon. Do you like them?"

Todd scarfed down two before answering with a garbled, "Definitely!"

"Now try the fudge!" Tracy opened her box, and Todd complied, stuffing the biggest piece into his mouth.

The girls laughed as he tried to swallow and compliment Tracy on the fudge at the same time.

He opened the CD next and said, "Thanks, Trace. You don't know how much I appreciate this."

"One more," Tracy said, handing him Christy's box.

Christy felt queasy. Would he like it? Would he ever wear it? Should she have given him a CD too, like Tracy had?

"Cool!" Todd held up the shirt, and Tracy added her *oohs* and *aahs*.

"Do you really like it?" Christy asked.

"Definitely!" Todd said, giving her a deep, warm look.

"That is really good, Christy," Tracy said. "She painted it herself, Todd. Did you know that?"

"No way! Really?"

Christy felt her cheeks turning red. She nodded, feeling relieved that he really seemed to like it.

Todd stood up, stepped over a pile of newspapers, and gave Christy a hug around the neck and then gave Tracy the same. "Thanks, Christy. Thanks, Tracy."

He snatched up another cookie and headed for the

kitchen. "Either of you want something to drink? We've got cranberry juice and 7-Up."

"Got milk?" Tracy asked with a laugh.

Todd stuck his head back into the living room with a grin on his face. "Nope. Drank the last of it this morning."

"Then I'll have 7-Up," Tracy called to him.

"Me too," Christy echoed.

"I have a strong urge to find the vacuum cleaner and go to work on this place," Tracy whispered while Todd was still in the kitchen. "It's such a mess."

For the first time ever, Christy felt sorry for Todd, and it surprised her. For so long he had made her feel all kinds of emotions, but she had never pitied him. Now seeing him in this messy, expensively decorated house and knowing he had been all alone for Christmas made her heart ache for him. How could his parents abandon him like that? And on Christmas?

Perhaps their breakfast on the beach had been a dream for him as well. She was seeing a whole new side of Todd, and she wanted so badly to tell him how deeply she cared for him.

"Can I put the CD on?" Tracy asked when Todd stepped back into the living room.

"Sure."

Tracy turned on the elaborate stereo and took out the CD that was already in the CD player. She looked at it before putting the new Debbie Stevens CD in and then yelled, "Todd! Why didn't you tell me you already had this CD?"

"It's cool," he said, handing Christy a can of 7-Up. "I'll keep one in the house and one in Gus the Bus."

"Did you put a CD player in Gus?" Tracy asked.

"No, but I plan to. One day."

"Well, Todd, if you hadn't taken the cellophane off, I could have taken it back and bought you something else. A different CD or something."

Todd stood next to Christy and said, "It's a Christmas present from you, Tracy. I would never take back anything one of my all-time friends gave me."

"Now that's good," Tracy said, turning to Christy. "'All-time friends.' What do you think of that?"

Christy thought for a moment. "It's all right, but not exactly it."

"Not exactly what?" Todd asked, plopping down next to her on the couch.

"On the way over we were trying to think of an expression for whatever it is that comes between 'like' and 'love' or between 'just friends' and 'in love.' Got anything better than 'all-time friends'?"

"Not me. I'm not the writer in this group. You are, Christy."

Christy put up her hands as if defending herself. "I don't have any great ideas."

"We'll have to work on that one," Tracy suggested. "And you know what else I'd like to do this week while we're all together? I'd like to talk about stuff in the Bible. You know, maybe everyone can read the same thing and then talk about it when we get together."

Todd and Christy both looked at her as if they weren't sure what to make of her suggestion.

"What do you want us to read?" Todd asked.

"How about Philippians? Or First John? Or some of the Psalms?"

"First John sounds good," Todd said.

"All right, good." Tracy looked pleased with herself.

"Do you want to do something tomorrow?" Christy blurted out. Todd and Tracy both looked at her, waiting for her to go on.

"I mean, you guys could come over, or we could all go do something together."

"Sure," Todd said without hesitating. "What do you want to do?"

"We could go to the movies," Tracy suggested. "That is, if there's anything worth seeing. Or we could rent a video and watch it at my house."

"Do you guys ever go ice-skating?" Christy asked. She had ice-skated every winter since she could remember, outside on the frozen pond with all her friends. California had to have indoor rinks somewhere where they could all go.

"That sounds like fun!" Tracy said. "Let's get everybody together and go tomorrow to that rink in Costa Mesa. If we all pitch in for gas, will you drive, Todd?"

"Sure. When do you want to go?"

"I don't know. About one or two. We could all meet at my house," Tracy said. "Let's meet around noon for lunch. My mom won't mind. Then we could all leave from there."

"Sounds cool. What time is it now?" Todd asked.

Tracy looked at her watch. "Oh, no, Christy! It's almost five."

"I have to go too," Todd said. "I'm going over to Doug's. I'll tell him about ice-skating tomorrow."

"Could I go with you to Doug's?" Tracy asked.

"Sure. Come on, Christy. I'll drop you off on the way."

They all hopped into Todd's old VW van, "Gus the Bus." Both girls squeezed into the front seat, with Christy closest to Todd. Christy couldn't help but smile to herself with memories of last summer when more than once she had been jealous of Tracy because Tracy had been the one sitting in the front seat and Christy had been in the back. Now they were sharing the seat and sharing their friendship with Todd. The three of them really, truly were "all-time friends" together. It was a wonderful thing to Christy, and it made her feel good deep inside.

When Todd pulled up in front of Bob and Marti's, he thanked Christy again for the shirt and cookies.

"I'm glad you like them," Christy said. She wanted to reach over and hug him and tell him she was sorry he'd been alone for most of Christmas. She wanted to whisper in his ear that she couldn't wait to see him again tomorrow. But all she did was smile and look into his clear, blue eyes and say, "Thanks for the ride."

Todd tilted his chin back, gave her his usual "Later," and then drove off with Tracy.

Christy stood on the curb and waved good-bye to her two "all-time friends." When she turned to walk back into Bob and Marti's house, her heart was full of anticipation. So what if her breakfast with Todd hadn't been all that special? Tomorrow they would go ice-skating, and he would hold her hand. He'd have to. It's very natural for people to hold hands when they skate. She knew how wonderful it felt to slip her hand into his. Even though it had been months, she remembered exactly what Todd's hand felt like. Tomorrow she'd feel it again: strong and warm and wonderful.

Smiling widely to herself, Christy opened the front door and stepped inside. *Todd and I really, truly are more than "in like." I just know it. Maybe we're even on our way to "in love."*

6

Skating Along

That evening at the dinner table, David squished his green beans with his fork and gave his opinion of shopping with Aunt Marti.

"She made me buy a pink shirt, Christy. Pink!" He scrunched up his nose in his favorite hamster look.

"David looks very good in muted colors. It isn't really pink. I'd say it was a light mauve tone," Aunt Marti said.

"It's pink," David muttered. "And the McDonald's we went to didn't even have a playground."

"You're getting a little too old for playgrounds, don't you think, dear?" Aunt Marti's smoothly made-up face seemed to twitch just a bit. Christy wondered how awful the experience had actually been. Who had been the most ornery—Marti or David?

"I know a playground down at Balboa for big kids," Uncle Bob said. "Why don't we go there tomorrow, David? If I can still play there, so can you."

David nodded and smiled, his mouth full of baked potato. It wasn't a pretty sight.

"Then Christy and I will spend the day shopping," Aunt Marti stated.

"I kind of already made some plans for tomorrow," Christy said slowly. "Tracy invited me over to her house at noon, and then a bunch of us are going ice-skating. Todd said he would drive. Would that be okay?"

"Sounds like fun," Uncle Bob said.

Aunt Marti put down her fork with an exaggerated thump. "I'm surprised, Christina, at how quickly you've managed to fill up your social calendar this week. Do you suppose you'll have any time to fit us into your plans?"

"We just decided today, Aunt Marti. I didn't know you had anything else planned!" *There was a time, dear aunt, when you pushed me out on the beach to make these new friends. Do you now object to my spending time with them?*

In a squeezed voice, Aunt Marti said, "Tell me, dear, are you available, say, the day after tomorrow? Perhaps we could go to lunch."

Christy glanced at Uncle Bob and then answered in a voice that came out too sweet, too bright: "Sure! That would be great."

Satisfied, Aunt Marti smiled, looked at her food, and slowly took another bite.

All Christy could think was, *A whole day. I'm going to end up spending a whole day with my aunt, and I could have been spending it with Todd.*

When Aunt Marti dropped Christy off at Tracy's house the next day she said, "Now remember, we've got plans for tomorrow, so please don't promise any of your friends that you'll do something with them. All right?"

Christy agreed and thanked her aunt for the ride, but

inside she felt soured. Her aunt had manipulated her all last summer, but now it irritated her to pieces. She no longer welcomed Aunt Marti's interference in her life.

Nevertheless, her dad had said she was to remember that she was a guest this week, and she was to fit into her aunt and uncle's plans. She would simply have to try harder.

Heather and Leslie opened the door and warmly greeted Christy. She stepped into the living room, where two guys were planted in front of the TV, playing a video game.

She could see Todd in the kitchen, helping Tracy and her mom make pizza. He sprinkled a handful of cheese onto the top before shoving another handful of cheese into his mouth. Tracy playfully punched him in the arm. Christy wondered if she should go into the kitchen or wait until Todd noticed her.

"Christy!" Doug suddenly stood in front of her. He had changed a lot since the summer. Home for Christmas vacation after his first semester at San Diego State, he looked like a college student. His blond hair was styled shorter than the last time she'd seen him. He wore a neatly pressed green shirt and was clean-shaven. The only thing that hadn't changed was the little boy look in his eyes when he grinned.

"Hi, Doug!"

"How are you?" He gave her an awkward hug around the neck and said, "Come over here and sit down. Tell me about Escondido. How's school? Do you like it better here than in Wisconsin?"

They chatted easily for a few minutes, with Doug turned sideways, resting his arm on the back of the couch. "You look good in blue," he said. "Makes your eyes look real clear."

Christy could feel herself blushing as she said, "Thanks."

Just then Todd walked into the living room. Christy caught a glimpse of him out of the corner of her eye. Was he coming over to talk to her? No, he went back into the kitchen.

Doug talked about school and his new truck. Then, out of nowhere, he said, "You know, Christy, I'm so glad you're here and that everything's going well for you!" He gave her another quick, awkward hug. It was a real "Doug" thing. He was always hugging people and trying to cheer them up and encourage them.

Just then, Tracy popped her head into the room. When her gaze fell on Doug and Christy hugging on the couch, she gave them a strange look that lasted for only an instant. Then she called out, "Come eat, you guys! Pizza's ready!"

They gathered in the kitchen around the counter, which was spread with soft drinks, paper plates, and three steaming pizzas. Doug reached over and snitched an olive. Christy playfully swatted his hand. She caught Tracy's gaze, and again, for a brief moment, Tracy looked mad.

"Let's pray, you guys," Brian suggested and took the hands of the people standing next to him around the counter.

The rest of them followed his gesture. Doug took Christy's hand as she reached for Heather's on the other side. Doug's hand felt strong, a little bit rough, but very warm.

The sensations confused her. They were supposed to be praying, like brothers and sisters, yet she felt a bombardment of mixed emotions.

I wish I were holding Todd's hand instead. Or do I? Doug is acting inter-

ested in me, but is he really? Why is Tracy looking mad? Was I supposed to
help her make the pizza? And why is she over there, next to Todd, when that's
where I want to be?

"Amen," Brian said. They dropped hands and dove for
the pizza.

Christy felt ashamed that she hadn't heard a word of
Brian's prayer. She slipped one slice of pizza onto her plate,
grabbed a can of soda pop, and found a chair at the kitchen
table next to Heather. She thought it would be good if she
kept her distance from the guys for a few minutes, until she
had her thoughts straight.

"Your hair looks cute," she said to Heather, who automatically patted the French braid Leslie had made.

"It feels as though it's about to fall out."

"Doesn't look like it," Christy said, examining the braid
more closely.

"Your hair is long enough to braid," Heather commented. "I can't believe it grew so fast!"

"I like it long," said a male voice.

Christy turned to see Todd sitting down next to her.

"What?" Heather said in a squeaky voice. "You like
Christy's hair long? When did you ever see it long?"

Todd took a bite of his pizza, the cheese stringing out.
Doug reached over and broke the string bridge with his finger before sitting down across from Christy. She felt excited
with the sudden attention, yet uncomfortable at the same
time.

Todd swallowed his wad of pizza and looked right at
Christy with an expression she didn't recognize. "Used to
be almost to her waist," he said. "I liked it long." Then he
took another bite of pizza.

Christy sat perfectly still, running the information through her mind. She came to California last summer with long hair but had it all whacked off the day before she met Todd. How would he know she used to have long hair?

"I liked it long too," Doug added.

Just then Tracy came over to the table and took the last chair, right next to Doug.

"What are you guys talking about?" she asked.

"Tracy," Heather said, sounding perplexed, "did you ever see Christy with long hair? These guys are being mean and saying they liked her better with long hair."

The girls looked at Christy, waiting for her to make sense of the conversation. The guys kept eating, glancing at each other as if they knew some great secret.

Christy quickly pulled an explanation together. "I had long hair the first few days I was here last summer, but I got it cut the day before I met all of you. I don't know when these guys saw it long, unless..." She stopped. "Oh, no. Were you the guys who made fun of my old bathing suit that day on the beach?" Christy looked at them with panic in her eyes.

"What bathing suit?" Tracy asked.

"What day?" Heather said. "What are you talking about?"

Doug and Todd kept eating, wearing their smirky little expressions. Christy looked as though she was about to throw something at them.

Doug must have realized her intentions because he quickly swallowed, leaned forward, and said, "We weren't the ones who made the rude comments. But we did notice you that day."

There was a pause, and then Doug added, "We definitely noticed you that day."

"You were kind of hard to miss," Todd mumbled before stuffing another bite of pizza past his upturned lips.

Doug nearly choked on his drink when Todd said it. He grabbed a napkin, covered his mouth and nose, and sputtered, "Rude, Todd! Rude!"

Christy wanted to run from the room and cry her eyes out. How could they do this to her? That was a horrible experience, the day the surfers had laughed at her "green bean" bathing suit. Why would Todd and Doug be so mean as to bring it up now? She lowered her head and blinked fast so the tears wouldn't come.

"Anybody else want some more pizza?" Todd said, getting up from his chair. Then, before he left the table, he leaned over and whispered in Christy's ear so no one else could hear, "I like your hair now, but I really liked it long." Then off he went to get more pizza.

Christy's heart pounded. She could still feel the sensation of his whisper, his warm breath on her neck. The welled-up tears instantly evaporated, but then the anger came. *Why do you always do this to me, Todd?* she thought. *You put me on this roller coaster, and the worst part is, you seem to enjoy it!*

Skinny Heather turned red in the face and pounded her hand on the table. "You guys are all a bunch of...you're all..."

"Gweeks?" Doug questioned and let out a hearty laugh.

Todd returned laughing too, looking as if he were having a great time.

"Well, maybe we girls just don't want to go ice-skating with all you 'gweeks.' What do you think, Tracy, Christy, should we leave these guys and go to the mall?"

"No!" Tracy said too quickly, and they all looked at her in surprise. "I mean, I already called the ice rink, and they're giving us a discount because we have more than eight people coming."

"We should make the guys go by themselves and pay the higher price," Heather said and then gave Todd and Doug a playful smirk. For emphasis she quickly stuck out her tongue at them.

"I wouldn't keep a dirty thing like that in my mouth either," Doug said.

Todd joined him in another boom of laughter. They were like that all the way to the ice-skating rink—like two eight-year-olds full of little boy tricks and jokes. It drove Christy crazy. She confided her frustration to Heather as they sat on a bench, watching the group skate to the blaring music.

"Todd is driving me crazy! He's acting like such a brat. I'm almost expecting him to pull a frog out of his pocket and chase me around the parking lot!"

"Do you really like him?" Heather asked. Wisps of her thin blond hair had come out of the braid and now danced around her face. She looked so innocent, so trustworthy.

"Can I tell you something?" Christy asked, lowering her voice.

"Of course." Heather's eyes grew wide in anticipation.

"I really, really, really like Todd. But I can't figure out where I stand with him. One day he acts as if he likes me; the next day he's a brat."

"That's because he doesn't know how much you like him! You're so cute and sweet and friendly with everybody,

I bet he has no idea that you're really interested in him more than, say, Doug."

"That's the crazy part," Christy confided. "I almost thought he was jealous at Tracy's because I was talking to Doug. But then he and Doug said all that embarrassing stuff, and I could have slugged both of them."

"You should have!" Heather said. "You know, I think that might be the way to go."

"What, physical abuse?"

"No." Heather giggled. "Get Todd jealous. He's not a real fast mover, you know."

"Yes, I know."

"So, motivate him. Flirt your face off with Doug, and Todd will see that he's going to lose you if he doesn't act quickly."

"I don't know, Heather. I'm not sure playing games is the way to go—with any guy."

"Just try it. What have you got to lose? Go ask Doug to skate and see what happens."

Christy shook her head hesitantly.

"What have you got to lose? Come on, Christy. Try it. Go!"

Christy reluctantly pegged her way across the floor on her ice skates and stood by the rail, watching the blur of people skating by. She saw Todd slowly skating on the outside with two junior high girls fluttering nearby, ready to pounce whenever he tumbled, which was quite often. Todd might be the tall, handsome champion surfer, but he was a klutz on ice skates. Christy figured it must be a different set of muscles or a different sense of balance. Whatever it was, she had it and Todd definitely did not. The junior high girls spotted him the minute he came in and had followed him around the rink all afternoon.

Christy smiled, remembering when she and Paula, her old best friend in Wisconsin, were that age. They used to hover around the cute older guys, dreaming big high school dreams and exaggerating the stories about the guys each time they retold them.

Now Christy was a big high-schooler. Was she still playing games? Was Heather's make-him-jealous idea as stupid as some of the ideas Christy and Paula had schemed up in junior high?

Just then the music stopped, the skaters cleared the ice, and the lights dimmed. The disc jockey announced a couples' skate.

Christy wished she were stepping out on the ice at that moment with Todd holding her hand, the way she had dreamed the day before.

"There you are," Doug said, suddenly coming up behind her. "I was looking for you. Want to skate?"

"I, well..." Christy hated it when she stammered like this. She didn't want to play a game to make Todd jealous, yet Doug had asked her, not the other way around. She glanced back at Heather, who was urging her with a wide-eyed expression to move forward.

"Come on!" Doug said, taking her by the hand. "You know how to skate, Christy. I saw you out there. Don't act like you don't."

Doug knew how to skate too. Forward, backward—she had even seen him do a halfway decent spin in the center of the floor earlier. Now they skated hand-in-hand around the dimly lit rink. They were smooth.

Doug said, "Let's try something." He pulled around in front of her so that he was skating backward. He put his hands on her waist, and she put hers on his upper arms. "You tell me if I'm going to crash, okay?"

"I hope you've done this before," Christy said tensely, "because I can only skate forward."

"No way! You can skate backward, can't you?"

"Look out!" Christy cautioned.

Doug glanced over his shoulder and barely missed two little kids who had just tumbled. "Close one! Good call! Here, I'll teach you how to skate backward."

For the rest of the couples' skate, Doug and Christy worked on their little routine. First Doug skated backward, then he would gently spin Christy around so she was going backward. At first she kept looking over her shoulder, but then she relaxed and had a great time, feeling like a ballet dancer gracefully slicing through the air. It was wonderful.

She looked for Todd but didn't see him. Was he watching her? What was he thinking?

The soft music came to an end, and the lights went back up. The floor flooded with noisy skaters. Doug directed Christy to the center of the rink to work out a spin in which Doug would twirl Christy around and she would end up in his other arm. It was so much fun Christy barely noticed when the lights dimmed again and "triples" were announced.

"Let's get another person so we can keep skating," Doug said. "There's Heather."

He pointed to a waving Heather at the sidelines and motioned for her to come out on the ice to join them. Heather grabbed Doug's free hand, and the three took off around the rink.

When Doug wasn't looking, Heather motioned to Christy as if to say, "Good work! You're flirting with Doug just the way I told you to!"

Christy was quiet. She had forgotten all about trying to make Todd jealous. She and Doug were just having fun. It was no big deal. She didn't even feel all that tingly about him holding her hand anymore. As a matter of fact, his hands were kind of sweaty.

"Look!" Heather squeaked and pointed to a threesome bumbling along in front of them.

It was Todd and two of the adoring junior-highers.

"Hey, dude," Doug called as they skimmed past, "nice crutches."

The girls giggled and tugged on Todd's arms, pulling him along. Todd looked absolutely miserable. Christy felt guilty and jealous. Guilty for being with Doug and, as crazy as it sounded, jealous of the junior high girls. What were those little squirts doing with her "boyfriend," anyway?

This was not the way she had hoped the day would be. It had to get better. It had to change back into the dream she'd imagined the day before, where Todd—and not Doug—was the one making her feel like a floating angel. This was not at all turning out the way Christy wanted it to. She had to talk to Todd.

7

The Hurt Puppy

Around five-thirty the group members turned in their skates and piled into Todd's van. A discussion ensued as to what they should do next—all go home or go to dinner or go to a movie and have popcorn and M&M's for dinner.

Christy felt like going home and starting the day over. She had spent the whole time at the ice rink with Doug and hadn't said one word to Todd. Sitting now in the front seat of Gus, she realized that this was the closest she had been to Todd all day. He looked okay—not mad or miserable but not great. Just okay.

The group voted on going to dinner at Richie's. Todd started up Gus and chugged out of the parking lot.

"I'd better call my aunt and uncle to make sure it's okay," Christy said softly.

Without turning to look at her, Todd, in his matter-of-fact way, said, "It's on the way. We'll stop by. If they say no, you're already home."

What's that supposed to mean? Christy thought. *That you don't want me to go? Are you hoping they'll say no so you can drop me off and be rid of me? Todd! I've waited months to see you, and now I can't even talk to you!*

When they pulled up in front of the house, Doug called after her, "Bring back some of those cookies you and Tracy made."

Christy hurried into the house and called out, "Uncle Bob?"

"In here," he answered from the den, where he sat with his feet up, reading the paper. The TV was on, and David was half watching it and half tinkering with his remote-control car.

"Everybody's out front waiting. They want to go to some place called Richie's for dinner. May I go with them?"

"Richie's, you say? Good choice. Sure. Here," he said, reaching into his pocket. "I've only got fifty dollars. Think that'll be enough?"

"Oh, that's too much. I only need eight or ten dollars, I think."

"Take the fifty. Treat your friends to my favorite at Richie's: Oreo Fantasy shake. It's a killer. Have fun!"

"Where's she going?" David called out as Christy dashed out the door.

She jumped into Gus with renewed vigor. "My uncle gave me fifty bucks and told me to treat everybody to some kind of Oreo shake."

Only Todd heard her. Everyone else was wrapped up in various conversations, and Heather was laughing loudly in the backseat.

"Cool," was all Todd said without looking at her.

Come on, Todd! she thought, annoyed. *Talk to me! What's wrong?*

Just then Doug leaned forward, his head between Christy and Todd, and said, "Where are the cookies?"

"There weren't any left."

"Those were great cookies," Doug said. "Didn't you think so, Todd?"

Todd nodded but didn't say anything.

Now Christy was getting mad. Why was he acting like such a baby?

"So," Doug continued, apparently not bothered by the tension that seemed to hang between Todd and Christy, "when do you want to go skating again, Christy? We were getting pretty good out there. Did you see us, Todd? What do you think? Not bad, huh?"

Todd's words came out slowly and deliberately. "You're good, Doug. You two looked real good together."

Christy had heard those words before. That same phrase had run through her mind a dozen times last night when she had dreamed about what it would be like to skate hand-in-hand with Todd, not with Doug! Todd wasn't supposed to say that. Somebody else was supposed to say that about her and Todd. Everything was turned around.

Todd pulled into a parking place next to the pier. The group tumbled out of the van, talking and laughing.

Doug opened Christy's door. "You coming?" he asked.

She climbed out and joined the gang marching down the pier. Todd led the pack, and Tracy was with Brian and Heather. Doug stayed right beside Christy.

The wind off the ocean whipped around them from every angle, chilling Christy to the bone. Diehard fishermen in down jackets lined the pier, their fishing poles jutting into the dark waters below. The crashing surf sprayed the air with a fine mist. Christy hugged herself, rubbing her arms to get warm.

"You cold?" Doug asked. Before she could answer, he slipped his jacket around her and left his arm around her shoulder, drawing her to his side.

Wait a minute! she thought. *Why is Doug doing this? What if somebody sees him? What if Todd sees him?*

She pulled away slightly, scanning the group ahead of them to see if anyone had noticed. They all still had their backs to them. Then, as if Doug could read her thoughts, he slipped his arm down. Funny. While they were ice-skating it didn't bother her that he held her hand or put his arm around her. Now it felt uncomfortable. She didn't know if he was doing it in a brotherly way because she was so cold or if he was acting as if they were a couple now.

What is wrong with me? Christy thought. *How come I'm so confused? First with Rick and now with Doug. And the only one I want to put his arm around me is Todd! But he won't even look at me.*

Doug hopped ahead of her a few steps and opened the door to Richie's, a small, charming diner at the end of the pier. It was a cozy place—inviting and warm—and looked like a snack bar from a fifties movie with its red vinyl seats at the booths and a long bar with red stools.

The group huddled together, waiting until the large corner booth opened up so they could all squeeze in. Christy hung back, hoping to arrange it so that she could sit by Todd. But Todd had already seated himself at the far end of the booth, with no room next to him.

Christy decided it was time to make her feelings known to Todd. He was the one she wanted to be with. She bravely walked over to his end of the booth, anticipating that he would scoot over or somehow make room for her. But he ignored her. She couldn't believe it. He totally ignored her.

"Christy," Doug called, "there's a place down here."

Fine! Christy thought angrily. *I'll go sit by you, Doug, and I'll laugh and have a good time and forget that Todd is even here.*

Tracy appeared at the booth and sized up the seating arrangement. She must have slipped into the rest room while they were playing musical chairs, because she had taken her hair out of its usual ponytail, and now it cascaded to her shoulders, smooth and pretty. Grabbing a chair, she planted it on the end, right next to Doug. Doug stepped away from the booth and let Christy slide in next to him so that he was on the end and between Tracy and Christy.

Tracy gave Christy a rude glare and said, "Nice jacket."

"It's Doug's," Christy said defensively. "It was freezing out there."

"I know," Tracy said with an icy edge to her voice.

I can't believe this is happening! Christy thought. *These are all my perfect, ideal, Christian friends, and they're ready to kill me. What's wrong with everybody?* Christy opened a menu and stared at it without seeing the words.

"Chili fries sound great tonight!" Doug said energetically.

"Those are so gross," Leslie said.

"Hey, Todd," Doug yelled across the table, "what's that one you always get here?"

"Beach Burger," Todd said flatly, catching Christy's glance at the very moment she happened to look up. He held her gaze. Then he did something with his eyes. He didn't really move his eyes or eyebrows, or maybe he did just a tiny bit. It looked like in the old movies when the hero searched the maiden's face, scanning desperately for an answer. Or was he asking for an apology for not making room for her to sit by him?

Todd's look, his unspoken message, was too piercing. Christy turned away and hid behind her menu. All she could see were his screaming silver-blue eyes saying, "What are you doing to me, Christy?"'

Is he upset about how the day turned out too? Christy thought hopefully. *Well, he certainly isn't doing much to change things!*

"And for you?" the waiter said, playfully tapping his pencil on Christy's menu. She looked up instantly and saw a guy in a white shirt with a black bow tie. He looked like a soda jerk out of *Happy Days*.

"Um, I guess I'll have a Beach Burger, and do you have Oreo shakes?"

"Oreo Fantasy," he said. "One of our specialties."

"I'll have one, then."

She sat quietly, watching Doug demonstrate to Tracy how to make a worm out of a paper straw wrapper. First he scrunched the wrapper real tight, like an accordion, and placed it on the table. Then, with the straw, he dripped water onto the "worm," and it grew instantly.

Tracy relaxed. "Is that what they teach you in college?" she teased, laughing and encouraging Doug's silly tricks.

Doug apparently loved it because he set to work on a magic trick with two quarters and a napkin.

Now Christy was the one left out, as Doug and Tracy worked to put his magic trick together. She thought Todd was looking at her, but when she casually glanced his way he wasn't. She remained quiet while all the others chatted around her. Halfheartedly nibbling at her hamburger, she couldn't even enjoy the celebrated Oreo Fantasy shake.

While the others ate and talked, she slipped out and went into the tiny bathroom. Her reflection in the mirror surprised her. Her hair fuzzed all over from the damp air, and her cheeks and nose were still red from the ice-skating. Her eye shadow had turned into a blue-brown crease in the middle of her eyelid. Her mascara had left dark smudges in the bottom corners of both eyes.

She quickly dampened a paper towel and tried to fix her eye makeup. Then, half talking to God and half talking to herself, she said, "Did You see how everything got messed up today? Of course You did. Well, I don't mean to be rude or anything, but I don't think this is how Your other Christians are supposed to be acting toward me."

She paused, looked at her reflection, and added, "Not that I've been doing such a great job of being everybody's friend, but at least I'm not being outright rude like Tracy."

Just then the bathroom door lurched opened, and Heather blew in breathlessly. "Christy, it's totally working! I can't believe this! I've never seen him act like this before."

"Who? Act like what?"

"Todd! He's acting like a hurt puppy. He's all mad at Doug. I can't believe how jealous he is!"

"But I don't want him to be jealous. I don't want him to be mad at anybody," Christy groaned. "Heather, it wasn't supposed to be like this."

"It wasn't?" Heather looked surprised.

"No! All this 'game' stuff doesn't work. Believe me."

"Of course it works. You skated with Doug, and Todd's jealous, isn't he?"

"Heather, I didn't skate with Doug to get Todd jealous,

like you told me to. I ended up skating with Doug because we both could skate, that's all."

"Oh really? And the jacket?" Heather eyed Doug's jacket, which Christy still had on.

"I was cold, and Doug offered me his jacket."

Heather rolled her eyes and put her hand on her hip. "Christy, make up your mind whose game you're going to play, because it sure looks to me as though you're going after Doug."

"I'm not. Honest."

"Well, don't tell me. Tell Todd."

"I'd love to tell Todd. There's a whole bunch of things I'd love to tell Todd! Only he's not talking to me at the moment!" Christy felt herself getting angrier and angrier at Heather.

Heather shrugged her shoulders and looked at her hair in the mirror. "I guess you shouldn't have made him jealous, then."

Christy threw her head back and closed her eyes. "Heather!"

"What?"

"First you tell me to make Todd jealous; then when he is and everybody is mad at me, you tell me I shouldn't have done it!"

"Well, how was I supposed to know? It seemed like a good idea. So what are you going to do?" Heather cocked her head to one side, looking like a little bird. It was hard to stay mad at anyone who looked that innocent.

"I don't know. I'll think of something."

They traversed the maze of tables back to their booth just as everyone was figuring out the bill.

"Here," Christy offered, pulling the fifty-dollar bill from her pocket and tossing it on the table. "Uncle Bob's contribution."

"Are you sure?" "Really?"

"Yeah, it's fine. Go ahead."

They decided to leave the waiter a big tip since the table was such a mess. One of the girls commented that the waiter had seen them pray together before they ate, and it would look pretty bad if they acted spiritual but weren't generous in thanking him for the service.

Christy hung back, waiting for Todd. They walked through the door together as Doug held it open for them. Todd didn't say anything to her, but he didn't walk away when Christy tried to fall into step with him. Tracy came up next to Christy, and Christy noticed that the expression on her face looked a little softer than when they had gone in.

As it turned out, the four of them—Todd, Christy, Doug, and Tracy—walked together down the pier, the girls next to each other in the middle. The wind sliced even deeper now, and Tracy said, "Man, it's cold tonight."

Christy immediately slipped out of Doug's jacket and said, "Here, Tracy. I warmed up a lot in there. Why don't you wear this now?" She meant it as a kind gesture to a good friend, but as Tracy slipped the jacket on she gave Christy a strange look as if Christy were intruding. Intruding into what? If Tracy was cold, then she wanted a jacket, right? Or else she wanted Doug to put his arm around her, which he hadn't done. Suddenly, the pieces of the puzzle all tumbled together, and Christy saw the whole picture.

Why didn't I see this before? she thought. *Tracy likes Doug!* He was the mystery boyfriend! And here Christy had been interfering all day. That's why Doug asked for more cookies. Tracy had gone to Doug's house yesterday with Todd and given him her box of cookies. No wonder Tracy was all upset at her for skating with Doug and wearing his jacket! *I can't believe I didn't figure this out sooner! What a relief to at least know what the problem is. Now, how am I going to patch everything up?*

Todd didn't say a word on the way home. He dropped Christy off first, which disappointed her.

Before getting out, Christy touched his arm and said softly so the others wouldn't hear, "Todd, could we talk sometime?"

He turned and looked at her, the hurt puppy sag still pulling at the corners of his eyes. In an annoyingly non-committal tone, he said, "Sure. Whenever."

Doug popped his head between them and said, "Do you want to do something tomorrow, Christy?"

She cringed. Turning her head slightly, Christy could see Tracy looking anything but pleased.

"I promised my aunt I'd spend some time with her tomorrow," Christy answered quickly.

"I know, you guys," Heather piped up. "Let's plan a New Year's party at my house. My mom won't mind. She'd rather have me home than out on New Year's. You want to? I mean we can do something tomorrow too, if you want to. But we should all get together for New Year's, don't you think?"

Everyone voiced approval and started throwing out suggestions. Christy searched Todd's expression for some indication of when she would see him again. He looked straight ahead and popped Gus into first gear.

"Later," was all he said.

Christy hopped out and slammed the passenger door so hard that she immediately felt as though she should apologize to poor Gus the Bus, who had done nothing to deserve such treatment.

"Sorry, Gus," she murmured as she stood shivering in the driveway, watching the van chug down the street, driving her all-time friends farther and farther away. "Guess everybody got treated a little unfairly today."

The Quiet Woman

Inside the house the twinkling white lights on the Christmas tree illuminated the living room. Everyone had gone to bed, leaving Christy alone with her thoughts.

What a disaster of a day! Will Todd call me tomorrow, or should I call him to say I'm sorry? But what did I actually do wrong? I didn't mean to spend so much time with Doug; it just turned out that way. Besides, Todd didn't make any effort to skate with me. Maybe I'm the one who should be feeling wounded, not him.

She meandered up to her room and flopped onto her bed. She noticed a letter on her pillow. It was from Alissa, a girl she had met last summer. Christy had admired Alissa and desired to be like her until she found out what Alissa was really like and how hard her life had been. They had written to each other several times, but Christy hadn't heard from her for months. If this letter was anything like Alissa's previous letters, it probably wasn't filled with good news.

Christy stretched out, took a deep breath, and began reading:

Dear Christy,

I lost your address in Escondido, so I hope this gets to you all right. I hope you and your family have a good Christmas. A lot has been going on in my life lately, and I feel as though you're about the only person I can tell all of this to. Please don't think I'm horrible, but Christy, I'm not innocent like you. I wish I were. The truth is, I'm pregnant.

Christy paused, trying to take in this news. Then she went on to finish the letter, but before she got to the bottom of the second page, tears came, making the words bleary.

I thought about having an abortion a few months ago because it seemed like it would make everything easier, and my problem would disappear. But like they say, "Two wrongs don't make a right." I know you must think I'm a terrible person, and I know I never should have gotten myself into this situation, but I did. A friend of mine had an abortion, and she said she wished she hadn't, because years later she still had nightmares about it. She told me that if she had to do it over again, she would have had the baby and then given it up for adoption. I think that's what I'm going to do—give the baby up for adoption....

Christy wiped away her tears before finishing the letter. She felt so bad for Alissa, but the end of the letter was a little more encouraging.

...I have only about three more months to go, so, as you can imagine, I look like a whale.

Remember how in your last letter you said that I should get a Bible and try to find some other Christians? I went to a Crisis Pregnancy Center, and my counselor, Frances, is a Christian. She's helping me and has given me a Bible. I've been going to church with her too. I knew you would be glad to hear that.

Thanks too for saying that you were praying for me. I could use some more prayers, if you think of it. I know it's not going to be easy, but I think I'm doing the right thing.

Well, that pretty much explains why I haven't written for a while. You don't have to write back or anything. I just wanted you to know about the baby, and I hope you'll be praying for me.

Alissa

After reading the letter, all Christy could do was pray. She wasn't sure exactly what to pray, but with tears for Alissa, Christy offered awkward requests to God until she fell asleep.

"Christy dear?" Aunt Marti tapped her long nails on the bedroom door. "Are you up yet?"

Christy barely lifted her head from the pillow. "Yes, Aunt Marti." Her voice came out froggy.

"Good. I thought we could leave in, say, half an hour?"

Christy thumped her head back into the center of the pillow. *Oh, yeah,* she thought. *"Shopping with Aunt Marti Day." How could I have forgotten?*

"I'll be ready," Christy called out, doubting if she could pull herself together in only half an hour yet determined not to upset her aunt today.

They left the house right on time, according to Aunt Marti's schedule, and Aunt Marti even approved of the jeans and sweater Christy had thrown on. It was the new Christmas sweater Marti had given her.

"Did you have a good time with your friends yesterday?"

"Yes." It wasn't the whole truth, but Christy didn't feel like going into the details with her aunt.

"It's certainly wonderful having Todd back, isn't it?"

"Um-hmm." Christy forced a tight smile. *Come on, Christy, don't say anything negative. Say what she wants to hear and you'll be okay.*

"And that cute little gal Tracy is just a doll, isn't she? Bob said you had a wonderful time making cookies together. I'm so glad you have good friends here, Christina. Dear, dear friends like that are hard to come by, you know."

Christy didn't say a word—not a word. But her mind was anything but quiet. *My "dear friends" are all ready to kick me out of their lives. It's never going to be the same with them again. Every piece that was left of my friendships from last summer is withered and mangled—just like all those dumb carnation petals I saved in that smelly coffee can. What am I supposed to do with a bunch of dried-up memories?*

Just then Aunt Marti stopped at a red light. The same red light, the same intersection where last summer, in the middle of the street, Todd had kissed her and given her the bouquet of white carnations. Christy couldn't swallow the wad of self-pity in her throat any longer. Turning her face to the window, she let the tears flow.

It lasted only a moment. The light turned green, Christy faked a coughing spell and fumbled in her purse for a tissue. With a few quick dabs and clearing of the throat, she had her emotions under control. Aunt Marti hadn't even noticed. What a contrast to last summer, when Christy had gushed her heartaches out all over the place and had willingly let her aunt pick up all the pieces.

Things had changed between them. She no longer

appreciated her aunt's dominating personality. Swallowing these emotions was a victory for Christy, and silently she congratulated herself on her maturity and control. Now, if only the incredibly painful knot in her stomach would go away.

"First thing on the schedule," Aunt Marti began, "is your nine-thirty appointment at Maurice's. He's going to be amazed to see how quickly your hair has grown!"

"You made an appointment for me to get my hair cut?"

"I knew you wouldn't mind. It's gotten so long, dear, you really are desperately in need of a cut."

"No way!" Christy popped off. "I am not getting my hair cut!"

Aunt Marti shot a stunned glance at Christy as she maneuvered through the parking lot at Fashion Island Shopping Center. "Christina, I'm surprised at you! What are you saying?"

"I'm saying I do not want to get my hair cut." She said each word slowly and deliberately. "I'm trying to grow my hair out again." She took a deep breath as Marti parked the Mercedes, clicked off the engine, and turned to face her. "You didn't even ask me, Aunt Marti. You could have at least asked me!"

Aunt Marti pulled back like a turtle disappearing into its shell. Her voice came out as controlled as Christy's but softer, more gracious. "I was trying to think of what was best for you, dear."

Silence reigned for a moment. Marti cleared her throat and then literally stuck her neck back out. "Why don't we keep your nine-thirty appointment for a simple wash and blow dry? Then, if you decide to have anything else done, you can tell Maurice exactly how you'd like your hair. Would that be agreeable to you?"

Christy wanted to scream out, "No, that would not be agreeable! Your interference in my life is not at all agreeable!" But she controlled her emotions and answered, "All right." It was no good appearing calm. The searing blob in her stomach grew and grew.

Maurice washed Christy's hair and chatted brightly with Aunt Marti. Christy didn't say a word. After the conditioning and rinsing, he wrapped a towel around her head and directed her to his styling area. Christy looked at herself in the mirror. Her expression was disturbing: hard and cold with clenched teeth. She didn't like it.

The words to a Debbie Stevens song she had heard at Todd's flashed into her mind, and she began to sing them inside her head, like a prayer:

> *Touch this heart, so full of pain,*
> *Heal it with Your love.*
> *Make it soft and warm again,*
> *Melt me with Your love.*
> *I don't want to push You away;*
> *Come back in,*
> *Come to stay.*
> *Make me tender, just like You,*
> *Melt me with Your love.*

Maurice removed the towel and fluffed up her hair with his fingers. "So long!" he exclaimed. "So badly in need of a trim. Next time do not wait so long before you come see me."

Christy met his gaze in the mirror, and she spoke gently

but firmly. "I'm letting my hair grow. I don't want it cut today."

"But, perhaps, just a tiny trim, then?" Maurice already had the scissors in his hand.

"No. I want it to grow."

Maurice and Aunt Marti exchanged glances in the mirror behind Christy. She felt awful. She didn't want to be a brat. *Make me tender, just like You, / Melt me with Your love.*

Maurice slapped the scissors down onto the counter and stepped briskly away from the chair. Aunt Marti shot her a look that said, "Oh, now you've done it! You've offended the best-known hairstylist in Newport Beach!"

Christy offered Marti a weak smile—not a mean smile, a nice smile, a soft smile. A smile that showed her heart—but not her determination—was melting. She knew what she wanted, and no one could change her mind.

Maurice plopped a large book of hairstyles in Christy's lap. He quickly thumbed through the section showing longer styles. "Like this?" he pointed to a picture of wavy, shoulder-length hair parted on the side. Carefully studying the picture, Christy melted a little more. "That's pretty. I like that style. But my hair doesn't have that much body. It just frizzes."

"Aha!" Maurice announced, snatching the large book and snapping it closed. "I shall give you a wave."

"You mean a perm?"

Aunt Marti stepped forward. "Christy, would you like to have a perm put in your hair today, darling?" She said it as though she were talking to a toddler, exaggerating each word, to make sure Christy was in agreement with the idea.

"I hadn't even thought of it, but I guess that would be

okay. That way I can keep my hair long."

Aunt Marti spread her lips in a tight smile. "As long as you're sure that's what you want, dear."

Christy felt the emotions gurgling inside her stomach again. "Yes, Aunt Martha. That's what I'd like. As long as it's just wavy like the picture. I don't want it curly."

"Yes, all right then," Aunt Marti said, sitting back down. "Okay. Good." She motioned for Maurice to go to work.

It seemed that everyone was relieved several hours later when Maurice stood back to admire his handiwork. Christy's hair looked good—really good—and she loved it. Even though the wave had drawn her hair up a little shorter, it made it look thick and full all around.

Christy shook hands with Maurice and thanked him, telling him what a great job he had done. He looked pleased. Aunt Marti looked pleased. "Would you like to do some shopping, Christy? Or should we grab a bite to eat?" Marti asked.

"Doesn't matter to me."

As if Christy had just relinquished the reins on a team of snorting horses, Aunt Marti snatched them up and off they thundered, in and out of small specialty shops. Christy found a clip for her hair, nail polish, a collapsible mirror for her purse, and a pair of black shoes on sale. Nothing too exciting, yet Aunt Marti seemed delighted with every choice Christy made. It was clear that anything Christy wanted, she could have.

But Christy didn't go wild, picking out clothes and accessories to her heart's content. She felt spoiled, and she didn't like that. She also felt controlled, and she really didn't like that. Plus, she didn't want to be shopping. She wanted to be back at the house, doing whatever she could to clear things up with Todd. And every minute she spent with her aunt seemed to be pulling her farther and farther away from him.

At two-thirty Aunt Marti announced it was time for lunch. Christy suggested they go home and make a salad, but Aunt Marti insisted they drive to Corona del Mar. She parked in front of a tiny restaurant on the Coast Highway called The Quiet Woman. The old English tavern sign hanging over the front door showed a headless woman. Apparently she was "the quiet woman."

Settling comfortably into their secluded booth, Aunt Marti ordered Veal Oscar for herself and the same for Christy before asking, "Does that sound good to you, Christy?"

"Sure. Doesn't matter." Actually, she would have preferred a hamburger. But it didn't matter, as long as they could have a nice, quick lunch, and she could get home and try to work out some of the complications in her life.

The waiter placed their beverages before them. Christy waited until he left before she quietly bowed her head to pray.

"You've really taken your religion to heart, haven't you, Christy?" Aunt Marti asked.

Christy felt a little embarrassed that her aunt figured out that she had been praying. "Our family always prays before meals," Christy said.

"Yes, I realize that, dear. However, I've noticed you do it even when your parents aren't around. It's something you do for yourself, and that's worthy of a compliment, don't you think?"

Christy shrugged. "I guess so. I never thought of praying as something a person would be complimented on."

Within minutes the waiter stood before them, delivering the savory dishes and filling their water glasses. Christy cautiously took a bite and decided the Veal Oscar tasted pretty good. Aunt Marti looked extraordinarily delighted with the meal and continued the conversation between tiny bites.

"I'm pleased to see how you're maturing, Christina. I must say, I had some concerns several months ago in Palm Springs when you and your girlfriends snuck out of the hotel room in the middle of the night."

Christy opened her mouth to defend herself, but Aunt Marti calmly waved her fork as a signal to just listen. "There's no need to discuss that night, and I wouldn't have even brought it up except to say that I'd like to have more input in your life."

Christy waited for her aunt to go on. She felt defensive, anticipating some kind of criticism, which Aunt Marti could dish out like no one else.

"I felt you were reluctant to spend this time with me today. Over the last few days you've been completely absorbed with your friends, and I can understand that. However, I feel you're making it difficult for me to get involved in your life. I'm proud of the way I see you taking a stand for what you want. But I would like it if you would discuss things with me more and ask my opinion. I truly feel that I can do for you and give to you what no one else can."

Christy squirmed uncomfortably. She loved her aunt, yet she never liked the way Marti tried to mother her.

"I don't know how to make it any clearer than to tell you, Christina, that you are the daughter I never had, and I see you as that—my daughter. I want only the very best for you. Do you think you can understand what I'm saying?"

Christy nodded. She understood perfectly. It was just that she didn't want another mother—or an agent or whatever it was that Aunt Marti saw herself as.

"I see great potential in you, dear. Perhaps more than what your parents see. I could truly make something out of you. You've got the figure, the face, the personality...why, you could really be somebody!"

Never before had compliments stung so cruelly. Aunt Marti charged on, apparently not reading the pain in Christy's face.

"I see you becoming the kind of young woman who stands out in a crowd. If you will only allow me to be more involved in your life, I can teach you how to become someone who can get anything she wants—a stunning young woman who makes a lasting impression. Someone like, well, like your friend from this summer. You know, Alissa."

Twang! Everything inside Christy snapped.

"Like Alissa? That's what you want? You want me to become like Alissa?"

"Lower your voice, dear."

"Ha!" Christy laughed aloud, then lowered her voice just a pinch. "It just so happens, Aunt Martha, that Alissa is pregnant!"

Aunt Marti's mouth dropped open, her eyes doubled in size.

"The baby will be born before she even graduates from high school. Is that what you want for me too?" By now the tears streamed down Christy's face. She didn't care who saw her or what they thought of her.

Not so with Aunt Marti. She rose swiftly, as if something were chasing her. Quickly fumbling with the check, she tossed it back on the table with a couple of twenty-dollar bills.

Christy wiped her eyes and followed her spooked aunt as she blazed a trail through the center of the restaurant and scurried to the car.

Now I've blown it! Why didn't I keep my mouth shut? Christy felt miserable.

Aunt Marti slammed the door and thrust the car forward into the flow of traffic. However, the traffic was clogged on the Coast Highway, causing them to travel a few feet, jerk to a stop, travel a few more feet, then come to another quick stop, with Aunt Marti's foot hard on the brake. At this rate it could take half an hour to get home.

Christy spoke up, anxious to smooth things over. "Can you see why I don't want to be like Alissa?"

Aunt Marti nodded without looking at Christy, then slammed on the brakes again.

"I just want to be myself," Christy said softly. "No, actually, it's more than that. I want to be the person God wants me to be."

"That's fine, Christina. Very noble. However..."—Marti paused and pressed extra hard on the brakes so the car lurched, as if for added emphasis—"...life doesn't always go the way you think it will or the way you want it to."

A heaviness hung between them. Christy knew Aunt Marti didn't understand. But then maybe Christy didn't understand completely either.

The car jerked to another stop, and Marti started

coughing. It was a fake, choking kind of cough. Christy thought she saw tears in her aunt's eyes.

What's wrong with me? Christy thought. *Why am I making everybody I know get mad at me? I can't do anything right!*

"Aunt Marti?" Christy felt emptied of all her determination. "I'm sorry. I didn't mean to upset you."

Marti didn't respond.

They drove the rest of the way home in agonizing silence. When they pulled into the driveway a yellow Toyota four-wheel-drive truck followed them and parked in front of the house. It was Doug's truck. David sat in the front seat beside him, all smiles.

"We had more fun than you did," David sang out. He bounded from the truck and met stone-faced Christy and Marti in the driveway. "We went skateboarding."

"David," Aunt Marti exclaimed, "you've ruined your brand-new jeans!" Angry words tumbled from her mouth. Christy knew that poor David was receiving verbal blows that were meant for her.

"I know, I kind of wiped out a couple of times," David said sheepishly, all the adventure draining from his voice.

"Go inside and change immediately!"

Without a word, David ran into the house. Christy felt awful for him.

Doug had slowly made his way to where Christy and Aunt Marti were standing, hanging back until the conflict passed. Marti turned to Doug and smiled; she was poised and charming and glossy.

Christy cleared her throat, harnessed her emotions, and quickly made the introductions, explaining that Doug was a friend of Todd's. Doug then said that he knew Christy had gone shopping today, but he thought he would swing by anyway. Since Christy wasn't back yet, he had taken David skateboarding.

Marti looked pleased and said, "How gracious of you, Doug. It's wonderful to meet you. Christy, why don't you invite your friend to stay for dinner, if he'd like? I'm not sure what's planned, but"—she turned to Doug, gushing with sweetness—"you're welcome to join us."

"Thanks," Doug said without committing himself.

Aunt Marti excused herself, and Christy and Doug stood in the driveway.

"Your hair looks nice," Doug said. "Did you have it fixed today or something?"

"I got a perm. I'm letting it grow," she said with a certain determined look in her eyes.

Doug half smiled and said, "Oh, yeah. You look good in long hair." Then he sniffed. "It smells like flowers or something."

"It's this conditioner stuff they put on my hair," Christy explained. She scooped up the end of her hair and pulled it toward her nose. "I think it smells like green apples."

"Is that what it is?" Doug said. Then, in a natural gesture, he put a hand on her shoulder and leaned over, nuzzling his nose into her hair right above her ear.

At that very second, Christy heard an all too familiar sound. She looked out at the street and caught a glimpse of Gus the Bus chugging past the house. *Oh no! What should I do?* she thought frantically. She couldn't see Todd's face, but she knew he had seen Doug leaning over her, smelling her hair. Todd sped on down the street as if he hadn't meant to stop at all.

"You're right," Doug said, pulling back, completely unaware of what had just happened. "It does smell like green apples."

Christy felt like yelling at him, but she stood in her frozen position and just stared past him at the back end of Gus turning at the corner. *I can't believe that just happened!*

"I stopped by so I could talk to you, if that's okay," Doug said.

"About what?" Christy snapped.

Doug pulled back a little and then said, "Well, could we sit inside my truck for a minute?"

"Okay, I guess so." Christy calmed herself down.

Once inside the cab of the Toyota, Christy's eyes kept darting up and down the street, just in case Todd returned. She wished he would, but then she wished he wouldn't, because everything felt so mixed up right now. She needed to deal with one thing at a time. Doug first.

"Well, I hope this doesn't come across the wrong way or anything. I'm not sure how to say it."

For the first time, Christy focused on Doug. He looked serious. "Go ahead, Doug. You can tell me."

When he hesitated she added, "I think you know you can trust me." Even as she heard the words come out of her mouth, Christy wasn't sure she knew what she was getting herself into.

"I know I can trust you," Doug said. "I noticed that when I first met you. You're very approachable. You make people feel as though they can come and talk to you about anything."

Oh sure! Real approachable, Christy thought. *Is that why everyone I know is furious with me at the moment?*

Then Christy remembered Alissa's letter. Alissa had poured out her heart, yet Christy barely knew her. Alissa had said, "I feel like you're about the only person I can tell all this to."

Doug jumped right in. "What I wanted to say is that, well, I'll just say it. I'm taking Tracy out tonight."

"You are?" Christy said excitedly. She impulsively leaned forward and grabbed him by the shoulders. "That's wonderful!"

Doug looked surprised and pulled back. Christy quickly let go. She didn't want Todd to drive by again and this time see *her* holding on to Doug in his truck.

"I wanted to tell you because, well, I care about you, and I didn't want it to hurt our friendship or anything."

"Don't worry. It won't hurt it at all. I'm glad you two are going out."

Doug still looked uncomfortable. "I guess I thought maybe after we went ice-skating and everything that, well, maybe something was starting between you and me, but I wasn't sure. I mean, I know how much you mean to Todd, and I'd never want to come between you two, but still, I feel as though you and I are starting to become good friends too, and I'd like that to keep growing." He had said everything in one breath and now drew in another breath of courage.

"So, what I want to say is that I want to get to be really good friends with you, and sometimes, if you go out with somebody, then everybody thinks you don't want to be friends with anybody else anymore and that you just want to spend time with that one person, since you're going out with them. You know what I mean?"

430 ● ● ● ● ● Robin Jones Gunn

He looked so sincere. Christy smiled for the first time in hours. She reached over and squeezed his hand. "Doug, I understand. Really. We can still be friends—really good friends—and just because you're dating Tracy, that won't change anything with us. It might even make it easier."

"What do you mean?"

Christy hesitated. "All I'll say is that I'm really, really, really glad you and Tracy are going out."

"Good," Doug said with a smile.

"Can I ask you one thing?" Christy said. "Does Todd know you and Tracy are going out tonight?"

"No. I haven't talked to him all day."

"Could you do me a favor and let him know?"

"Sure. Why?"

"Just so that he'll know. Okay?"

"Okay." Doug reached over and touched her hair again. "What do they do? Put electrical wires in your hair and hook you up to a generator or something to make your hair puff?"

Christy gave him a look of playful disgust and gently tugged away. "Doug, you need a sister to educate you in the finer areas of life when it comes to women and manners. As a matter of fact, you and Todd both could use a sister."

"You interested in taking the position?"

"Maybe," she answered playfully.

Doug burst out laughing, focusing on the window behind Christy. She turned to see her brother making a grotesque face and drooling on the truck window.

"Then again," Christy said dryly, "it could be I have all the brothers I need at the moment."

9

Confiding in Mom

Christy did a lot of thinking that night. Tomorrow her parents were coming back, which meant she needed to clear things up with her aunt. She had only a few more days with her beach friends, and she had to talk to Todd. Plus, she had to make sure everything was okay between her and Tracy. And she wanted to write Alissa right away, but she wasn't sure what to say. The whole muddled mess made her sick to her stomach.

She decided to start with Todd. Slipping on her robe and new fuzzy bunny slippers, she marched to the phone in her aunt and uncle's bedroom. They were downstairs watching TV with David, and she knew she'd have more privacy up here than downstairs. Bravely dialing Todd's number, she coached herself to say whatever came to mind first. All she had to do was get the conversation going and let Todd take it from there.

It rang four, then five times before a deep male voice answered. It wasn't Todd's voice. His dad's, maybe?

Christy opened her mouth and...nothing came out.

She quickly slammed down the receiver, then stared at the phone as though it were a familiar pet that had just bitten her. It all happened so quickly, and she felt so ridiculous. She didn't dare call him back.

Why did I do that? Why is my heart pounding so fast?

Christy flopped back onto the bed and let out a blurt of nervous laughter, laughing at herself.

So much for brave and daring and getting everything all cleared up with Todd!

Like a meek little mouse, Christy scurried back to her bedroom, her fuzzy slippers leaving tufts of white fluff on the hallway carpet behind her.

She tried calling Todd twice the next morning, but each time she hung up before it even rang.

What is my problem?

Heather called around noon and had all kinds of exciting news about how the party was shaping up for the next night.

"Have you talked to anyone else today about the party?" Christy asked.

"Like who?" Heather seemed to know what Christy was getting at, but Heather also seemed to enjoy making Christy spell it out.

"Well, has Todd said for sure that he's going? I really have to talk to him, Heather."

"Why don't you call him?"

"I tried, but..."

"Okay. I'll call him; then I'll call you back and tell you what he says."

"You don't have to, Heather."

"No, I need to call him anyhow, so if I happen to mention that you've been trying to get ahold of him, it won't be a big deal."

Christy sighed into the phone.

"I'll call him right now, okay?"

"I guess." Christy heaved another sigh. "I don't want things to get any more complicated than they already are."

"Don't worry. Everything will work out fine. Look how wonderful everything is for Doug and Tracy. Tonight he's having dinner over at Tracy's house. Isn't that great? I told her to have her mom invite him."

"That's great!" Deep down Christy meant it, but right now it didn't help to know that Doug and Tracy were together. Their problems might have been solved, but hers weren't. She still hadn't smoothed things over with Tracy, and all this stuff with Heather calling Todd was just part of the games again—games Heather loved to play, but games Christy wasn't so sure she wanted to get caught up in. These games hadn't helped her progress much with Todd in the past.

Why can't I be bold and up front like Doug? He was incredibly caring yesterday when he came over and talked to me privately just to make sure he wouldn't hurt my feelings by going out with Tracy. And Doug is the only one whose personality hasn't changed drastically during the last few days. He acted the same way toward me when he skated with me as he did when he told me he was going to go out with another girl. Now that's an all-time friend. Why can't I be like that?

When Heather called back a few minutes later, she had disturbing news. "Todd said he might not make it to the party. He said he was going to a dinner tomorrow night."

"A dinner? With his dad?"

"He didn't say, but he kind of made it sound like a date or something."

Christy's heart sank.

"I'm sorry, Christy," Heather said.

"That's okay. I just didn't know he was dating anyone."

"He's not, as far as I know. Maybe somebody set him up—you know, an out-of-town cousin of his dad's boss here for the holidays."

"Great."

"But I told him you were trying to get ahold of him. He said his dad just got back from Switzerland, so he's been hanging around the house, spending time with his dad. Maybe you should try calling him again."

"Why doesn't he try calling me, huh? Would that be too much to ask?"

"Don't get so defensive! I tried, okay?"

"I'm sorry, Heather. I know you tried. Thanks. It's just that I thought he was going to be at your party, and that would be the perfect time for me to talk to him."

"Well, he said he was going to this dinner thing, but after that he might come by. Why don't you call and ask him yourself?"

"I should."

But she didn't. She couldn't—at least not right away. Right now her feelings, worn thin, couldn't handle another blow if Todd didn't respond the way she needed him to. She knew she should call him.

But she put it off and retreated to the family room, avoiding contact with Aunt Marti and everyone else in the world by tuning into the TV. There, alone, she spent most of the day watching old movies and eating anything she could find—anything, that is, except international cheese.

Christy's parents arrived in the late afternoon, right

during the last five minutes of *Captain January*, a Shirley Temple movie Christy had never seen before.

"Christy!" her dad called out as they came into the house. "Please come here and help carry in these bags."

"Okay! In a minute," she called back, her attention glued to the TV.

Dad stood in the doorway of the den and said, "I really need your help now, Christy."

"Okay. I'm coming." Christy jumped up and hurried out to the car. She knew that tone in her dad's voice and didn't want to get him upset.

"Where should I put it, Dad?" Christy asked when she walked back into the house.

"Downstairs guest room," he answered on his way to the kitchen.

Christy hurried, hoping to catch the final minutes of *Captain January*. She pushed open the bedroom door with her shoulder and stopped. There on the bed lay her mother with her foot in a cast.

"Mom, what happened?"

"It's really nothing. I slipped and fell yesterday. A hairline fracture. Doesn't even hurt, but the doctor wanted me to stay off it."

"Mom, I didn't know."

"It wasn't worth calling to tell everyone. It's not that bad." Mom pushed back her graying brown hair and smiled. "Your dad would probably have me in the hospital by now if the doctor hadn't convinced him I was all right." She propped a pillow behind her back and said, "Thanks for bringing in my bag. So, tell me, did you have a good week?"

Then, as if Christy were four years old again, she climbed onto the bed, buried her head in her mom's shoulder, and cried her eyes out.

The tears lasted only a few minutes. Christy pulled up her head, wiped her eyes, and, feeling ridiculous, apologized over and over. *How could I have fallen apart so suddenly?* she thought.

Her mom smiled and handed her a tissue. It had been a long time since they had shared a transparent moment like this. Mom said softly, "Must have been a pretty bad week."

Christy hesitated. "I guess it wasn't all that bad. It's just that everyone is mad at me. And then I came in here, and you're in a cast and I didn't even know." She looked away. "Oh, Mom! My whole life is falling apart."

"You want to tell me about it?"

Christy usually didn't tell her mom many of the details about what was going on with her friendships, but now that all the doors were opened between them, she decided to go for it.

In one long sentence, Christy explained all about Todd and about Tracy's being jealous of her and about Doug and how that had worked out, sort of; but she still hadn't seen Tracy, and Heather was having a party tomorrow night, but Todd might not come.

"What time is this party?" Mom asked. "And where is it?"

Christy told her and then asked, "I can go, can't I? I have to talk to Todd—I mean, if he comes. But I mostly need to talk to Tracy and make sure she understands I wasn't trying to get Doug away from her."

"I suppose you can go. It sounds as though everything

will work itself out, once you see your friends and have a chance to talk."

Christy nibbled nervously on her fingernail.

"You don't look too convinced of that," her mom said. "By the way, your hair looks very nice. Did Marti take you to have it done?"

Christy nodded. "Except we kind of got in an argument at lunch, and we're still both sort of avoiding each other."

"What happened?"

Christy never thought it could be this easy to talk with her mom. Probably because an opportunity like this had never come up. Or maybe because she never tried, because she had assumed her mom wouldn't understand. But what had Uncle Bob said on Christmas morning? Something about her parents being young once. And her mom grew up with Marti. Of course she would understand how hard it was to communicate with her sometimes.

Christy told her about Maurice's and how Aunt Marti had told her at lunch that she was the daughter she had never had. Mom's usually clear blue-gray eyes clouded.

"What else did Marti tell you?" she said.

"That she wished I were like Alissa, a girl I met here this summer."

"Yes," her mom said thoughtfully, "I remember Marti's mentioning her before."

"Mom," Christy said, looking her in the eyes, "I got a letter from Alissa a few days ago, and she told me a whole bunch of stuff." Christy paused and then plunged in. "Mom, Alissa is pregnant."

Mom looked serious in a soft, understanding way.

"When she found out," Christy continued, "she went to

a counseling center. See, in the last letter I wrote her, I told her I was praying for her and that maybe she could find some other Christians. So she called around until she found this pregnancy center that is run by Christians, and they've been helping her."

Mom listened intently.

"She also said that her counselor at the pregnancy center, a lady named Frances, was taking her to church. That was about the only good news in the whole letter."

"Where does Alissa live?"

"In Boston, with her grandmother. Her dad's dead, and her mom is in an alcoholic rehabilitation center."

"Oh, my," Mom sympathized, shaking her head. "Did you tell Marti all this?"

"No." Christy hung her head. "When Aunt Marti told me she wanted to make me into somebody like Alissa, I blurted out the part about her being pregnant."

"What was Marti's reaction?"

"She wouldn't talk to me. I apologized, but she's barely talked to me since."

Mom leaned forward on the bed, stuffed a pillow under her cast, and then sat up as straight as possible. "Christy, there's something you should know."

Now it was Mom's turn to be open and honest, and Christy wasn't sure what to expect.

"Marti had a daughter once." Mom's words came out painfully soft. "A week before you were born, Marti gave birth to a baby girl."

Christy stared at her mom in disbelief.

"The baby was three months premature and was born severely brain damaged. The doctors did what they could, but the baby died." Mom paused, then added, "Christy, you were born the next morning."

Christy let the tears flow. "I never knew. Mom, how come you never told me?"

"It isn't something Marti ever talks about—with anyone."

"Why didn't they have another baby?"

"They tried. Even though the doctor advised against it, they tried. Marti wasn't able to conceive."

"Why?" Christy felt a rush of a whole string of emotions she had never before felt for her aunt.

"Well..." Mom chose her words carefully. "Sometimes a person makes a decision that seems the easiest or best at the moment, but later they find that choice had a price."

"I don't understand."

Mom paused and said, "If Marti opens this topic up with you sometime, then you ask her about it, all right?"

Christy remained quiet, remembering a collage of conversations, arguments, and actions of her aunt's that hadn't made sense until this moment. No wonder Marti said Christy was the daughter she never had. She was more like the replacement for the daughter Marti had and then lost.

"Mom? Did they name her, the baby?"

A gentle, endearing expression swept across her mom's face. "Johanna. Johanna Grace. She was named after our grandmother, your great-grandmother."

"Johanna," Christy repeated. "That's pretty."

Mom nodded. "It was almost your middle name. Your father and I planned to name you Christina Johanna. But after little Johanna passed away, well..."

Christy blotted the last few runaway tears and then

shook her head. "This is kind of freaky, Mom. I mean, finding out I almost had a different middle name and that I had a cousin I never knew about. Are there any other big family secrets I should know?"

Mom thought for a minute. "I think those are the only ones you need to know at this point. I never would have told you about Johanna, but I felt it would help you understand your aunt better. She truly loves you, Christy. I think you know that. You don't have to go along with everything she has in mind for you, but do understand that she's acting out of a motherly instinct. You mean an awful lot to her."

Just then Dad stepped into the guest room and asked, "Can I get you anything?"

"No, thanks, I'm fine. It feels much better propped up like this." Mom pointed to her pillow-elevated cast.

"Dad," Christy said, turning around on the bed and facing him, "I was wondering if I could go to my friend Heather's house tomorrow night. She's having a New Year's party. Her parents will be there and everything."

Dad sat down on the edge of the bed and shook his head. "I don't like the idea of your being out on New Year's Eve."

"But I'll be completely safe at Heather's house. It's not very far from here. And it's the last chance I'll have to see all my friends."

"Your aunt just told me you spent most of your week with your friends," Dad said.

"Not really. We went ice-skating one day. That was all." Christy was worried. It looked as though her dad wasn't going to let her go to Heather's party, and that meant she might not see Todd again.

"Let me give it some thought, Christy. We don't know your friends here or what their home situations are like."

Christy's heart sank deeper and deeper. *He might really say no, and then what am I going to do?*

"We can talk about this later, Christy," Mom said. "Would you do me a favor and see if Marti needs help getting dinner going?"

"From the looks of it, it's all ready," Dad said.

"All ready? What are we having?" Mom asked.

"Judging by what I saw on the counter, we're having a buffet of international cheeses."

Mom groaned and shook her head.

"Oh, please," Christy said, "anything but that!"

10

Wrong Number

Actually, they had chicken for dinner. Or maybe it would be more accurate to say that Christy was a chicken at dinner. She intended to bring up the subject of Heather's party again, with a sneaky, back-door approach. She thought that if Uncle Bob heard about the invitation, he might talk her dad into letting her go. But she chickened out.

After dinner the three "boys" went out front to play with David's remote-control car. Christy cleared the table by herself and loaded the dishwasher while her mom and Aunt Marti talked in the living room. Marti had barely looked Christy in the eye since their conflict the day before, and that bothered Christy a lot. She didn't know if she should apologize again or let it rest.

The solitude of the kitchen helped Christy think through some of the heavy thoughts that relentlessly pounded her. It seemed as though every relationship she had was on "hold" right now. Sprinkling the dish soap into the dishwasher, she closed the door and snapped the "On" switch. The machine whirred, and Christy leaned against the counter, wishing she could wash away the uncomfortable events of the past week as easily as the dishwasher cleaned the dishes.

The phone rang. It rang two more times, and Christy answered it.

"Hello?"

"Hey, Christy. How's it going?"

"Todd?"

"Yeah. How's it going?"

Christy leaned against the counter. After all her schemes to talk to him, now she couldn't think of what to say. "It's going okay, I guess."

"You sure?" Todd asked, his voice calm and even.

Christy hesitated. *What should I say? The truth?*

"Actually, things have been better." *There. That was truthful.*

One of those terrible pauses followed—a pause that made Christy feel completely insecure, thinking that Todd must be sitting there on the other end wishing he'd never called in the first place.

"Tracy said you wanted me to call you," Todd said.

"Tracy?"

"Actually, she said that Heather said that you told her that you wanted me to call you."

Oh, no! Not another one of these triangles!

Christy carried the cordless phone over to the kitchen table and sat down, her free hand supporting her forehead. "Not really, Todd. I mean, I wanted to talk to you. As a matter of fact, I've wanted to talk to you all week. I guess it just hasn't worked out. I didn't tell anyone to relay any message to you, though. At least, not the way it sounds like I did."

Todd didn't say anything.

Christy felt like she needed to speak up and tell him how she felt. "Todd? I want you to know that…"

Just then Aunt Marti bustled into the kitchen, and Christy instantly silenced her heart and her words.

"Yes?" Todd prodded.

Christy turned away from her aunt, who was retrieving a diet soda from the refrigerator. Calmly getting up from the table and moving over to the window, Christy pretended to be watching her dad maneuver the remote-control car around the driveway. With her voice lowered she continued. "It's just that this week hasn't exactly gone the way I hoped it would. I thought we'd have more time together."

"I know."

That's all you're going to say, Todd? "I know"? I'm pouring my heart out here, and all you say is "I know"?

Another awkward pause. Then Todd spoke as if he had worked hard and long at choosing the right words.

"This week didn't exactly go the way I thought it would either. But you know what? It's okay. Everything is going to work out. As far as I'm concerned, nothing's changed."

That was all he said. She kept waiting for him to go on, to explain how everything was going to work out. Would he set a time and say that he was coming over so they could work everything out? No, he wasn't saying anything or committing to anything. Aunt Marti slid a glass into the ice cube dispenser in the door of the refrigerator. The ice clanged loudly.

"Sounds as though I'd better let you go," Todd said.

"Oh, no, that's okay." Christy watched her aunt leave the kitchen. "It's all right. What were you going to say?"

"I don't want to keep you from your family or anything."

"It's okay, really, Todd. You're not keeping me from
anything."

"We can talk more when I see you. I think I'd better let
you go. Later, Christy."

"When?" Christy demanded. "When are we going to
talk more?"

But Todd didn't answer. All she got was the dial tone
buzzing in her ear. *What do you mean, "Later"? Todd! What did you
mean, "Nothing's changed"? Todd!*

Christy marched across the kitchen floor, returned the
phone to its cradle, and then bustled into the dining room.
There she suddenly came face-to-face with her aunt, each
of them looking the other in the eye. Neither of them said
anything at first.

Then Aunt Marti lowered her head, her glass of soda in
her hand, and mumbled, "Excuse me, dear."

Christy couldn't stand the alienation—the icy distance
between them. "Wait a minute, Aunt Marti."

Marti turned.

The frustration with Todd filled Christy with boldness,
although the words tumbled out without much finesse.
"Aunt Marti, Mom told me about Johanna, and I'm really
sorry. I never knew."

Marti's expression grew pinched and fierce. "She what!"

Christy stood her ground and tried to soften her
approach. "Mom told me about your baby girl and how—"

"She had no right to tell you that!"

"Well, I'm glad she did because it helped me understand why you do so much for me and why you—"

Marti sharply drew up her index finger and wagged it inches from Christy's nose, growling through clenched teeth. "You don't understand a thing, Christina. Not a thing!"

Then she pivoted on her heels and marched off to her bedroom, leaving Christy alone in the dining room. She could hear the back door open and her dad's voice filling the kitchen. Christy fled upstairs to her room, shattered to the core and determined to stay away from everyone.

Wasn't talking supposed to clear up conflicts? Weren't people supposed to get their feelings out in the open? Then why did it become more of a mess when she talked to her aunt? And why, oh why did she feel more confused and frustrated after talking to Todd?

What am I doing wrong? Christy thought in despair. Throwing herself on the bed and curling up in an angry ball, she let all her thoughts go racing around and around. When they slowed long enough for her to recognize them as more than blurs and flashes, she carefully tried to sort them all out. The quiet helped her calm down.

After a long while, Christy reached for her Bible. She turned to the book of 1 John, since Tracy had suggested they all read it that week. That obviously wasn't going to happen, but Christy thought maybe she should try reading the short book. About halfway through the first chapter she remembered a verse she had seen in Doug's truck. It was written out on a three-by-five card and attached to his visor. It was something about God knowing our thoughts, and she remembered it being in Psalm 130-something.

Christy found Psalm 130 and started reading verse one: "'Out of the depths I cry to you, O Lord.'"

Boy, that's sure how I feel tonight.

She kept reading chapter after chapter. Some of the verses didn't make any sense at all, and she skipped some parts. But then she came to Psalm 139 and found Doug's verses, one through four: "O Lord, you have searched me and you know me. You know when I sit and when I rise; you perceive my thoughts from afar. You discern my going out and my lying down; you are familiar with all my ways. Before a word is on my tongue you know it completely, O Lord."

Closing her Bible, she lay back with her hands behind her head and stared at the ceiling. "Lord, if You already know what I'm thinking and what I'm going to say, then why do You let me blow it all the time? Why can't You control my life a little better? Every day I have to keep coming back and coming back and telling You how I messed up. Don't You get tired of it? Couldn't I just do things right for once, so I wouldn't have to keep asking You for a second chance? I don't want all this agony with my friends and family. I want everything to work out smoothly. And I want You to be happy with me."

She meant that prayer. She meant it with all her heart. And she knew God had heard her. After all, He knew all her thoughts, didn't He?

Then why was everything the same the next morning? Nothing seemed to have changed. Aunt Marti ignored Christy at breakfast. The subject of the party didn't come up on its own, and Dad didn't seem overly approachable, so Christy bit her tongue and waited.

Then, when she had a moment alone with her mom, she told her how she had mentioned Johanna to Aunt Marti the night before and how much it had angered Marti. She was hoping to open the door to a deep, meaningful talk with her mom again.

Mom only groaned and shook her head. "Why, oh why did you say anything, Christy? I didn't tell you so that you could throw it back at Martha."

"I didn't throw it at her. I mean, I wasn't trying to. I wanted her to know that I knew."

"Why?"

"Because it changed everything for me. Now I understand her a lot better, and I know why she treats me the way she does. You said that I could ask her about it."

"No, no, no, no, no. What I said was that if Marti ever opens up the topic that she could tell you the details because I don't feel I have the liberty to do that. For now, we'd be better off dropping the whole subject."

"Okay. I'm sorry. I didn't mean to—"

"I know you didn't," Mom said softly. "Would you mind handing me that pillow over there?"

She pointed to a throw pillow on the corner chair in the living room. Christy picked it up and handed it to her mom, who stuffed it under her cast.

"Mom?" Christy ventured. "Do you think I'll be able to go to the party at Heather's tonight?"

"I don't think so, Christy. Maybe next year, when you're older."

"But, Mom, I really need to see my friends and talk to them like I told you." Surely her mom would sympathize and see how important this was to Christy. She could talk her dad into it, couldn't she?

"I know it'll be disappointing, Christy. But there will be

other New Year's parties. I'd say the best thing you could do would be to call Tracy and Todd and try to work things out over the phone."

What a crushing blow! What had Uncle Bob said about her parents being teenagers once? Well, maybe they were, once. But at this moment, Christy could not believe her mother or father ever had been typical teens. If they had been, they would see the importance of the whole situation.

The more Christy thought about it, the more she realized she had better take her mom's advice or else she'd go back home tomorrow and have missed the opportunity to talk to either of them.

But why did she have to be the one to call them? Why couldn't Todd just call and have a normal conversation? Why did he have to be so confusing?

Christy finally decided that maybe she should go ahead and call Tracy and Todd. It would be better than going back to Escondido with everything completely unresolved. It couldn't hurt. Slipping upstairs, she drew in a breath of courage and dialed Tracy's number.

"Hello?" It was Tracy's mom.

"Is Tracy there?"

"No, she's out with some friends. Would you like to leave a message?"

"Do you know when she'll be back?"

"This afternoon sometime."

"I guess I'll try calling her then. Thanks. Bye."

Christy hung up and stared at the phone. It was now or never. She had to call Todd. He answered on the first ring, and she bravely said, "Hi, Todd?"

"Yeah?"

"Hi, it's Christy."

"I know."

"Could I talk to you for a minute?"

"Sure."

What is all that noise in the background? "Todd, I was wondering if you were going to Heather's party tonight."

"Maybe."

"Well, I'd really like to have a chance to talk to you. I'm going home tomorrow."

"Okay."

Come on, Todd! Can't you answer in more than one-word sentences? And what is all the commotion in the background? "So, when can we talk?"

He answered with half a laugh, "Later."

Christy lost it. "What do you mean, 'Later'? Is it too much to ask you for a straight answer? What is all this, 'Yeah, okay, maybe'? Why can't you ever commit to anything?"

Todd didn't respond. She had never yelled at him before. She could hear him breathing, and then she clearly heard Doug's voice in the background say, "Come on, Todd! You going to sit on the phone all day?"

So Doug was there. That meant Tracy must be too. All the "all-time friends" got together at Todd's, except no one thought to invite her. That hurt!

Suddenly she realized that she had told herself for months that her relationship with Todd was unchanging, but that wasn't true. She didn't know where she stood with him. Ever!

"Hey, Christy—" Todd began, but she cut him off with words she didn't plan on saying and regretted as soon as she let them spill out.

"Oh, excuse me," she said, sounding bitter and cold. "I must have the wrong number. I thought you were somebody else."

She slammed down the receiver and burst into tears. An instant later the phone rang. She let it ring twice before controlling her shaking voice and answering.

"What's going on?" Todd asked.

She couldn't answer.

"Christy?" His voice softened and cut through to her heart. "I don't know what's going on, but whatever I did to tick you off like this, hey, I'm sorry, all right?"

"It's not your fault, Todd." She blinked and swallowed the tears. "It's just me. Really. I'm sorry I bothered you."

"You didn't 'bother' me." Todd sounded irritated; then he mellowed out and said, "Listen, let's just let it go for now. We'll talk some more later, okay?" It was a statement. One of Todd's "this is how it is" factual statements. It left Christy feeling even more empty.

"Okay," she said hoarsely. Then, flippantly, she used Todd's own word back at him: "Later," and she slammed down the receiver.

So just when are we going to talk, Todd? You have all your friends over today, and tonight you have some big date. And even if, by some miracle, my parents let me go to Heather's party, would we even be able to talk then? Or are you going to bring your date with you—if you even show up, that is!

Suddenly David burst into the bedroom. "Christy? Oh there you are. You want to go out and play volleyball on the beach?"

"No."

"You want to ride bikes?"

"No!"

"Come on! Let's go out on the beach."

"I don't want to, David. Just leave me alone, okay?"

"I bet you'd go out if Todd were there!"

Christy sprang to her feet and shoved David out of her way. "Don't ever say that name to me again!"

She stormed from the room as David chanted after her, "Toddy, Toddy, Toddy, Toddy-Woddy, Toddy!"

11

The Mandolin Player

"*Christy?*" Uncle Bob's voice was extra gentle through her closed door. "I wanted to let you know we're having some company for dinner tonight. It's sort of a tradition. We have a formal dinner every New Year's Eve. You'll need to dress up."

She didn't want to dress up. She didn't want to eat dinner. And she certainly didn't want to go to Heather's party. She was convinced that she had no true friends in Newport Beach. She would be better off going home, although things weren't much better there, were they? Every time she was around people, she made them and herself miserable. Why couldn't her life be nice and calm and simple and uncomplicated?

A few minutes later her dad's thick hand pounded on the door. "Christy?"

She sat up straight and cleared her throat. "Yes?"

Dad opened the door and came over and sat next to her on the bed. "About this party at your girlfriend's house tonight. I've given it some thought and talked it over with your mother. We've decided that you can go."

"Well, I don't really want to go now," Christy said in a mousy voice.

Her dad looked at her in disbelief, then shook his head. "You might change your mind later. Just make sure you put your best dress on and join us for dinner at six, all right?"

Christy nodded. She made no attempt to go enjoy her last day of Christmas vacation. Instead she stayed in her room, struggling with herself, her dreamlike approach to life, her anger and frustration, and the way she felt like she was always failing God, no matter how hard she tried.

This week had turned out to be a great disappointment. Her Christian friends had let her down, Todd had left her completely disillusioned, and the whole thing with Alissa's and Marti's secrets left her weak and empty. That's how she felt. Empty. Completely empty.

At 5:15 she glanced at the clock and decided the battle needed to come to an end. Honestly, openly, she prayed, "You know what I'm thinking, don't You, God? You know everything I'm feeling. So why does it have to be like this? I hate falling flat on my face all the time."

A picture came to Christy's mind, something she had seen while shopping the other day with Aunt Marti. A darling little girl in pink tennies was shopping with her mommy. She had blond hair and pudgy cheeks and was just learning to walk. The mother put the toddler down while she looked through a rack of clothes. The toddler took about five wobbly steps before falling down, nose first. The mom scooped up her little angel, who was wailing loud enough for all to hear, kissed her on the nose, and then put her back down.

Christy thought the little girl would have stayed seated where the mom put her. But no, she stopped crying, stood up, and took six or seven more awkward steps until she touched her mommy. There she stood, smiling and holding on to her mother's leg.

Now Christy saw herself as that little girl, trying so hard to walk yet falling every time. "Time for me to get up and try again, isn't it, God?"

Feeling renewed enough to face the family, she sprang into action and showered and dressed in record time. The only really nice dress she had with her was a black one Aunt Marti had bought for her in Palm Springs last fall. It was definitely a party dress, even if the only party she would be going to was downstairs with a bunch of "old raisin" friends of Bob and Marti's.

The dress made her look older than fifteen—all her friends said so. Her dad, who was always telling her to "slow down," didn't approve of dresses that made her look older than she was—like the blue one Aunt Marti had bought her last summer. Christy had worn it a few months ago to church and then out to lunch with Rick and some of his friends, and her dad had not been happy. Well, the black one was the only nice dress she had with her, and her father had said, "Put on your best dress."

At six o'clock David knocked on her bedroom door. "I'm supposed to come get you," he said.

Christy swung the door open, and the first thing, the only thing, she saw was David's blinking bow tie. "David, you can't wear that!"

"Why not? I'll turn it off. Nobody will even know it blinks. Look, I even wore this dumb pink shirt." He opened his jacket to give the full view of the shirt, but all Christy noticed were the tie wires.

"Come here," Christy said, shaking her head. "If you're going to be rigged, at least hide your wires."

In a few minutes she had David completely rewired. As she tucked his collar down in the back, David squeezed the button in his pocket, causing his tie to blink twice.

Christy smiled. "I'm sorry about earlier, David. I shouldn't have shoved you. You are my favorite hamster, you know."

"Oh yeah?" David said with a smirk on his face. "Well, you're my favorite beetle."

"Beetle?" She scrunched up her nose.

"You look like a beetle—a black beetle. You're all dressed in black with all that dark stuff on your eyes. You look like a beetle."

Christy rushed over to the mirror in the hallway. Maybe he was right about the eye liner. She never could figure out how to put it on without it getting smeared or globby. Why did it always look good on the girls in the magazines? She quickly dabbed it off her eyelids.

"Come on," David said. "I can hear music down there. Real music."

David was right. As they swept down the stairs together, Christy was certain that the song "Greensleeves" came from a real instrument, not the stereo. And it sounded like a mandolin.

Christy and David saw their mom and dad, dressed nicely but not too formally, seated by the Christmas tree; the hundreds of twinkling lights in the dimly lit room played fancifully across Mom's dark sweater. Uncle Bob, dressed in a black tuxedo with a sapphire blue cummerbund, stood by the fire with a glass of eggnog in his hand. The three adults turned when they saw David and Christy approach the entryway, and Aunt Marti stepped around the corner, dazzling in a sapphire blue gown with silver sequins.

"Don't you two look marvelous! Look, Bob, Christy has on the dress I got for her in Palm Springs. Doesn't she look wonderful?"

Christy looked to her dad to see if he approved. He didn't. She could tell. But he smiled and said, "You sure these two are my kids? I don't ever remember my kids looking like that."

Everyone chuckled, and the music kept playing. Christy stepped into the living room, curious to see where the sweet melody was coming from. A musician, dressed in a black tux, sat in the dimly lit corner by the window, his head down, playing a mandolin.

Christy stood by the couch, listening and enjoying the end of the song. When the mandolin player plucked the last chord, he lifted his head. The gaze from his screaming silver-blue eyes shot across the room and sliced Christy right through the heart.

"Todd?" she whispered.

Todd stood and playfully gave a bow, then fixed his gaze back on Christy. She froze.

"Um, Mom, Dad? Have you met Todd?"

"Yes, we did earlier," Mom said.

"Hey, dude!" David greeted Todd and rushed over to give him a high five.

"Surprised?" Aunt Marti asked, sidling up next to Christy; her expression, her hair, and her dress all shimmered.

Christy nodded, fixing her attention back on Todd. He looked incredibly handsome.

"Good," Aunt Marti stated, apparently quite pleased with her prearranged New Year's surprise. Or had Uncle Bob set this up?

A tiny crystal bell sounded from the dining room.

"Ah!" Aunt Marti looked even more pleased with herself. "Dinner is served. Shall we?"

Then, as if this were some royal ball, Marti offered her hand to Bob, and he graciously escorted her to the dining room. Dad hoisted his wife from her chair with about as much grace as a dairyman lifting a lame calf. They both laughed, and David picked up the crutches and held them for his mother.

Without saying anything, Todd stepped forward and offered Christy his arm as he played along with the "escorting to dinner" game. She slipped her arm through his hesitantly.

"You okay?" Todd asked softly.

She nodded. "Todd? About today on the phone, I'm sorry."

"Hey. Don't worry about it."

But she did worry about it. She had completely given up on their relationship. In her imagination, Todd had been practically engaged to some other girl whom he was going to have dinner with tonight. She never guessed that she was the girl or that this was the dinner he was going to. She felt completely humbled.

At the dining room table, Todd pulled out her chair, and Christy seated herself. Then he sat next to her, swishing the white cloth napkin into his lap as if he dined like this every night.

Christy tried very hard to relax. Todd seemed fully himself, quite at home in a tux at a formal dinner. She never would have imagined it. There was so much she didn't know about Todd.

A maid or some kind of caterer brought in bowls of steaming soup: cream of broccoli. Bob and Marti both eased their spoons into their soup, then noticed that no one else followed.

"Ah, yes!" Bob declared, setting down his spoon. "Would you offer thanks for us, Norm?"

Dad stood and prayed for the food and for the coming year, gave thanks for the past year, and prayed one by one for each person around the table. Christy had never heard him pray so eloquently.

Ever since they had moved to Escondido and become involved in their church as a family, a lot of things had seemed to come alive for them.

"Well, Norman, you've certainly become the preacher," Marti exclaimed after he said, "Amen."

Dad sipped his soup. His bushy eyebrows pushed together like two caterpillars in a head-on collision. "Anyone can pray, Martha. And there certainly is plenty to pray about these days."

Marti didn't reply.

"'Course," Dad continued, "even if you're a little rusty at it, it never hurts to give it another try."

Marti slowly lowered her spoon. She didn't look offended, merely determined to have the last word. "Some of us have given prayer and God a second try and a third. But then we wise up." She lifted her spoon for emphasis. "And give up!"

Oh no! Christy thought. *Not now, you guys! Don't get into an argument over spiritual stuff now. Not in front of Todd!*

Christy had seen standoffs like this between her parents and aunt and uncle before. She had had her own conflicts with them whenever she talked about her commitment to the Lord. But then Todd changed everything.

"That's what I like about God," he said in his matter-of-fact way, crushing a cracker into his soup. "We might give up on God, but He never gives up on us."

"I'm not so sure about that," Bob said.

"You remember King David?" Todd asked. "In the Bible? He was called 'a man after God's own heart.' But he blew it big time: adultery, murder. Still, God didn't give up on him."

No one said anything. They kept eating, politely listening.

"And Moses," Todd continued. "Remember him? Great leader, right? Well, he killed an Egyptian. Then there's Abraham. He lied—said his wife was his sister so that some king would spare him and take his wife instead."

"What a jerk!" Christy interjected.

"Yeah? Well, Abraham did the same thing twice. Still, he's called 'the friend of God.'"

"So, what you're saying," Bob summed up, "is that the people in the Bible were all sinners, not saints. They weren't really heroes. Only imperfect people like the rest of us."

"I don't think that's what he meant," Mom said.

"No, that's exactly what I meant," Todd said. "Like Peter. The guy spent three years living with Jesus, and then the night of Christ's trial, Peter wimps out in front of a girl and says he doesn't even know the Lord. But Christ didn't give up on him."

"I certainly didn't intend for us to have a religious discussion over dinner," Marti said, lifting a bell and ringing it.

The maid appeared and cleared the soup bowls.

"Spinach salad with hot bacon dressing," Marti announced as the salad was served.

"So you believe, Todd, that God doesn't give up on people; rather, people give up on God?" Bob asked.

Christy couldn't tell if her uncle was agreeing with Todd or trying to trap him.

Todd nodded. "Of course, it's all in the surrender. Our surrender to God. Because even though we blow it, God will forgive us. But only if we surrender and ask Him for that forgiveness."

"Except you have to be sorry," David piped up. "They told us that in Sunday school. You have to be sorry for what you did, not just sorry that you got caught." He pushed up his glasses and put a whole cracker into his mouth.

Mom and Dad exchanged looks of amazement at their little David. Christy couldn't believe they were all talking about God and no one was stopping them or arguing.

Bob said, "Do you think, Todd, that these people you listed from the Bible deserved a second chance, or should they have been punished for what they did—the murders and everything?"

"They deserved to die. We all deserve to die."

"But God gave them a second chance?" Bob questioned.

"And a third and fourth and so on. See, even after a person becomes a Christian, he still blows it," Todd said.

"Then what's the point?" Marti asked, looking irritated yet sounding sweet. "If people are no better off 'saved' or 'unsaved' because they're all 'sinners,' as you say, then why do you 'born-again' people—and I don't mean that offensively, really—but why do you insist that people aren't Christians unless they've been, well, 'born again'?"

Mom and Dad exchanged glances of uncertainty, Bob looked at Todd, and Christy thought, *You know, Aunt Marti, that's a pretty good question. This week it sure doesn't seem to matter if my friends are Christians or not—especially Tracy. Everything got messed up even though we're all Christians.*

Todd leaned back in his chair, and Christy knew he was about to give one of his famous examples. She loved listening to him talk at times like this, and she loved his illustrations.

"It's like a baby. When a baby tries to walk, he falls down."

Christy immediately thought of the toddler she had seen while shopping with Marti.

"Babies don't give up just because they fall. They keep trying until they get better at it. But see, a baby wouldn't even try to walk if he were never born."

Christy thought she saw Marti's face flinch slightly, but she kept listening.

"That's like becoming a Christian. At first you still fall a lot because you're just learning to walk with the Lord. The more you grow, the better you get at it. But you have to be 'born again,' because the spirit side of your life can't grow if it's never been born."

Christy put down her fork and stared at her plate, seeing only a blur of colors. *That's it! That's why I've been falling all the time. I'm just learning. I'll get better as I grow more. It's okay. God under-stands, and He's right there to pick me up every time I tell Him I'm sorry.* She felt like jumping up and dancing around the table, saying, "I'm not a failure! God gives me second chances!"

"So, Todd, my boy," Bob challenged, "the next ques-tion is, when do you believe a person runs out of second chances with God?"

"You don't." Todd looked at Marti. "You only run out of time."

Marti gave Todd a puzzled look as he concluded, "If you die without ever surrendering your heart to the Lord, then the Bible says you'll be separated from Him forever."

Todd got the same tight, watery-eyed expression Christy had seen on his face at Shawn's funeral last summer. He looked down and said deliberately, "There are no second chances in hell."

Marti choked on a spinach leaf, and Bob looked disap-pointed, as if he figured he and Todd could carry on this theological discussion with no conclusions being drawn and no feathers being ruffled. Not so. From the moments of silent munching that followed it seemed apparent that Todd had given them all something to think about.

"This salad is delicious," Mom said cheerfully. "Did you say it's hot bacon dressing? It's so good."

Marti slowly pulled back into her take-charge mode, and by the time they cut into their stuffed Cornish game hens, she led the conversation.

"How long have you played the mandolin, Todd?"

"Couple of years. I've played guitar since I was six or seven."

"And where did you take lessons?"

"My dad taught me."

"And what does your dad do?" Bob asked.

"International sales for a computer company in Irvine."

"I thought you told me once that he was a hippie," Christy said, and Todd laughed.

"He was, but then he discovered money."

Here was a whole area of Todd's life Christy knew nothing about. There was so much more she wanted to learn about him. She started to relax and feel a little less guilty about how she had talked to him on the phone earlier. Yet the nagging questions remained: *Where do I stand with Todd? Exactly where is our relationship going? Did he come tonight out of courtesy to Marti, or did he really want to be with me?*

12

A Time to Talk

"That was delicious," Mom praised her sister as they all rose from the table.

"Shall we have coffee in the living room?" Marti suggested.

They entered the living room and found the manger scene had been moved to the side of the coffee table. In the center sat a silver tray with a silver coffee pot, sugar and creamer, and china cups and saucers. A tray of candies and little round cookies covered with powdered sugar sat next to the coffee service.

"Can I have some candy?" David asked.

"Help yourself," Bob said.

David stuffed a whole piece of chocolate into his mouth, and for the first time during the evening he squeezed his hidden button. The tie flashed on and off, drawing everyone's attention.

"Yum, yum!" David said, blinking the tie and enjoying all the attention as they laughed at him.

Marti poured coffee, Christy nibbled on a powdered

sugar cookie, and Todd played another song for them. When he finished, Dad said, "Isn't it time you got going?"

Christy looked at Todd. He smiled and shook Dad's hand.

"Thank you, sir. What time would you like Christy home?"

"Twelve-thirty."

We're going to Heather's party? I can't believe this! Christy thought. *My parents are letting me go with Todd!*

"Are you going to the party now? Can I go? Please? Can I go too?" David whined.

"No, sir," Dad said.

"Aw, why not?"

"This is Christy's night, son. Your chance will come soon enough."

Slipping into the hallway, Christy smiled and thought, *God, You knew about this all along, didn't You? Why was I so paranoid about everything?*

Marti followed her. "Christy, I wondered if you would like to borrow some earrings for your special night."

"Sure," Christy answered, eager to do whatever she could to mend her relationship with her aunt.

"Here." Marti held out a blue velvet box and said, "These are very special earrings. Your uncle gave them to me on our tenth anniversary. We celebrated in Paris that year, and he gave them to me in a little sidewalk café on the Champs-Elysées."

"Paris? Really?" Christy opened the box and exclaimed, "Oh, they're beautiful!" Lifting the exquisite diamond and pearl cluster earrings, she said, "Are you sure it's okay for me to wear these?"

"Of course, Christy. Now don't spoil my fun by saying you won't wear them. It's my way of contributing something special to your memorable evening."

"Thanks, Aunt Marti. I really appreciate it."

The two exchanged warm smiles.

Then, as Marti helped Christy fasten the earrings, she spoke softly. "This was a difficult week for me, Christina. You have a way of getting to the core of a person; did you know that?"

Christy shook her head.

"Hold still," Marti cautioned.

"I wanted to apologize for all the things I said that upset you," Christy said. "I don't know when to be quiet. Maybe I should be more like the quiet woman on the sign at that restaurant."

"No, dear," Marti said. "You keep being yourself. You have tenacity, Christy, and I don't want you to ever lose that."

"I'm not sure I know what that is, but I hope it's good."

Marti brushed a spot of powdered sugar from Christy's cheek, "Yes, it's good." Then, focusing on the earrings more than she needed to, Marti said, "Tenacious women are good at giving second chances."

Christy desperately wanted to say something deep and tender, like in the movies, but all that came to mind was, "Well, then you must be a tenacious woman too. Maybe that's where I get it from."

"Possibly."

"Ready?" Todd asked, stepping toward them.

"Yes," Christy said, giving Marti a quick hug. "Thanks for being like a second mom to me, Aunt Marti. I really appreciate you. And thanks for letting me wear your earrings."

"You two get going now," Marti said, snapping out of the tender moment. "I'm certain it goes without saying, but Todd, if you have too much to drink, don't try to drive home. We'll be up, so you call us, okay?"

Todd began to laugh, but then he saw that Marti was serious. "Don't worry. I don't drink. Honest."

"Well, it is New Year's, and you don't know what Heather might have at this party."

"If you knew Heather, you wouldn't even think that," Christy said. Then she realized her aunt must be remembering a party Christy went to last summer where the alcohol and drugs were plentiful. That was an experience Christy never wanted to repeat.

"Don't worry," Todd said. "We'll be fine."

Christy waved to her family in the living room and noticed that David was drowning his sorrows in the remainder of the chocolates, his silly tie blinking off and on.

Sorry, David, but this time you can't take him away, Christy thought. *Finally, Todd and I are going to be together.*

Christy had so much she wanted to talk to Todd about, yet, oddly enough, they drove the first few blocks in silence. She wanted to get the conversation going, but now that they were finally alone she couldn't think of a thing to say. Did he feel strange too?

Just then Todd stopped at a red light. Christy glanced out the front windshield. It was their intersection! This is where he kissed her last summer. Did he remember? Was he thinking the same thing? She glanced at him cautiously. He was looking straight ahead.

The light turned green, and Todd sped on.

"I wanted to ask you something," Todd said, breaking the stillness.

Good! Finally! He's going to start the conversation!

"I've been thinking a lot about Alissa lately. Have you heard from her?"

Alissa! You've been thinking about Alissa? What about us?

"Actually," Christy said stiffly, "I got a letter from her the other day."

"How's she doing?"

"Not so well," Christy said, letting down her guard and choosing to give the news to Todd slowly. "She asked me to pray for her. She's going through a rough time right now."

"She needs the Lord," Todd stated.

"I agree," Christy said as they pulled into a tight parking spot at the end of Heather's block. "But she also needs people in her life who can help and support her while she goes through all this."

"Goes through what?" Todd asked. He turned off the engine and faced Christy.

"Todd, she's pregnant."

"How pregnant?"

"What do you mean?"

"How many months along?"

"Five or six. Why?"

"I knew it!" Todd hooted, popping the palm of his hand against the steering wheel. "Man, this is great!"

"Todd!" Christy couldn't believe his reaction. "I just said she's having a baby!"

Todd kept smiling. "You know what, Christy? It's Shawn's baby."

"Shawn's? How do you know?"

"She's five or six months along, right? Well, count backward."

"I don't know. I thought it might be that other guy's—Erik. The one with the black Porsche who she met at Shawn's party."

"Nope, it's Shawn's."

"How do you know that?"

"I know Erik. He never went to bed with her. He tried, but he never did."

Christy thought back to the day Erik had come to Alissa's house and was upset when he found Christy there.

"I wonder if that's why Erik said all those mean things to Alissa the day she left."

"Could be." Todd leaned back in his seat. The glow from the streetlight washed over his face, showing his contented expression.

"Todd, you should see your face right now. I think this whole thing is awful, and you're smiling. I mean, can you imagine how hard it must be for Alissa being pregnant, with no parents around to support her? And she can't even tell the baby's father because he's dead!"

"Don't you see?" Todd said, leaning forward. "She's giving that baby life. Shawn's baby! She could have aborted it. But she chose to give it life!"

"Todd, she got pregnant! That's not such a noble thing. And you're acting as if she's a heroine. From my perspective, she blew it, and now she's suffering the consequences."

"Right. She is. But don't we all blow it sometimes, in one way or another?"

"Well, yes, but—"

"Doesn't God forgive us and give us second chances?"

"I don't know if she's asked God to forgive her."

"True, and that is the first step," Todd agreed. "But she didn't try to solve the problem by having an abortion. She's going to give that little soul a life, and who knows what that kid is going to be when he grows up? He could be the greatest evangelist the world has ever known!"

"What makes you think it's going to be a 'he'?"

"Okay, *she's* going to become the greatest evangelist the world has ever known!" Todd smiled and then looked serious again. "Man, we've got to pray for her and the baby. We need to pray that she'll meet some Christians who will help her out."

"She did meet some." Christy explained about Frances and the Crisis Pregnancy Center. As she did, Todd's expression grew into a full smile.

"Man, this is incredible!"

"Todd, I still don't see why you're so happy about this. I didn't think sin was something Christians were supposed to get all excited about."

Todd laughed at her in a warm kind of way. "I'm not excited about the sin, Christy. You're absolutely right. Shawn and Alissa should never have gone to bed together. That was totally wrong. At the time, I knew about it, and it ate me up inside."

"You knew?"

"Yeah. But the thing is, God's not limited by their mistakes. Don't you see? Shawn and Alissa created a human life. A soul! Even though what they did was wrong, they made something that is going to last forever. A soul!" Todd looked really excited, as though he was about to shout or something. "A soul, Christy! Even angels can't do that!"

Christy's eyes grew wide. Todd amazed her. He absolutely amazed her.

Todd looked at Christy with a new expression: a pleased look. "You do realize, don't you, that Alissa went to that pregnancy center and looked for a Christian because of you. You might have been the one who really saved that baby's life."

Christy shook her head. "I didn't do anything."

"You showed Alissa that you loved her and cared about her. You were a true friend. And that is something." Todd smiled, his dimples showing in the dim light. "Come on," he said. "We'd better get over to the party. Stay there. I'll get your door."

Being with Todd, even though they talked about Alissa the whole time, warmed Christy. She felt as though she had come into a warm house on a cold day. The anger, hurt, and confusion she had felt toward him that afternoon had thawed, melted, and washed away.

When Todd opened the van door and took her hand to help her out, she felt like she'd just been given a second chance with Todd. And maybe that was what kept all lasting friendships going: lots of second chances.

Todd kept holding Christy's hand for the half-block walk to Heather's house. It didn't matter to Christy if they ever defined their relationship. She didn't need to know where she stood with Todd. Not when she had her hand in his and they were this close.

"Well," Heather exclaimed when she swung open the door, "we were wondering when you two were going to show up. You guys look like you're going to the prom."

Christy felt her cheeks turning red, and Todd looked as though he weren't used to having attention drawn to what he was wearing either.

"Where did you get the tux?" Heather asked.

"My mom. I had to have it for her wedding. She's one of those people who thinks, 'Why rent when you can buy?'"

"Well, you both look like you should be on the cover of some magazine. And Christy, those earrings are unbelievably sparkly. Are they real diamonds?"

"Yes. They're my aunt's."

Heather *ooh*ed and *aah*ed while Todd stepped down into the living room and started talking to the guys. Tracy, who had been sitting next to Doug on the couch, came over to Christy.

"Hi," Tracy said. She looked pretty tonight in her pink sweater, with her hair curled full around her heart-shaped face. "Could we go in the kitchen for a minute, Christy?"

"Sure," Christy said, following her to the corner of the kitchen by the window.

"I need to apologize, Christy. I was rude to you that night at Richie's, and I'm sorry."

"It's okay, Tracy. Don't worry about it."

"You sure? No hard feelings?"

"Yes, I'm definitely sure. And you need to know that I honestly wasn't trying to upset you when I skated with Doug. I didn't know you liked him!"

Tracy's face broke into her bright smile. "I know. I didn't tell you, remember?"

"Well, maybe you should have," Christy said with a laugh. "Then I would have stayed far away from him!"

Tracy reached over and took Christy's arm. "No, I don't

ever want you to stay away from Doug or any of these guys just because I like one of them or somebody else likes one of them. I want all of us to be able to hang out together and not play jealousy games. And that's what made me so mad at myself the other day. That's exactly what I ended up doing at the skating rink! Isn't that dumb?"

"No. I know exactly how it can happen. I've been there."

"Well, Christy, if you ever see me doing that again, promise you'll slap me," Tracy said.

They both laughed.

"Only if you promise you'll slap me too," Christy said, still laughing. "I got caught up in playing games too, and I'm really sorry, Tracy."

"It's okay. Let's just start over from here."

Just then Doug came up to them. "Christy, you look really nice tonight."

Impulsively, Christy put her arm around Doug's neck, the way he always hugged everybody else, and she gave him a quick hug. Then she quickly turned to Tracy. "That was okay, wasn't it?"

"Of course!" Tracy said. "That's how I want us all to be."

"What was that for?" Doug asked.

"That was for being the most considerate guy I know."

Doug looked at Tracy. "Did I send her flowers without knowing it?"

"No, no, no," Christy said. "When you came over and told me you were taking Tracy out and said that you still wanted to be friends with me, I thought that was the sweetest thing any guy could ever do. You made it possible for me to still feel comfortable around you, even though you and Tracy are together now."

"Wow," Doug said, "that's awesome, Christy."

Heather popped her head around the corner at that moment and said, "Awesome? You still use that word, Doug? Didn't they teach you any new words in college?"

"Hey! *Awesome* is an awesome word!"

"Come on, you guys," Brian called from the living room. "We've got the game all set up."

Tracy and Christy exchanged glances.

"Don't slap me," Tracy teased. "This isn't the kind of game I meant for you to slap me over."

Christy laughed and joined the rest of her all-time friends in the living room.

13

Forever

Christy ended up on the team with Heather, Doug, Tracy, and Brian. Todd was on the opposite team. It was a word-guessing game in which they drew with felt pens on a big, white easel pad. Within fifteen minutes, Todd's team was way ahead.

"These phrases are too hard for my team," Heather whined. "Don't they have any with 'awesome' or 'dude' in them? Doug would guess those a whole lot faster!"

They laughed, and Doug jumped up, grabbed Heather by the shoulders, and shouted, "Come on, you guys, let's throw her in the pool."

Todd and the other guys jumped up and grabbed Heather. She screamed and kicked until they put her back down.

Christy watched Todd, trying hard to remember exactly what it was that afternoon that made her want to scratch him off her list of friends forever. He was everybody's friend, but she was special to him. He had proved that by putting together their breakfast on the beach and by coming to dinner tonight. Why did she need to define their relationship? It was more than "like" and not truly "in love." They were somewhere in-between.

Around eleven o'clock Heather rounded everyone up and directed them to the backyard, where a fire blazed in an in-ground fire pit a few yards from the swimming pool. Heather handed out marshmallows and coat hangers and had graham crackers and chocolate bars on the picnic table behind them. The gang set to work making s'mores.

Doug started acting silly, bending his coat hanger in half. "Trace," he called, "hand me two marshmallows. Where's Todd? Where did he go?"

Todd called from the picnic table, "Yo, Doug, over here."

Then Doug stood up with the coat hanger across his head and marshmallows attached to either end so they covered his ears. "Todd," he hollered, "check it out! Number fifteen. Earmuffs."

Todd laughed until the graham cracker in his hand crumbled into dust. As he held his side, tears streamed down his face. Christy had never seen him crack up like that.

"I don't get it," Heather said, looking at Doug and then at Todd.

"It's this stupid book," Tracy explained, shaking her head. "Todd gave it to Doug for Christmas."

"Todd gave one of those books to Doug?" Christy asked.

"Yes, have you seen it? All about what to do with dead hamsters," Tracy said.

"Ewwww!" Heather squealed. "That's gross."

"Yes, I've seen it," Christy replied. She poked her coat hanger into the fire and toasted her marshmallows.

"Todd gave me the same book," Tracy said disgustedly. "Don't you think a guy would have to be pretty strange to give a girl a book like that?"

"Yes, he would," Christy agreed. "Definitely strange." Christy stared into the amber flame and thought about Rick. *Guys give joke gifts like that to their buddies. Rick must see me as a buddy. But then why did he kiss me? You don't kiss your buddies.*

That's when Christy decided that she and Rick were buddies. They had pushed their relationship into something it wasn't by trying to be romantic. Not that they couldn't end up going out someday. But they definitely weren't at that point now. And it was silly to pretend they were or to let other people convince them they were. She liked Rick, and she wanted to go back to being buddies—to give their friendship a second chance. To just let it be what it was without trying to make it something it wasn't.

Christy felt as though a weight had been lifted off her shoulders. She knew what she had done was wrong. Even though she wasn't sure how to fix it, she wouldn't give up until she figured it out. After all, she was tenacious, wasn't she?

While Christy was lost in thought, her marshmallows burned, but she didn't mind. She peeled off the burned part and tried again, roasting the sticky white insides. That's how she always toasted them on purpose when she was a kid. She knew how to burn and peel for layer after layer until only the core of the marshmallow was left.

"Look out! Yours are on fire!" Todd said, coming up next to her, his eyes still sparkly from the laughter tears.

Christy pulled her hanger out of the fire and blew. As Todd watched, she peeled the top layer off and popped it into her mouth.

"Trying to give that marshmallow a second chance, I see," Todd teased when he saw her stick it back in the fire.

Christy said, "I think everybody deserves a second chance, even marshmallows."

Just then Doug trotted into the backyard with a big box in his arms. "Look, you guys, sparklers! I've had them since the Fourth of July. Let's see if they still work."

They all finished up their sticky s'mores and grabbed sparklers and lit them in the fire pit. Suddenly flashes of glittering light were everywhere. The group laughed and swished sparklers in the air. The fireworks lasted for only a few minutes, and then everyone tossed the sparkler sticks into the fire pit. A few people went inside while others roasted one last marshmallow.

Christy joined the group inside and was standing by the kitchen sink, washing her hands, when Todd came up behind her and said, "You about ready to go?"

She gave him a surprised look. "It's not midnight yet. Don't you want to stay?"

"I said I'd have you home by twelve-thirty. I think we should go now."

"Okay," Christy said, still not sure why they were leaving so early. They said good-bye to Heather and the rest of the group.

Todd maneuvered Gus out of the tight parking spot, and Christy said, "Thanks so much for tonight, Todd. For coming to dinner and taking me to the party."

"But you would have liked to have known ahead of

time what was going on, right?" Todd asked.

Christy was surprised that he guessed her feelings so accurately. "I like being surprised, but, yes, I guess I got pretty insecure over when I'd see you and when we'd be able to talk."

"That's why we left Heather's early. I wanted to make sure everything was cleared up between us."

"Is it?" Christy asked.

"As far as I'm concerned it is. Nothing's changed. Is everything okay with you?"

Christy leaned back. "This is probably really stupid to ask, and I'll probably regret it, but, Todd, what hasn't changed? I mean, what are we?"

"What are we?" he repeated, glancing in her direction.

"Are we just friends or more than friends or buddies or what?"

"I don't think there's a word for it. It's something between 'friends' and 'boyfriend-girlfriend,' like you and Tracy were saying the other day at my house."

"So, what does that mean?" Christy hoped she wasn't pushing this too far.

"It means I really care about you, Christy. It also means I don't want to cut you off from any of your other friends."

"Like when we went ice-skating?"

"Exactly. You and Doug were having a great time together. I didn't want to come between you. But to be honest, I felt pretty sorry for myself. I guess I assumed you and I would be together that afternoon."

Christy felt awful when he said that. "Todd, I wanted to be with you that day too. I guess I also had big expectations of what the day should have been like. Everything got messed up. And then the next day, when you drove by and Doug was smelling my hair—"

Todd laughed. "Is that what he was doing?"

Christy nodded. "I got a perm that day, and my hair smelled like green apples."

Todd laughed again. "Man, when I drove by and saw you two I felt as though I'd been eating green apples!"

Christy laughed. "Todd, I'm sorry everything got so mixed up."

"I think it was good. It made me think through a bunch of stuff. I ran into your uncle later at the gas station, and he invited me for dinner tonight. Said I'd probably be able to take you to Heather's party if I asked your dad in person, which I did this afternoon. When your dad said it was okay, I was going to ask you because you sounded freaked when you called. But David told me you were in your room and that he wasn't supposed to ever mention my name to you again." Todd grinned, and Christy hung her head.

"I can't believe this! I was in my room all upset over nothing, and the whole time you were downstairs. Can you believe that? I feel so immature right now."

"That's all right. That's kind of how I was that night at Richie's."

They were both quiet for a few minutes; then Christy said, "I guess we still don't know what we are."

"We're friends, Christy. True friends. Real friends. What that means exactly, I guess we'll have to figure out as we go along. One thing I know for sure is that no matter what happens to either of us, no matter what the future holds, we're going to be friends forever."

Christy's voice came out delicate and sincere. "Todd, I

feel the same way. No matter where we are between 'like' and 'love,' and no matter where we end up, I want to be your friend forever too."

At that instant, Todd pulled up at a red light. Without any warning he stopped Gus, opened his door, hopped out, and ran to Christy's side. Yanking her door open, he grabbed her by the hand and said, "I can't believe it. This is perfect!"

"What?" Christy squawked. "Todd! What are you doing?"

Taking Christy by the hand, Todd tugged her out of the van and led her to the front of Gus the Bus, where the headlights spotlighted them.

"This is it!" he said. "This is where we are. Somewhere in the middle. Kind of like being right in the middle of the street."

Christy's eyes shot past Todd to the stoplight. Then it hit her—this was "their" intersection! They were standing right in the middle of their intersection on New Year's Eve, dressed in their best clothes and stopping traffic.

"Todd!" Christy laughed. "This is crazy!"

"I know," he said. "Isn't it great?" Then Todd reached inside his tux and pulled out a small, rectangular box wrapped with a white ribbon. Excitedly, like a little boy, he said, "I didn't know when to give this to you, but, hey, now's as good a time as any. Go ahead, open it."

Cars zipped past them, and Christy kept laughing. Only Todd would do this. She tore off the ribbon and paper. Inside the box she found a delicate gold ID bracelet. "Todd, it's beautiful!"

"Read what it says."

She held it toward the headlights and read the engraved inscription: " 'Forever.' Oh, Todd, this is so perfect. I love it! Thank you so much. It's exactly what we were just saying about being friends forever."

"You noticed that too?"

The light turned green, and the car behind them honked. Todd stepped around the van and waved them past like a patrolman.

Christy knew the passengers were staring at her, standing there in her fancy black dress, with her aunt's real diamond earrings, clutching the gift box in one hand and the gold bracelet in the other. But she didn't care.

At that very moment Christy knew where she was for perhaps one of the first times in her life. She was right in the middle of the street, right in the middle of her relationship with Todd, and that's right where she wanted to be—nothing more, nothing less. And right now nothing else mattered.

"Let me help you put it on," Todd said eagerly, stepping back to Christy's side. He slipped the bracelet around her wrist, pinched the tiny clasp open, and tried several times before securing it around her wrist.

Then Todd took Christy's hand in his and said, "I really mean it, Chris. No matter what the future holds, no matter how many other guys you go out with or how many miles separate us, a part of you will always be right here." He patted his chest.

"You're in my heart," he continued. "You're my friend. I honestly don't know where we go from here, but I'm not worried. God knows. All I know is we're going to spend eternity together with Him. This bracelet is my way of saying, 'Here's my friendship. I promise it to you. It's yours forever.'"

Christy melted. She never imagined Todd had such a romantic side to him. Yet it wasn't all emotions. It was solid and well thought out. The amazing thing was, although she felt incredibly close to Todd at this moment, she also felt incredibly close to God.

Suddenly a loud boom echoed from a few blocks over, followed by honks and hoots and a screaming cherry bomb sailing through the air.

"Must be midnight," Christy said. "Happy New Year, Todd."

He smiled and wrapped his arms around her. "Happy forever, Christy."

Then he kissed her, twice. First on the lips, quick and tender, in the middle of the street, in front of Gus's head-lights. The second kiss came after hustling her back to her side of the van and opening her door. He kissed her this time on the right side of her forehead, partly in her hair, partly on her eyebrow. It was sweet—a tender, caring, pro-tective kind of kiss.

Todd ran to his side of the van, waving at the car behind them and shouting, "Happy New Year to you too, buddy!" He popped Gus into gear, and they charged through the intersection, barely making it through before the light turned red.

Christy twisted her wrist back and forth, watching her bracelet catch glimmers of light. "I love this bracelet, Todd."

His jaw stuck out a little more than usual with a proud, satisfied look. "I'm glad you do. Sorry it's late. It was supposed to be your Christmas present, but it took me a while to figure out what to have engraved on it."

"How did you think of 'Forever'?"

"Believe it or not, I got it out of First John. Remember Tracy said she wanted us to read it and talk about what we learned when we got together? Well, even though that never happened, I read it through a couple of times."

"I read it too," Christy said. "Well, not all of it, but I started it."

"What I got out of it was that God's love for us goes on forever, and that's how He wants us to love each other."

Christy knew Todd was right. She also knew she'd learned a little about being more loving to her friends and family week. That thought made her feel sad at the opportunities that were lost. "It's too bad we never got to all talk about it together."

Todd shrugged. "Tracy said the same thing when she and Doug were over this afternoon. They wanted to go with me to pick up your gift at the jeweler's, and then they came over to help me wrap it. I told her there's always the next time we're all together."

Christy realized that was why Doug and Tracy were at Todd's house when she called. They weren't having a special get-together and leaving her out. They were helping Todd with her present. Now she felt even worse about the things she had said to him on the phone. But that was in the past. Todd had already told her it was okay. She knew they needed to move forward and start fresh in this brand-new year.

"Thanks, Todd," Christy said, reaching over and squeezing his shoulder.

"Sure. You're welcome."

"I mean, thanks for the bracelet, but thanks too for not giving up on me, even though I acted like a brat."

"Hey, I already forgave you. Let's leave it back there, all right?" He nodded over his shoulder. "Let's give us a second chance."

They pulled up in front of Bob and Marti's, and Todd came around to open her door. Slipping his arm around her shoulders, they walked slowly to the front door.

Todd tilted his head back, looked up, and stopped walking. Christy put her arm around his waist and looked up too. The night sky stretched above them like a long, extravagant garment of black velvet dotted with thousands of glittering diamonds.

"It's beautiful," Christy murmured.

"You know," Todd said, "that's where God scatters our sins when we confess them to Him. He says, 'As far as the east is from the west,' that's how far He's removed from us all the stuff we've done wrong."

They gazed at the vastness in quiet awe.

"When I was little," Christy said softly, "I used to think that the sky at night was a big, black blanket that separated heaven from earth, and the stars were a whole bunch of little pinholes that the angels poked in the blanket so they could look down on us."

Todd squeezed her shoulder and gave a little chuckle. "Sometimes, Christy, you totally amaze me."

"Oh yeah?" she said, pulling away just enough so she could face him. "Most of the time, Todd, you 'totally amaze me'!"

"Good," he replied, confidently pulling her back to his side and walking up to the front door. "That's the way it should be. Hey, do you think your aunt and uncle would mind if I went in, even though it's late? I left my mandolin in the living room."

"I'm sure it's okay," Christy said. "My aunt might even give you a sobriety test."

They both laughed and went in, finding her whole family still up, sitting in the den. As soon as they walked in, Dad looked at his watch.

"You're early," he said.

"Should we leave and come back?" Christy teased.

"Of course not!" Mom said, turning her head from her stretched-out position on the couch. "How was the party?"

"It was great!" Christy said. "We played some games, then roasted marshmallows outside over a fire pit. Doug brought a big box of sparklers, and that was really fun."

"I must say, that's a much better way to welcome the new year than to drink yourselves silly!" Marti commented. "You should be thankful for such good friends, Christy."

"I am," she said, smiling at Todd. "Believe me, I am."

Todd returned the smile and said, "I need to pick up my mandolin. Is it still in the living room?"

"Why, yes, it is," Marti said.

Then Todd did something that made Christy feel proud. He walked over and shook hands with her dad and with Bob, then kissed Marti on the cheek and thanked her for the dinner. He slapped high five with David and leaned over and gave Christy's mother a quick peck on the cheek too.

"Thanks for letting me be a part of your family tonight," Todd said.

Perhaps only Christy knew how much being with family on the holidays meant to Todd.

"You're welcome at our house anytime," Marti said graciously. "And I mean that."

"Same goes for us," Dad said.

Christy couldn't believe her ears! *Is my father actually inviting Todd to come down to our house?*

"You'll have to come to Escondido sometime and see us," Dad said. Christy knew he meant it.

"Thanks. I'll do that. I'd better get going. Happy New Year, everyone." Todd slipped into the living room while Christy waited for him at the front door. With his mandolin in one hand, Todd gave her a one-armed hug and said, "I guess I'll have to come down to Escondido sometime."

"You heard what my dad said. You're welcome anytime."

Todd opened the front door, then turned and said, "Well, I'll see you, then."

"Later?" Christy teased.

Todd smiled and said, "Yeah, later, Chris." He leaned over and gave her one of his warm, brotherly kisses on her temple, partly in her hair. Then, as he closed the door, he said with a slight wink, "Green apples, huh?"

The door was all the way closed before Christy understood, and when she did she laughed aloud. Her heart felt as it never had before: warmed, happy, content.

"Don't worry, everybody! He only kissed her on the head," David reported in a blaring voice to the others in the den. His scrunched-up nose stuck out from around the corner.

"Why, you little hamster!" Christy yelled and chased him through the dining room and into the kitchen. "I'm going to short-circuit your bow tie!"

"Just try, Beetle Face," David challenged from behind the kitchen counter.

"That's enough, you two!" Dad's voice boomed from the hallway. "It's time for bed for both of you."

Regaining her dignity, Christy smoothed back her hair and paraded past her dad with David hot on her trail, still trying to torment her.

"Good night, everyone!" she called from the bottom stair. "And good night, David," she said, turning to face him. "I hope you don't dream about big black beetles that like to eat little hamsters!"

His face puckered up, and he said, "Oh yeah? Well, I hope that…" He searched for some jab. "I hope that…that you don't dream at all!"

Christy turned and floated up the stairs, murmuring, "Who needs to dream?" *Tonight was real life, and it was better than any dream.*

Then, just to make sure tonight really happened, she reached for her wrist and ran her finger over the etched "Forever" on her smooth, gold bracelet. *Forever, Lord.* Her heart melted into the words as she prayed them. *No matter what happens, no matter what You've got planned for me, no matter how things end up for Todd and me, I want You to know that I am Yours. I'm Yours, God. Yours forever.*

Can't get enough of ROBIN JONES GUNN!

Christy Miller COLLECTION

●●●●● **VOLUME 2**

Book 4: Surprise Endings

With prom just around the corner, Christy gets swept away making plans for her dress and the entire event. But her dreams turn to bitter disappointment when her parents tell her she won't be allowed to attend, and Christy watches in tears as Todd takes another girl. Can Christy leave a space in her heart for God to fill, or will she keep looking to others for her happiness?

Book 5: Island Dreamer

Celebrating her sixteenth birthday in Maui and holding hands in the moonlight with handsome Todd don't exactly meet Christy's romantic expectations. The problem? Her best friend Paula. As soon as Paula sees Todd, she never takes her baby-blues off the goal of winning him. Can Christy put aside her jealousy and fears? And will Todd choose Christy and their longstanding relationship over Paula and her flirty maneuvers?

Book 6: A Heart Full of Hope

Christy's starting her junior year going steady with a handsome guy who carefully plans each date to show Christy she's wonderful. And Christy is dazzled by him. But when her parents restrict her activities and insist Christy find a job, her boyfriend is upset by her parents' strict rules. Can he and Christy work out their problems? Or will her parents ruin everything?

Christy Miller

COLLECTION

● ● ● ● ● **VOLUME 3**

Book 7: True Friends

When Christy finds herself on a ski slope in Lake Tahoe in the arms of a handsome ski instructor, she is suddenly pulled into the "in" crowd, while Katie is left out. And when Katie discovers some of the kids are up to no good, she expects Christy to help expose them rather than support her newfound friends. Can Christy and Katie patch up their damaged friendship?

Book 8: Starry Night

When Christy's ex-boyfriend, Rick, seems interested in Katie, Christy and Katie's relationship changes. Then an old friendship takes on new meaning, and Christy wonders why she never before saw Doug as the prince he is. All of these relationships collide, leaving Christy wondering what is happening. Will she end up counting stars with Rick or Doug?

Book 9: Seventeen Wishes

Working as a camp counselor is not how Christy envisioned spending her summer. Before long, she is up to her ears with kids who won't obey her, camp rules to remember, and an embarrassing incident that makes her the camp joke. Then a moonlight canoe cruise with a handsome counselor leads Christy to make some decisions about her future and trust that God knows what's best for her. What will she be wishing as she blows out the candles on her birthday cake?

Christy Miller COLLECTION

VOLUME 4

Book 10: A Time to Cherish

Juggling the stress of not having enough time with Todd, trying to understand Katie's relationship with Michael, and making Doug happy forces Christy to evaluate what's most important to her. Can Christy find a way to keep her friendship with Katie even though they're not in agreement on much anymore?

Book 11: Sweet Dreams

Christy is relieved her senior year is over. She and Katie have made up, and Christy's dreams of growing closer to Todd are coming true. Suddenly, Christy finds herself having to make what might be the most difficult decision of her life—one that could end every sweet dream she ever possessed. Will Christy find the strength to do what she knows is right?

Book 12: A Promise Is Forever

On a European mission trip with her friends, Christy can just see herself traveling across different countries and talking to new friends, like Sierra Jensen. But when tensions among the group set in, memories of Todd constantly swim in Christy's mind. Then she's sent to Spain alone while her friends travel elsewhere. Will Christy face her fears of the future? And can she truly trust that God has great things planned for her even when all seems lost?

Don't Miss the Next Chapter in Christy Miller's Unforgettable Life!

Follow Christy and Todd through the struggles, lessons, and changes that life in college will bring. Concentrating on her studies, Christy spends a year abroad in Europe and returns to campus at Rancho Corona University. Will Todd be waiting for her? CHRISTY AND TODD: THE COLLEGE YEARS follows Christy into her next chapter as she makes decisions about life and love.

CHRISTY AND TODD: THE COLLEGE YEARS by Robin Jones Gunn

Until Tomorrow • As You Wish • I Promise

Check out Robin Jones Gunn's new online shop!

Books, clothing, posters and more

You're going to love shopping at Robin's Nest Shop, author Robin Jones Gunn's new online store for books and more! The shop includes books from all of her collections—Christy Miller & Friends, the Glenbrooke Series, the Sisterchicks® Series, and her children's and gift books. You'll find audiobooks, MP3, posters, T-shirts, including the popular "I Love Todd" T-shirt, and special offers, too.

Secure and private, you can shop and pay for your items online—and they're delivered directly to you.

Click and shop at: http://shop.robingunn.com

A portion of the proceeds from all items sold at Robin's Nest Shop will be donated to various ministries around the world.

About the Author

Just like Christy, Robin Jones Gunn was born in Wisconsin and lived on a dairy farm. Her father was a school teacher and moved his family to southern California when Robin was five years old. She grew up in Orange County with one older sister and one younger brother. The three Jones kids graduated from Santa Ana High School and spent their summers on the beach with a bunch of wonderful "God-lover" friends. Robin didn't meet her "Todd" until after she'd gone to Biola University for two years and had an unforgettable season in Europe, which included transporting Bibles to underground churches in the former Soviet Union and attending Capernwray Bible School in Austria.

As her passion for ministering to teenagers grew, Robin assisted more with the youth group at her church. It was on a bike ride for middle schoolers that Robin met Ross. After they married, they spent the next two decades working together in youth ministry. God blessed them with a son and then a daughter. When her children were young, Robin would rise at 3 a.m. when the house was quiet, make a pot of tea, and write pages and pages about Christy and Todd. She then read those pages to the girls in the youth group, and they gave her advice on what needed to be changed. It took two years and ten rejections before *Summer Promise* was accepted for publication. Since its release in 1988, *Summer Promise* along with the rest of the Christy Miller and Sierra Jensen series have sold over 2.3 million copies and can be found in a dozen translations all over the world.

Now that her children are grown and Robin's husband has a new career as a counselor, Robin continues to travel and tell stories about best friends and God-lovers. Her popular Glenbrooke series tracks the love stories of some of Christy Miller's friends. Her books *Gentle Passages* and *The Fine China Plate* are dearly appreciated by mothers everywhere. Robin's best-selling Sisterchicks novels hatched a whole trend of lighthearted books about friendship and midlife adventures. Who knows what stories she'll write next?

You are warmly invited to visit Robin's websites at: www.robingunn.com and www.sisterchicks.com. And to all the Peculiar Treasures everywhere, Robin sends you an invisible Philippians 1:7 coconut and says, "I hold you in my heart."